Temporal Revolution

La Révolution Series - Book 1

Robert Cruise

Copyright ©, Robert Cruise, 2024

Disclaimer

Any events or characters depicted in this work are entirely fictional.
Any resemblance to actual people or event is purely coincidental.

All rights reserved.
Any reproduction of this written work, in part or in whole, is prohibited without permission from the publisher.

For more information, contact the publisher at
AdlerSealPublishing@Gmail.com

First Edition July 2024
IBSN 978-1-0688331-6-8

Adler Seal Publishing

TABLE OF CONTENTS

Table of Contents	3
Tribute Page	4
Revolutionary Timeline	5
Revolutionary Calendar	8
Chapter One	12
Chapter Two	35
Chapter Three	65
Chapter Four	91
Chapter Five	113
Chapter Six	147
Chapter Seven	188
Chapter Eight	230
Chapter Nine	263
Chapter Ten	302
Chapter Eleven	337

TRIBUTE PAGE

FOR JACOB

In these pages, you'll find more than just words; you'll discover the reflections and dreams of a heart that has missed precious moments with you. Life, in its unpredictable flow, sometimes pulls us apart, leaving spaces we yearn to fill. This book is a bridge across those gaps—a testament to the unwavering love that distance cannot diminish.

As you turn each page, know that each word is steeped in the hope of reclaimed time. I am grateful for every moment we share and look forward to those yet to come. May this book serve as a promise from my heart to yours: to cherish and make up for the times we have lost.

With all my love,

Revolutionary Timeline

The French Revolution, a pivotal period in world history that reshaped France and influenced many other nations, can be divided into several distinct periods, each marked by significant political, social, and cultural changes. Here's a detailed breakdown using precise dates:

The Ancien Régime Ends (1789)

Estates-General and National Assembly (5 May - 9 July 1789): The Estates-General was convened in May 1789, the first such meeting since 1614. It was composed of representatives from the three estates: the clergy (First Estate), the nobility (Second Estate), and the common people (Third Estate). Disputes over voting procedures led to the Third Estate forming the National Assembly on 17 June, marking the initial shift of power from the monarchy to the populace.

Tennis Court Oath (20 June 1789): Members of the Third Estate vowed not to disband until a new constitution was established.

Storming of the Bastille (14 July 1789): This event, where a Parisian crowd stormed the Bastille prison, symbolises the uprising against the monarchy and the beginning of the Revolution.

The Moderate Phase (1789-1792)

Declaration of the Rights of Man and of the Citizen (26 August 1789): A fundamental document of the French Revolution, it outlined individual and communal rights at a time when revolutionary ideals were spreading across France.

Women's March on Versailles (5-6 October 1789): Thousands of Parisian women marched to Versailles to demand bread and compel King Louis XVI to move to Paris, effectively decreasing the king's power.

Civil Constitution of the Clergy (12 July 1790): This law transformed the Roman Catholic Church in France into a branch of the state and caused a deep rift between revolutionary and religious authorities.

Flight to Varennes (20-21 June 1791): The king's unsuccessful attempt to escape Paris radicalised public opinion and led to a surge in republicanism.

The Radical Phase (1792-1794)

Declaration of War against Austria (20 April 1792): Initiated by revolutionary leaders who suspected the king of plotting with the Austrians.

September Massacres (2-6 September 1792): Spontaneous mob killings of suspected royalists and opponents of the revolution.

Monarchy Abolished and First French Republic (21 September 1792): The monarchy was abolished following the Storming of the Tuileries Palace and France was declared a Republic.

Reign of Terror (5 September 1793 - 28 July 1794): Led by Robespierre and the Committee of Public Safety, this period was marked by mass executions, political purges, and a war against anti-revolutionary forces.

Execution of Louis XVI (21 January 1793): The king was executed by guillotine, underlining the irreversible break from monarchical rule.

Fall of Robespierre (27 July 1794): His arrest and execution marked the end of the Reign of Terror.

The Directory (1795-1799)

Establishment of the Directory (27 October 1795): A five-member committee which ruled France. This period was characterised by a constitution that balanced power between the legislature and executives but was marked by corruption and inefficiency.

Coup of 18 Brumaire (9 November 1799): Napoleon Bonaparte's coup d'état overthrew the Directory and replaced it with the Consulate, signaling the end of the revolutionary government and the beginning of Napoleonic rule.

These phases show the evolution from an absolute monarchy to a radical republic and finally to an authoritarian consulate, illustrating the dynamic and often violent nature of the French Revolution. Each period reflects a shift in political power and public sentiment, leading to profound changes in French society.

Revolutionary Calendar

The decision by France to change its calendar during the Revolution is a fascinating example of how political and cultural transformations can manifest in seemingly mundane aspects of daily life, such as the measurement of time. This change was deeply symbolic and served multiple purposes, from erasing old royalist influences to promoting the values and ideals of the new Republic. Here's a detailed exploration of the reasons behind this significant shift.

Erasing the Old Regime: The French Revolution, which began in 1789, was fundamentally about replacing the old socio-political order with something radically different. The revolutionaries sought to remove all traces of the monarchy and the aristocracy in French society. The calendar, used by everyone in their daily lives, was a symbolic representation of the old system's culture and history. By transforming the calendar, the revolutionaries aimed to break with the past and establish a new era that reflected the revolutionary values.

Symbolising a New Era: The revolutionary government wanted to create a calendar that would not only mark the passage of time but also symbolise the new society they envisioned. The introduction of the French Republican Calendar in 1793 was a way to signify the birth of a new political and social order, rooted in Enlightenment ideals of rationality, secularism, and equality.

Promoting Rationality and Secularism: The design of the new calendar reflected the Enlightenment's emphasis on reason and knowledge. It was designed by a committee of prominent mathematicians and astronomers, including the famous mathematician and astronomer Charles-Gilbert Romme. The calendar was structured around the decimal system, which was part of a broader push to metricate measurements in France. Weeks were replaced with "décades" of ten days each, aiming to rationalise how weeks were structured. Each day was divided into ten hours, each hour into 100 decimal minutes, and each decimal minute into 100 decimal seconds.

Moreover, the revolutionary calendar, or known officially as the French Republican Calendar, was overtly secular. It removed all religious and royal connotations present in the Gregorian calendar, which was named after Pope Gregory XIII. The new names for the months reflected seasonal changes and agricultural cycles—like Vendémiaire (from French vendange, meaning grape harvest) for the beginning of autumn, or Nivôse (from Latin nivosus, meaning snowy) for the snowy period. This secular approach was part of a wider effort to reduce the influence of the Catholic Church and ensure the separation of church and state.

Unifying the Nation: The calendar reform also aimed at cultural standardisation and unity across France, which was a patchwork of regional dialects, customs, and local calendars. The new calendar was part of a broader campaign to centralise and standardise various aspects of life in France, from the legal system to measurements, and even to the language. By introducing a uniform calendar, the revolutionary government sought to foster a sense of shared identity and common purpose among the French people.

Political Control: The new calendar also served as a tool for political control. By redefining the structure of the week and eliminating Sundays, the calendar disrupted traditional weekly church attendance, weakening the Church's influence on public life. The ten-day décades included a day of rest and celebration on the tenth day, which was intended to replace Sunday as the day of leisure, thereby detaching leisure from religious observance.

The Return to the Gregorian Calendar: Despite these intentions, the Republican Calendar was not widely beloved or deeply rooted in French society. It faced practical issues, such as the disruption of traditional weekly markets and the mismatch with religious and cultural practises. Moreover, the 10-day week proved unpopular as it reduced the number of traditional rest days. After Napoleon's rise to power, he recognised the calendar's unpopularity and inefficiency, leading to its abandonment in 1806, when France reverted to the Gregorian calendar.

Additional Notes:

Year Naming: The years in the Revolutionary Calendar were numbered from the proclamation of the Republic on 22 September 1792, which was declared as the beginning of Year I.

Days of the Week: The Revolutionary Calendar also abolished the traditional 7-day week, replacing it with a 10-day week (décade) to reduce the influence of the Christian week with its sabbath.

Leap Year Handling: The system handled leap years by adding a leap day, called "le jour de la révolution" or the day of the revolution, at the end of the year in Fructidor every four years.

Calendar Abandonment: The Revolutionary Calendar was officially abandoned by Napoleon on 1 January 1806, and France reverted to the Gregorian calendar.

Revolutionary Calendar to Gregorian Calendar Conversion Chart

Revolutionary Calendar	Gregorian Calendar	Season
Vendémiaire	September 22 - October 21	Autumn
Brumaire	October 22 - November 20	Autumn
Frimaire	November 21 - December 20	Autumn
Nivôse	December 21 - January 19	Winter
Pluviôse	January 20 - February 18	Winter
Ventôse	February 19 - March 20	Winter
Germinal	March 21 - April 19	Spring
Floréal	April 20 - May 19	Spring
Prairial	May 20 - June 18	Spring
Messidor	June 19 - July 18	Summer
Thermidor	July 19 - August 17	Summer
Fructidor	August 18 - September 16	Summer

Chapter One

In early 1789, Paris teetered on the edge of change. Beneath its grand façade, tension brewed in the streets and along the Seine. Pierre Moreau, a clockmaker with a visionary spirit, sensed the growing discontent in his beloved city.

Pierre was of medium height, and his build reflected more intellectual pursuits than physical labour. His hair, streaked with silver, and deep brown eyes hinted at years of meticulous work and revolutionary ideas. His face, lined with age and experience, bore the marks of a life dedicated to quiet determination. A neatly trimmed beard framed his jaw, adding to his dignified appearance. Pierre's calloused and scarred hands moved with the precision of an artist, each motion deliberate and measured.

He dressed, favouring practical clothing over displays of wealth. His workshop mirrored his personality—organised chaos with tools and timepieces scattered about, each holding a place in his daily routine.

Pierre's mind constantly buzzed with innovative ideas, continually seeking ways to improve life for others. He dreamed of a world where society functioned as seamlessly as his clocks, each part working harmoniously for the greater good. Despite the turmoil, he remained steadfast, believing that even the smallest cog could drive monumental change.

One day, Pierre was working on his latest project, 'Decimal Time', when his wife, Claire Fountaine, entered, holding a trembling newspaper. "They've called for the Estates-General to convene," she announced. "It's been nearly two centuries since the last one."

Pierre looked up, a mix of concern and curiosity in his eyes. "The Third Estate will finally have a voice again," he mused. "Perhaps this is the opportunity for change we've hoped for, Claire. For the people, for Henri, and maybe even for my theories on time."

Deeply aware of the common folk's suffering, Claire felt a blend of excitement and apprehension. "But do you think they will listen, Pierre? The nobility and the clergy have had their way for too long."

Pierre stood, stretching from hours at his workbench. "It is a beginning," he said with determination. "Every gear must align perfectly for the clock to work. Maybe now, the gears of our society will finally begin to turn as they should."

Claire was a woman of quiet strength with auburn hair streaked with grey, usually pulled into a neat bun. Her warm hazel eyes reflected understanding and compassion. Her face, marked by age and worry, still held a soft beauty. High cheekbones and a delicate nose gave her an air of grace, while her smile, though often tinged with sadness, could light up a room.

Though not as calloused as Pierre's, her hands bore signs of domestic responsibilities and quiet activism. She dressed in modest, well-made clothing, reflecting her pragmatic nature but with an understated elegance.

Deeply empathetic, Claire always attuned to others' needs and pains. She possessed a sharp intellect and a keen sense of justice, often discussing societal issues with Pierre. Despite their hardships, Claire's optimism never wavered. She believed in a better future for all oppressed people, providing unwavering support and strength to her family.

Together, they pondered the significance of the Estates-General. It was not just a meeting but a harbinger of change. In their modest home, surrounded by sketches of gears and celestial charts, they felt history's weight pressing close.

As Pierre turned back to his work, the ticking of his clocks echoed the nation's heartbeat, each beat a second closer to revolution. With a careful hand, he rolled up his diagrams, the lines and numbers a outline for not just a new way of measuring time, but perhaps, a new era. The coming months would reveal if the gears of change would grind forward or seize under centuries-old rust.

—

The air was thick with the murmur of discontent and the rustle of pamphlets in the busy streets of Paris. News of the convening Estates-General spread like wildfire, igniting discussions in cafes, markets, and the dim corners of workshops like Pierre's.

Pierre, wiping the soot from his hands, joined his old friend Lucien at the local café, a hub for the city's restless intellectual ferment. Lucien, a scholar of some repute and a staunch advocate for the rights of the Third Estate, shook his head grimly as he unfolded the newspaper. "Look at this, Pierre," he said, pointing at the printed call. "The King asks for our grievances to be penned, yet what guarantee do we have that our voices will be heard?"

Pierre sipped his coffee, the bitter taste grounding his thoughts. "It's a start, Lucien. Every cog in the machine is essential. We are being given a tool; how we use it will determine its worth."

Around them, the voices of other patrons rose and fell in passionate waves. The notions of liberty, fiscal reform, and equality were debated fiercely. Pierre listened, his mind weaving through the complexities of political reform and his own theories of temporal reform. Decimal Time wasn't just about redefining the hours of the day; it was about revolutionising how society itself was organised and functioned.

"You're not just a clockmaker, Pierre," Lucien remarked, observing his friend's thoughtful expression. "You're a revolutionary in your own right. But remember, ideas are the first victims in a struggle for change."

Pierre nodded, acknowledging the truth in Lucien's words. "And yet, without new ideas, there is no true change. Just as our clocks must be set right to mark the time accurately, so too must our society find a new rhythm."

Their discussion was interrupted by the clamour outside. A group of pamphleteers passed by, their voices loud and insistent, distributing papers that called for fair representation and just taxation. The clamour was not just noise but the sound of change, of gears beginning to turn, slowly, perhaps too slowly for some, but moving nonetheless.

As Pierre returned to his workshop, *Moreau Horlogerie*, the echo of the café's debates rang in his ears. He looked at his diagrams, spread out like a battlefield of ideas on his workbench. Each line, each number, represented more than a measure of time—they were a measure of hope, a diagram for a future where time and society were aligned more equitably.

The weight of the coming Estates-General hung over Paris like the thick clouds that promised rain. Pierre knew that what was crafted in those sessions would affect every citizen, from the poorest farmer to the wealthiest noble. And in his heart, he carried a flicker of hope that perhaps, this time, change was truly at hand.

—

The streets of Paris were alive with the pulse of growing discontent as May approached. Pierre found himself frequently at the heart of these surges, not just as a participant, but as a keen observer, absorbing the undercurrents that would soon direct the tide of revolution.

One evening, as he shut the doors of his workshop, the distant sounds of a heated discussion drew him towards the local square, where a crowd had gathered under the flickering light of lanterns. The air was charged, electric with the collective energy of the people, each word spoken adding fuel to the blazing fire of change.

At the centre of the assembly, a young orator with fiery eyes and a voice that carried across the crowd articulated the grievances of the Third Estate. "We are the backbone of this nation, yet we are bent and broken under the weight of taxes and indifference," he proclaimed, his hands cutting through the chill night air.

Pierre edged closer, his ears straining to catch every word, every inflection. Around him, faces illuminated by lantern light nodded in agreement, murmurs of approval rising like a wave. He could feel the shift, the momentous energy that comes from shared purpose and collective outrage.

Turning to a neighbour, a baker whose flour-stained apron marked his trade as clearly as the tools did Pierre's, he asked, "Do you think they will listen to us now?"

The baker's expression was a mix of hope and scepticism. "Listen? Perhaps. Change? That remains to be seen. But speaking out, that's the start."

Pierre nodded, his thoughts drifting to his own projects, his designs not just for clocks but for a society that valued every second of a man's labour equally. "Change starts with a single tick, a moment that pushes the hands forward," he mused aloud, more to himself than to his companion.

As the crowd began to disperse, a plan was hatched among whispers. A meeting would be held, they said, in the days to come, not just to air grievances but to form a response to any dismissal from the King or his advisors. Pierre knew he would be there, not just to observe this time, but to participate.

Walking back through the cobblestone streets to his home, Pierre felt the weight of impending change. He understood that the coming days would shape not just his life but the lives of all in France. The Estates-General was no longer just a distant political assembly; it was the spark that could ignite the powder keg on which they all sat.

In his study later that night, the dim light from his lamp cast long shadows across the plans for his latest invention. The detailed diagrams for his decimal clock lay spread out before him, each line a testament to his belief in order and reason. Yet, outside his window, the disorder of the world seemed at odds with the precision of his designs. Pierre couldn't help but wonder if a new measurement of time could ever bring the equity he dreamed of, or if it would be lost in the tumult of the coming revolution.

—

As spring unfurled its tender leaves over Paris, the atmosphere within the city walls grew tenser with each passing day. The Third Estate, brimming with a mix of hope and unrest, found themselves repeatedly stifled by the ancient protocols that governed the Estates-General. In the midst of this, Pierre Moreau's workshop became a lesser-known hub of whispered strategising.

On one such afternoon, Pierre stood by his workbench, the components of a clock laid out before him like a scattered constellation. His hands moved deftly, but his mind was elsewhere; caught in the currents of change swirling through Paris. His friend, Jacques, a fellow enthusiast of enlightenment ideas, burst through the door, his face alight with urgency.

"They've done it again, Pierre! The proposals of the Third Estate dismissed outright," Jacques announced, slamming a stack of papers on the cluttered table. "They treat us as if the voice of the common man is but a murmur against the roar of the aristocracy."

Pierre set down his tools, his brow furrowed. "It's clear then," he replied, his voice measured, "our hopes for peaceful reform are dimming with each rebuff. What is being said among the others?"

Jacques leaned closer, lowering his voice despite the privacy of the workshop. "There's talk of taking matters into our own hands, of drafting our declaration. The air is ripe for something bold, something definitive."

The notion of a declaration sparked a flame in Pierre's chest. He was a man of gears and measurements, but the mechanics of society were proving to be a more complex puzzle—one that required a solution of its own. "A declaration could be the lever that shifts the balance," Pierre mused, his mind alight with the possibilities.

"Exactly!" Jacques agreed, pacing the room. "We meet tonight at Jean's. We'll draft our grievances and resolutions. You must come,

Pierre. Your insight into the intricacies of systems—the way things work—will be invaluable."

Pierre nodded, a sense of resolve settling over him. He was no stranger to the intricate dance of cogs and wheels that brought synchrony out of chaos. Perhaps, he pondered, these skills could yet serve a greater purpose.

As dusk fell and the streets of Paris whispered with the secrets of revolution, Pierre locked up his workshop. The tools of his trade lay dormant on the bench, silent witnesses to the transition of their master from craftsman to revolutionary. Walking through the narrow alleys towards the meeting, Pierre felt the weight of the moment on his shoulders. Tonight, they would pen a document that could perhaps change the course of history, or at the very least, echo the beating heart of a nation yearning for justice.

The room at Jean's was dimly lit, thick with tobacco smoke and the low murmur of conspiratorial voices. Pierre entered, greeted by nods and solemn faces. Around the table, men of various dispositions—artisans like himself, lawyers, small businessmen—all united by a common vision of a just society. As they set to work, drafting their declaration, the quills scratching against the parchment seemed to Pierre like the ticking of a clock, counting down the seconds to a new era.

Each word written, each sentence crafted, was a step away from subjugation and towards something grand, something equitable. Pierre, amidst the excitement, felt a profound connection to these men and their shared cause. Here, in the flickering candlelight, a new time was being schemed—a time where every man's voice might be heard equally, measured not by birth but by merit.

As the clock tower struck midnight, the document began to take shape, a testament to the collective will of the Third Estate. Pierre leaned back in his chair, his eyes passing over the assembled faces. Here, in this room, the gears of change were turning, and he was a part of the mechanism, integral and indispensable.

—

The spring of 1789 saw not only the blooming of flowers across the French countryside but also the flowering of revolutionary enthusiasm among its people. In Versailles, the grandeur of the palace stood in stark contrast to the growing discontent among the masses. As the Estates-General convened, Pierre Moreau, a man whose life had been dedicated to the precision of timekeeping, found himself measuring the pulse of a nation on the brink of upheaval.

On a particularly crisp morning, Pierre, along with Jacques and several of their compatriots from the Third Estate, made their way to a modest inn not far from the grand halls where the Estates-General met. The inn's common room was abuzz with talk of taxes, grain prices, and rights—topics that had become as common as the bread they shared.

"The nobility remains obstinate," grumbled a burly farmer named Martin as he joined Pierre at a worn wooden table. "They're blind to the struggles of the common folk. How long before all of France is starved or silenced?"

Pierre nodded, his gaze thoughtful as he sipped his weak ale. "It's not just food and taxes," he began, setting down his cup. "It's about time—our time. We toil from sunup till sundown, and for what? To fill the coffers of those who wouldn't spare a thought for our plight."

The men around the table leaned in, their expressions a mix of curiosity and confusion. Pierre, heavily influenced by Enlightenment thinking, continued, his voice low but firm, "Consider this: what if our days were not governed by the sun but by a system where every hour, every minute counted equally for everyone? Decimal time—ten hours in a day, one hundred minutes in an hour, each minute one hundred seconds long. Imagine how it would simplify trade, streamline work, make every man's time as valuable as the next."

The idea sparked interest and debate among the group. Some dismissed it as fanciful, while others, like Jacques, saw the revolutionary potential. "That's the kind of thinking that could rebuild France," Jacques exclaimed, his eyes alight with revolutionary zeal. "Not just reforming our governance but transforming our very conception of time itself!"

As they debated, the discussions around them grew louder, more animated. News had arrived of the King's reluctance to address the Third Estate's grievances directly, fuelling the fires of discontent. Pierre listened, his mind weaving together the threads of political reform and his vision for decimal time. It wasn't just about clocks and schedules; it was about equity, about reshaping society so that every man's hour was his own, free from the dictates of tradition and the inequality of birth.

As the meeting drew to a close, Pierre and his friends prepared to return to the tumult of the Estates-General. They left the inn with a sense of purpose, their minds occupied with plans both grand and intricate. The conversation continued in hushed tones as they walked through the verdant gardens of Versailles, the beauty of the surroundings a stark backdrop to their revolutionary discourse.

Pierre felt a resolve solidifying within him as the palace loomed ahead. The Estates-General might be a battleground of wills between the estates, but for Pierre and his companions, it was also a crucible for change. As they entered the grand hall, the echo of their steps mingled with the clamour of voices, each man there a small piece in the bigger puzzle of history, each man there part of a time that was slowly but inevitably ticking towards revolution.

—

Late May 1789, Versailles was not just a symbol of royal extravagance, but now a theatre of burgeoning dissent. Within this ornate backdrop, Pierre Moreau found himself among a throng of thinkers and workers converging in a less opulent corner of the city, a place where ideas brewed as heated as the coffee in their cups.

Amidst the rustic charm of a local café, conversations veered from the obstinance of the Second Estate to the radical pamphlets that slipped through the city like whispers of revolt. Pierre, with his plans for decimal time, listened more than he spoke, absorbing the mixture of hope and outrage that filled the air.

"You see, Pierre," said Jacques, gesturing with a intensity, "it's not merely about who pays the taxes. It's about who holds the power to decide. We're talking about a fundamental shift—from rule by divine right to governance by the people's consent."

Pierre nodded thoughtfully, his mind aligning the principles of equity in timekeeping with those of political representation. "And just as we seek fairness in representation, we should also seek it in the measurement of our days. A decimal system aligns perfectly with this new era of logic and reason."

A murmur of agreement passed among their group. The idea of restructuring time itself seemed a fitting metaphor for their larger aspirations. It was a conversation that stretched well into the evening, with each argument polished by the passionate discourse.

As the night deepened, the room was thick with the scent of tobacco and a palpable sense of revolutionary zeal. Conversation among the gathered throng swirled energetically, reflecting the charged atmosphere. Suddenly, a courier burst through the door, breathless with urgent news from the palace. The King, pressed by the unyielding stalemate at the Estates-General, had conceded a pivotal change: the verification of credentials would now proceed by individual count rather than by estate.

This was no minor triumph; it was a significant fracture in the formidable structure of the *Ancien Régime*. Previously, the nobility and clergy could dominate decisions by sheer virtue of their estate's status, overshadowing the vast yet fragmented Third Estate. Now, each delegate's vote carried equal weight, empowering the commoners and signaling a move toward a more equitable system. The room erupted into murmurs of approval and speculative whispers, as all present sensed the shifting tides of power.

"This is it, Pierre! The momentum we needed," exclaimed Jacques, his eyes bright under the flicker of the oil lamps. "Tomorrow, we push even harder. The Third Estate needs to stand firm."

Pierre left the café in the cool night air, his thoughts racing. The parallels between his scientific endeavours and the political struggle were clearer than ever. Both sought to dismantle outdated structures, proposing in their place a system more rational, more equitable.

As he walked through the dimly lit streets of Versailles, the distant clatter of carriage wheels on cobblestones reminded him that the old world was still very much alive. Yet, the winds of change were palpable, carrying with them the promise of a storm. Pierre knew that what lay ahead was fraught with uncertainty, but like the precision gears of a clock, every small movement was essential to the greater mechanism of revolution.

With the Third Estate feeling more empowered, Pierre sensed the threshold of something momentous. He understood that his participation, though philosophical, was as vital as the most vocal agitator's. Tomorrow, he would be there, not just as an observer, but as a voice of the Third Estate in the crafting of history.

—

Early June 1789, within the hallowed yet fraught halls of St-Louis Church in Versailles, murmurs of defiance filled the air as Pierre Moreau joined the burgeoning ranks of the Third Estate. The group, no longer willing to bow to the dictates of a crumbling *Ancien Régime*, was on the brink of a declaration that would echo through the ages.

Pierre, amidst the throng of commoners, merchants, and intellectuals, felt a surge of solidarity that transcended his scientific endeavours. Here, gathered under the vaulted ceilings stained with the light of dawn, was a collective that might reshape France.

"Can you believe it, Pierre? Today we may very well set the course for a new France," whispered Lucien, a fellow scholar and ally, as they edged closer to the front, where voices raised not just in volume but in conviction.

"The King's refusal to listen will be his undoing. We demand a national assembly, and by God, we shall have it," responded another voice, firm and resonant, cutting through the low tones of conspiracy.

As the deputies of the Third Estate convened, the air tinged with the sharp scent of anticipation and the underlying fear of royal retribution, Pierre's thoughts returned to his diagram designs for decimal time. How fitting, he mused, that his plans for an equitable measure of time might align with the very day they would demand equality from their governance.

The meeting unfolded with rapid urgency. Speeches were delivered with impassioned eloquence, each word a thread in the fabric of a new society they hoped to weave. Jean-Sylvain Bailly, esteemed as both a scientist and a statesman, emerged as a leader, his voice echoing off the stone walls, calling for unity and resolve.

"The formation of a National Assembly is not just our right; it is our duty," Bailly declared, his gaze sweeping over the assembled deputies. "Let us bind ourselves by an oath, here in this tennis court, to not disband until we have given France a constitution."

The crowd erupted, the sound a resounding affirmation of their shared purpose. Pierre, caught in the swell of a revolutionary craze, felt his heart beat in rhythm with the promises of change. Here was a momentum no royal edict could halt.

As they prepared to take the Tennis Court Oath, Pierre glanced around at the determined faces of his compatriots. This was more than a political act; it was a profound pledge for progress, a statement of the people's power.

The oath, solemn and binding, was taken amidst a chorus of voices, each deputy laying a hand upon the makeshift ledger that served as their testament. Pierre, with a steady hand and a clear eye towards the future, signed his name. It was a signature not just for himself, but for the principles of rationality, equality, and time measured not by the whims of kings, but by the needs of the people.

As they dispersed, the weight of their defiance heavy in the air, Pierre knew that they had crossed an irrevocable line. The Revolution loomed on the horizon, a spectre of the violence that might follow. Yet, for now, the unity and ideals of the Tennis Court Oath offered a beacon of hope.

He walked back through the streets of Versailles, the echo of their collective vow resonating deeply within him. The revolution, like his clocks, would move forward, second by second, towards an unknown but inevitable reformation.

—

As June 1789 waxed into its later days, the air in Versailles was thick with the scent of impending change. The corridors of power whispered of the defiance shown at the Tennis Court, where men like Pierre had stood firm against the tyranny of a faltering monarch.

Pierre found himself at a small café near the Palace, a quiet spot favoured by intellectuals and writers. Across from him sat Marianne Beaulieu, a sharp-minded journalist whose pen was as fierce as her spirit. Their conversation flowed from the implications of the Tennis Court Oath to the broader strokes of revolution.

"Do you think Louis has understood the message yet?" Marianne asked, her eyes alight with a mix of hope and scepticism. Her quill never far, ready to capture the essence of the revolution in ink.

Pierre stirred his coffee, his mind racing with thoughts of decimal time and democratic ideals. "The King is isolated, surrounded by advisers clinging to old ways. But the Oath… it's a beacon. It's undeniable even to him."

Their dialogue was interrupted by a courier, breathless from haste, who handed Pierre a folded note. With furrowed brow, he read the message: a summons to join a clandestine meeting of minds, planning the next steps of action, no doubt spurred by the day's earlier defiance.

Marianne watched him, her journalistic instincts piqued. "More plans for the future?" she queried, a note of excitement threading her voice.

"Indeed," Pierre replied, tucking the note into his coat. "Tonight, we discuss not just the structure of our new assembly but the scaffold of a new society. Care to join? Your pen might prove mightier than any sword in this fight."

With a nod, Marianne agreed, her presence at such a gathering a bridge between the spoken word and the populace's ears.

As dusk settled over Versailles, Pierre and Marianne made their way to a secluded manor house on the edge of the city. Inside, the atmosphere was charged with anticipation and determination. Gathered there were leaders of the Third Estate, intellectuals, and a smattering of sympathetic nobles, all united by a common cause.

The discussions were spirited, with voices raised not in discord but in passionate debate. Plans were laid for maintaining momentum, for ensuring that the flame kindled at the Tennis Court Oath would not be extinguished by royal diktat or military might.

Pierre contributed his vision of a rational, equitable society, using his ideas on decimal time as an analogy for the precise and fair restructuring of society itself. "Just as my concepts aim to divide the day into equal parts, we must also ensure equality under the law," he argued, his voice resonant with conviction.

As the meeting drew to a close, resolutions made and alliances strengthened, Pierre felt a profound sense of purpose. He and Marianne stepped out into the cool night, the stars above indifferent spectators to the human drama unfolding below.

Marianne turned to him, her expression thoughtful. "Pierre, this revolution, it's about more than just freedom from tyranny, isn't it?

It's about defining what we stand for, not just what we stand against."

Pierre nodded, his gaze fixed on the distant glow of Paris. "Exactly. And it's about ensuring that whatever we build on the ruins of the old regime, it must be something enduring, just, and truly revolutionary."

With the echoes of unity from the day's oath lingering in their ears, they parted ways, each to their tasks—Pierre to refine his plans for a new measure of time, Marianne to her desk, where she would narrate the day's events for posterity. The revolution was more than a change of rulers; it was a rewriting of the very concept of governance, a systemic change for a new age drawn in the bold strokes of hope and the finer lines of prudence.

—

As June bled into July 1789, the streets of Paris simmered with the heat of summer and revolutionary enthusiasm. Pierre, ever attuned to the city's pulse, sensed the rising unrest that even the thick walls of his workshop could not muffle.

Walking through the bustling market of Les Halles, he overheard vendors and commoners alike speaking in hushed, urgent tones. "The King's soldiers are doubling," one bread seller muttered to her neighbour, her eyes darting nervously. "What's next for us, then? Will bread be just a memory?"

Pierre paused, absorbing the charged atmosphere. It was here among the common people that the true temper of the revolution brewed, not just in the salons and secretive meetings of the intellectuals. Turning a corner, he stumbled upon a small crowd gathered around a fiery orator, his words slicing through the air like a sharpened guillotine.

"Brothers and sisters," the orator proclaimed, "the time has come to demand what is rightfully ours! Will we starve while the royals feast on our labour?"

The crowd roared in agreement, a raw, powerful sound that resonated with Pierre's own revolutionary zeal. He felt Marianne's hand on his arm, pulling him closer to hear over the clamour.

"This is the voice of Paris itself," she whispered, her voice vibrant with excitement. "The storm is near, Pierre. Can you not feel it?"

Pierre nodded, his gaze fixed on the orator. "Yes, and we must ensure our cause remains just, not just angry," he replied, the weight of his responsibility pressing upon him.

Later that evening, as he and Marianne shared a modest dinner in a quiet tavern with Jacque and a few other intellectuals, they discussed the day's events, weaving their personal hopes into the broader tapestry of revolutionary change. "It's all leading to something imminent, Pierre. The Bastille, perhaps?" Marianne mused, her quill poised above her journal, ready to document history as they spoke.

Jacque leaned forward, his eyes gleaming with anticipation. "The tension in the air is palpable," he remarked. "Diderot's writings on freedom, Condorcet's visions of progress, and Rousseau's social contract are resonating with the people like never before. We are on the brink of a seismic shift."

Pierre leaned back, his mind racing with possibilities. "The Bastille would be symbolic, certainly. A fortress of oppression toppled would send a message far beyond the borders of Paris."

Their conversation was a blend of strategy and philosophy, weaving together personal and political themes. They discussed the future, envisioning a France where both individuals and societal values were measured and cherished equally, every moment and every person significant.

As they left the tavern, the streets of Paris whispered around them, the city alive with the restless dreams of its people. Pierre felt a resolve hardening within him, fortified by Marianne's fearless spirit and the palpable yearning for change that thrummed through the cobblestones beneath their feet.

Heading back to his workshop, the night air thick with the promise of rain and revolution, Pierre knew that the coming days would test the mettle of all who dared to dream of a different world. But for now, he had plans to perfect, ideas to propagate, for when the dawn came, it would illuminate not just the flaws of the old order, but the design for the new.

—

By early July 1789, the simmering discontent in Paris had begun to boil. Pierre, after a long day at his workshop among gears and pendulums, sensed the growing restlessness as he walked through the streets, now thick with the voices of an agitated populace. He stopped by a familiar tavern, where the air buzzed not just with the clamour of clinking glasses but with the intense discussions of impending action.

As Pierre leaned against the worn wooden bar, a robust figure detached from the shadowy corner of the room and approached him. It was Lucien; his face etched with both excitement and concern. "Pierre, have you heard? The King has dismissed Necker. They say it's a signal that he will dissolve the National Assembly. The city is on edge." Jacques Necker was a prominent figure in the Estates-General serving as the Director-General of Finance and advocating for economic reforms.

Pierre's brow furrowed as he absorbed the news, the gravity of the situation settling in. "That's ill news indeed. Necker's dismissal could only inflame the tensions. We must be ready for what comes next."

The tavern's atmosphere thickened with the arrival of more patrons, whispers of a march to the Bastille prison circulating among the crowd. Pierre listened, his mind racing with the implications. "A march on the Bastille would be bold, indeed. It's a fortress but also a symbol. To take it would be to shake the very foundations of the monarchy."

Lucien nodded, clapping Pierre on the shoulder. "True, but it would also be dangerous. We must think carefully about our next steps. Are you with us?"

Pierre glanced around the room, the determined faces of his compatriots bolstering his resolve. "I am," he affirmed, his voice steady. "I may not wield a musket, but my support is yours. As a revolutionary and a pacifist, I believe we stand at the brink of something profound."

As they spoke, plans began to form, the strategy for the coming days taking shape amidst the din of the tavern. Pierre knew that his role as an intellectual and a maker of time was symbolic. His support lent credibility to the cause, bridging the gap between action and ideology.

Leaving the tavern, the night air felt charged, the distant rumble of unrest like the ticking of a giant clock, counting down to a momentous event. Pierre walked home through the restless streets of Paris, his mind occupied with thoughts of liberty and justice, the weight of his decision pressing upon him like the leaden gears of his clocks.

Each step brought him closer to a future uncertain yet inevitable, the spirit of revolution growing stronger with the passing of each day. As he entered his home, the soft glow of candlelight and the sight of Claire waiting anxiously reminded him of what was at stake. In her embrace, Pierre found not just comfort but a shared resolve to see through the tumult, their fates intertwined with the revolution's unpredictable heart.

—

July 1789 saw Paris on the edge of eruption. Pierre, drawn by an inexorable pull towards the heart of the city's burgeoning unrest, found himself outside an intense assembly at a local guild hall. Leaning against a shadowed column, he eavesdropped on the heated discourse spilling from the open doors.

A voice, loud and impassioned, cut through the cacophony. "Brothers, the dismissal of Necker is a declaration of war against us! We cannot let this pass. The Bastille, laden with gunpowder and arms, stands not just as a prison but as a symbol of royal tyranny!"

Pierre felt a chill despite the summer heat. The Bastille—a daunting fortress with a reputation as dark as its dungeons. He scribbled notes, the mechanics of his mind linking the strategic value to the symbolic power it held. His heart raced; the idea of capturing such a stronghold seemed as audacious as it was dangerous.

A plan was taking shape among the crowd, the strategy bold and fraught with peril. "At dawn, we gather at the square. We arm ourselves and march. The Bastille will fall by the hand of the people!"

Murmurs of agreement swelled into a chorus of determined shouts. Pierre, absorbing the gravity of the moment, knew this was a pivotal point. The success or failure of such an endeavour could very well dictate the momentum of the revolution.

As the crowd dispersed, Pierre remained still, lost in thought. The night air was thick with the promise of conflict, the distant sounds of Paris restless and expectant. He needed to document this, to capture the essence of the rebellion in its nascent stage. His role as an observer felt suddenly paramount, a duty to record the course of history unfolding before him.

Walking back through the dimly lit streets, Pierre's mind was a whirl of cogitations. At home, he relayed everything to Claire, who listened with a mix of awe and apprehension. "Pierre, this is history in the making," she whispered, her voice steady but her eyes wide with the shared realisation of the gravity of their times.

"Yes, and tomorrow, I will go to the square. Not to fight, but to witness, to record. This is the chronicle of our age, and it must be preserved," Pierre responded, his resolve firm.

That night, as they retired beneath the uneasy stillness that had enveloped Paris, Pierre lay awake, the burden of the coming day weighing heavily on him. The ticking of his own clock, usually a reassuring presence, now resembled the steady drip of rainwater through a leaky roof, each drop foretelling the unavoidable storm.

In the grey predawn light, Pierre set out with his son Henri, his tools of trade—a journal and a quill—his weapons against the tide of forgetfulness. The streets were already buzzing with activity, the spirit of agitation pervaded with anticipation and fear.

As they reached the square, the crowd was swelling, a living, breathing entity with one collective heartbeat. Pierre found a spot, an observer's perch, and began to write. The first rays of the sun lit the page as he chronicled the moment—the poised tension, the passionate faces, the palpable bravery tinged with fear.

Today, he was not just a horologist but a historian, capturing the pulse of a revolution that would redefine the fabric of their society. The storming of the Bastille was not just an event; it was a declaration, a severing of chains, and Pierre Moreau, in documenting it, ensured it would never be forgotten.

Chapter Two

On the 14th of July, 1789, the streets of Paris, already simmering with the heat of an oppressive summer, boiled over with the rage of its citizens. Amidst this chaotic ferment, Pierre Moreau, a clockmaker by trade and a thinker by nature, was swept up in the tide of insurrection that led to the storming of the Bastille prison.

As a roughly 1,000-strong crowd surged towards the fortress, Pierre watched with his son Henri clutching his hand with awe and fear. The formidable prison that had long stood as a symbol of royal tyranny was now besieged by a mass of bodies, each person driven by a desperate hunger for liberty and justice. The governor of the Bastille, confronted by this wave of humanity, initially attempted to negotiate.

Negotiations quickly fell through, and with the assistance of some French Guards who brought artillery, the storming of the Bastille commenced.

The air was thick with the smoke of musket fire and the clamour of iron against stone. Shouts of "Down with tyranny!" merged with the cries of the wounded, creating a dissonance that echoed off the city's stone buildings. Pierre's mind raced through this din, concerned not just for his and his son's safety but with the implications of this monumental day. As a man devoted to the principles of order and precision, the chaos was jarring, yet its purpose resonated deeply with his yearnings for change.

With each cannon blast that shook the walls of the Bastille, it seemed as though the very foundation of the *Ancien Régime* was crumbling. To Henri, only fourteen and wide-eyed at the spectacle, his father's grip was the only stable thing in a world turned upside down.

As the final resistance of the fortress faltered and the gates were breached, the crowd's fury gave way to jubilation. Seeing the guards surrender and the prisoners being freed, Pierre felt a complex swirl of triumph and trepidation. What would come of this upheaval? How would the principles of reason and time, which he held dear, measure in this new era?

That evening, as he returned home with Henri through streets still reverberating with the tumult and passion of revolution, Pierre reflected on the Enlightenment ideals that shaped his thoughts. Just as principles of reason and logic provide a foundation for understanding the natural world, society must establish equilibrium after such upheaval. In this emerging chaos, he saw his challenge: to aid in crafting a world where knowledge—and perhaps humanity itself—could be more precisely comprehended and appreciated.

The storming of the Bastille represented the dismantling of physical barriers and the fracturing of an ancient regime. For Pierre, it signalled the start of a new era, one in which every moment was a testament to the relentless advance of ideas and the continuous quest for a fairer society. As he recounted the day's events to Claire, his wife, that evening, his voice conveyed both the burden of duty and the glimmer of potential. The Revolution had commenced, and with it, the opportunity to shape the essence of time into an instrument for liberty and advancement.

—

In the days following the storming of the Bastille, Paris remained a city in flux, simmering with newfound freedoms and the unsettled dust of rebellion. For Pierre Moreau, the events of 14 July 1789 had planted seeds of profound reflection. As he returned to the comforting regularity of his clockmaker's workshop, the rhythmic ticking of gears and pendulums provided a stark contrast to the erratic pulse of the city outside.

Sitting at his workbench, with tools arranged meticulously, Pierre reflected on the day the Bastille fell. Each component of his clocks, carefully crafted and aligned, echoed his aspirations for France's future—shaped by the rational and revolutionary concept of a universal time zone across the entire French metropole. This idea, which Pierre had long considered, aimed not only to standardise the measurement of time but also to harmonise it with the new principles propelling the nation forward.

Henri had apprenticed with his father since he could walk, but his lessons in horology had only recently begun. The chatter of Parisians outside spoke of liberty, a concept as compelling and intricate as the mechanisms on his worktable. Pierre's son, Henri, often sat beside him, soaking in his father's quiet wisdom. To Henri, the unfolding events were an exciting spectacle of change; to Pierre, they were a summons to reshape society.

At fourteen, Henri was a lanky youth on the brink of adolescence, his slender frame suggesting future strength. His tousled dark hair framed a face alive with curiosity and a budding sense of purpose. His deep brown eyes, reminiscent of his father's but brighter with idealism, reflected his fascination with both the mechanics of clocks and the revolutionary ideas enveloping Paris.

His hands, still soft but precise, showed the early promise of a skilled craftsman. Guided by his father and innate talent, Henri adeptly managed the delicate components of timepieces, his nimble fingers moving naturally.

Dressed simply in practical clothes—plain shirts and sturdy trousers marked by his work—Henri exuded a quiet confidence that hinted at a maturity beyond his years.

Deeply attuned to the transformative times, Henri's youthful face bore a seriousness that belied his age. He was keenly interested in the broader discussions of liberty and justice. He actively engaged with his father, Pierre, to explore how society and clocks could be refined and improved.

In the quiet moments of the workshop, Henri's focus was unwavering. He listened intently to Pierre's instructions, absorbing the technical skills and philosophical musings his father shared. To Henri, each clock tick was not just a measure of time but a step towards a future where every second could bring about change.

On one such afternoon, as Pierre explained the intricacies of a clock's escapement to Henri, he drew a parallel that captured the boy's imagination. "Just as this mechanism governs the release of these gears, so must laws govern man. Without such structure, there is only chaos," he explained, his words punctuated by the soft clicks of the clock.

During these discussions, news of the National Assembly's latest decree reached Pierre's ears. The Declaration of the Rights of Man and the Citizen, proclaimed in late August 1789, resonated deeply with him. This document, an outline for moral and political conduct, mirrored the precision and clarity he sought in his work.

As Pierre read through the articles of the Declaration, his mind alighted on the possibilities it heralded. "Liberty, property, security, and resistance to oppression," he read aloud to Claire and Henri one evening, his voice imbued with hope and caution. The concepts were revolutionary, but their implementation would require the kind of exactitude and care that he applied to his timepieces.

The dialogue at home that evening was rich with debate and speculation. Claire, ever practical, voiced concerns about the tumult such sweeping changes might bring. Henri, inspired by his father's ideals, imagined a world ruled by the principles of equality and reason.

As summer gave way to autumn, Paris continued to seethe with revolutionary fervour. Amidst his reflections, Pierre maintained a correspondence with fellow intellectuals, discussing earnestly how the principles of the Declaration might be applied universally, including within his own domain of timekeeping.

In his letters, Pierre championed the idea of a universal standard as a cornerstone for societal order, transcending beyond just the concept of time to encompass all facets of life. He viewed this universality as essential, a means to embody the Revolution's plea for rationality and uniformity across all systems. "To standardise our units, whether for time, currency, or measurements, is to bring coherence to daily life, simplifying transactions and aligning our practices with the natural order," he wrote. For Pierre, establishing order was crucial, yet he recognised the inherent challenge of harmonising this with the prevailing chaos of revolutionary change.

As the summer of 1789 drew close, Pierre's workshop was a forge for his mechanical experiments and revolutionary thoughts. With each adjustment and calibration, he perceived the potential for society to be reformed and function as coherently as the mechanisms he crafted. Yet, the outside world defied predictability, and Pierre understood that the journey towards societal reform was laden with dangers and opportunities. His role in this transformative era was defined, though the final results were as uncertain as the future.

—

As the zeal of the summer's revolutionary activities began to meld into the fabric of daily life in Paris, Pierre Moreau became increasingly involved in the intellectual ferment that the Declaration of the Rights of Man and the Citizen had ignited. Late September 1789 brought crisp air and clearer heads as the city adjusted to its new rhythm of liberty and debates.

In his workshop, nestled in the heart of a bustling Parisian street, Pierre's discussions often extended beyond the mere mechanics of clocks. Pierre seized the opportunity to discuss the broader implications of France's new moral compass with each visitor, be it a fellow artisan or a curious neighbour. "Consider this," Pierre would begin, holding up a cog, "each tooth must engage precisely for the whole mechanism to function. So too must each citizen engage with these new rights and responsibilities for our society to thrive."

One evening, as Pierre pondered the workings of the Enlightenment alongside Henri, he shared a thought. "Consider the steady and reliable principles of reason and justice, my boy," he said, "These are the heartbeat of our Republic. Just as the heart sustains the body with every beat, so must these principles guide our nation with unwavering commitment."

Claire, well-versed in Pierre's penchant for drawing parallels between abstract concepts and societal structures, listened to his analogies with admiration and a measure of scepticism. Her engagement with his intellectual pursuits was deep and personal, yet she often pondered his theories' real-world applicability. While supportive of Pierre's aspirations, she remained cautious about how they could be realistically implemented.

"Pierre," she remarked one evening while they prepared dinner, "these ideas are honourable, but how do we align them with the ongoing power struggles? Not everyone perceives the same truth in your analogies."

Pierre pondered her query carefully. "That lies at the heart of our endeavour," he replied, his actions deliberate as he prepared their meal. "The theory is robust, but its execution is intricate. It underscores the need for education and understanding to ensure these principles translate from mere words into tangible actions in our society."

In the tumultuous summer of 1789, with the reverberations of the Bastille's fall still echoing through Paris, the National Assembly was swiftly carving a new trajectory for France and originating from the deep-seated grievances and dynamic meetings of the Estates-General, the Assembly jade taken a decisive stand in June. Delegates from the Third Estate, historically marginalised by a voting system that granted equal weight to each estate regardless of size, joined forces with like-minded members of the clergy and nobility. Together, they declared themselves the National Assembly, pledging allegiance not to the entrenched societal divides but to the rights and welfare of the populace at large.

They envisaged a France ruled by laws they would draft, starkly contrasting the long-standing monarchical authority. This pivotal transformation marked the beginning of a representative government, evolving from a society stratified by social estates to one unified by common citizenship and mutual rights. Energised by the revolutionary zeal that had brought down the Bastille, the National Assembly rapidly introduced radical reforms. They abolished feudal privileges, formulated the Declaration of the Rights of Man and the Citizen, and established the foundations for a constitutional monarchy. These decisive actions not only reshaped the political contours of France but also paved the way for the more profound and enduring changes of the Revolution that were still to unfold.

The conversation at the Moreau household deepened as the National Assembly continued to meet, wrestling with applying these newly declared rights. Pierre followed each development keenly, often receiving newspapers and pamphlets from friends within the Assembly. He read excerpts aloud to his family, discussing each article's implications on their lives and his work.

On one such occasion, as October painted the leaves golden, Pierre read about the debates on property rights, a crucial aspect of the Declaration that resonated with his professional concerns about intellectual property in his timekeeping inventions. "See here, Henri," Pierre pointed out, "the property right is deemed sacred, as is one's labour. This directly supports the protection of our designs and inventions as much as any land or title."

The dialogue often extended into the night, candles burning low as they dissected each part of the Declaration, relating it to everyday experiences and Pierre's visions of decimal time. Inspired by his father's passion, Henri began to sketch his own ideas, drawing parallels between the mechanics of clocks and the mechanics of democracy.

—

As the leaves began to fall in early October 1789, the political landscape of France transformed with the seasons. Often engrossed in the intricacies of his craft, Pierre Moreau drew numerous metaphors from the complex workings of his creations and the evolving events of the French Revolution. His keen observations of the mechanical and social mechanisms gave him a unique perspective on the tumultuous changes sweeping the nation.

In the days following the Declaration of the Rights of Man and of the Citizen, Paris was both turbulent and exhilarated. In his shop, Pierre Moreau, discussing this monumental event with local merchants, drew on Enlightenment thinking to explain its significance. "Gentlemen," Pierre began, setting aside his tools, "each article of our Declaration lays the groundwork for justice and equality, much like the principles of logic and reason underpin the advancements of our age."

Learning from life rather than formal schooling, Henri absorbed the lively debates and teachings that filled his father's workshop. This space served as his classroom, where Pierre and Claire, embracing the spirit of the Enlightenment, delighted in imparting every bit of knowledge they could to their son.

One crisp morning, as autumn's chill permeated the air, a heated debate took hold among the patrons. Monsieur Garnier, a local baker, brandished a pamphlet, his frustration evident. "But how can we uphold these rights when the King feasts while his people starve?" he challenged, his face as flushed as the season's leaves.

With a reassuring gesture, Pierre responded, "Monsieur Garnier, achieving this is akin to seeking equilibrium in philosophical debate. We must balance power with the needs of the people. Our Declaration serves as a benchmark, ensuring that the King and his citizens are held accountable to the same standards of justice."

Later that week, Pierre and Henri attended a session of the National Assembly. Standing at the back of the crowded hall, they felt the electric anticipation of change. Pierre whispered to Henri, "Observe and listen. These men are defining the nation's future, akin to philosophers shaping the contours of thought."

The Assembly's debates were passionate, the voices of representatives from across France ebbing and flowing in intense discussions over the Declaration's interpretation, each striving to align the new laws with their principles.

Back at his workshop, inspired by the vigour of the National Assembly, Pierre returned to his bench with a fresh perspective. Innovatively, he began constructing a new clock with a unique design symbolising the balance of power. "This clock," Pierre reflected aloud as Henri assisted him, "will feature dual pendulums, each moving in synchrony to maintain time, just as our nation strives to harmonise freedom and governance."

As the weeks passed, news of the Assembly's resolutions filtered down to the common folk, sparking discussions in markets, taverns, and homes. Pierre often found himself at the centre of these discussions, offering explanations that drew parallels between his mechanical creations and the political mechanisms of the new society.

One evening, while Pierre and his family were gathered for supper, Claire looked at her husband, energised by the revolutionary spirit yet wary of the rapid changes. "Pierre, do you think these changes will last?" she asked, handing him the bread.

Pierre paused, his expression thoughtful. "I believe they have to, Claire. For our son's sake and all the children of France. We're laying the foundations for a new epoch and must ensure it remains steady."

At that moment, under the gentle glow of the candlelight reflecting off the sincere faces of his family, Pierre felt a deep connection to the revolution. It represented more than just a struggle for power or a legal transformation; it was a profound reshaping of society's core values, a chance to align the nation's spirit with the enduring principles of justice and rational thought.

—

The autumn of 1789 saw Paris awash with the colours of change; even the trees in the Palais-Royal seemed to shed their leaves in solidarity with a nation shedding its past. Amidst this transformative backdrop, Pierre Moreau and his son Henri ventured into the city's heart, where the air thrummed with the revolutionary enthusiasm of a people emboldened by newfound liberties.

As they walked through the bustling streets, Pierre explained the significance of the recent upheavals to Henri, whose keen eyes absorbed every vibrant detail. "See, Henri, how do the people speak openly and debate intensely? This is the essence of liberty—freedom of speech, a fundamental right newly inscribed in our Declaration," Pierre noted, pointing towards a group of animated citizens gathered around a speaker in a corner of the square.

The father and son paused to listen. The speaker, a robust woman with a commanding presence, passionately quoted from the Declaration of the Rights of Man and of the Citizen. "Men are born and remain free and equal in rights!" she declared, her voice resonating off the stone buildings, her words galvanising the crowd into cheers.

Pierre leaned down to whisper to Henri, "These words, my son, are not just ideals; they are the principles that propel our nation forward now. Just as each element in a system must work together, so too must these ideals interlock for our society to function effectively."

Continuing their walk, they stopped at a local printer's shop where freshly printed copies of the Declaration were being sold. Pierre bought one and handed it to Henri. "Keep this safe," he instructed, "for this document now shapes the era we live in, as fundamentally as the foundations of our society."

As evening approached, they returned home through streets buzzing with revolutionary intensity. At their modest dining table, Claire Fontaine laid out a simple supper, and the family sat down, the document placed centrally like a revered text. Over their meal, they delved into the articles of the Declaration, each family member sharing their hopes and concerns for the future.

"It says here," Henri pointed out, his finger tracing the lines of text, "'The aim of all political association is the preservation of the natural and imprescriptible rights of man.' What does 'imprescriptible' mean, Father?"

Pierre smiled, pleased by his son's curiosity. "It means rights that cannot be taken away or forfeited, Henri. It's the idea that some rights are so fundamental that no one can strip them from us—not a king, not a government."

That night, Pierre sat at his workbench with the Declaration open beside him. Inspired by its powerful ideals, he began sketching a new clock design, embedding motifs that represented liberty, equality, and fraternity. As he drew, he reflected aloud, "This clock will do more than mark time; it will celebrate a pivotal moment when our very understanding of time was transformed."

In the tranquil late hours, surrounded by the subtle ticking of clocks, Pierre felt deeply connected to the evolving spirit of his country—a nation in the process of profoundly reshaping its core values, with liberty at the forefront. His work as a clockmaker, once simply a trade, had evolved into an echo of the revolution, each passing minute and hour a testament to a nation courageously redefining its identity.

As November 1789 progressed, the very fabric of French society underwent a profound transformation, influenced by a new set of revolutionary ideals. On a clear, brisk morning, Pierre Moreau was meticulously engaged at his workbench, finely tuning the delicate components of a clock. This was not merely a functional item; it was a symbolically charged gift for a member of the newly established National Assembly. The clock's face was artfully adorned with symbols of the Tricolour, emblematic of the intense enthusiasm for change that had gripped Paris.

The Tricolour, a powerful representation of the French Revolution, consists of blue, white, and red. These colours were imbued with deep meaning: blue and red, the traditional colours of Paris, flanked the white, symbolising the monarchy. Together, they stood for the new alliance between the people and the royal powers, embodying the revolutionary ideals of liberty, equality, and fraternity. The incorporation of the Tricolour into everyday objects like Pierre's clock demonstrated the depth of the revolution's influence on French culture, showing how the new national sentiment had permeated even the minutiae of daily life.

Henri, always inquisitive, watched his father at work, absorbing his methodical approach to each task. "Father," Henri asked, his brow furrowed with thought, "how do these new ideas integrate into our lives? Will our lives change because of them?" His question reflected the revolutionary curiosity that Pierre had encouraged in him.

Pierre paused, setting aside his tools with deliberate care. "Everything is interconnected, Henri. Just as Voltaire argued for reason and Montesquieu for the separation of powers, these new laws and rights touch every aspect of our lives. We are entering an era shaped by Enlightenment thinking, where every citizen is urged to consider the common good over individual desires. This shift in perspective is as transformative as any change we might observe in our daily routines or governance."

The conversation was interrupted by a knock at the door. Claire answered it to find their neighbour, Monsieur Dupont, who was visibly agitated. "Pierre, have you heard? The Assembly is debating something monumental today—something about the Church and its lands. It's all anyone can talk about in the market."

Inviting Monsieur Dupont in, Pierre offered him a seat. The three adults and young Henri gathered around the kitchen table, the morning light spilling across the maps and newspapers strewn about. "They're considering turning all ecclesiastical properties into national assets," Dupont explained, his voice a mixture of excitement and concern. "It's a bold move, one that will surely send ripples through every parish and estate in France."

Reminded of the days before Henri was born when she regularly held salons, Claire served a pot of tea, the steam rising in the quiet room as they discussed the implications of such decisions. Life as a wife and mother had quietly taken over her days. Henri listened intently, the adults' words painting a vivid picture of the shifting societal landscape.

"Imagine the resources, Pierre," Dupont continued, his hands animated. "They could fund our military, reduce the national debt, and support the poor. But it will anger the Church, and many devout folks as well."

Pierre nodded thoughtfully. "It's a decisive step, but a necessary one if we are to truly reform our nation. The Church has long held wealth and power that could be better used for the public good. This is similar to improving a system to ensure every part contributes effectively to the whole."

After Dupont left, Pierre returned to his workbench, the ideas from their discussion intertwining with his ongoing project. He began sketching a new clock design, incorporating symbols like the tricolour, a plough, and a grapevine—representations of the common man and the rewards of his toil, symbols soon to gain recognition in the new social order.

Henri, meanwhile, was also drawing, his paper slowly filling with his interpretation of a clock. Inspired by the day's conversations and his father's innovative spirit, he said, "One day, I'll build clocks that do more than measure time. They will narrate the saga of our nation, its trials, and its triumphs."

Pierre glanced over, his face lighting up with a smile. "And that, my son, will be a true revolution." As they continued their work side by side, the workshop seemed alive with the promise of the new era. Each tick from the surrounding clocks was not just a marker of time, but a steady drumbeat of human progress and potential.

—

As the autumn of 1789 faded into winter, the streets of Paris, still echoing with the chaos of the Bastille's downfall, thrummed with a new rhythm of hope and anticipation. In his workshop, Pierre Moreau, with keen precision and thoughtful expression, carved not only gears but also conversations around the nascent ideals now shaping France. The Declaration of the Rights of Man and of the Citizen, promulgated on the 26th of August, had unfurled a canvas of possibilities for every Frenchman and woman.

Despite Pierre having read it to him countless times, the passion Henri saw in his father made every reading a story in itself. On a crisp morning in early December, Pierre, his fingers stained with ink and oil, paused to read the declaration aloud to Henri, who listened with the intense concentration of youth on the brink of understanding. "Men are born and remain free and equal in rights," Pierre recited, his voice imbuing each word with weight, feeling the depth of their meaning ripple through the air.

Henri's eyes widened. "Does that mean everyone, Father? Even people like Monsieur Dupont, and—"

"And us, yes," Pierre affirmed, his hand resting on his son's shoulder. "It means that the law must protect everyone equally. Imagine, Henri, a society where it isn't the lineage of your birth but the merit of your deeds that defines you."

Claire entered the workshop, her apron dusted with flour from the morning's baking, adding, "It's a promise of what France could become, if only we can hold these ideals close and act upon them."

Their conversation was interrupted by a knock at the door. It was their neighbour, Madame Bertin, a widow who often sought repairs for her late husband's watch—a delicate piece that Pierre treated with the utmost care. Today, however, concern etched her face, and her hands clutched a folded copy of the declaration.

"Pierre, Claire," she began, her voice wavering, "how can we rely on these words to endure? The nobles and the king, will they not cling to their privileges?"

Pierre accepted the document from her, handling it as carefully as if it were a precious manuscript. He spread it on his workbench, meeting her worried look with a composed assurance. "Indeed, they might resist," he acknowledged, his tone both calm and resolute. "But we are witnessing a shift, Madame Bertin. More than just the physical walls of the Bastille have fallen; it's the mental barriers that have crumbled. We've seen what's possible when collective will aligns."

Bolstered by her neighbours' steadfastness, Madame Bertin nodded, a flicker of hope igniting in her eyes. "Then we must cling to these words and bring them to life. For my children, and for yours, Henri."

After Madame Bertin left, feeling reassured, Pierre returned to his workbench with Henri at his side. They commenced constructing a new clock, its face not only marked with the hours but also adorned with emblems of liberty and equality—visible symbols of the new epoch they were entering.

"That clock, Father," Henri observed keenly, touching the symbols lightly, "will it indicate when the promises are fulfilled?"

"It might, in a manner," Pierre replied, his laughter soft. "But more importantly, it will remind us that liberty, like time, requires constant diligence. We must protect them both, incessantly. Remember, Henri, with freedom comes the challenge of ensuring it is not misused. Our vigilance must never falter."

As the day dimmed to evening, the ticking of the newly assembled clock merged with the distant sounds of a revitalised Paris, each tick a step towards the future they dared to envision together.

—

By late December 1789, the tangible shifts in France's political landscape had spread to the lamp-lit alleys of Pierre's neighbourhood. The crisp winter air carried the excited whispers of transformation, echoing from the bustling marketplaces to the quiet cafes where scholars and laymen alike engaged in spirited debates. Pierre, always an observer, found these discussions invaluable, both fueling his intellectual curiosity and inspiring his craftsmanship.

One evening, as he meticulously adjusted the gears of a watch—a piece belonging to a member of the newly formed National

Assembly—Pierre's thoughts wandered to the recent decrees issued by this burgeoning entity. The Assembly had moved decisively, abolishing feudal privileges in a night that would echo through history. On 4 August 1789, they declared the end of serfdom, tithes, and feudal dues, dismantling the centuries-old privileges of the nobility and clergy. This night marked a seismic shift, reshaping the very foundation of French society and affirming the principles of equality and liberty that had ignited the revolution. The decrees of that night were a collective leap towards a society free from the chains of old hierarchies, paving the way for a new order based on the rights of man.

Henri, now more aware of the undercurrents shaping their world, often joined these discussions, his keen young mind absorbing the ideals of liberty and equality that filled the room. "Father," Henri queried one day, as they walked past the Seine, watching the leaves drift by in the gentle flow, "why do the people believe these changes will hold? The king still sits at his throne, does he not?"

Pierre considered his son's question, recognising the depth of observation Henri had developed. "True, the king remains, but the power, the true power, now begins to stir in the hands of the people. Like this river, it might be diverted, but it cannot be stopped without spilling over its banks."

As the new year dawned, Pierre found himself at a local tavern, a place alive not just with the aroma of spiced wine but with fervent debates over the Declaration of the Rights of Man and of the Citizen. The tavern was a microcosm where abstract ideas became concrete, discussed passionately by people from diverse backgrounds.

A robust man, a butcher by trade, punctuated his point by slamming his fist on the table, causing the tankards to rattle. "Rights are well and good on paper," he declared, "but how do we ensure these are more than just words?"

Pierre, taking a thoughtful sip of his drink, responded, "It is our collective responsibility to animate these principles. We must remain vigilant, ensuring that each individual, every neighbour, lives by and respects these rights."

The conversation continued as the wind outside picked up, swirling snow around the cobblestones in an intricate dance, reflecting the restless spirit of the times.

That night, as Pierre walked home under the soft glow of street lamps, he contemplated the nature of time. It was both constant and subjective, something both measured and experienced. His own role as a clockmaker seemed a fitting parallel to the revolution unfolding around him. Each component of a clock must operate in synchrony to accurately track time.

The same precision and collaboration were necessary for the revolutionary changes to last. As he unlocked his door to the warmth of his home where Claire and Henri waited, Pierre's resolve deepened. Just as he dedicated himself to the craft of horology, he would commit to the ideals set forth by the revolution—a commitment to progress, equality, and the relentless forward march of time towards a brighter future.

—

January 1790 saw Pierre immersed in a sea of political tumult that swirled around Paris like the winter mists along the Seine. As the city emerged from the New Year's celebrations, an undercurrent of unease permeated the air. There was a palpable sense that the old ways were being dismantled piece by piece and reshaped in the flames of revolutionary passion.

On a cold evening, as frost sparkled on the city streets beneath the glow of oil lamps, Pierre made his way to a meeting in a dimly lit hall near the Marais district, close to his home and workshop. The room was filled with the thick smoke of tobacco and the rich scent of mulled wine, yet these aromas couldn't obscure the underlying tension of anxiety and determination that filled the air.

"The Declaration of the Rights of Man and of the Citizen must be more than words," declared a young journalist, his voice ringing with passion as he slammed a copy of the document on the wooden table. "It must translate into action, into laws that govern fairly and justly!"

Pierre, leaning against the back wall, watched the scene unfold, his mind racing with the implications of each spoken word. His own work, the creation of decimal time, seemed now more than ever a symbol of the rational and equitable society he hoped France would become. The precise and equal division of hours and minutes mirrored the call for equality under the law.

Henri often accompanied his father, as Pierre felt these were valuable opportunities to teach and nurture Henri's education. Listening with intense fascination, Henri's learning extended far beyond the pages of books, coming alive in the flurry of discussions among those dedicated to transforming their nation. Barely a teenager, Henri was witnessing history unfold right before his eyes.

As the debate moved from philosophical ideals to practical applications, Pierre chimed in, his voice steady and clear. "If we are to truly embrace these rights, let us also adopt a system of time that reflects our new values. Time is still fragmented, with each town operating on its own schedule. Decimal time is not merely about the mechanics of clocks; it is about unifying our daily lives, making time itself democratic and universal. It ensures that no matter where one is in France, the rhythm of the day is the same for all, embodying the equality we strive for."

When someone inquired, "What is decimal time?" Pierre's eyes sparkled with eagerness. He took the opportunity to explain succinctly. "Decimal time restructures our day into 10 hours, each hour into 100 minutes, and each minute into 100 seconds. It's designed to make timekeeping simpler by harmonising it with the metric system, which uses units of ten."

The room quieted briefly as the listeners absorbed Pierre's explanation. Then, a wave of applause emerged—not overwhelming, but filled with respect for the clockmaker's innovative vision.

Later, as Pierre and Henri walked home beneath the starlit sky, Henri glanced up at his father. "Father, do you think people will embrace your ideas about time?"

Pierre responded, looking down at his son with a gentle smile, illuminated by the street lamps. "I believe, Henri, that our ideas are akin to seeds. Some may sprout swiftly; others take time to mature. But all will grow, provided we tend to them."

Approaching their home, they heard the night watchmen's calls resonating through the streets, maintaining order and safety in the nocturnal hours. Inside, Claire welcomed them with a warm hearth and the comforting scent of freshly baked bread. The family convened around the dinner table, not just sharing food but also the warmth of collective ideals and hopes for a future forged by revolutionary change. Each tick from Pierre's clocks underscored the relentless advance of time, ushering them towards a new year ripe with possibilities for further groundbreaking transformations.

—

Mid-January 1790 brought with it the biting cold that swept through the streets of Paris, but within the chambers of the newly formed National Assembly, the air was thick with debates and declarations that shaped the furnace of revolutionary France. Amidst this, Pierre, his mind often preoccupied with the gears and springs of clocks, found himself increasingly drawn to the gears of political change.

On a particularly frosty morning, Pierre attended a session of the Assembly, his interest piqued by discussions that would lay the foundational principles of the new constitution. The Assembly hall buzzed with the voices of deputies arguing fervently about the rights of man and the future of the French nation.

As Pierre watched from the visitor's gallery, a deputy from the Third Estate, his voice resonant and commanding, spoke passionately about the need for liberty and equality to permeate every aspect of French life. "These rights are not just the privileges of the few but the inalienable rights of all," he proclaimed, his words echoing off the stone walls.

The voices erupted when someone from the gallery yelled, "How can these rights be for all when in the colonies we still employ slavery?" The question hung in the air, a stark reminder of the contradictions and challenges that lay ahead for the revolutionaries.

Henri, who had been allowed to accompany his father, listened intently, his youthful eyes wide as the concepts of freedom and equality were debated with an ardour he had never witnessed. He looked up at his father and whispered, "Father, will the new time you speak of be part of this change?"

Pierre smiled, gently ruffling his son's hair. "I hope so, Henri. Just as our nation seeks to recalibrate its course, we must also reconsider how we measure our days and nights. Clocks across France should be synchronised for the efficiency of the nation, and Decimal Time would facilitate this transition perfectly. It's about equality—making every hour and every minute equal, mirroring how each person's rights should be."

As the day unfolded, discussions intensified. Pierre and Henri listened to debates over the abolition of feudal privileges, the overhaul of the tax system, and the integration of the Declaration of the Rights of Man and of the Citizen into the constitution. Each topic was a line in the narrative of their country's transformation.

Leaving the Assembly as the evening set in and Parisian street lamps flickered to life, Pierre felt a wave of optimism. The crisp air felt less biting as he and Henri strolled home, their conversation spanning not just the intricacies of horology but the principles of democracy, reflecting thinkers like Rousseau's advocacy for political equality and Montesquieu's ideas on the separation of powers.

At home, Claire embraced them warmly, eager to hear about the day's events. As they sat around their modest dinner table, Pierre animated the discussions from the Assembly, each word painting the portrait of a nation fervently sketching its identity.

"The world we knew is changing, Claire," Pierre reflected. "And perhaps, through our small contributions, we can help steer that change."

Claire nodded, her face a canvas of concern and pride. "Then let us remain unwavering, Pierre. For Henri, for our future."

With Henri absorbing so much from his father, Claire contemplated reviving her local ladies' salons. That evening, as they gathered by the fire, the family felt the weight of history unfurling around them. Outside, the streets of Paris lay quiet under the frost, but inside, the flame of revolutionary fervour blazed, ignited by the belief in a dawn heralded by the chime of equality's clock.

—

As February 1790 enveloped Paris in its frosty embrace, the National Assembly was a hub of frenzied activity, echoing the determined spirit that had gripped the nation. Inspired by Enlightenment ideals, the deputies called for proposals to infuse rational and progressive thought into the restructuring of French society. Pierre, buoyed by this revolutionary zeal, saw a precious opportunity to advocate for his concept of decimal time.

In his workshop, amidst clocks and watches at various stages of assembly, Pierre often paused in deep thought. His workspace, adorned with sketches and mathematical calculations, testified to his diligent pursuit. Observing him one evening, his wife, Claire, commented, "The Assembly's call—it's a beacon for your ideas, Pierre. It's time they emerged from the shadows of outdated prejudices."

Pierre nodded, his eyes reflecting both determination and concern. "Yes, my love. Tomorrow, I'll present a plan that embodies the principles they value—equality, uniformity, and rationality."

The next day, Pierre, carrying his rolled parchments, navigated the bustling streets of Paris, where a palpable sense of anticipation hung in the air, hinting at the profound changes reshaping their world.

Upon entering the Assembly, Pierre was surrounded by a gathering of intellectuals, philosophers, and reformists, all eager to shape the new societal order. When his moment came, he addressed the Assembly with a calm tone, filled with intensity.

"Esteemed deputies, the revolution has recalibrated our societal framework, heralding a new epoch. Let us ensure our methods of measuring time are as revolutionary as the changes we strive for. Decimal time, by dividing the day into ten hours, each hour into one hundred minutes, and each minute into one hundred seconds, not only aligns with the decimal structure of our new currency but also embodies the uniformity we seek to instill across all aspects of French life.

This revolution has already seen the *Académie des Sciences* develop the metric system—a unified measurement system based on rational principles and natural constants, reflecting our ideals of uniformity and rationality. In a similar vein, adopting decimal time would synchronise the towns and cities across the entire French metropolis, promoting efficiency and order in our daily lives."

The Assembly, initially filled with subdued murmurs, fell into contemplative silence. Pierre's proposal resonated, striking a chord with their philosophical and practical considerations. Henri, who had accompanied his father, watched with proud admiration as nods of approval began to spread through the chamber.

Stepping outside, Pierre harboured cautious optimism. The deputies had committed to thoroughly evaluating his proposal. "Regardless of their decision, you've sparked a vital discussion, Father," Henri remarked, looking up at him with respect.

"That's all we can strive for, my son. To ignite thought, challenge the status quo, and possibly illuminate a path forward," Pierre responded, his hand resting supportively on Henri's shoulder.

As they walked home, the city whispered of impending change. Every resonant footstep on the cobblestones, every distant call from the riverbanks spoke of a society in flux, a world where ideas like Pierre's might redefine the rhythm of daily life.

That evening, as the National Assembly remained abuzz with debates on Enlightenment-inspired proposals, the Moreau family gathered around their dinner table, lit not only by the flickering candles but also by vibrant discussions about the future—a future where time itself could reflect the ideals of liberty, equality, and fraternity. Claire steered the conversation, not just focusing on the measurement of time but also on her passionate subjects of social justice and education.

—

By late April 1790, Paris resonated with the vibrations of change, the impassioned debates of the National Assembly reverberating through the city. In this charged atmosphere, Pierre Moreau found the perfect moment to advance his innovative ideas on timekeeping.

Within their cosy home in Marais, nestled in a quiet Parisian alley, the Moreau family convened for an evening discussion. Candlelight flickered across the room, illuminating Pierre's scattered papers and meticulous designs. His proposal, deeply intertwined with revolutionary calls for rationalisation and equality, represented more than just technical innovation; it symbolised the dawn of a new societal order.

"As the Assembly deliberates our future, so must we," Pierre declared with measured enthusiasm. Henri, well accustomed to his father's reflective conversations, listened intently, imagining a society guided by the logical rhythm of decimal time.

Claire, always supportive yet pragmatic, raised a critical point, "And the common folk, Pierre? How will you persuade them to adopt a rhythm entirely foreign to them?"

"Through education," Pierre responded, acknowledging the challenge. "We must demonstrate how this new system reflects our core values. *Liberté, égalité, fraternité*—these must extend to our very conception of time."

Fuelled by the lively discussions from the Assembly, Henri suggested, "Perhaps we could organise public demonstrations, Father. Letting people see and experience your clocks might bridge their understanding of decimal time."

Pierre smiled at his son's enthusiasm. "An excellent idea, Henri! We shall begin in the marketplaces, where the pulse of daily life is most evident."

In the following weeks, Pierre and Henri devoted themselves to constructing models of decimal clocks. These were not merely timekeepers but beacons of a new era. Each clock was crafted with precision, its face divided into ten segments for hours, with further divisions for minutes, subtly educating its viewers in the new time system through its very design.

Together, they painstakingly assembled each component, embedding within them the revolutionary promise of rationality and equality. Each movement of the hands was a step towards enlightenment, a commitment to the principles of liberty and fraternity.

The day of the first public demonstration at Place Royale arrived. Henri watched, proud and inspired by his father's conviction. A crowd formed, curious yet sceptical, as Pierre unveiled his creation.

"Observe, citizens! Just as our Republic has discarded tyranny, so must we cast aside the old timekeeping methods. Embrace a system that aligns with the logic our new society deserves!" Pierre proclaimed.

The response was mixed, typical of any profound change. Yet, seeds of curiosity were planted. Conversations ignited in cafes, debates sparked in salons, and the notion of decimal time gradually infiltrated Parisian thought.

That evening, as Pierre and Henri trundled a cart laden with prototype clocks through the cobbled streets of Paris, the city around them buzzed with the spirit of enlightenment and reform. Eager for rational and innovative ideas, the National Assembly had called upon all citizens to contribute, and the Moreaus, with their cart full of intricate timepieces, were answering that call.

Back at his workbench, Pierre composed a letter to the Assembly. His writing was deliberate, infused with a firm resolve. He outlined his vision for decimal time, framing it not just as a scientific improvement but as a societal revolution, reflecting the highest ideals of the Revolution.

Sealing the letter, the distant chimes of Notre Dame blended with the steady ticking of his decimal clock. This symphony of old and new was a sound thick with the promise of tomorrow. For Pierre Moreau, this was merely the beginning of his mission to transform society's rhythm, his determination echoing the relentless advance of the revolution itself.

—

As the spring of 1790 waned, marking a period of ideological renewal, the National Assembly, galvanised by the revolutionary tide, resolved to embed Enlightenment principles into the fabric of French society. On a brisk morning in late August, they gathered to debate proposals that would transform lofty ideals of liberty and equality into practical reforms.

In central Paris, Pierre Moreau, buoyed by a renewed sense of mission, prepared to attend a pivotal session. The Assembly had summoned thinkers and pioneers to contribute, and with his plans for decimal time under his arm, Pierre felt the significance of this moment deeply. This was no mere presentation; it was an appeal for reason in an age balanced precariously between turmoil and order.

Watching his father organise the papers, Henri, deeply involved both as an apprentice and a devoted son, voiced a concern tinged with youthful innocence and curiosity. "Father, do you think they will grasp the importance of aligning time with the principles of the revolution?"

Pierre reassured him with a gentle hand on his shoulder. "It's not solely about comprehension, my son, but about envisioning a future governed by reason's natural order. Our clocks are just the start."

As they ventured towards the Assembly, Paris pulsed with the jubilant energy of a city reborn. Vendors announced new decrees, and citizens engaged in endless debate on street corners and in cafés. The city was a living canvas, ready for the strokes that would paint the new France.

Upon entering the grandiose hall, the magnitude of the assembly struck Pierre. Surrounded by France's keenest advocates for freedom, he was poised to champion a temporal revolution. The chamber buzzed with the anticipation of those united by the goal to remould their world.

Called to the podium, Pierre addressed the hushed crowd, laying out his diagrams. The detailed diagrams of his clocks, designed to mark time anew, lay before the assembly.

"Citizens," he started, his voice firm, "we stand at the dawn of a new era, where each aspect of our society must mirror our revolutionary values. The way we measure our days, our work, our lives, should be as rational and equitable as the society we aim to create."

Pierre spoke passionately against the tyranny of traditional timekeeping, constrained by outdated customs and inequitable measurements, advocating for a system where each hour, minute, and second was equal, understandable, and divisible by ten. "Decimal time," he asserted, "concerns not just the mechanics of clocks but the very mechanics of society—efficient, equitable, and enlightened."

His speech sparked lively debates among the assembly members. Some nodded thoughtfully, intrigued by the idea of standardising time as they standardised measures and weights. Others expressed scepticism, cautious of the disruption such a fundamental change might entail.

Nevertheless, Pierre's presentation planted seeds of contemplation. The Assembly decided to review the proposal more thoroughly.

Exiting the Assembly, Pierre felt a blend of excitement and anxiety. The road ahead was strewn with challenges, yet the admiring, hopeful gaze of Henri provided reassurance. Together, they would traverse the uncertain landscape of this new era, guided by the stars of reason and the relentless drive for progress.

Stepping back into the sunlight of Paris, the city throbbed with the constant rhythm of change. In the distance, Notre Dame's bells tolled the time in their traditional manner, soon perhaps to be superseded. But for Pierre Moreau, those peals were a summons to the future—a future where time itself would stand as a testament to the revolutionary ideals.

Chapter Three

By May 1790, Pierre Moreau was deeply absorbed in establishing his revolutionary decimal clock at the bustling Place Royale marketplace. The day unfolded with the crispness and precision Pierre aimed to introduce through his innovation. The marketplace thrummed with activity; vendors announced their offerings, the air tinged with the aroma of freshly baked bread and ripe fruits. Stalls brimmed with vibrant produce, and the rhythm of horse-drawn carts enriched the lively scene.

Fifteenth-year-old Henri, exuding the earnestness of youth, eagerly assisted his father, handing him tools and absorbing the conceptual foundations of the decimal clock. Around them, the curiosity of onlookers grew as they paused in their daily errands, intrigued by the clock's unique design and Pierre's passionate explanations. The air was charged with a blend of scepticism and curiosity as the rhythmic ticking of the clock heralded a new order in a world ripe for change.

"As we construct this clock, Henri, we mirror the nation's transformation," Pierre explained, securing a brass cog. "While the Assembly debates the Civil Constitution, we redefine time itself, making it orderly and universally applicable across the French metropole."

Henri absorbed his father's words, the significance of the task deepening his understanding as his craftsmanship skills grew. The city buzzed with the energy of change, stoked by memories of the

Bastille's fall, which spurred conversations about aligning daily life with the ideals of liberty and reason.

"This clock transcends mere timekeeping, Henri," Pierre continued, his eyes alight with a visionary's zeal. "It heralds a new era marked by precision and a reformed way of thinking and living."

As they worked, discussions about ecclesiastical reform filled the air, resonating with the market's bustling energy. Pierre seized these moments to teach Henri, drawing analogies between the restructuring of time and societal reform, each aimed at fostering a rational and enlightened France. This approach highlighted the theoretical underpinnings of the decimal clock as not only a technological innovation but a philosophical embodiment of the revolution's drive towards unity, standardisation, and enlightenment, pivotal in establishing a universal timezone that would bind the nation under a single rhythmic pulse.

—

As the sweltering heat of July 1790 enveloped Paris, the National Assembly was deep in vigorous debates over the Civil Constitution of the Clergy. The city streets resonated with intense discussions and dissent, mirroring the controversies echoing through the Assembly's chambers. Meanwhile, Pierre, a devotee of Enlightenment thinking and a secular thinker was, in his workshop, focused on the diagrams of his decimal clock—a project inspired by the broad sweep of reforms and his commitment to the rational and egalitarian ideals forming the new France.

"Look here, Henri," Pierre gestured towards the detailed diagrams. "Each component must align precisely, reflecting how our society must function. Just as the Assembly seeks to recalibrate our clergy to integrate better with secular governance, we too must ensure every part of this clock works in harmony."

Now familiar with his father's penchant for drawing parallels between their mechanical work and the political shifts, Henri listened intently. The workshop had become more than a place of craft for him; it was a classroom where lessons in clockwork melded with dialogues on philosophy and statecraft.

Pierre spoke of the Assembly's recent actions as they assembled the clock. "The Civil Constitution aims to transform the clergy into civil servants. It's a contentious move, but it captures the spirit of the Enlightenment—promoting rationality, order, and equality before the law. We also advocate these principles through our work on decimal time."

Henri passed a finely polished gear to his father, their hands meeting briefly—a quiet moment of unity in their shared endeavour. "Do you think the people will readily accept these changes, Father?" he inquired, his voice carrying the collective uncertainty of Parisians.

Pierre fitted the gear into the clock's core, securing it precisely. "Change often encounters resistance, Henri. But just as we aim to enlighten the public on the merits of decimal time through our demonstrations, so must the Assembly effectively communicate and showcase the advantages of these reforms."

As evening approached, the silhouette of the nearly completed clock stood prominently in the dimming workshop light. Oil lamps softly illuminated the space, casting long shadows across the walls adorned with diagrams and neatly arranged tools. The aroma of sawdust and metal shavings filled the air, a testament to the hours dedicated to their craft. With its sophisticated gears and polished brass, the clock symbolised more than a mere timekeeper; it was a beacon of the new order Pierre envisioned sweeping across France.

Outside, the pulsating energy of revolution filled the city, each day ushering in fresh challenges and transformations. Inside, Pierre and Henri persisted in their work, the consistent ticking of their creation a steady echo of time's relentless march and the unyielding progress of human endeavours.

—

By early autumn of 1790, Pierre's workshop was alive with the sounds of industry and vibrant discussions on France's transformation. This space served as a hub for those with progressive values. It hosted Claire's intellectual salons one evening a week in the backroom, where discussions flourished around the philosophical and political currents of the era.

Meanwhile, the market square clock at Place Royale, an impressive structure of gleaming brass and intricately painted dials, gradually came together, symbolising the change Pierre envisioned and Henri was helping to manifest. The streets of Paris buzzed with the energy of revolution and reform, filled with the aroma of freshly baked bread and the rhythmic clatter of horse-drawn carts on cobblestones.

One crisp morning, Pierre adjusted his spectacles, examining a challenging component of the clock. Noticeably taller and more confident, Henri presented him with a customised tool. "It should fit better, Father. I modified it to match the adjustments you made to the diagram last week."

Pierre smiled, accepting the tool. "Excellent work, Henri. You've become skilled at anticipating the needs of our projects, much like how our Assembly must foresee the needs of France." His voice carried the gravitas of a mentor. "Every decision in our clock's creation mirrors a decree from the Assembly—carefully considered, debated, and implemented with precision to fulfil its intended role."

Henri nodded, absorbing the lesson as they aligned the final gear. News of the Assembly's latest debates wafted through the open workshop doors, carried by the lively crowds outside discussing upcoming legislation and proposed radical changes to governance and everyday life.

Amid the workshop's clamour, Pierre steered the conversation towards a significant political development, skillfully linking it to their mechanical endeavours. "Consider the Civil Constitution of the Clergy, Henri. In the same way we construct this clock to regulate the time, the Assembly is restructuring the Church to align with the new societal framework. It's a contentious, complex, delicate task demanding careful balance to function properly without causing upheaval."

Henri appeared contemplative, his expression reflecting the complexity of the issue. "But not everyone supports the changes, Father. The priests in our district are split. Some embrace the oversight, while others see it infringing on their beliefs."

"Precisely, Henri," Pierre replied, continuing his work. "That's where clear explanation and persuasion are essential. We must articulate the benefits of our work and demonstrate its value, just as our leaders must explain and justify their reforms to the populace."

The clock chimed for the first time, its tones clear and resonant above the square's din—a triumphant moment. Pierre and Henri shared a look of mutual satisfaction, a connection in their common pursuit.

"This clock, Henri," Pierre gestured broadly, "does more than just mark the hours. It will educate the people on the benefits of orderly, rational change, just as the Assembly seeks to steer France towards a more structured, enlightened future."

As daylight waned, their conversation turned to the practicalities of their next steps, both in mechanics and philosophy. The clock in the square stood not merely as a timekeeper but as a metaphor for their aspirations, a focal point for community education, and a testament to the ongoing revolution in timekeeping and societal thought.

—

As 1790 progressed, the political landscape of Paris vibrated with the rhythm of radical change, with daily debates that resonated from the Assembly halls and spilt into the streets. In this dynamic backdrop, Pierre found his arena not within the governmental halls but amongst the hearts and minds of those who gathered daily to witness the construction of the monumental clock in the market square.

On a crisp November morning, a crowd encircled the square, their breaths misting in the cold air as they watched Pierre and Henri attach the intricate hands of the decimal clock. Seizing the moment, Pierre stepped onto a makeshift platform to address the onlookers.

"Ladies and gentlemen," Pierre began, his voice resonant and assured, "as our great nation embarks on a new era, this clock represents a new method to measure our days in harmony with the rationality and precision that underpin our revolutionary principles."

As Henri passed tools to his father, he observed Pierre skillfully captivate the audience. Pierre elaborated, "Consider the metric system, proposed by the *Académie des Sciences* to our Assembly, grounded in the natural order, simplifying and standardising measurements for everyone. Decimal time follows the same philosophy; it simplifies, standardises, and unites."

A man in the crowd, identifiable as a baker by his flour-dusted apron, challenged, "But why change how we tell time? What's wrong with the old way?"

Pierre responded with a knowing smile, prepared for such resistance. "Just as our nation strives to cast off the shackles of an outdated monarchy to embrace liberty, equality, and fraternity, we must also re-evaluate old customs that tether us to inefficiency and confusion. Decimal time offers us a chance to align our daily lives with what is rational and logical."

Murmurs rippled through the crowd, a mix of nods of agreement and sceptical frowns. Pierre recognised the challenge of changing long-established habits, yet he was poised to defend his vision with as much vigour as any politician.

"Envision a day divided into ten hours, each hour into one hundred minutes. Consider the symmetry, the simplicity. Just as we are reshaping our government, so too can we transform how we measure our lives."

As the conversation unfolded, Henri admired his father's passion, understanding more clearly the link between the clock's mechanics and society's dynamics. He saw the clock as a timekeeping device and a metaphor for progress and enlightenment.

The clock's construction continued over the following months, each component symbolising potential transformation. The debates Pierre sparked in the square became a regular fixture, drawing more people into discussions about time and the sweeping reforms reshaping their lives.

By the late fall of 1790, the clock towered majestically over the square, nearing completion. It had become more than just a technological marvel; it was a beacon for the new era, drawing people as powerfully as the revolution had pulled them toward a new order. The clock was merely a curious novelty; to others, it was a profound revelation. It successfully initiated a social dialogue about the merits of Pierre's ideology, stimulating discussions and debates on the rational restructuring of time and society.

Pierre's dialogues frequently extended to other revolutionary changes, such as the Civil Constitution of the Clergy, illustrating the need to recalibrate societal frameworks analogous to the precise adjustments required for the clock's optimal function.

As Pierre and Henri installed the final pieces, the clock transcended its role as a mere project; it became a symbol of their aspirations, a focal point for their ideals, and a tangible manifestation of the change Pierre hoped to instil in the hearts of his fellow citizens.

—

The marketplace clock at Place Royale had become a beacon of innovation and Enlightenment thought, perfectly woven into the fabric of the community's daily life. Pierre, often seen with hands marked by the day's labour, worked diligently alongside Henri, who was quickly honing his skills under his father's watchful eye. Around them, the square buzzed with activity, reflecting the enthusiasm of the revolution as citizens engaged in vigorous debates over the transformative ideas reshaping their nation.

On an exceptionally crisp morning, while Pierre was fine-tuning the clock's pendulum—a task demanding quiet and precision—he caught wind of a lively discussion among market-goers. They debated the proposed Revolutionary Calendar, a system that, like his clock, aimed to rationalise and detach timekeeping from religious and royal traditions.

Seizing the opportunity to promote the principles behind decimal time, Pierre paused his work and approached the crowd, wiping his hands on his apron. "Citizens," he began, his voice firm yet inviting, "this clock does more than mark the passing hours; it symbolises the rhythm of our new society—one founded on reason rather than tradition."

As people gathered around, Pierre elaborated, "As we debate new ways to structure our days and seasons, we must also rethink how we measure our hours and minutes. Decimal time complements the Revolutionary Calendar, streamlining our daily routines into universally understandable and applicable units."

The crowd listened with varying degrees of intrigue and scepticism. A seamstress in the group voiced her concern, "But how can we adapt to such changes? They appear so radical."

Pierre responded with an encouraging smile. "Change indeed poses challenges, madame. Yet, consider the metric system, which is now being adopted—it initially seemed foreign but brings clarity and unity. This clock," he gestured towards the impressive structure, "will make time a shared language for all French citizens, aligning with our new government's efforts to unite us under common ideals."

As the dialogue unfolded, Henri observed the crowd's reactions, absorbing not only the technical aspects of clockmaking but also his father's art of persuasion and public engagement. The young apprentice took mental notes on the technical tweaks required for the clock and the public's concerns, preparing himself to engage in such discussions.

Pierre drew a powerful analogy with the sun at its peak, casting the long shadow of the clock across the square. "As this clock's shadow tracks the sun's path, so does our revolution signal a new epoch in human history. Let us meet these changes not with apprehension but with the resolve to redefine our concept of time."

After the crowd began to disperse, a few remained, their faces alight with curiosity and intrigue for further discussion. Pierre and Henri resumed their work, adjusting gears and polishing the brass hands, each tick of the clock a step towards realising Pierre's vision.

Their efforts echoed the broader societal shifts, with each advancement in their craft mirroring the revolutionary zeal that animated the streets of Paris. Working side by side, father and son didn't just measure time; they were actively shaping a future informed by Enlightenment principles and the relentless progression of time itself.

—

By the winter of 1790, the public square in Paris had transformed into a daily spectacle at midday when the five chimes of Pierre's decimal clock marked the day's division. Citizens, becoming accustomed to the sound, would pause in their activities—some in admiration, others still perplexed by the rhythmic proclamation of decimal time. Now skilled in maintaining the mechanism, Henri often took the lead on adjustments, with his proud father observing his expertise.

On a crisp December day, as snowflakes began to adorn the cobblestones, Pierre organised a demonstration for local Assembly members intrigued by this innovative time-keeping approach. The square, bustling with vendors selling hot chestnuts and children playing near the fountain, provided a vibrant backdrop for the severe discussions unfolding under the clock's shadow.

Pierre initiated his demonstration by delineating the principles of decimal time, effortlessly integrating the advantages of the metric system, which was gradually gaining acceptance. "Just as we have adopted a uniform system for measuring distance, we should establish a standardised, nationwide time measurement. It simplifies trade, education, and daily routines," Pierre articulated, his voice resonating against the stone buildings.

A progressive young Assembly member responded thoughtfully, "And how do you propose we implement this system nationally? It's a forward-thinking concept but could meet resistance."

With a prepared smile, Pierre replied, "Through education and gradual adoption. We start with the young, still malleable to new ideas. We initiate here in Paris, demonstrate its benefits, and then expand to other cities." He gestured expansively around the square. "Imagine every city synchronised to a single, rational time system. The efficiency in communication and coordination would be unprecedented."

Henri, actively participating beside the clock, distributed leaflets that detailed the clock's design and the logic behind decimal time. His role had evolved beyond an apprentice to an advocate, a representative of a new generation pushing the boundaries of the revolution.

As the Assembly members departed, immersed in contemplation and debate, an older man approached Pierre, his face marked by scepticism. "Monsieur, this is all very innovative, but why change what is not broken? Our traditional methods have served us well."

Pierre acknowledged the challenge respectfully. "Consider, monsieur, how the revolution seeks to improve upon the past, not just in governance but across all facets of life. Decimal time isn't merely a new way to segment the day; it symbolises order and reason, the pillars of our current reforms."

The man mulled over Pierre's words while watching Henri enthusiastically engage a group of children with the clockwork. The older man's chuckle, sparked by the youth's passion, hinted at acknowledging the inevitable shift when championed with such zeal.

That evening, as Pierre and Henri strolled home through the snow-laden streets, they reflected on the day's interactions. Henri, ever curious, asked, "Father, do you think they grasped the importance? Will they consider our proposal seriously?"

Pierre placed a reassuring hand on his son's shoulder, feeling the crisp winter air. "Whether they stand with us now or come around in time, we've cast a stone across the water, Henri. Each ripple it creates reaches further, affecting more than the last. Our role is to keep the momentum going and to ensure each wave builds upon the last until the whole surface is transformed."

As they turned a corner, their modest home's lights spilt onto the snowy path. Inside, warmth awaited, but outside, the chilly air thrummed with the spirit of change, each breath a reminder of the ongoing revolution.

—

In March, Paris was alive with debates; pamphleteers were heralding their documents on everything from education reform to the abolition of slavery. Amid this setting, Pierre, deeply committed to promoting decimal time, found a valuable ally in Monsieur Lefèvre, a member of the Assembly who shared his vision of rationalising daily life through scientific and mathematical principles.

One radiant afternoon, Pierre and Henri established a public exhibition in the bustling market square under the shadow of the prototype decimal clock that dominated the scene. Henri, increasingly confident and articulate, led the explanation of the clock's mechanics to an engrossed audience, his voice rising above the market din.

"Monsieur Lefèvre, much like my father, believes that decimal time will foster a unity essential for the Republic," Henri asserted, gesturing towards the detailed diagrams on display. "Like the Revolutionary Calendar aims to restructure our year, decimal time seeks to simplify and unify our daily timekeeping."

A mixture of curious onlookers and sceptics in the crowd exchanged murmurs. From the back, Pierre observed Henri tackle the questions with a wisdom that belied his youth.

A market vendor, overtly sceptical, challenged, "Why change what everyone already understands?"

Henri, channelling the composure his father had modelled, replied, "Because, monsieur, simplification signifies progress. Our current time system is rooted in ancient traditions, not rationality. Decimal time, aligning with the decimal system in our new currency and measurements is about introducing logic into every aspect of our lives."

As Henri spoke, Pierre noticed Monsieur Lefèvre approaching, his expression one of keen interest. The politician congratulated Henri warmly as the presentation concluded. "Excellent work, young man! Your father has imparted his wisdom well. We shall delve deeper into this at the Assembly. This initiative can potentially position France as a leader in thought and revolution across Europe."

Grateful for the support, Pierre invited Lefèvre to join them for dinner, seizing the chance to discuss strategies for advocating their initiative. That evening, their modest dining room transformed into a lively strategy room.

During the meal, Lefèvre outlined the anticipated challenges. "You must prepare to confront significant resistance, Pierre. Traditions are deeply cherished here. Your scientific approach, though commendable, needs to be interwoven with the practicalities of daily life."

Ever eager to contribute, Henri suggested, "Perhaps we could prepare pamphlets for distribution at public forums, articulating the benefits in simple, relatable terms?"

"An excellent proposal," Lefèvre concurred with enthusiasm. "Education will indeed be our most potent tool. The populace must perceive the practical advantages, not merely the theoretical ones."

As the discussion extended into the night, Pierre was buoyed by optimism. The forthcoming months promised rigorous endeavour, yet the possibility of revolutionising the time framework invigorated him. Henri, slipping away to the workshop momentarily, returned with a small, newly crafted decimal clock.

"For Monsieur Lefèvre," Henri announced, presenting it. "A model to accompany you to the Assembly."

Lefèvre accepted the gift with genuine appreciation. "This will indeed aid our cause. A tangible example often resonates more profoundly than the most heartened oratory."

As Lefèvre departed into the chilly night, the Moreau home remained bathed in the warmth of collective conviction and revolutionary zeal. Looking out at the street, Henri contemplated the forthcoming months, aware they stood on the brink of something truly monumental.

—

Pierre's workshop was illuminated through the frost-kissed windows, a warm sanctuary against the biting cold outside and within, the sound of metal clinking against metal filled the air as Pierre and his son Henri, now fully embraced as his father's apprentice, meticulously assembled another section on a decimal clock. The workbench was littered with gears and springs, each a component in their visionary timekeeping system.

Pierre, examining a finely crafted cog, shared his insights. "Henri, precision lies not only in where each piece fits but also in understanding its purpose. This clock isn't just about marking time; it reflects the rhythm of a new epoch."

Surrounded by timepieces since childhood, Henri, now sixteen and notably taller, had matured into a skilled apprentice. His grasp of the craft had deepened, shaped by his father's guidance.

As Henri handled the clock components with increasing confidence, he remarked, "It's akin to the debates in the Assembly; each legislation must integrate precisely to ensure the Republic progresses smoothly."

Pleased by his son's analogy, Pierre's face lit up with pride. Watching Henri's assured hands at work, he saw the mechanical skill and a growing comprehension of their broader impact.

"Yes, exactly!" Pierre exclaimed, pulling out a stack of papers from his coat. "Here's the proposal I've prepared for the Assembly. It details how decimal time complements the Revolutionary Calendar. I'll present it tomorrow, hoping they'll recognise the need for a standardised approach to time, much like we've achieved with weights and measures."

The following morning, Pierre stood before a committee of the National Assembly, his refined public speaking skills on full display. Over recent months, his ability to engage and persuade had been honed in the lively debates of Place Royale.

"Gentlemen, as we reforge our nation on the principles of equality and reason, let us also consider rationalising time. Decimal time provides a systematic approach, reflecting our collective zeal for order and efficiency."

The Assembly members listened, a mix of intrigue and scepticism among them. Drawing on the disorder of inconsistent timekeeping and its societal implications, Pierre's argument was compelling.

During a speech to the National Assembly in 1790, Pierre Moreau passionately presented his vision for reforming the measurement of time across France:

"Envision a society where every citizen, irrespective of their status, measures their day by a uniform standard, where time itself mirrors our revolutionary ideals," Pierre begins, gesturing emphatically to emphasise his points.

He then explains the current state of timekeeping, "Presently, the concept of a standardised time does not exist, and the time of day varies significantly from one city to another across our nation. Each locality sets its clocks according to solar time, meaning that noon is the point at which the sun is at its highest in the sky, directly overhead. This method results in variations because the actual solar noon occurs at different times in different places due to geographical differences."

Through his speech, Pierre underscores the importance of adopting a standardised system of time that aligns with the principles of liberty, equality, and fraternity. He advocates for a reform that would unify the nation further and facilitate the transition into a modern Republic.

Meanwhile, Henri waited anxiously in the corridor, overhearing snippets of conversation about the radical reforms under consideration. He understood the resistance from conservative elements within the Assembly to such a transformative idea.

When the session concluded, Pierre emerged, his expression sombre. Henri approached eagerly. "Father, how did it go?"

Pierre sighed his hand reassuringly on Henri's shoulder. "As expected, Henri. While some are receptive, others find it too radical, too unsettling. But we persevere. This is merely one step in our journey towards enlightenment."

As they walked through the bustling Paris streets, the sound of traditional clocks ringing in the distance seemed almost defiant. Pierre pondered not just mechanical adjustments but also strategic shifts.

"We need a more direct approach, Henri. If the public sees the value of decimal time firsthand, the Assembly will have to reconsider," Pierre mused.

Inspired by his father's resolve, Henri agreed. "Let's start with the marketplace clock. Making the change visible might help them see its benefits."

Together, they planned their next moves, undaunted by the political obstacles. For Pierre and Henri, promoting a unified time measurement in revolutionary France was more than a technical challenge—it was about establishing a new rhythm for the future.

—

Spring 1791 found Paris astir with revolutionary zeal, but a distinct revolution was being nurtured within Pierre's workshop. Illuminated by the warm glow of oil lamps, Pierre and Henri were engrossed in crafting the intricate mechanisms of the decimal clock. Each gear and spring represented a time segment and a piece of the new society Pierre envisaged.

One evening, amidst the clutter of tools and sketches, Henri, his youthful face marked by deep concentration, paused and looked up. "Father, how will people react to this new time system? It represents such a fundamental shift."

Pierre wiped his brow and considered the question. "Change often meets resistance, Henri, but acceptance is born from understanding. We must educate them and demonstrate the advantages. This clock," he gestured towards the grand assembly of cogs and wheels, "will act as a public tutorial." They could transport a large yet portable clock around Paris to reach and engage a wider audience.

A few days later, an ideal opportunity presented itself. A local market festival was scheduled, and Pierre secured a booth. Amid the colourful chaos of vendors and entertainers, they positioned their model of the decimal clock. Armed with a stack of leaflets, Pierre was ready to engage the gathering crowd, drawn by the novelty of their invention.

"This clock," Pierre began, his voice carrying over the crowd's murmurs, "divides the day into ten hours, each hour into one hundred minutes, and each minute into one hundred seconds. It simplifies time, just as the metric system simplifies our measurements."

An intrigued middle-aged shopper stepped forward, voicing a common scepticism. "But why change the way we measure the day? Doesn't this complicate things?"

With a patient smile, Pierre replied, "Consider this—our current system is based on ancient Babylonian mathematics, which is somewhat arbitrary. By aligning our time with the new systems of weights and measures, we streamline all aspects of daily life, bringing us in step with the rational ideals of our Republic."

As Pierre explained, Henri demonstrated the clock's mechanics, highlighting the smooth progression of its hands. The crowd's initial scepticism gradually transformed into murmurs of appreciation, sparking discussions and debates among them.

Later, as the market square emptied, Pierre and Henri packed away their booth. Henri, looking contemplative, asked, "Do you think they understood, Father?"

"Some did, and more will," Pierre answered, securing their equipment. "Lasting change takes time, and the adoption of decimal time is no exception. But today, we've sown seeds."

Walking home past Notre Dame, whose bells chimed the late hour, Pierre glanced up at the cathedral and the stars above. "The stars follow nature's laws, Henri. We assign them names and measures to understand our world. One day, our measurements will align more closely with nature, just as our Republic seeks to align with the principles of liberty and reason."

Back at his desk that evening, Pierre penned another treatise on decimal time, inspired by the day's interactions. His words were crafted not merely to persuade but to enlighten, striving to extend the reach of reason further into the heart of the revolution.

As dawn broke over the rooftops of Paris, the city was bathed in a new light, symbolising the fresh hope Pierre harboured for his vision of decimal time.

By June 1791, Paris was a crucible of revolutionary transformation, its streets alive with the clamour of citizens eager for sweeping changes across all spectrums of daily life. Amid this tumultuous atmosphere, Pierre's push to institutionalise decimal time as part of these reforms was gaining momentum, driven by the collective desire to sever ties with the past.

In a cramped room filled with influential members of the Assembly, Pierre stood poised, his attire plain but his presence formidable. Beside him, Henri watched, filled with pride and nervous anticipation.

"Ladies and gentlemen," Pierre began, his voice unwavering, "as we reshape our nation, we must also revolutionise how we measure time. Decimal time is not just a scientific innovation—it embodies the Enlightenment ideals of rationality and equality that this revolution champions. Just as we have adopted the metric system, we should also streamline our concept of time."

He presented a visual comparison between the proposed decimal clock and a traditional clock, highlighting the new system's simplicity against the old's outdated complexity.

"Pierre pointed to the new design, "This model represents simplicity and unity. It promises streamlined commerce, education, and daily interactions by introducing a universal time zone that unifies the entire French metropolis under a single time standard."

The assembly murmured, some nods of approval mingling with hesitant murmurs. A provincial delegate raised a concern, "Monsieur Moreau, your vision is compelling, but the implementation across France seems daunting. How will we manage the costs and the massive effort of re-education?"

Acknowledging the validity of the concerns, Pierre responded, "Indeed, the transition presents challenges. However, consider the long-term advantages: a unified time system enhances the efficiency of our scientific endeavours, eases daily interactions, and sends a powerful message about our commitment to progress and modernity. This initiative could also be integrated into the broader educational reforms already under discussion."

As the debate unfolded, Henri circulated among the attendees, distributing detailed pamphlets outlining decimal time's practical benefits. His discussions were spirited, echoing his father's passion and increasingly resonant with his growing advocacy skills.

Meanwhile, news of King Louis XVI's failed attempt to flee to Varennes stirred further unrest outside. On the night of 20-21 June 1791, the king's botched escape to the town of Varennes, intending to regroup with loyalist forces, had backfired spectacularly, bringing him and his family back to Paris under guard, deepening public distrust and solidifying the revolutionary fervour.

Seizing on the moment's symbolic weight, Pierre drew a parallel between the king's actions and the need for progressive change in timekeeping. "The flight to Varennes underscores the futility of clinging to outdated practices. Just as the monarchy's failure to adapt has led to its crisis, so will our society struggle if we ignore the need for rational and progressive reforms in measuring our time. Today, we stand at a crossroads to adopt a system that mirrors our revolutionary values of liberty and equality."

Later that day, Pierre rallied the citizens at a spontaneous gathering in a local café. "The king's attempt to reverse our revolution highlights why we must push forward with our reforms. Let's embrace a new time system reflecting our revolutionary aspirations."

This analogy struck a chord with the crowd, linking the political shift to a conceptual leap in timekeeping. Observing the crowd's reactions, Henri felt a profound connection between the revolutionary ideologies and their practical implementation.

Walking home under the Parisian stars, Pierre reflected on the day's events with Henri. "Today, we've not only championed a new way of measuring time but have embedded it deeply into the fabric of our revolution. Our efforts are more than just about advancing clockwork; they symbolise the dawn of a new era."

Under the starlit sky, Pierre and Henri weren't merely spectators of history; they were actively forging it, crafting a future where time itself would be a testament to the ideals of the French Revolution.

—

As June 1791 ended, France was on the precipice of further political disruption. In this climate of uncertainty, Pierre intensified his advocacy for decimal time, aligning it closely with the revolutionary shifts engulfing the nation.

In the aftermath of the Flight to Varennes, the disillusionment with the monarchy surged, echoing through Paris with a momentum reminiscent of the storming of the Bastille. Against this backdrop, the grand clock at Place Royale, constructed by Pierre and Henri, became a marvel of engineering and a focal point for the revolutionary spirit.

Standing tall in the market square, the clock drew crowds that were both curious and idealistic, their interests piqued by the novel concept of decimal time. It was here, amidst the buzz of the square, that Pierre took the opportunity to connect deeply with the citizens, transforming each exhibition and explanation of the clock's workings into a significant event.

"Observe, Henri," Pierre would often say, gesturing towards the intricate mechanisms of their creation, "each movement is precise, each setting intentional. This clock does more than measure time; it symbolises our dedication to a rational, organised society."

Henri, whose expertise and confidence had grown under his father's guidance, adeptly handled the clock's demonstrations. He had become a proficient spokesman for their cause, eloquently explaining how the clock's regularity and precision mirrored the revolution's aspirations for order and equality.

Their efforts were timely. As news of the king's botched escape spread, more Parisians were drawn to Place Royale, eager to witness the symbol of change—the decimal clock—that promised a new way of life aligned with revolutionary values. Pierre seized these moments to deepen the public's understanding of how decimal time could fundamentally transform society, reinforcing the clock's role as a beacon of the new era they were striving to build.

"Fellow citizens, just as our quest for liberty cannot be restrained, we must liberate ourselves from the inconsistencies of traditional timekeeping. Let us adopt a system that mirrors our new principles—equality, rationality, unity. Decimal time simplifies the day into intervals that are easily understood and shared equally by all."

His speeches resonated with the audience, stirring a mix of agreement, curiosity, and scepticism. The newspaper *Le Moniteur Universel*, keen to reflect the city's evolving dynamics, frequently featured articles on Pierre's initiatives, sometimes quoting him directly, other times analysing the feasibility of his ideas.

Amid this flurry of activities, an invitation arrived for Pierre to address the Assembly—a pivotal opportunity to advocate for decimal time not only to the public but also to those with the authority to implement it nationally. As the date of his presentation drew near, Pierre prepared meticulously, recognising the moment's significance.

The night before his scheduled speech, Pierre and Henri reviewed their workshop's critical points by candlelight. Pierre, usually animated when discussing decimal time, appeared tense, the strain of their late-night preparations evident.

"Remember, Henri, it's not solely about proving that decimal time is effective—it's about persuading them of its necessity for the Republic," Pierre stated, his gaze intense yet fatigued.

Henri observed his father, and the mix of dedication and exhaustion was evident on his face. "Father, you've created more than a clock. You've introduced a new perspective on time itself."

Pierre smiled, his hand resting on Henri's shoulder. "And you, my son, have been instrumental. Tomorrow, we stand before the Assembly as craftsmen and pioneers."

As they left their workshop for the night, walking towards their modest apartment in the Marais, the streets of Paris thrummed with the restless energy of a nation on the cusp of further change. With the quiet ticking of their decimal clock in the background, Pierre and Henri prepared for a day that might herald a new chapter in the French Revolution.

—

As the National Assembly dealt with the fallout from Varennes, Pierre prepared for an important speech. Scheduled on the anniversary of the Civil Constitution of the Clergy, July 1791, his address was an opportunity to link the need for time-keeping reform with broader revolutionary changes.

The night before his speech, Pierre and Henri reviewed their strategy by candlelight in their workshop. "Tomorrow is about more than just introducing a new clock or calendar, Henri," Pierre reflected. "It's about presenting a vision of order and predictability in these chaotic times. It's about showing that every minute counts in the new France we strive to build."

Henri nodded his experience over the past year, deepening his understanding of their mission. "They'll see the sense in your words, Father. Decimal time is not just a new measure; it's a declaration of our values."

As Pierre addressed the Assembly the following day, he passionately argued for adopting decimal time, tying it to the revolutionary aspirations of liberty, equality, and fraternity. He spoke as both an inventor and a committed citizen, eager to see his innovations contribute to the Republic's renewal.

"As we redefine our government and our society, let us also redefine how we measure time," Pierre concluded, his voice echoing in the chamber filled with attentive deputies.

Initially met with hesitation, his proposal gradually sparked interest and discussion among the legislators, many of whom were keen to establish a new society distinctly different from the *Ancien Régime*.

Leaving the Assembly, the buzz of conversation that followed them was a blend of curiosity and cautious optimism. Pierre and Henri walked back through the changing streets of Paris, the cityscape a vivid tableau of the ongoing revolution.

In that defining moment, as the hands of the grand clock in Place Royale ticked in its novel rhythm, it mirrored the nation's journey towards a new dawn, marking time in a way that epitomised the revolutionary spirit sweeping across France.

Chapter Four

In the summer of 1791, as Paris simmered with revolutionary change, Pierre Moreau and his son, Henri, became central figures in a movement that fundamentally sought to alter the concept of time. Their promotion of decimal time resonated with the sweeping reforms transforming the Republic. Pierre's commitment to his vision was steadfast. At the same time, Henri, now sixteen, took on more prominent roles, articulating the nuances of their system at public forums that attracted crowds eager to embrace new ideas.

At home, however, concern mingled with their ambition. Claire, Pierre's wife, felt uneasy about their increasing prominence. Her salons, a weekly feature in their workshop, had become a sounding board for the anxieties brewing within revolutionary Paris. Late one evening, she shared her worries with Pierre, "Our family is becoming a symbol, and with that comes both reverence and suspicion."

As Pierre grappled with personal dilemmas, Paris's political climate grew increasingly charged. The Assembly was a hotbed of intense debates and radical propositions, reflecting the city's deep divisions. Within this vibrant atmosphere, Maximilien Robespierre, a leading figure among the Jacobins and an advocate for liberty, equality, and fraternity, recognised the potential in Pierre's work. Intrigued by the philosophical implications of decimal time, Robespierre saw Pierre's efforts as a way to advance the rational science that could guide the Republic towards true enlightenment.

Having risen to prominence as a radical faction within the French Revolution, the Jacobins were known for advocating republican values and a centralised state. Their origins in the former Jacobin friars' monastery in Paris lent their name a historical echo that contrasted sharply with their progressive aims, which included championing the rights of the less privileged and advocating for universal male suffrage.

Robespierre's support brought Pierre into the inner circles of revolutionary power and closer to the Revolution's more dangerous currents. During one assembly, as Pierre presented a model of the grand clock intended for the market square, Robespierre quietly cautioned, "Your clock measures more than time, Pierre; it measures our societal evolution. Ensure it aligns with the pulse of our new Republic." This remark left Pierre pondering the more profound implications of his work.

Throughout the year, as Pierre and Henri continued to advocate for decimal time, each presentation and public lecture they conducted was met with enthusiastic reception but also rigorous scrutiny. They attracted attention from supportive citizens and those who viewed their innovative ideas as potential threats.

Henri, growing under both his father's guidance and Robespierre's watchful presence, began to grasp the intricate connections between their technological pursuits and the broader mechanics of political power. One evening, reflecting on the day's events, he asked, "Father, is our clock then pivotal to the nation's fate?"

Observing his son's development with pride and concern, Pierre responded thoughtfully, "It might well be, Henri. Yet, we must navigate cautiously, for as we adjust the flow of time, we must also be mindful of its impact on history."

This dialogue underlined the dual nature of their undertaking—not only were they redefining the measure of time but also participating in shaping a new societal order, where each tick of their revolutionary clock echoed the transformative beats of the French Revolution.

—

As the summer of 1791 intensified, the vibrant streets of Paris were alive with the sounds of change. Distinguished among those advocating revolutionary reforms, Pierre Moreau found himself deeply engaged in a whirlwind of activities. His days were filled with legislative meetings, public demonstrations of his decimal clock, and secretive discussions with figures like Maximilien Robespierre. Each tick of the experimental clock in Place Royale seemed to synchronise with the city's rapidly beating heart of revolution.

Amidst this tumult, Henri, matching the growing scale of their ambitions, assumed a role beyond his years. Under the guidance of his father and influenced by the city's radical intellectuals, he evolved from apprentice to visionary. Together, Pierre and Henri crafted compelling arguments, likening the order, rationality, and fairness of decimal time to the natural rights espoused by Enlightenment thinkers.

However, not everyone was convinced by their proposals. With perhaps a clearer perspective than Pierre—her insights sharpened by the exchanges at her weekly salons—Claire Fontaine sensed the increasing dangers. The political atmosphere teetered on a knife-edge, and Pierre's prominence placed him in a precarious position. One quiet evening, in the seclusion of their study, she expressed her apprehensions, "You are steering the currents of change, Pierre, but remember, those who stir the waters often find themselves swept away by the tides."

Despite Claire's warnings, the thrill of potential recognition propelled them forward. In August, the Assembly became an arena of heated debate. Invited to speak, Pierre stood before a divided audience and articulated his vision. "Consider a revolution in how we measure time," he proposed, unveiling a model of the grand public clock. "Envision a society where time summons us not to servitude under church or monarch but to the ideals of liberty, equality, and fraternity."

His presentation sparked support and scepticism, sending ripples through the halls of power. Outside, the public discourse fractured, rumours of counter-revolutionary conspiracies intermingled with debates about the nation's future direction.

During this period, Robespierre, increasingly viewed as the custodian of revolutionary integrity, showed a particular interest in Pierre's endeavours. His visits to the workshop, *Moreau Horlogerie*, became more frequent, with each session being dense with discussions on the intersection of science and societal progress. "Your clock," Robespierre reflected on one occasion, "represents more than a mere measurement device; it is a gauge of our advancement towards an ideal republic."

As the month waned, Pierre and Henri, amid piles of diagrams and mechanical parts, dedicated long nights to their project. What they were creating transcended mere machinery; it was a manifesto crafted from metal and gears, symbolising their belief in a rational and structured future. Yet, as they delved deeper into their work, the shadows outside their workshop lengthened, and the voices of dissent grew more strident. Pausing to look out over Paris's rooftops, Henri sensed their task's weight. "We are forging more than just timekeepers, Father," he mused, his gaze returning to the scattered designs before him. "We are shaping the very fabric of time itself," fully embodying his father's revolutionary ethos.

As August waned, the revolutionary spirit that had captivated Paris reached new heights. The Moreau family found themselves at the heart of a society in flux, with Pierre and Henri's efforts to promote decimal time becoming entwined with broader political movements. Their concept, a symbol of progress and reason, resonated with the revolutionary ideals sweeping through the city, drawing the attention of influential figures, including members of the burgeoning Jacobin Club.

Maximilien Robespierre, a meticulous and increasingly influential figure within the Jacobins, began to see in Pierre a kindred spirit—an innovator whose ideas could symbolise the rational restructuring of society. Despite his ambitions, Robespierre tended to perceive some ideas as threats to the new revolutionary order in Paris. Their discussions, which initially centred on the symbolism of decimal time, gradually ventured into deeper ideological territories. With his ascetic demeanour and penetrating gaze, Robespierre spoke passionately about the need for a revolution in governance and how citizens perceived and measured their lives.

"Your work," Robespierre told Pierre during a visit to their workshop, "epitomises the Enlightenment's greatest strengths—clarity, precision, and equality. Just as we seek to eliminate the old regime's arbitrariness in law and order, so must we standardise time measurement across France."

Henri, keenly observant, listened intently as discussions unfolded. He was absorbing the technical skills his father taught him and the revolutionary ideology that permeated their home. This era of endless possibilities shaped Henri's youth, leading him to ponder the philosophical implications of time in the context of freedom and control.

Meanwhile, Claire, the matriarch, remained a step back from Pierre's public pursuits, allowing her to watch over her husband and son during the turbulent times taking shape. Always observant and pragmatic, she viewed the growing prominence of Pierre and Henri with a mix of pride and apprehension. The streets buzzed with talk of legislative changes and public debates, and the Moreau name was increasingly mentioned with both admiration and hints of envy and suspicion. In the dim light of their parlour, she confided her worries to her closest friend, saying, "For every supporter they have, there's someone else who views their success as a threat." From her position as a less public figure, she was uniquely attuned to the underlying currents of the revolution.

―

In September 1791, as the king's grip on power became nothing more than a hapless figurehead, Paris was awash with debates and clashes. Amid this tumult, the Moreau family reached a pivotal point. Their work on the decimal clock had ignited the imaginations of many, symbolising a new era of rationalism and order amidst the chaos.

In their bustling workshop, the steady tick of the nearly completed grand clock mirrored the city's intense atmosphere. Outside, voices of revolution mingled with whispers of danger. With Henri's diligent assistance inside, Pierre made the final adjustments to the intricate mechanism that promised to set the tempo for their new world.

Always wise and cautious, Claire maintained a measured distance from Pierre's fervour over decimal time, her insights into the political landscape sharpened by her weekly salons. While she appreciated their achievements, her pride was tinged with concern. The visibility that came with their success brought accolades and scrutiny. In a political climate that was becoming increasingly volatile, Pierre's prominent role as a proponent of this new measure of time made him a distinguished and vulnerable figure.

During this period, the influence of Maximilien Robespierre and the Jacobins proliferated. Their calls for justice and equality struck a chord with the public. Once a marginal figure, Robespierre had now become a pivotal presence, pushing for radical and sweeping reforms to purify the Republic.

One evening, as they gathered in their dining room, the discussion naturally drifted towards the political storms engulfing Paris. Robespierre, present as a guest, spoke eloquently about the necessity for a new moral and temporal framework. "The fabric of our society must be rewoven," he asserted, his intensity captivating those gathered. "Your decimal clock, Pierre, is more than a timekeeping device; it symbolises the new order. Just as we aim to cleanse our Republic, we must redefine our perception of time."

Now mature beyond his years, Henri absorbed every word, keenly aware of the weight of their undertaking. The symbolism was clear to him—their clock could either unify the nation or make them targets for those resistant to change.

As summer transitioned into autumn, the atmosphere in Place de la Révolution was not only filled with the lingering warmth of late summer but also thick with palpable anticipation. Paris, a city buzzing with rumours and conspiracies, felt like a powder keg ready to explode. The upcoming public unveiling of the decimal clock in the square was eagerly awaited, seen not just as a demonstration of technological innovation but also as a rallying point for those advocating for a rational and orderly revolution.

Every tick of the clock in their workshop was a stark reminder of time slipping away, drawing them closer to the launch and the unpredictable responses it might elicit. Pierre and Henri, motivated by a commitment to progress and unnerved by the potential backlash, pressed on with determination and apprehension.

—

As late September 1791 unfolded, the streets of Paris thrummed with the energy of revolution. The city's boulevards, alive with animated discussions and the rustle of wind through the leaves, echoed the fevered pace of change. Amidst this atmosphere of rampant idealism, Pierre Moreau and his son, Henri, pushed forward with their decimal clock project. This venture increasingly aligned them with the political sentiment sweeping the city.

In their workshop in the vibrant Marais district, the clock—destined for the newly named Place de la Révolution—became more than a device to measure hours; it was a monument to the new era they envisioned. Each adjustment Pierre made to the clock's gears and springs was done with meticulous care, ensuring flawless operation as a symbol of progress.

"Father, do you think people will grasp what this represents?" Henri pondered aloud one afternoon, his voice resonating against the stone walls crowded with tools and diagrams.

"They will, eventually," Pierre reassured him, blending hope with caution. "Change is gradual for those steeped in old traditions. Our clock isn't just about tracking hours; it represents a new way of conceptualising time."

Meanwhile, Claire Fontaine, Pierre's wife, expressed growing concerns about their rising prominence, especially during her weekly salons. Despite her pride in their work, the visibility they were garnering made her uneasy amidst such unpredictable times. The revolutionary zeal was lifting them to a precarious height, and the increasingly strident tones from figures like Robespierre and the

Jacobins regarding counter-revolutionaries only heightened her anxiety.

"High visibility in such times can be as perilous as obscurity," she confided to her sister in their quiet kitchen. "I worry for Pierre and Henri, not just because of the monarchy's remnants but from those who claim to be our allies."

Her fears were not without merit. As Pierre and Henri's profiles rose, so did their interactions with vital revolutionary figures, including the enigmatic and powerful Maximilien Robespierre. Robespierre, both revered and feared, saw in Pierre's initiatives the embodiment of the rational and scientific principles he held dear.

"Monsieur Moreau, your work aligns closely with our Republic's vision," Robespierre observed during a visit to their workshop, his piercing gaze sweeping across the assortment of mechanical components. "Time, measured and managed like the resources that sustain us, can be a tool for promoting equality and order."

Pierre, aware of the dual implications of Robespierre's words, responded with careful diplomacy. "Our aim is simply to enhance the lives of our citizens through a clearer understanding of natural laws," he said, cautiously sidestepping a direct political endorsement.

As the warmth of summer gave way to the crisp air of early autumn, the political climate in Paris grew increasingly charged. Rumours of dissent and secretive plots wove through the city's fabric, placing the Moreau family at a crossroads between their revolutionary ideals and the stark realities of the era.

Each day, the unveiling of their latest decimal clock drew closer, symbolising the passage of time and counting down to an uncertain climax. Amidst these rising tensions, the lives of the Moreau family were woven ever more tightly with the fate of the Revolution, their personal and public existences intertwined with the transformative currents of their time.

—

Amid the changing allegiances and hushed conversations of political intrigue, Pierre Moreau's workshop emerged as a hub of innovation and philosophical debate. As the revolutionary landscape transformed, the significance of his decimal clock extended beyond mechanical innovation to embody the Enlightenment principles of rationality and equality.

On a brisk October morning, as the marketplace stirred with the early hustle of vendors and the rumble of carts, Pierre and Henri made subtle adjustments to their clock. The air around them was charged with a sense of expectation, mirroring the anxious mood of Paris itself.

"Father, the people seem uneasy today," Henri noted, handing Pierre a tool, his voice reflecting his growing awareness of the societal undercurrents.

"Indeed, the city pulses with the anticipation of change, restless and charged," Pierre responded, aware of the broader implications of their work. His project had captured the attention of the city's intellectuals and was now drawing the eyes of its political leaders.

Meanwhile, in a secluded room, Maximilien Robespierre discussed the symbolic potential of the Moreaus' clock with his Jacobin colleagues. "This clock could mark the steady pulse of the Republic, a beacon of order and enlightenment," he suggested, his eyes reflecting intense conviction.

As they continued their work, Claire Fontaine, feeling the mounting pressure of their increasing prominence, conferred in hushed tones with a journalist friend, Marianne Beaulieu. "Be wary, Claire. Pierre and Henri are now more than inventors; they are symbols, and symbols are potent and vulnerable," she cautioned, emphasising the precariousness of their position.

At the square, as the clock approached completion, the discourse around time mingled with debates on liberty and governance. Pierre seized this moment to engage with his fellow citizens. "Time moves forward without bias; let it remind our leaders to act with fairness and justice," he declared to an attentive crowd, his words resonating with the themes of impartiality and progress.

As October wore on, the atmosphere in Paris shifted palpably. The scrutiny of the Jacobins grew more pronounced, and the city bristled with a mix of hope and suspicion. Whispers of a registry of enemies to the revolution circulated, adding to the tension.

Deeply involved yet contemplative, Henri voiced his concerns during a quiet moment in their workshop. "Father, are we risking too much for this vision of a rationalised time?" he asked, his expression shadowed by the workshop's dim light.

Pierre looked at his son, a mix of paternal protectiveness and pride swelling within him. "To forge the future, we must sometimes stand in the spotlight, regardless of its glare," he answered, his voice steady yet uncertain.

—

November 1791 in Paris carried the unmistakable bite of winter's approach. The leaves, once vibrant, now crunched underfoot as the city was enveloped in the stark contrasts of revolution. Amidst these transformative times, Pierre Moreau and his son Henri stood amidst a society on the brink of redefinition, their lives mirroring the more significant shifts in the mechanics of timekeeping and the very structure of the Republic itself.

Pierre, a man driven more by his passion for scientific advancement than a desire for recognition, found himself increasingly in the public eye—a position he both appreciated for its influence and feared for its dangers. With each public demonstration of his innovative timepiece, the crowd's enthusiasm grew, but so did the attention from political factions and royalist detractors.

Claire, Pierre's wife, though proud of the advances her husband and son were making, maintained a cautious perspective. She observed the shifting political currents with growing concern, aware of the risks associated with their rising visibility. In the quiet of their home, she warned, "Remember, not all eyes that watch us are friendly."

At gatherings in cafés and meeting halls where the nation's fate was debated, Pierre's contributions to the rational measurement of time were increasingly noted. Maximilien Robespierre, whose influence was growing by the day, saw in Pierre's decimal clock a symbol of the order and rationality he sought to impose on France. "The precision of Moreau's clock mirrors the precision we need in our governance," Robespierre remarked during a meeting, reflecting both admiration and a strategic calculation of the clock's symbolic power.

Meanwhile, Pierre and Henri, somewhat removed from the depths of political intrigue, focused on completing another clock. This new clock was designed not just as a functional timekeeper but as a marker of the revolutionary changes proposed by the Assembly, aligning with the proposed revolutionary calendar.

However, the streets of Paris were far from safe, and the political atmosphere was tense. Pierre's visibility made him a target for scrutiny and suspicion. During a visit to the Assembly, he was confronted by a group of sans-culottes emblematic of the radical elements of the revolution. These working-class militants were pivotal in pressing for profound societal changes.

One particularly outspoken sans-culotte challenged Pierre directly, his tone suspicious and aggressive. "Why should we trust your new order of time?" he demanded, reflecting the broader unease with rapid changes and the distrust of those perceived to be in positions of influence.

Recognising the critical need to align his innovations with the revolution's ideals, Pierre appealed to the principles of equality and unity. "Just as all citizens are born free and equal, so should everyone share equally in the time measurement. My clock promotes a democracy of time," he argued, striving to connect his technological innovation to the core values of the revolution.

While fraught with tension, this encounter underscored Pierre's dual role as both an inventor and a revolutionary thinker, intertwining his technological advancements with the ideological battles of the era. However, the incident also highlighted the precariousness of his situation, as Claire's earlier warnings seemed ever more prescient.

As late November 1791 deepened, the air in Paris crackled with the tension of impending winter and revolutionary extremism. News of a slave revolution in Saint-Domingue trickled into the city, igniting fierce debates among the burgeoning abolitionist circles and adding another layer of complexity to the already charged atmosphere. Amidst this backdrop, Henri Moreau, who had grown into his role with a swift and severe dedication, felt the dual burdens of innovation and protection heavily upon his shoulders. Working alongside his father, Pierre, he honed his skills as a craftsman and emerged as a vigilant sentinel for their family's legacy. Each demonstration of their groundbreaking timekeeping technology carried the potential to stir the public's imagination or provoke dissent, reminding Henri of the delicate balance they must maintain in these transformative times.

—

In the sweltering July of 1792, Paris was alive with revolutionary energy. At the centre of this dynamic upheaval were Pierre Moreau and his son Henri, whose grand clocks in Place Royale and Place de la Révolution stood as bold symbols of the new era they envisioned —one shaped by the principles of the Enlightenment and the relentless pursuit of progress.

Henri, now seventeen, had grown remarkably under Pierre's mentorship, mastering the technical skills and embracing the philosophical depth of their work on decimal time aligning with the ideals of reason, order, and equality championed by the Enlightenment thinkers.

As the days passed, the political landscape of Paris grew tenser. Public debates and private conversations alike were charged with a sense of urgency and a demand for deep-seated changes. In this charged atmosphere, Maximilien Robespierre, a rising figure within the revolutionary leadership, began to align himself with the Moreaus' vision. Robespierre, known for his rigorous commitment to the revolution's ideals, saw the decimal clock as a powerful metaphor for the new order he hoped to establish.

However, the widespread acclaim for the Moreaus' work also brought sharper scrutiny from various factions within the burgeoning political arena. The Jacobins, in particular, saw the clock as a testament to revolutionary progress but were wary of its potential misuse by conservative forces clinging to the past.

One morning, during a public demonstration of a clock's new features, which included a calendar mechanism aligned with the proposed revolutionary calendar, the event was briefly interrupted by a group of Jacobin supporters. They praised the clock's symbolism but expressed concerns about its adoption across different strata of society. "This clock must be the people's clock, a beacon of the new France, not a relic of the old order," one outspoken member declared.

Quickly understanding the political undercurrents, Henri addressed the crowd with a maturity beyond his years. He spoke about the universality of decimal time, envisaging a France where everyone, irrespective of class, would share the same rhythm of life, unifying the nation under a common temporal framework.

As the day ended, Pierre and Henri, illuminated by the soft glow of Parisian street lamps, reflected on the events. Pierre shared with Henri the importance of their work transcending mere mechanics to embody revolutionary ideals. "Our clock does not just count moments; it counts the progress of our ideals, the heartbeat of the Republic," he explained, his voice imbued with hope and caution.

Walking through the lamp-lit streets, the Moreaus felt the weight of their contributions to this pivotal moment in history. Their invention, a product of Enlightenment thinking, had become intertwined with the very fabric of the revolution, holding the potential to either unify or divide, depending on how the tides of political change would turn.

—

A dynamic blend of hope and unease marked the summer of 1792 in Paris. The city, vibrant and full of contrasts, was alive with the chaotic pace of the revolution. The streets echoed with the determined footsteps of its citizens and the distant rumble of cannon fire, a testament to the significant mobilisation efforts underway. In April 1792, the revolutionary government declared war on Austria, beginning the War of the First Coalition. This exacerbated political tensions within France, intensifying the atmosphere as the revolutionary armies and the National Guard were actively engaged in drills and exercises, including the use of artillery. This preparation was critical as the new revolutionary government fortified the city and the nascent republic against the looming threats of both internal and external adversaries.

The debates and discussions were not confined to military strategies; pamphleteers were heralding their documents on everything from education reform to the abolition of slavery, adding to the robust push for reform. In this charged environment, Pierre, deeply committed to promoting decimal time, found a valuable ally in Monsieur Lefèvre, a member of the Assembly who shared his vision of rationalising daily life through scientific and mathematical principles. Together, they navigated the complex political landscape, advocating for changes that they believed would bring order and efficiency to the chaotic times.

Amid this backdrop of preparation and defence, the atmosphere in Paris was electrified with tension and anticipation. Smoke hung in the air, blending with the pervasive scent of apprehension and the exhilaration of revolutionary change.

Pierre Moreau's workshop had become a nexus of innovation and secret political discussions in a humble corner of the city. By August, the sound of the decimal clock, crafted by Pierre and his son Henri, echoed the city's tumultuous rhythm. With its precise engineering and groundbreaking concept, this clock was a manifesto in itself, symbolising the rational reordering of time and society. It represented a bold leap beyond mere scientific achievement into societal transformation.

On the fateful day of 10 August 1792, events escalated dramatically, marking a pivotal chapter in French history. The insurrection of the Tuileries Palace by the National Guard and revolutionary forces signalled the definitive collapse of monarchical power. The battle was fierce; smoke billowed, and the air filled with the sharp scent of gunpowder and the cries of combatants. The palace was breached, the royal family fled for their lives, and the monarchy's fall triggered a cascade of profound changes across the nation.

In the Moreau household, the significance of these events was deeply felt. Pierre, hands marred by oil and soot, and Henri, with a resolute expression, grasped that their creation had taken on a profound new role. The decimal clock was no longer just a timekeeping device; it had become a beacon for the new era, a symbol of the universal and rational principles they hoped would govern the future of France.

Following the fall of the Tuileries, the city's revolutionary intensity surged. The September Massacres began on 2 September 1792, a brutal purge of those suspected of counter-revolutionary sympathies, filling Paris with an atmosphere of fear and suspicion.

Amidst this tumult, Claire Fontaine, Pierre's wife and Henri's mother, watched with pride and concern. Her salons, held in the softly lit backroom of the workshop, had become crucial gatherings for intellectual and revolutionary debate. Figures from various sectors of society convened in this candlelit space, engaging in spirited discussions about the unfolding events and the nation's future.

Claire's salons served dual purposes: they were forums for debate and a protective measure for her family. She recognised the precarious balance between prominence and peril in a city where notoriety could be as dangerous as obscurity. Her attentive gaze during these discussions and the creases of worry on her brow reflected her acute awareness of the revolutionary government's paranoia, which saw potential foes in every dissenting voice. The flickering candles cast long, foreboding shadows mirrored the pervasive uncertainty of their times as Claire navigated the complex terrain of revolutionary Paris with vigilance and foresight.

Amid the charged atmosphere of Paris in 1792, Maximilien Robespierre's influence became increasingly significant. His name was now intertwined with his push for revolutionary justice and the emerging terror that shadowed it.

Robespierre's visits to the Moreau workshop, once infrequent and brief, grew more regular and purposeful. His intense scrutiny and articulate speeches hinted at an underlying threat. He saw the decimal clock as a timekeeper and a symbol for his vision of a rational, virtuous Republic.

One sweltering late summer afternoon, as the city buzzed with unrest, Robespierre entered the workshop. The consistent ticking of the clock punctuated the air, a constant reminder of time's unyielding progress. "Monsieur Moreau," he began, his voice both serene and authoritative, "your invention is more than a tool for measuring time; it embodies the reformation of our society—a society guided by the principles of reason and scientific rationality rather than the caprices of hereditary rule."

Recognising Robespierre's statement's gravity, Pierre responded with a thoughtful nod. Although deeply invested in the philosophical implications of his work, he remained cautious about its potential political exploitation. Outside, the atmosphere of Paris was electric as the abolition of the monarchy drew near. The streets brimmed with citizens passionately discussing the nation's future, with many debates evolving into spontaneous political assemblies.

Ever more engaged with the political ferment, Henri was frequently at these gatherings, his youthful enthusiasm moderated by the complexity of the discussions.

Claire, always concerned for her family's safety, often accompanied Henri, providing guidance laced with caution. She understood that the intensity of youthful idealism could lead to impulsiveness, which is especially dangerous in such unpredictable times. Her involvement in the revolutionary effort was pragmatic, aiming to keep their contributions impactful yet circumspect.

As September dawned, the city's sense of expectation intensified. The newly convened National Convention was deep in deliberations, setting the course for the revolution. The palpable tension hung heavy over Paris, with its residents poised on the edge of their seats, awaiting the decision to determine the monarchy's destiny.

On the morning of 21 September 1792, a hush settled over Paris. The streets, typically bustling, quieted as if the city braced for a monumental shift. The Moreau family—Pierre, his son Henri, and Claire—prepared to join the crowds converging on Place Royale, now the symbolic epicentre of revolutionary pursuits.

Dressed but with dignity, they navigated the winding streets, passing buildings scarred by recent conflicts. As they neared the square, the energy shifted; the air became electric with the mixed emotions of the crowd—hope, anxiety, determination—all palpable. Groups gathered, buzzing with conversation, occasionally punctuated by cheers from speakers who captured the crowd's imagination.

Arriving at Place Royale, they found themselves amid a sea of humanity united by a shared desire for change. Revolutionary banners fluttered, and the Triclour dominated the scene, symbolising the struggle and aspirations of the people. As the crowd swelled, people from all walks of life stood together, waiting for the pivotal announcement.

At noon, as sunlight bathed the square, a profound silence fell. The delegates of the National Convention took to the stage. With a declaration that resonated through the square, the president announced, "The National Convention decrees the abolition of the monarchy!" The response was immediate—a thunderous roar, emotions spilling over as tears and joyous embraces marked the historic moment.

Henri, inspired and hopeful, turned to his parents. "This is the beginning," he stated, his voice resonant with conviction.

Pierre, placing a reassuring hand on Henri's shoulder, replied, "Indeed, it is, Henri. Yet the path ahead will be strewn with challenges. We must stay vigilant and committed to our principles."

Her eyes were reflective with unshed tears, and Claire added, "The monarchy's fall is a significant step, but it's merely the start. We must strive relentlessly to see the ideals of liberty, equality, and fraternity realised."

As the assembly dispersed, the Moreaus returned to their workshop, the rhythmic ticking of the decimal clock a backdrop to their thoughts. The events of the day had left an indelible mark on them. This precise and relentless clock wasn't just a keeper of time but a symbol of the ongoing march towards a rational and equitable society.

That evening, under the twilight sky of Paris, they gathered in their workshop, surrounded by the familiar scent of oil and metal, the remnants of their day's work. The clock ticked on, each movement marking the close of an era and the dawn of a new one.

They sat in the glow of candlelight, contemplating the day's significance. The abolition of the monarchy was a milestone, heralding new challenges and a future filled with uncertainties. Yet, at that moment, the Moreaus were united by a resolve to contribute to creating a new society based on the Enlightenment ideals they cherished.

As the candles dwindled, casting a soft light in the workshop, the steady tick of the decimal clock was a constant reminder of the ongoing revolution—a revolution not just of political institutions but of time itself. With each tick, they reaffirmed their commitment to shaping this new world, prepared to meet the future, one tick at a time.

—

On 22 September 1792, Paris awoke to a new era. The streets, still resonating with the echoes of the previous night's jubilation over the proclamation of the Republic, carried a palpable sense of renewal. Despite the exhaustion from the celebrations and his presentation, Pierre Moreau rose with a renewed sense of purpose. The fall of the monarchy heralded new possibilities for his decimal time project.

The workshop was quiet that morning, with tools and sketches untouched as Pierre and Henri paused to consider the historical weight of the moment. Henri, matching his father's enthusiasm but clouded with anxiety about the future, voiced his concerns. "What now, Father? How will the Republic receive our ideas?" he asked, seeking reassurance in the uncertain dawn of this new era.

Pierre, gazing out the window at the Parisians passing by, each face etched with a blend of resolve and uncertainty, responded thoughtfully. "We align with the pulse of the Republic, Henri. Our work on decimal time complements the revolutionary calendar; it's rational, orderly, and democratic. We must continue to showcase its value, not just as a method for measuring time but as a symbol of the new societal order," he explained, his voice unwavering.

Outside, the city buzzed with discussions and debates about the future implications of the new government, the roles of key figures like Maximilien Robespierre, and the rise of the Jacobins, whose growing influence stirred both admiration and apprehension.

Claire sensed a blend of pride and concern. The previous night's successful demonstration had thrust their family into an unwelcome spotlight. As Pierre joined her, she quietly shared her apprehensions. "Pierre, tread carefully. Our ideas now intersect with broader movements, and not everyone might embrace this change as we do."

Acknowledging the validity of Claire's concerns, Pierre spent the day with Henri fine-tuning a decimal clock model, preparing for further demonstrations to convince the new government's influential figures. Meanwhile, in the political arenas of Paris, Robespierre and the Jacobins were tightening their grip on power, their vision for the future of the Republic proving to be as radical as Pierre's proposals.

As dusk fell, the streets filled with Parisians keen to discuss the day's events again. The Moreau family joined their neighbours, engaging in the vibrant discussions that surged around them. Pierre seized the opportunity to promote his decimal time system, linking it to the nascent ideals of the Republic, stressing that innovation and unity were paramount.

Henri observed intently, absorbing not only the intricacies of timekeeping but also the nuances of persuasion during tumultuous times. He noted how his father intertwined the revolution in governance with the revolution in timekeeping, underscoring the preciousness of every moment of change.

Chapter Five

On the morning of September 23, 1792, the air over Paris was crisp, tinged with the smell of change and the rustle of dry leaves swirling through the cobbled streets. In these transformative days, Pierre Moreau and his seventeen-year-old son, Henri, found themselves at the heart of a city thrumming with vibrant calls for new beginnings.

Pierre, a visionary horologist, saw the seismic shift in the political landscape as an opportunity to advocate for his revolutionary idea of Decimal Time. The recent ousting of the monarchy and the declaration of the French Republic had primed society for radical reforms, even in the measurement and perception of time. Henri, no longer the boy who once marvelled at his father's intricate clockwork but now his skilled and insightful partner, adeptly navigated complex discussions with the public and emerging political figures.

Their forums had become a nexus of intellectual exchange, frequently hosting members of the nascent National Convention, drawn by the allure of Decimal Time's promise to embody the revolutionary ideals of equality and rationality. Pierre held his forums in the vibrant Palais Royal, attracting a melange of thinkers, radicals, and sceptics eager to see how reshaping the very concept of time could further the revolution's aims.

"As we redefine time, so must we redefine society," Pierre often proclaims during these gatherings, his voice echoing off the stone walls, stirring his audience. Watching from the sidelines, Henri saw the fire of idealism reflected in the eyes of the attendees—a mixture of resolve and curiosity that fueled his own passion.

The political atmosphere, however, was as charged as the intellectual intrigue of the forums. The National Convention, which had convened just days before on September 20th, was a hotbed of factionalism, with the moderate Girondins and the radical Montagnards vying for control. These groups debated governance and the principles that should guide the new republic amidst the looming threat of counter-revolution.

Though primarily a man of gears and springs, Pierre found himself increasingly caught in the political currents. His advocacy for Decimal Time, initially a cultural and scientific cause, had morphed into a political statement, aligning him with radical elements favouring deep societal reform.

Henri, for his part, penned his reflections during these heady days. "The revolution asks of us more than we anticipated," he wrote in his diary. "It demands not just our skills but our very souls. As Father speaks of reordering time, so too must we consider the reordering of our lives and loyalties."

The debates surrounding the adoption of the Revolutionary Calendar, proposing a complete overhaul of the year divorced from royal and religious traditions, mirrored Pierre's struggles. This was no coincidence but a parallel campaign—his and the republic's efforts to liberate society from the shackles of the past, proposing a new, rational structure for life itself.

As the leaves turned and the air grew colder, the discussions in Pierre's workshop and the halls of the Convention drew sharper, more urgent. "To recalibrate time is to recalibrate power," Pierre argued one evening, his eyes intense. "What is time but the measure of our lives? And what is revolution but life demanding to be measured anew?"

Henri, sitting across from him, scribbled these words down. They were not just witnessing history but threading it through the fabric of time, each tick of the clock a step into uncertainty and possibility. As the shadows of the season stretched longer, so did the shadows of their endeavour, each moment heavy with the weight of futures yet unformed.

—

As the calm winds of autumn swept through Paris in 1792, bringing a drop in temperature and stirring the currents of political upheaval, Pierre Moreau and his son Henri found themselves deeply intertwined in the revolutionary excitement sweeping the nation. Their workshop in the heart of Paris became a crucible of innovation and political discourse as they advocated for a radical idea: Decimal Time. Inspired by Enlightenment thinkers like Voltaire and Rousseau, who championed reason and equality, Pierre and Henri aimed to reshape how time was measured and how it reflected the values of the newly formed French Republic.

The workshop was cluttered with gears, pendulums, and papers scattered about, the air thick with the smell of oil and metal. Amid this chaos, the father and son duo worked to integrate Decimal Time with the Revolutionary Calendar, believing that timekeeping should mirror the revolution's principles by being logical, consistent, and egalitarian—reflecting a break from the past just as the calendar did.

"Henri, take a look at this," Pierre said, pointing to a new diagram on the wall. "This design improves the mechanics of our decimal clock, making it more efficient."

Carefully examining the complex gears and springs before him, Henri nodded in approval. "This could enhance how accurately we measure and represent time, Father. It's a significant step forward in clock design."

However, their revolutionary project did not go unnoticed. The growing influence of the Jacobin Club, initially seen as a protector of the Republic's ideals, began to stir unease among the populace. The Jacobins' increasing dominance highlighted the complexities of revolutionary power dynamics. At a bustling meeting of the Jacobin Club, Robespierre, a central figure, discussed the potential of Decimal Time.

"Citizens," Robespierre declared, his voice echoing in the crowded hall, "just as we have reset society, we must also reset our clocks. Decimal Time is not merely about measurement but order and equality. It is about structuring our society so every citizen can understand and access."

Pierre's project gained prominence, buoyed by Robespierre's support, but also attracted scrutiny from political adversaries wary of too much change. This period was marked by Henri's reflections in his diary, noting the precariousness of their situation—how their innovations drew both admiration and suspicion, symbolising broader tensions within the revolution.

As they prepared a new Decimal Clock prototype for public unveiling at the Hôtel de Ville, Pierre and Henri planned to distribute similar prototypes across Paris. This strategic deployment was meant to embed their concept deeply within the revolutionary fabric of the city, making Decimal Time a common standard that symbolised a new era of rationalism and equality.

The unveiling day arrived, and the Hôtel de Ville buzzed with anticipation. Crowds gathered, murmurs of curiosity mixing with whispers of dissent. Pierre addressed the assembly with a steady voice, unveiling the gleaming brass and polished wood of the Decimal Clock.

"Behold, a clock not bound by ancient tradition but inspired by our new-found liberty. Let every tick remind us of our freedom; every tick pushes us towards equality."

The mounting anxiety about their work and its implications was palpable as they navigated the increasingly charged atmosphere of Paris. The scrutiny from the Jacobins, vigilant against dissent, underscored the risks involved in their advocacy. Henri's quiet reflections during this time highlighted the personal stakes of their public efforts, capturing the essence of their struggle to align their technological innovations with the ideological battles shaping the Republic.

In these revolutionary times, every discussion and demonstration of Decimal Time became a moment of political expression, linking Pierre and Henri to the mechanics of clocks and the heart of the French Revolution's tumultuous journey towards a new societal order. As the shadows of the guillotine loomed ever more prominent, their quest to recalibrate time itself intertwined irrevocably with the fates of those driving the relentless wheel of revolution.

—

As the chill of October 1792 swept through Paris, the Moreau family found themselves entwined with the tide of the French Revolution, now advocating for Decimal Time amidst the political fervour. In their bustling workshop, filled with the scent of oil and metal and the clutter of gears and plans, Pierre Moreau and his son Henri prepared for a pivotal presentation at the National Convention. The city outside mirrored their anticipation, alive with the sounds of newsboys and the rustle of political pamphlets.

Henri, arranging materials with meticulous care, broke the morning's silence. "Father, do you think they'll truly listen today?" His voice, tinged with nervous anticipation, echoed slightly in the cool air of the workshop.

Securing a bundle of diagrams, Pierre placed a reassuring hand on Henri's shoulder. "They must, Henri. Decimal Time is logical—it's what a rational, new France needs," he stated with calm determination.

They went to the Convention, where the political landscape was charged with recent victories and ongoing struggles. Inside, the divide was palpable: the Girondins called for cautious reform, while the Jacobins, led by the intense Maximilien Robespierre, pushed for radical, sweeping changes.

Pierre stepped up, his voice filling the hall. "Ladies and gentlemen, as we discuss casting aside the old calendar, should we not also abandon the archaic divisions of day and night dictated by monarchs? Let us measure our days with reason as we measure our lands."

His words stirred a mixed reaction. Some delegates, recognising the alignment of Decimal Time with revolutionary ideals, applauded. Others, however, murmured in dissent, wary of too much change too swiftly. Robespierre's intense scrutiny from the crowd added a layer of tension, his reaction crucial and unreadable.

After the session, a group of deputies, Girondins and Jacobins, approached the Moreaus. "Monsieur Moreau, your proposal intrigues, yet in such turbulent times, is it prudent to alter even our concept of time?" one deputy inquired, his voice a blend of curiosity and concern.

"Change, especially now, grounds us in reason during tumultuous times," Pierre responded, his confidence unshaken. "What better symbol of our break from the past than a new system of time that mirrors our revolutionary values?"

Returning to their workshop, Henri reflected on the day's events and their roles, which seemed to evolve beyond mere clockmaking. "It appears our craft makes us revolutionaries, too," he observed.

Pierre chuckled softly, his eyes twinkling with humour and seriousness. "Debating isn't the same as aspiring to politics, Henri. But let's hope our revolution keeps us far from the guillotine."

The overarching anxiety of Paris shaded their journey back. Their high-profile advocacy had not only garnered support but had also attracted the Jacobins' intense scrutiny, placing them in a precarious position. Their commitment to rationality and progress, though in line with the revolution, risked dangerous misconstruction in the volatile atmosphere.

Through every tick of their innovative clocks, the Moreaus marked time and the pulse of a city and a nation at the crossroads of profound change.

—

As the crisp autumn air of 1792 transitioned into the bitter chill of winter, Paris felt the grip of both the cold and the intensifying political tensions. Deep engrossed in their visionary endeavour, Pierre Moreau and his son Henri found themselves at the heart of the revolutionary currents sweeping through the city. Their workshop, usually a beacon of innovation and precision, was now a stark contrast to the volatile streets outside, buzzing with the meticulous work of perfecting the decimal clock—a symbol of the new order they aspired to inspire.

On a freezing November evening, their focus on the intricate designs of their clock was abruptly interrupted by a hurried knock at the door. Jeanne, a devout Jacobin sympathiser and friend, stood breathless in the doorway, her cheeks reddened from the cold. "There's an urgent session at the Convention tonight," she said, her voice tense with urgency. "They're discussing reforms, including the measurement of time."

The significance of the moment was not lost on Pierre and Henri. Swiftly gathering their coats and papers, they braced themselves against the cold, their minds racing with the implications of the meeting. The quiet streets echoed their footsteps and the tense anticipation of the discussions ahead.

Upon entering the Convention, they were met with an electric atmosphere of anticipation and apprehension. Robespierre spoke, his voice commanding as he talked about unity and control—themes that echoed deeply within Pierre's aspirations for his decimal clock. As the discussion turned to the topic of time restructuring, Pierre found his moment to speak, stepping forward with a clarity of purpose.

"Ladies and gentlemen," Pierre began, his voice resonant in the crowded hall, "if we are to rebuild our society on liberty, equality, and fraternity, should we not also consider a new way to measure our lives? Let us embrace Decimal Time—not just as a measurement, but as a symbol of the rationality and order we strive to establish."

His plea was met with a mixed reaction. While some assembly members nodded in agreement, intrigued by the revolutionary potential of Decimal Time, others whispered among themselves, sceptical of the sweeping changes it proposed during such volatile times.

After the session, as they stepped back into the night, Henri expressed his worries to his father. "Do you think they understood our vision, Father? Or do they see it as just another upheaval?"

Pierre looked at his son, a gentle smile softening his features. "Understanding may take time, Henri. But remember, every great change begins with a bold idea. And sometimes, persistence is as important as the idea itself."

Their walk back to the workshop was sombre, shadowed by the looming presence of the guillotine in the distance—a grim reminder of the difficult path they tread. Revolutionary France, with its insatiable desire for change, was also a place where ideals could be as dangerous as they were transformative.

Unbeknownst to the Moreaus, their advocacy for Decimal Time had not gone unnoticed. In the dimly lit corridors of power and whispered discussions behind closed doors, their names were carefully noted, a stark reminder that in times of revolution, the clocks they sought to reset might be counting down their fates.

—

On a brisk November morning in 1792, Paris was a city in the throes of transformation. As the new French Republic sought to redefine every aspect of life, Pierre Moreau and his son Henri emerged as pioneers at the intersection of time and revolution. Their vision for Decimal Time—an entirely new way to mark the hours of the day—sought to align the rhythms of daily life with the revolutionary ideals of rationality and equality.

That morning, the cobblestone streets bustled with energy as the Moreaus made their way to a critical session of the National Convention. Invited to present their innovations, they carried with them not just mechanical prototypes but also the hope of embedding their new system into the very fabric of the new society.

Arriving at the grand hall, they were greeted by the anxious murmurs of delegates and the scratch of quills on parchment. The room's anticipation was palpable as Pierre set up their latest decimal clock model. Feeling the weight of the moment, Henri leaned in towards his father, his voice barely a whisper amidst the din, "Do you believe they're ready for this, Father? Ready to redefine time itself?"

Adjusting the gleaming hands of the clock, Pierre responded with a reassuring firmness. "They must be, Henri. Our Republic prides itself on enlightenment, and what is more enlightened than reforming the very measure of our lives to reflect our new values?"

The session commenced with fervent debates echoing around the ornate chamber. When Pierre was called upon, he stepped forward, the clock ticking methodically beside him. With a calm clarity, he began, "Citizens, delegates, consider this—our Republic has embraced the metric system for its logic and universality. Should we not seek the same clarity in our perception of time? Decimal Time offers this, simplifying our lives in alignment with natural laws and our new principles."

The assembly listened, some nodding in agreement while others whispered sceptically. Madame Beaufort, a delegate known for her sharp intellect, spoke with an authoritative grace, "If we claim to be architects of a new world, why cling to the remnants of the old in our daily lives? Let us embrace this change, not out of fear of the new but for its promise."

As the debates stretched into the afternoon, the Moreaus felt the tide of opinion shifting, slowly but perceptibly. Discussions spilt out into the corridors and across the squares of Paris, where the promise of Decimal Time stirred public imagination and debate.

Days they turned into weeks of consultations, public demonstrations, and endless discussions. The Moreaus, once mere clockmakers, found themselves at the heart of revolutionary politics, navigating the dangerous waters of radical change and conservative resistance.

One evening, in the quiet of their workshop, Henri reflected on their journey, "Father, have we set forth a clockwork revolution?"

Looking over a diagram, his eyes weary yet bright with resolve, Pierre replied, "Perhaps, my son. And like any mechanism we create, its true test will come with time. We must continue to advocate, to educate, and to refine. Our work, like the revolution, is ongoing."

In their pursuit of a more rational world, the Moreaus pressed on, driven by the belief that time, like society, could be reimagined and reformed. Their legacy, woven into the fabric of the revolution, would tick forward, marking the endless pursuit of progress and enlightenment.

—

On a frost-laden Christmas morning in 1792, Pierre Moreau and his son Henri navigated the cobblestone streets of Paris, wrapped tightly against the chill. Their destination was a meeting at the Jacobin Club, the vibrant heart of intellectual and revolutionary activity, where the air buzzed with the ideals of Enlightenment thought and the sharp tang of tobacco smoke.

A wave of heated discussions washed over them as they entered the club. The recent attempts to introduce decimal clocks throughout

Paris had stirred a spectrum of reactions. Some praised the clocks for their logical consistency with Enlightenment principles, while others grappled with adjusting their daily routines to a fundamentally different system.

Observing the divide, Henri remarked to his father, "It seems our clocks do more than measure time; they challenge perceptions." They found seats as the clamour subsided into attentive silence for the speaker.

Robespierre took the floor, his presence commanding immediate attention. He spoke passionately about the Republic's virtues and the necessity of vigilance against its enemies. His stirring rhetoric was laced with an ominous tone that hinted at the extreme measures his leadership would later embody.

When it was Pierre's turn, he stood, the embodiment of calm rationality, and spoke of Decimal Time. "In shedding the chaotic vestiges of monarchy, our daily lives too must reflect the order and precision we strive for in our Republic," he proposed, his voice resonant in the hushed room.

The debate that followed was intense. Supporters argued that Decimal Time, like the metric system, was essential for rationally restructuring society. Detractors deemed it an unwelcome complication in an already tumultuous era. Pierre addressed each concern with the patience and clarity of a dedicated scholar.

Post-discussion, walking through the shadowed streets, Henri expressed his anxieties about their efforts. "Are we merely sowing seeds in barren soil?" he questioned.

Pierre responded with thoughtful optimism, "Understanding precedes acceptance. Our role is to plant these seeds. Their flourishing may take time, but the effort is worthy."

In the days that followed, the Moreaus doubled their efforts, hosting workshops and public forums to educate Parisians about the benefits of Decimal Time. They distributed pamphlets and engaged directly with the community, hoping to ease the transition to this new system.

However, the execution of Louis XVI in January 1793 cast a long shadow over Paris, escalating the tension and suspicion. The vibrant debates of the Jacobin Club now often gave way to fears of betrayal and the ever-looming guillotine, a grim symbol of the new order.

Despite the growing dangers, Pierre and Henri persevered with their advocacy, driven by their deep commitment to Enlightenment ideals. Yet, as they prepared for another presentation in February, the threat of arrest became ever more tangible.

Adjusting the mechanism of a decimal clock in their workshop, Henri voiced his concern, "Father, with each passing second, are we drawing closer to danger?"

Pierre, fixing a steady gaze on the clock, replied firmly, "Indeed, the shadows grow longer, but our mission remains clear. We must not let fear deter our pursuit of reason and enlightenment. We stand firm, champions of a rational future."

Outside, the winds whispered through the streets of Paris, rustling the pages of their notes and echoing the steady ticking of the decimal clock—a constant reminder of time's relentless march amidst a world on the edge of profound change.

—

By the 10th of March 1793, the streets of Paris echoed with a resonant mix of revolutionary zeal and creeping fear as the city grappled with its rapidly changing political landscape. Pierre Moreau and his son Henri, deeply committed to revolutionising the concept of time, were aware that their advocacy for decimal time placed them in the storm's vortex.

On this significant day, the Revolutionary Tribunal was established under Robespierre's stringent oversight, intensifying the dread that permeated the air. It was designed as a swift means to suppress counter-revolutionary actions, casting a shadow over the city. Yet, amidst these daunting developments, Pierre continued to champion the cause of decimal time, linking the necessity for societal restructuring to reform how time was measured and observed.

In the secluded backroom of a Montmartre café, lit dimly by the flicker of oil lamps, Pierre convened a meeting with a group of ardent supporters. "We are ushered into a new era that demands we abandon the monarchical past, not just in governance but in how we measure our very days," Pierre asserted passionately. "Our revolutionary values must be reflected in our conception of time itself."

Maturing into a forceful advocate, Henri took on the mantle of educating the public. Through forums and talks, he explained the utility of the decimal time system. "Imagine a day not arbitrarily divided into twenty-four hours but into ten equal parts—decides, mirroring the decimal system already adopted in our commerce and other measurements," he told an intrigued audience.

However, their forward-thinking campaign was not without its adversaries. The atmosphere, thick with the suspicion fostered by influential radical groups like the Jacobins and Cordeliers, made their mission difficult. Amidst gatherings teeming with spies, Pierre and Henri were forced to constantly alter their venues and cloak their language in layers of caution.

After one such meeting, stepping out into the brisk March evening, they came across flyers plastering the city walls, advocating the proposed Revolutionary Calendar. Henri looked at these with a complex mix of pride and worry. "It's beginning, Father. The change we've envisioned is taking root," he noted, his voice a mix of excitement and apprehension.

Heartened yet prudent, Pierre responded, "These are treacherous times, Henri. While our intentions align with the principles of the Republic, the volatility of the moment could twist even the purest goals into threats. We must tread carefully."

The following day, at a public demonstration in the Place de la Révolution, Pierre and Henri displayed their decimal clocks against the backdrop of their Grand Decimal Clock. They laid out several smaller prototypes and began to educate the gathering crowd about the mechanics and advantages of their designs. The event attracted a mix of curious onlookers and passersby. However, the presence of several prominent Jacobins with sombre expressions served as a reminder of the ongoing political tensions. Nearby, the guillotine cast a formidable shadow over the scene, underscoring the high stakes of the period.

As Pierre explained the clock's workings, breaking down the divisions of decis and cents, a young Jacobin approached discreetly. "Citizen Moreau, your innovations are indeed revolutionary, but be cautious—every new idea is scrutinised for its adherence to the principles of the Republic," he whispered before melting back into the crowd.

As they walked home under a cloudy sky that evening, Henri voiced his concerns, "Are we moving too fast, Father? Could our zeal be our undoing?"

Feeling the weight of their precarious situation yet unwavering in his belief, Pierre reassured him, "No, Henri. We are on the right path. It is the world that is out of step. We must persevere, for progress waits for no one, and time marches on relentlessly as we seek to redefine it."

Their resolve, shaped by idealism and now tested by the encroaching shadows of the Reign of Terror, would face severe trials in the days to come as they navigated their destiny against the relentless ticking of their revolutionary clocks.

—

On the brisk morning of 27 March 1793, the early signs of spring in Paris contrasted sharply with the tightening grip of Robespierre's regime. The streets, alive with the stirrings of new growth, buzzed with Paris, which developed during the revolution yet also whispered fear and suspicion. Amid this complex backdrop, Pierre Moreau and his son Henri were determined to advocate for their radical concept: the integration of decimal time into the new French Republic.

Their efforts, filled with hope and hazard, led them to organise a public demonstration in a bustling square near the Marais. The square, framed by budding trees and the architecture of progress, served as an amphitheatre for their cause.

Pierre stood before the crowd, his mastery of the speech not unmatched, his voice carrying conviction as he unfolded the concept of decimal time. "Citizens," he began, the timbre of his voice echoing off the stone, "as our Republic has cast off the shackles of tyranny, so too must we shed the archaic chains of timekeeping that bind us to the past. Embrace a system that reflects our revolutionary ideals: logical, decimal, equitable."

Henri, distributing pamphlets, added, "Envision a day not arbitrarily divided but logically structured into 10 hours, each hour into 100 minutes, and each minute into 100 seconds. Such precision brings harmony and efficiency, mirroring the rational order we strive for in our new society."

However, not all were moved by the promise of reform. A group of sans-culottes, symbolic of the revolution's radical core, approached with scepticism. "How does reordering our clocks benefit the common man?" one demanded, his brow furrowed under his Phrygian cap.

Understanding their support's critical nature, Pierre replied with careful rhetoric. "Consider this: a rational approach to time offers clarity, a measurement free from royalist influence, aligning with our ideals of liberty and equality. It is more than a clock change—it symbolises our freedom."

While some nodded in agreement, others remained unconvinced, whispering among themselves. An elderly washerwoman, her face etched with the trials of revolutionary Paris, pulled Henri aside. "Young master," she murmured, her voice low, "change invites challenge. Tread carefully, for not all are ready to embrace such novelty, even when it promises progress."

The encounter left an unsettling residue as Pierre and Henri retreated from the square. The city's mood was a barometer of the political climate, increasingly charged with paranoia and the pursuit of purity. With the establishment of the Revolutionary Tribunal, whispers of lists and loyalty tests grew louder, and the Moreaus realised their advocacy might soon place them in peril.

A few days later, a promising and perilous opportunity arose. A letter arrived, sealed with the Tricolour, inviting them to present their decimal clock to a subcommittee of the National Convention. This could be their moment to secure the future of their project or, should they falter, mark them as enemies of the new order.

The night before the presentation, they gathered in their workshop, surrounded by the tools of their trade and the weight of their ambition. "Tomorrow, we stand before our peers not just as horologists but as revolutionaries," Pierre said, his hands steady despite the tremor in his heart.

Henri, his resolve bolstered by his father's courage, nodded. "We advocate for a reason, for progress. May the Convention see the clarity of our purpose."

As dawn broke over Paris the following day, the Moreaus made their way to the Convention, the cobblestones cold and damp beneath their feet, the rhythmic tick of their prototype clock in Henri's bag a reminder of time's relentless march. They were ready to make their case, aware that their fate was intertwined with the revolutionary clock they hoped to set ticking across France.

—

On the brisk morning of 21 April 1793, the streets of Paris were alive with the palpable tension of political upheaval and the chilling aftermath of recent arrests by the newly minted Committee of Public Safety. Amidst this backdrop of anxiety and distrust, Pierre and Henri Moreau prepared for a crucial public demonstration in a subdued corner of the city, determined to advocate for the adoption of decimal time amidst the growing shadows of surveillance and repression.

Henri meticulously adjusted the mechanisms of their latest decimal clock model, his hands steady despite the turmoil swirling around them. "We must not falter, Father," he murmured, his voice a low blend of resolve and worry. "Our mission to revolutionise time itself cannot be silenced by fear."

Pierre, observing the modest crowd gathering around their setup, nodded in solemn agreement. "Indeed, Henri. Yet, caution is paramount. Our clock is not merely a tool; it has become a symbol of the change we champion—a change that, as we have seen, carries its dangers."

The demonstration began with Pierre eloquently presenting the merits of decimal time, explaining how it mirrored the Republic's revolutionary values by simplifying the daily measure of life into a logical, equitable, and transparent system. The crowd listened, intrigued yet visibly tense, as the implications of adopting such a system during these uncertain times hung heavily in the air.

A sceptical voice from the back challenged them. "Your time changes with the political winds, citizen Moreau. How can we trust a measure as shifting as the tides?" asked a man adorned with the red cap of the sans-culottes, his tone a mix of curiosity and challenge.

Pierre addressed the man with a calm, steady demeanour. "Citizen, just as our Republic seeks to establish a new order based on equality and reason, so too does decimal time propose to standardise our days and nights in alignment with natural laws. It is a step towards democratising time, making it as accessible and rational as the rights we fight for."

The question sparked a broader discussion among the attendees, with Pierre and Henri addressing concerns and further explaining their system's benefits. Each interaction was careful and deliberate, designed to educate and reassure rather than provoke.

As the crowd began to disperse, a thoughtful young woman approached Pierre. "Monsieur Moreau, I appreciate the ideals behind your proposal, but in these times of fear, how can you assure us that this new system won't be turned against us as another means of control?"

Pierre pondered her question seriously before replying, "Mademoiselle, any innovation can be misused if wielded by the wrong hands. Our goal is to embed decimal time so deeply within the fabric of our society that it serves as a foundation for transparency and regularity, reflective of our revolutionary ideals of liberty and fairness."

The woman nodded, her expression a blend of reassurance and lingering concern as she walked away. Henri watched her go, then turned to his father. "The path we tread is fraught with peril, Father. Yet, I believe the light of reason will guide us through these dark times."

As they packed away their demonstration materials under the setting sun, the tolling of the distant Notre Dame bells reminded them of the passage of time—both the old and the new. Pierre looked over at Henri, a resolute spark in his eyes. "Let us continue, my son. Even as the shadows lengthen, our work lights a candle in the darkness."

Their conversation continued quietly as they made their way back through the cobblestone streets, each step a testament to their commitment to change how the world measures time and uphold the values for which the Revolution purportedly stood. Amidst the uncertainty of the political climate, the ticking of their decimal clock was a steadfast reminder of progress, a beacon of hope in a time fraught with danger.

—

On the morning of June 10, 1793, as the early summer sun filtered through the Parisian skyline, a tense atmosphere hung palpably over the city. The Committee of Public Safety increasingly dominated the political landscape under Robespierre's strict oversight, casting long shadows of fear and suspicion. Amid these oppressive vibes, Pierre Moreau and his son Henri were resolute in their revolutionary mission to reform time measurement.

They planned to meet with a small group of forward-thinking members from the National Convention. This discreet gathering was set in the secluded garden of Café Tranquille—a place that, despite its tranquillity, felt the weight of revolutionary fears just beyond its walls. Henri, mature beyond his eighteen years and acutely aware of the stakes, helped his father prepare the latest model of their decimal clock, a symbol of rationality meant to usher in a new era of order and efficiency.

As the key members began to arrive, cloaked in discretion and anonymity, Pierre adjusted the positioning of his prototype. "This isn't merely about innovation in timekeeping; it's about anchoring the very essence of the Republic in rationality and unity," Pierre explained to Henri in hushed tones, laying out pamphlets and diagrams for their presentation.

With the attendees settled Pierre began his advocacy with passion. "Imagine a France where time itself is a bastion of the Enlightenment—systematic, logical, freeing us from the relics of royal excess," he proposed passionately, pointing to the elegant simplicity of his timepieces that divided the day into ten hours.

A delegate, intrigued but cautious, raised a point that reflected the undercurrents of fear among many. "While your intentions are noble, Moreau, in these precarious times, even the most well-meaning innovations could be misconstrued as threats by those who now wield power. Robespierre sees deception in his own shadow."

Pierre, seasoned in navigating the treacherous waters of revolutionary politics, acknowledged the concern. "True, yet consider how aligning time with the Republic's principles could reinforce our collective commitment to a new societal order. This system could streamline governance, enhancing transparency and efficiency—tenets dear to our current leadership."

The following discussion was animated, with questions and ponderings about the practical implementations and implications of such a radical change. Taking his father's cues, Henri adeptly addressed the technical inquiries, illustrating how the new time system could integrate into everyday life and governance.

As the meeting concluded with cautious optimism and promises of further deliberation, Pierre and Henri gathered their materials, feeling a mixture of accomplishment and apprehension. They walked back through the bustling streets of Paris, reflecting on the day's events.

"Father, do you think they understood the depth of what we're proposing? This isn't just about changing how we tell time but transforming society itself?" Henri asked a slight unease in his voice.

Gazing at the sun setting over the city, Pierre replied thoughtfully, "We've laid the foundation, Henri. Just like building a structure, it now requires patience and meticulous attention. And no matter the immediate results, we've sparked an essential dialogue that questions the structure of our daily lives."

As they continued their walk, the distant echoes of the day's revolutionary clamour mingled with their thoughts. The potential of their project to truly align with the new ideals of the Republic or to falter under the weight of suspicion and political intrigue loomed large. Yet, driven by a steadfast belief in Enlightenment ideals and the transformative power of rationality, Pierre and Henri remained committed to their vision, ready to face whatever challenges the next day might bring in a city at the heart of a revolution.

—

On the crisp morning of 21 September 1793, as the whispers of autumn began to weave through the bustling streets of Paris, the city itself teetered on the brink of revolutionary fervour and oppressive dread. Fueled by a vision to alter how time was perceived and measured fundamentally, Pierre Moreau and his son Henri found themselves caught in the throes of these turbulent times.

Their mission for the day was clear yet fraught with danger: they were to meet with a sympathetic printer nestled in a hidden corner of Paris. This discreet workshop, filled with the pungent aroma of fresh ink and the rustle of paper, promised a beacon of hope. Here, pamphlets detailing Moreaus' innovative decimal time system will be produced and designed to educate the public on its merits before the impending official adoption of the Revolutionary Calendar.

As they approached the modest entrance of the printer's shop, Henri couldn't help but voice his concern, the weight of their secret task evident in his hushed tones. "Father, are we certain we can trust him?" he asked, scanning their surroundings for any sign of unwanted attention.

Pierre placed a reassuring hand on his son's shoulder, his confidence unshaken. "We must, Henri. Allies like him will help us turn the tide of understanding. This is about more than just redefining units of time; it's about aligning our very society with the principles of the Revolution—liberty, equality, and rational order."

Within the safe confines of the shop, they met with the printer, a man whose eyes flickered with the same zealous hope for change. Together, they reviewed the final proofs of the pamphlets. The compelling documents laid out the rationale for restructuring the day into ten hours, each hour into one hundred minutes, and each minute into one hundred seconds—a reflection of the new, decimalised way of life the Republic sought to embody.

As they finalised their plans, the printer spoke with cautious optimism. "I'll have these ready and distributed under the cover of darkness. We must move quickly and quietly," he insisted, aware of the growing shadows cast by Robespierre's Committee of Public Safety.

Leaving the printer's shop, Pierre and Henri blended back into the crowded streets, the echoes of the revolutionary Paris around them. They passed by pamphleteers proclaiming the values of the proposed calendar, a visual testament to the changing times. Inspired yet contemplative, Henri shared his hopes and fears with his father. "Do you think the people are ready for this, Father? To embrace such a fundamental change?"

Pierre, ever the philosopher, responded with a thoughtful gaze towards the horizon. "Change is like the dawn, Henri. At first, it is almost invisible, yet soon, it illuminates everything. Our task is to be the harbingers of this new light."

Their conversation meandered through the Enlightenment ideals underpinning their project—reason, equality, and the pursuit of a more orderly society. As they discussed, they were keenly aware of their precarious path. The political climate of Paris was becoming ever more fraught, with suspicion and intrigue weaving through the very fabric of daily life.

As they returned to their workshop, the streets of Paris alive with the chaotic dance of revolution and routine, Pierre and Henri remained resolute. They were not merely horologists but architects of time and change; their innovations were poised to tick in rhythm with the heartbeat of a new era.

Their journey was more than a mere adjustment of clocks; it was an attempt to recalibrate society. And as the sun set over Paris, marking the end of another day in the new Republic, the Moreaus were ready to face whatever challenges lay ahead, driven by a steadfast commitment to enlightenment and progress.

—

As October 1793 unfurled, Paris throbbed with a palpable tension. Under the austere rule of Robespierre, the Committee of Public Safety had cast its shadow far and wide, infiltrating every facet of public and private life. Amid this oppressive atmosphere, Pierre and Henri Moreau clung tenaciously to their mission. They sought not just to advocate for but to integrate decimal time into the Republic's new fabric—a vision they saw as crucial to the broader Enlightenment ideals of rationality and universality.

On a brisk morning laden with the promise of change, the Moreaus prepared for a clandestine assembly. This meeting was pivotal in a secluded location known only to their most trusted allies. It was their chance to secure backing for decimal time, advocating for a system that stripped away ancient temporal divisions in favour of a logical, equitable structure that could potentially unite a nation.

In the dim, musty confines of Café Paisible's cellar—a sanctuary from the pervasive surveillance of the Jacobins—Pierre and Henri unfurled their latest revisions. During the presentation, they demonstrated a thorough interaction between the decimal time system and the proposed changes to the calendar, emphasising their integration as parts of a cohesive whole. They hoped the audience would perceive the decimal time and the new calendar as complementary elements, reinforcing each other to support the revolutionary ideals of liberty and equality—now more critical than ever.

Henri took the lead, his voice steady, infused with a clarity honed through meticulous preparation. "This new measure of time is not just a schedule—it embodies the principles of the Revolution. It simplifies, unifies, and democratises. Each hour, minute, and second under decimal time mirrors the ideals we strive for."

The assembly—a blend of deputies and forward-thinking intellectuals—engaged in spirited discussions. They debated the practical implications and the profound societal adjustments required. Despite the palpable risks of such a radical change, the mood was cautiously optimistic. The idea of harmonising time with revolutionary values struck a chord, echoing the Enlightenment's call for reason and progress.

An influential deputy, sensing the profound implications, voiced his conditional support. "If framed correctly, this could become a potent emblem of our new order—rational, equitable, and unmistakably French."

As the meeting dispersed, Pierre and Henri emerged into the streets, now washed in the pale dawn light, feeling hope and apprehension. Their path through the awakening city turned philosophical as Henri pondered the broader impact of their work.

"Father, do you think society will truly embrace this change?" Henri's question, filled with both awe and uncertainty, highlighted the transformative potential of their endeavour against the unpredictable backdrop of revolutionary France.

Pierre, seasoned yet optimistic, replied with a thoughtful tone. "Change of this magnitude takes time, Henri. But history is often kind to ideas born of reason. We must press on, driven by the necessity of our vision and the belief in a more rational, equitable world."

Their conversation continued as they navigated the cobblestone streets, each step a testament to their resolve. The Moreaus, with their prototype ticking steadily in a satchel, were more than mere spectators of history; they were shapers of it, actively moulding the temporal contours of a new era.

Their commitment to decimal time transcended technical innovation. It was a declaration of faith in the enduring power of Enlightenment principles—a vision of a society governed by logic and equity, marked by each revolutionary second that passed.

—

On the brisk morning of 4 October 1793, as autumn's chill gripped Paris, Pierre Moreau and his son Henri prepared for a crucial presentation at the National Convention. The city, a canvas of revolutionary fear and oppressive tension, watched as Robespierre's Committee of Public Safety tightened its grip on dissenters. Amidst this backdrop, Pierre and Henri readied themselves to propose their radical innovation.

As they made their way through the maze of streets, laden with the scent of fallen leaves and the murmurs of discontent, Pierre rehearsed his points. "This morning, we align the republic's pulse through our proposal for Decimal Time," he explained to Henri, his voice steady but underscored by the weight of the day's importance. Their plan extended beyond mere mechanics; it was an endeavour to synchronise the nation under a unified and rational time system, mirroring the revolutionary ideals.

Pierre, with practised eloquence, linked the Enlightenment's ideals of rationality and equality to the benefits of Decimal Time. "By standardising how we measure time, we offer a tool that enhances the rationality and unity of the Republic," he argued, presenting Decimal Time as a natural extension of the revolutionary changes sweeping across France.

Henri supplemented his father's points with practical demonstrations, showing how Decimal Time could simplify daily transactions and governmental operations, reinforcing the deputies' understanding of its potential benefits.

The discussions that followed were thoughtful, reflecting the assembly's internal conflict—balancing the proposal's merits against the risks of endorsing a project in such a scrutinised regime. The tension in the room was palpable, a stark reminder of the broader dangers faced by those pushing for reform during the Reign of Terror.

After the meeting, as they walked through the dimly lit streets of Paris, Pierre and Henri reflected on the gravity of their situation. "The path we have chosen is fraught with challenges, but necessary for the advancement of reason and equality," Pierre remarked, his voice a mix of resolve and concern.

Henri, looking up at the muted stars above, felt a mix of pride and apprehension. "We are not merely participants in this revolution; we are its architects, shaping time itself to reflect the new values of our society," he responded, his optimism tempered by the reality of their precarious position.

Their discussion underscored the dual nature of their quest: as much a technical endeavour to revolutionise timekeeping as it was a philosophical commitment to the principles of the Enlightenment. As they disappeared into the night, their conversation about the future of Decimal Time continued, a symbol of their unwavering commitment to progress despite the shadows cast by the guillotine.

—

As the brisk October winds of 1793 swept through the bustling streets of Paris, Pierre and Henri Moreau prepared for another day shrouded in both ambition and caution. The chilling grip of Robespierre's Committee of Public Safety cast a formidable shadow over the city, suffusing the vibrant clamour of the Revolution with a palpable tension that touched every corner of public and private life.

On the morning of 7 October, nestled in the back room of a dimly lit tavern in the Marais district—a haven for those whose revolutionary intensity was matched only by their need for discretion—Pierre and Henri debated their next steps. They were keenly aware of the precariousness of their endeavour.

"The alignment of Decimal Time with the Revolutionary Calendar is no mere coincidence," Pierre explained to Henri, his voice low but certain. "It represents the embodiment of our revolution's principles—rationality, universality, a complete break from the *Ancien Régime*."

Their strategy session was abruptly interrupted by a soft, urgent knock at the door. It was Clarisse Leblanc, a trusted ally and fellow advocate for Enlightenment ideals. She slipped inside, her face etched with concern. "Jean Dupont has been arrested," she whispered, the news hanging heavily in the air. Jean's arrest was a stark reminder of the dangers they all faced—any deviation from the Jacobin-approved line could brand one a counter-revolutionary.

Despite the risks, Pierre and Henri resolved to press forward. They planned to distribute pamphlets covertly at the National Convention, hoping to sway more deputies to their cause. The pamphlets, rich with explanations of how Decimal Time could streamline commerce, governance, and daily life, argued for a rational restructuring of society from the ground up.

By 9 October, the atmosphere in Paris had shifted; the streets were quieter, the usual lively debates and discussions muted by a collective wariness. Disguised as merchants, Pierre and Henri moved stealthily through the Rue Saint-Honoré, distributing their revolutionary literature to a network of sympathetic deputies and intellectuals who shared their vision for a reformed France.

That evening, back at their workshop, Pierre recorded the day's events in his journal under the light of a flickering candle. "9 October 1793—Today, we sowed seeds of change amidst the shadows of fear," he wrote, his hand steady but his heart heavy with the gravity of their task.

As the city of Paris settled into the night, the Moreaus' commitment to their revolutionary project remained unwavering. They were driven not just by the desire to innovate but by the deeper mission to embed Enlightenment principles into the very fabric of the new Republic. Despite the omnipresent threat of the Committee, they pressed on, their efforts a testament to the enduring power of ideas and the belief that reason could ultimately reshape society.

—

On the brisk morning of 29 Vendémiaire, Year II (20 October 1793), under the newly established French Republican Calendar, Paris was abuzz with revolutionary fervour. Pierre and Henri Moreau, despite the overshadowing threats from Robespierre's Committee of Public Safety, were pivotal in pushing for a monumental reform—Decimal Time. This reform aimed to unify the nation under a rational measure of time, aligning perfectly with the revolutionary values of logic and equality.

The crowd around the Palais Bourbon was a tapestry of excitement and apprehension. The National Convention, poised to make history, declared the adoption of Decimal Time alongside the Revolutionary Calendar. The announcement was met with mixed reactions—while many embraced the change, others murmured with uncertainty about the implications of such a radical shift.

"In line with the principles of universality and rationality, we decree the adoption of Decimal Time, aligning our days with our revolutionary ideals. Let us all reset our clocks as we reset our nation, marking a new era from the Republic's dawn," announced a leading deputy, his voice resonating across the gathered crowd.

Pierre and Henri, standing among their compatriots, felt a surge of both triumph and trepidation. This decree not only validated their tireless advocacy but also marked them as key architects of a contentious transformation. Henri's reassuring grip on Pierre's shoulder served as a silent acknowledgment of the challenging path they had navigated together.

The decree prompted the Moreaus to consider their next steps. That evening, in the seclusion of their workshop, they celebrated their success with modesty and discussed educational strategies to promote Decimal Time. They recognised the necessity of widespread understanding to ensure the public's seamless transition to the new system.

"We must approach this with clarity and patience. It's imperative that everyone grasps the benefits and functionality of Decimal Time to truly appreciate its value," Pierre explained, his eyes alight with the foresight of a visionary.

Aware of the precariousness of their position under Robespierre's increasingly suspicious regime, Henri cautioned, "Visibility has its dangers, especially now. We must engage the public subtly, ensuring our efforts are seen as an enhancement of the Republic, not a challenge to its stability."

Resolved to forge ahead, they planned to distribute leaflets the next day, which would dual-date in both the new French Republican and the traditional Gregorian calendars to aid in the transition. They hoped these leaflets would elucidate the practicalities and advantages of Decimal Time, easing the populace into this new era.

As the first light of dawn streaked across Paris the following morning, Pierre penned a thoughtful entry in his journal. He reflected on the weight of their contributions to a redefined era—an era that would be measured not just by the passage of days but by the progress towards a society governed by reason and enlightenment ideals. Their dedication to this cause, despite the looming threats of the Terror, underscored their commitment to a future where time itself was a democratised commodity, accessible and equal for all citizens of the new Republic.

—

On 2 Brumaire, Year II (23 October 1793), as the chill of autumn swept through Paris, Pierre Moreau and his son Henri stepped into the heart of a city on the brink of a temporal revolution. The newly introduced Republican Calendar and Decimal Time, embodying the Enlightenment values of rationality and uniformity, stirred a mix of excitement and unease among the Parisians. Pierre, a passionate advocate for these changes, prepared to address a gathering at the Place de la Révolution, hoping to sway the public's opinion in favour of this new system.

The cobbled square, usually bustling with the day's commerce and conversation, had transformed into a forum of anticipation. As Henri distributed pamphlets detailing the advantages of Decimal Time, Pierre climbed onto an improvised platform. The crowd, a mosaic of curious faces, looked on with a blend of skepticism and interest.

"Citizens of the Republic," Pierre began, his voice cutting through the morning air with an urgency that matched the times, "on this day, 2 Brumaire, we stand on the cusp of a new era. The Decimal Time is not merely about changing how we measure our days but about aligning our society with the unerring principles of reason, equality, and transparency."

His words resonated across the square, invoking nods and murmurs of agreement from some, while others whispered their doubts. The atmosphere was electric with the palpable tension of change.

As the crowd dispersed, Henri leaned close to his father, his voice low. "We must proceed with caution, Father. Our visibility could make us targets, especially with the Committee of Public Safety watching closely."

That evening, in the dimly lit backroom of a secluded tavern, Pierre and Henri met with a group of intellectuals and reform advocates. The flickering candlelight cast long shadows as they discussed the future of Decimal Time, strategising on overcoming the widespread resistance.

"The clocks are reset, but the true challenge is changing minds," Pierre stated, his finger tracing routes on a map of France. "We need to demonstrate that this system is not an imposition but an enhancement of daily life."

Henri, thoughtful, added, "Our journey will take us from Lyon to Marseille. Despite the risks of bandits and political dissent, we must spread our message of rational reform."

In the weeks that followed, the Moreaus traveled, engaging with communities, debating in public squares, and distributing leaflets. Each town presented its own challenges, but slowly, signs of acceptance emerged. Public clocks were synchronised, and discussions about Decimal Time became commonplace in market squares and salons.

Throughout their travels, Pierre kept a detailed journal, documenting their progress and the shifting sentiments of the people. "Today, we are not merely participants but architects of change. As the Republic's heart beats to the rhythm of progress, so does ours."

Their campaign, fraught with dangers and challenges, was more than a mission to standardise time—it was an endeavour to cement the values of the Revolution in the very fabric of daily life. Through speeches and debates, they confronted old traditions, advocating for a system that promised not just uniformity but a renewed sense of communal identity.

The legacy of their work, though precarious in the shadow of the Committee, became a testament to their commitment. As the months passed, Decimal Time started to take root, altering not just how the French measured their hours but also how they viewed their place in an evolving world.

Chapter Six

On the brisk morning of 6 Brumaire, Year II (27 October 1793), the small workshop in Paris, nestled within a cobblestoned street that echoed with the subtle sounds of a city under the watch of revolutionary zeal, was a hive of focused activity. Pierre Moreau and his son, Henri, were immersed in their latest endeavour—a clock that embraced the newly introduced decimal time concept, symbolising the French Republic's efforts to rationalise daily life nationwide.

Pierre, a seasoned clockmaker whose life had been dedicated to the precision of timekeeping, viewed this project not just as a technical challenge but as a civic duty. "Henri, this clock is more than a tool; it's a beacon of the new era. By standardising time, we unify France under a common rhythm that transcends regional disparities and binds us in our revolutionary ideals."

Henri, whose recent years had tempered his youthful optimism into a more measured determination, was all too aware of the political undercurrents their work invited. "Father, do you believe the Committee appreciates the gravity of our task? Or do they see an implicit critique of their authority in our endeavours?"

The workshop door creaked, admitting Étienne Rochefort, a fellow artisan known for his meticulous craftsmanship and a staunch ally in their scientific pursuits. His entrance dispelled the lingering fog of apprehension as he quickly surveyed their progress. "Pierre, Henri,

I've just come from the Palais Royal. Rumours abound that the Committee of Public Safety is tightening its grip on those who deal with innovation. They fear the seeds of subversion may be hidden within our noblest intentions."

The mention of the Committee stiffened Henri's resolve. "Our work is for the Republic to streamline the complexities of daily life into a logical framework. Surely, rationality cannot be deemed counter-revolutionary?"

Étienne's gaze was grim as he adjusted his spectacles, a sign of the seriousness of the discussion. "It's not the rationality they fear, but the autonomy it grants. A populace that agrees on timeless relies on the government's proclamations to structure their day."

Pierre pondered this as he polished a brass gear, the soft cloth gliding over the metal in thoughtful strokes. "Then we must tread with caution but not abandon our course. We are architects of time, builders of a new foundation for our Republic. If we are to face scrutiny, let it be for a cause that will outlast us."

As night fell and the streets of Paris dimmed under the careful watch of patrolling guards, the candlelight in the Moreaus' workshop cast long shadows against the walls lined with clockworks and tools. The gentle tick of the partially completed decimal clock served as a reminder of the relentless march of time—a time they were now defining.

Looking over a set of complex diagrams for the clock's mechanism, Henri shared his reflection with his father. "In redefining time, we redefine how history is recorded. Are we merely keeping time or setting the pace for future generations?"

Pierre, his eyes alight with pride and solemnity, placed his hand on his son's shoulder. "Both, Henri. We are entrusted with a profound task. Let each moment we measure be a testament to our fidelity to the Republic and a step towards a unified future."

Their conversation was punctuated by the distant chimes of Notre Dame, ringing out the old hour and soon replaced by their new metric. The stars overhead bore silent witness to the quiet resolve of the father and son as they continued their work, the revolution outside their door starkly contrasted with the meticulous order within. The Moreaus were not just marking time; they were defining an epoch.

—

In the shadowed corridors of the Committee of Public Safety on 7 Brumaire, Year II (28 October 1793), the atmosphere was thick with the smoke of extinguished candles and the heavier weight of suspicion. Sitting at the head of a long, sad table, Maximilien Robespierre addressed his deputies with a steely resolve that belied the early morning hour.

"Citizens, our Republic is under threat not only from external foes but from within, cloaked in the guise of progress and innovation. We must scrutinise every shadow, for in shadows hide not just men but potentially dangerous ideas," Robespierre declared, his gaze piercing through the dim light.

Among the deputies, Louis Antoine Saint-Just, ever the ardent supporter of Robespierre's stringent measures, nodded in agreement. "Indeed, Maximilien, it is our duty to illuminate these shadows. While laudable for their precision, the recent advancements in timekeeping could also serve darker purposes."

The topic shifted towards *Moreau Horlogerie, whose work on decimal clocks* caught the Committee's vigilant eye. "The Moreaus, though seemingly aligned with our revolutionary ideals, must be watched closely. Their clocks do more than measure time; they could potentially measure the pulse of dissent," Saint-Just added, his voice carrying an edge of urgency.

Robespierre leaned forward, his hands clasped tightly before him. "I know the family; I have dined with them", Robespierre recalled, "Bring me more information on Pierre and his family. If their intentions are pure, they have nothing to fear. However, if they seek to use their creations as a cover for subversion, they shall face the full wrath of our justice."

As the meeting adjourned, Georges Couthon, another key member of the Committee, approached Robespierre. "Maximilien, while vigilance is paramount, we must also ensure that we do not stifle the scientific spirit that fuels our Republic's progress. We should tread carefully, lest alienate those whose only crime is curiosity."

Robespierre considered this, his expression unreadable. "Georges, our revolution was born out of the desire to overthrow tyranny, not to replace it with another form. We will monitor the Moreaus but not act without concrete evidence. Let them continue their work for now, but let them also be aware that the eyes of the Committee see everything."

Back in the Moreau workshop, unaware of their scrutiny, the clockmakers discussed the mechanics of their latest clock design, striving to align each gear and spring with the Republic's decimal system.

"Henri, remember, precision is key. Our clocks are not just instruments of time but symbols of the new order we embrace," Pierre instructed, his hand guiding his son through the delicate assembly.

Henri, his brow furrowed in concentration, nodded. "I understand, Father. But it seems with each tick, we draw more attention. It's as if our clocks are winding up the very springs of suspicion."

Pierre sighed, placing a reassuring hand on Henri's shoulder. "Let our work speak for itself, my son. We build these clocks not for recognition but for the Republic, to aid in rationalising daily life. If our intentions are clear, our consciences are clear."

That night, as the city of Paris lay under a blanket of silence, the ticking of the Moreau's clocks filled their workshop—a constant, rhythmic reminder of the unstoppable march of time and the relentless scrutiny that followed each second.

—

On 9 Brumaire, Year II (30 October 1793), the Committee for Public Safety's chamber was steeped in the low murmur of cautious discussions as the grey light of dawn filtered through heavy drapes. Sitting at the centre of a semi-circle, Robespierre adjusted his glasses before addressing his deputies. Today's agenda focused sharply on the scrutiny of intellectuals and innovators, with Pierre Moreau and his son Henri featuring prominently.

"Citizens, the very essence of our Republic is at stake when those we trust to further our ideals might instead harbour thoughts of regression," Robespierre began, his tone measured but underlined with a thread of urgency. "We have observed the Moreaus closely. Their work aligns with our principles in theory, but the practical application might prove a breeding ground for counter-revolutionary sentiments."

Bertrand Barère, known for his eloquence, leaned forward, interjecting, "Maximilien, while we must guard against dissent, must we also remind ourselves of the importance of innovation? The

Moreaus' work on decimal time could symbolise the rationalism we champion."

Robespierre nodded slowly, his eyes narrowing slightly as he considered Barère's point. "Indeed, Bertrand, rationalism is our guiding light, but we must not be blinded. Innovation should not lead to idolatry or, worse, to independence of thought that challenges the unity we strive for."

He turned to Antoine Saint-Just, who had been silent until now. "Antoine, you have studied the reports. What is your assessment of the Moreaus' activities and their influence amongst the populace?"

Saint-Just replied, calm yet firm, "The Moreaus are craftsmen of note, certainly. Their clocks are discussed in both hushed tones and open admiration. However, this admiration can turn into a rallying point, a symbol that might be twisted against us. We must ensure their loyalty is beyond question."

The discussion shifted as Robespierre proposed an action. "Let us then initiate a discreet inquiry. We will send agents to verify the true nature of their discussions and the company they keep. If their loyalty is confirmed, we shall continue to support their work. If not, they must be neutralised."

As the committee members murmured their assent, the meeting adjourned with the resolve to uphold the safety of the Republic, even if it meant casting a shadow over its most brilliant minds.

Meanwhile, the clockmakers were oblivious to the deepening scrutiny across the city in Moreau Horlogerie. The workshop was cluttered with tools and parts of clocks, sketches of gears and mechanisms strewn about. Henri was meticulously working on a new model, his hands steady despite the growing chill that Brumaire brought.

"Father, how do you think the people will adapt to decimal time once all our clocks are in public spaces?" Henri asked, not looking up from his workbench.

While overseeing his son's work, Pierre replied thoughtfully, "Change is always met with resistance, Henri, but also with curiosity. Our clocks offer a new way of seeing time, a more rational approach that mirrors the new society we are building."

Just then, a gentle knock at the door broke their concentration. It was Claude Monnet, a fellow artisan and friend. Claude and Pierre had apprenticed together when they were younger. His face was concerned as he entered, shaking off the autumn leaves clinging to his coat.

"Pierre, Henri, you must be careful," Claude whispered, glancing around the cluttered space as if the walls themselves might listen. "There are whispers that the Committee sees your work as more than innovation. They fear it could inspire thoughts of independence among the citizens."

Henri frowned, setting down his tools. "But our work is for the Republic, for all betterment. How can this be seen as a threat?"

Pierre sighed, placing a reassuring hand on his son's shoulder. "Even the purest intentions can be misinterpreted in times of great upheaval. We must tread carefully, continue our work, but be mindful of how it is perceived."

As Claude left, Pierre and Henri returned to their work with renewed caution. The clocks around them seemed louder now, each tick a reminder of the precarious times they navigated.

—

The Committee for Public Safety's headquarters were abuzz with activity as the cold winds of 12 Brumaire, Year II (2 November 1793) swept through Paris, carrying whispers of distrust and the chill of suspicion. Robespierre met with his deputies in the dimly lit, austere room, the candlelight casting long shadows over their intense discussions. Today, the conversation centred around the monitoring of intellectuals and potential disruptors of the revolutionary order.

"Citizens, we stand on the brink of true transformation, yet we are surrounded by those who might use our reforms to undermine us," Robespierre stated, his eyes flitting across the dossier of reports before him. Among them, the activities of Pierre Moreau and his son Henri were highlighted, marked by a discreet red line.

Georges Couthon, always a staunch supporter of Robespierre's methods, leaned forward, his voice low but persistent, "Maximilien, the Moreaus, though innovative, wield the kind of influence through their craft that could catalyse undesirable sentiments. Their clocks do more than measure time; they could measure dissent's pulse."

Robespierre nodded, his expression grave. "Precisely, Georges. We must ensure their allegiance is to the Republic. Surveillance must be subtle yet comprehensive. Jean-Marie, what is the latest from our agents?"

Jean-Marie Collot d'Herbois, tasked with overseeing the surveillance operations, responded, "We have agents placed discreetly near the Moreau workshop. Their interactions and visitors are being logged. So far, nothing overtly subversive has been recorded, but their popularity is undeniable, and that alone warrants a close watch."

"Let us intensify our efforts. Perhaps their correspondence might reveal more. They must not feel the net tightening, lest they withdraw into the shadows," Robespierre concluded, his directive clear.

Meanwhile, in the Moreau workshop, the atmosphere was thick with the metallic scent of machinery and oil. Pierre and Henri, engrossed in their designs, remained unaware of the encroaching shadow of surveillance. Henri, ever the curious mind, broached a topic that had been lingering in his thoughts.

"Father, do you ever feel as though our endeavour to redefine time places us at odds with those who seek to control it?" Henri's question hung in the air, mingled with the ticking of the clocks that filled the room.

Pierre paused, considering the implications. "Time is the one constant that all wish to master, Henri. But remember, we aim to align it with the Republic's principles of equality and rationality. We innovate not to control but to liberate."

As they continued their work outside, the eyes of the Committee's agents watched. Notes detailing the visitors to the workshop, the deliveries of materials, and even the rhythms of work within the walls of Moreau's haven of horology were taken.

That evening, as Henri locked the workshop door, he couldn't shake off the feeling of being watched. He voiced his concerns to Pierre as they went home through the brisk November air.

"Father, the streets feel different these days. Eyes seem to follow us. Could the Committee be that interested in our clocks?"

Pierre, racing with the implications of Henri's intuition, replied with a measured calm, "We must proceed with caution, Henri. Our clocks could be seen as symbols—of progress or defiance. Let us hope they are viewed as the former."

Back at their modest home, the Moreaus discussed their strategy. "We'll continue our work, but let's keep our discussions and plans within these walls," Pierre decided, the weight of their situation settling heavily upon him. "Trust is now a commodity as scarce as peace, and we must spend it wisely."

In the shadows of the evening, the agents made their way back to the Committee, their reports ready to be delivered. The Moreaus, marked by their brilliance and now shadowed by suspicion, continued their work, unaware of how closely their contributions to the Republic were being scrutinised.

As 12 Brumaire, Year II (2 November 1793) drew to a close, the dance of innovation and intrigue continued, each tick of the Moreau's clocks echoing through the corridors of power and the cobbled streets of a restless Paris.

—

In the shadowed halls of the Committee for Public Safety, the air was tense with the promise of revolutionary justice. The day, marked in the Revolutionary Calendar as 14 Brumaire, Year II, bore the Gregorian echo of the 4th of November 1793, a date of growing shadows and deepening chills, both meteorological and political.

Sitting at the head of a long, sad table, Maximilien Robespierre surveyed the documents before him. His deputies, equally grave, waited for his lead. Today's agenda was particularly delicate: the scrutiny of cultural and scientific advancements under the new Republic, with specific attention to the Moreau's decimal clocks.

"Citizens," Robespierre began, his voice steady yet imbued with an undercurrent of urgency, "the Republic thrives on the purity of its purpose. Yet, some might use the guise of progress to mask their treacheries. We must consider the implications of every innovation."

Bertrand Barère, always eloquent, took up the thread. "Indeed, Maximilien. The case of Pierre Moreau and his son Henri is peculiar. Their clocks do not merely tell time; they propose changing its measurement. Such ambition could either serve the Republic or destabilise it."

Robespierre nodded, his gaze sharp. "Has there been any indication of malcontent or disloyalty from them?"

Louis Antoine de Saint-Just, younger but no less severe, responded, "Not directly, Citizen Robespierre. However, their workshops have become a gathering place for many, including known radicals. The influence they wield is not insignificant."

"Then we must be vigilant," Robespierre declared. "Let us deploy a few trusted agents to mingle in these gatherings. They should not appear as spies but as patrons interested in the sciences. We must discern if these clockmakers' intentions align with our revolutionary ideals."

The plan set, the room's atmosphere grew heavier, each member aware of the gravity of their duties. Surveillance was a tool wielded with precision, and they intended to use it effectively.

Meanwhile, across the city, the clinking of gears and clocks ticking in the Moreau workshop filled the air with a rhythmic symphony of industry. The clockmakers, engrossed in their craft, discussed the finer points of a new design.

Henri, with a furrowed brow, expressed his concerns. "Father, do you think the new mechanisms for the public square's clock could be seen as too bold? We are altering how people perceive their entire day."

Meticulous in his work, Pierre paused to consider his son's words. "Innovation often frightens those accustomed to old ways, Henri. But our purpose is clear—we advance timekeeping to benefit the Republic. Our clocks symbolise order and rationality, the very foundations of our new society."

Unbeknownst to them, outside, the agents assigned by the Committee began their subtle surveillance. Dressed as everyday Parisians, they noted all who entered and left the workshop, documenting conversations overheard and gauging the mood of the gatherings.

As the day waned, the agents' notes grew more detailed. While there was no overt evidence of subversion, Pierre and Henri's influence was undeniable. Their ability to draw crowds, even under the guise of discussing horology, posed a potential risk in the eyes of the Committee.

Back at his modest home, Pierre shared his reservations with Henri that evening. "We must be cautious, my son. Our role in this new era is not just to mark time but to ensure our work does not alarm those who watch over us."

Henri nodded, the gravity of their situation settling upon his young shoulders. "Perhaps we could hold a presentation and invite members of the Committee to see our work firsthand? If they understand our intentions, they might view us more favourably."

Pierre considered this, a spark of hope flickering in his thoughtful eyes. "A wise suggestion, Henri. Transparency might indeed be our best defence."

As night enveloped Paris, the Moreaus prepared for the days ahead, unaware of the full extent of the Committee's watchful eyes but conscious of the need to tread carefully. The gears of their clocks were not the only ones turning in the city; the gears of political machinations were also at work, setting the stage for a confrontation between old fears and new hopes.

—

As dawn stretched its pale fingers over Paris, the city stirred under unease. It was 16 Brumaire, Year II (6 November 1793), a day that would further entrench the fears and hopes of a nation consuming itself with its revolutionary zeal.

Robespierre convened an urgent session with his closest deputies within the austere confines of the Committee for Public Safety's chambers. The walls, lined with maps and lists, seemed to close in as the weight of their task loomed large.

"Citizens," Robespierre began, his voice a low thrum of urgency, "the Republic is beset by enemies, both seen and unseen. Our vigilance must be absolute." He paused, his gaze piercing each man around the table. "The activities of certain citizens under the guise of progress, such as the Moreau clockmakers, require our particular attention."

Maximilien Robespierre was a slender man of average height, with a powdered wig framing his sharp, angular features at the height of the Reign of Terror. His penetrating blue eyes conveyed relentless intensity, and his pale complexion gave him an almost spectral presence. He was always impeccably dressed and wore the revolutionary Tricolour cockade pinned to his coat, symbolising his unwavering dedication to the Republic.

Despite his frail body, Georges Couthon, a man of sharp intellect, shifted in his seat. "Citizen Robespierre, the Moreaus' influence grows, not through overt political actions, but subtly through their craft. Their clocks do more than measure time; they redefine it. Could this not be construed as an attempt to control a fundamental aspect of daily life?"

Robespierre nodded slowly, his lips a thin line. "Indeed, Citizen Couthon. We must discern whether their intentions align with the revolutionary ideals or mask deeper, perhaps counter-revolutionary, ambitions."

Another member, Saint-Just, known for his ruthless dedication to the revolutionary cause, added, "I propose a closer examination of their workshops. To understand their true purpose, we must see these clocks and their makers up close."

"Very well," Robespierre consented, a flicker of resolve crossing his features. "Arrange a visit under the pretence of interest in their technological advancements. We must not alarm them unduly — at least not yet."

Meanwhile, across the city, the Moreaus continued their meticulous craft in their workshop. The soft clinking of metal and the steady ticking of clocks filled the air with a kind of music, the rhythm of innovation.

Henri, his hands steady as he installed a new gear, spoke thoughtfully, "Father, these clocks — do you think they could ever truly change the world?"

Pierre, looking up from his sketches, considered his son's question. "Henri, every revolution begins with a change in perception. By reshaping how people view and measure their time, we are, in a way, influencing how they view their lives. It's a small but powerful thing."

Their philosophical musings were interrupted by a knock at the door. Pierre tensed, a wary glance exchanged with his son. Henri moved to answer it, his movements cautious.

Standing at the threshold was a small delegation led by a man Henri recognised from the pamphlets circulated in Paris — a deputy of the Committee for Public Safety. "Good day, Citizen Moreau. I am François Louis, accompanied by experts from the Committee. We've come to see your renowned clocks."

François Louis exuded an air of authority and meticulousness, his presence both commanding and unsettling. He was of medium build, with sharp eyes that missed nothing and a demeanour that suggested he was always calculating, constantly assessing. His neatly trimmed hair and impeccably pressed clothing added to his intimidating aura, making it clear that he was used to getting answers and obedience. As he extended his hand to Pierre, the room seemed to grow colder, the weight of his scrutiny pressing down on everyone present.

Pierre, recovering from his initial apprehension, welcomed them warmly. "Of course, citizens. Please, come in." As he led them around the workshop, Pierre explained the mechanisms and philosophy behind their designs.

While outwardly impressed, the delegates exchanged subtle glances, their true mission masked beneath a veneer of curiosity. They asked probing questions, not just about how the clocks worked, but about the Moreaus' views on the new time decrees and their impact on society.

After the visit, as the delegation departed with polite nods, Henri couldn't shake a feeling of unease. "Father, do you think they believed us? That we are merely artisans?"

Cleaning away the remnants of their day's work, Pierre sighed deeply. "I am not sure, Henri. But today, we did more than showcase our clocks. We entered a much larger arena, whether we intended to or not."

That evening, as Robespierre received the delegation's report, his expression remained unreadable. "Keep a close watch on the Moreaus," he instructed. "They are either the clockmakers of a new era or the timekeepers of dissent."

As the Revolutionary calendar marked the end of another day, the ticking of the Moreau's clocks echoed through their workshop, a reminder of time's relentless march — a march that, in revolutionary Paris, could lead to innovation or insurrection.

—

The morning light had barely touched the cobblestone streets of Paris when the Committee of Public Safety convened once again. It was 21 Brumaire, Year II (11 November 1793), a date marked by the Committee's ever-tightening grip on the citizenry, spearheaded by Maximilien Robespierre.

Within the chill, shadowy confines of their meeting room, where papers littered every surface and maps lined the walls, Robespierre addressed his deputies sternly. "We have watched the Moreau workshop closely. Their work, though innovative, straddles the delicate line between revolutionary advancement and potential subversion. What have we learnt from our latest observations?"

A deputy, Antoine Louis, known for his meticulous note-taking, replied, "Citizen Robespierre, our agents observed nothing overtly seditious. However, the influence of the Moreau clocks is undeniable—they are beginning to mark time throughout Paris, and their rhetoric about changing societal perceptions through timekeeping warrants further scrutiny."

Jean-Marie Collot d'Herbois, another member, leaned forward, his voice cautious, "Might their intentions not align with our revolutionary goals? After all, they propagate the ideals of rationality and order through their craft."

Robespierre, his eyes narrowing, considered this. "It is precisely their potential to influence that concerns me. If their ideology spreads unchecked, it could mould public perception in ways we cannot control. We must ensure their narrative remains within the boundaries acceptable for the Republic."

The conversation shifted as Bertrand Barère, a skilled orator, said, "Perhaps we should invite Pierre Moreau to speak at the Convention. Let him articulate his vision under our supervision. This will also allow us to gauge the reaction of the deputies and the populace."

Robespierre nodded, "Arrange it, Citizen Barère. But let us also prepare a contingency plan. We cannot afford to be seen as stifling innovation, yet we must guard against any doctrine that might sow seeds of dissent."

Meanwhile, in their bustling workshop across the city, the clockmakers were unaware of the storm gathering around them. They continued their work with a dedication that had become their trademark, the rhythmic ticking of their creations a counterpoint to the chaos of the outside world.

At just eighteen years old, Henri had mastered clockmaking under his father's guidance and was keenly aware of the time's social and political events. As he adjusted a clock mechanism, his brow furrowed in concentration; he said, "Father, do you ever think about the legacy of our clocks? What they will mean for future generations?"

Pausing in his work, Pierre replied thoughtfully, "I do, Henri. I believe our clocks will stand as monuments to this turbulent era—a testament to the idea that even in times of upheaval, there can be moments of clarity and purpose."

Their discussion was abruptly interrupted by the arrival of a messenger, a young boy breathless from his hurried journey. "Monsieur Moreau, you are summoned to speak at the National Convention. They wish to hear of your work and its implications for the new temporal order."

Pierre exchanged a look with Henri, a mix of pride and trepidation crossing his features. "It seems our time to enter the light has come sooner than expected."

As the day progressed and the hour of the meeting drew near, Pierre prepared his notes; each word weighed with the gravity of the opportunity and the risk it posed. Ever his father's staunchest supporter, Henri rehearsed with him, ensuring that every argument was perfected.

The shadows lengthened as they made their way to the Convention hall, the streets alive with the murmurs of citizens and the sharp calls of street vendors. Inside the hall, the atmosphere was electric with anticipation and the underlying current of revolutionary spirit.

As Pierre took his place before the assembly, his heart beat steadily, much like the clocks he crafted. He began, "Citizens, deputies, we stand today as artisans and architects of time. Our clocks do not simply count hours; they measure the progress of our Republic."

The assembly listened, rapt, as Pierre eloquently described his vision. But in the hall's shadows, Robespierre's agents watched and listened, their minds calculating the impact of every word spoken.

As the session concluded, the air was thick with applause and contemplative silence. The Moreaus, their message delivered, could only hope that the seeds they had planted would bear fruit in a manner true to their intentions.

That night, as they returned to their workshop, the streets of Paris seemed to whisper with the echoes of the day's events. In the sanctuary of their workspace, surrounded by the gentle ticking of their clocks, Pierre and Henri pondered the future—a future as uncertain as it was promising. Like their clocks, the revolution moved inexorably forward, marking time in a world forever changed.

—

As the frosty dawn of 22 Brumaire, Year II (12 November 1793) broke over Paris, the chill in the air was a mere echo of the cold scrutiny from the Committee of Public Safety. Inside their sombre meeting chamber, Maximilien Robespierre convened with his most trusted deputies, their faces reflecting the gravity of their relentless vigilance.

Robespierre's stern yet thoughtful countenance initiated the proceedings with a pressing issue. "Citizens, the matter of Pierre Moreau and his timekeeping innovations requires our continued attention. While no overt subversions have been uncovered, the influence he wields through his creations remains a concern."

Louis Antoine Saint-Just, known for his radical views, added, "The very precision of these clocks, their ability to redefine temporal measurement, could metaphorically reset the populace's minds. We must consider not just the creator but the potential for these creations to inspire ideologies contrary to revolutionary principles."

Georges Couthon, another key ally of Robespierre and known for his more measured approach, interjected, "Yet, citizen Robespierre, should we not also champion advancements that propel our Republic forward? If Moreau's intentions align with our revolutionary ideals, might his innovations not serve to further our cause?"

Robespierre nodded slightly, acknowledging the point. "Indeed, Citizen Couthon, but we must tread carefully. Let us deploy a few more of our trusted agents to infiltrate the circles around Moreau. They should gauge the public sentiment and the discussions these clocks spark amongst the citizens."

Meanwhile, across the city, in their workshop, the Moreaus were unaware of the intensifying gaze of the Committee. They continued their diligent work, and the click and clack of gears provided a steady backdrop to their discourse.

Henri, his curiosity piqued by the diverse reactions their clocks had begun to elicit, posed a question to his father. "Do you think, Father, that our clocks could change how people think about not just time but governance itself?"

Pausing to adjust a particularly stubborn gear, Pierre contemplated deeply before responding. "Every tool of change, Henri, holds grand and dangerous potential. Our clocks mark time impartially, yet how society uses that time can sway the course of governance."

Back at the Committee, the decision was made to send agents to the forthcoming public forum the Moreau's were planning at their decimal clock in the Place de la Révolution. Robespierre, always strategic, declared, "We shall observe not just the clock but the crowd. The people's reaction will tell us much about the potency of Moreau's influence."

Despite the French government's decrees about adopting the Decimal Clock, the Moreaus knew they still needed to sell the idea to the public to effect actual social and temporal change.

As the sun climbed higher, casting long shadows over the Parisian landscape, the Moreaus prepared for their public forum. Acutely aware of the event's significance, Pierre meticulously reviewed every detail of the presentation. Ever his father's diligent assistant, Henri ensured that the mechanism functioned flawlessly.

The square slowly filled with curious onlookers, academics, and several discreetly placed agents of the Committee. As Pierre started to speak, the crowd's murmurs grew into a cacophony of awe and debate.

Pierre addressed the gathering calmly yet resonantly, "Citizens, behold a tool that measures our new Republic's time—decimal, rational, and democratic. Let it mark a new era of enlightenment where every citizen can measure their day by the same rational principles that guide our revolution."

In the crowd, an agent of the Committee, disguised as a tradesman, noted the reactions: nods of approval, whispers of dissent, and the unmissable undercurrent of revolutionary zeal. His report would later paint a vivid picture of the event's atmosphere—a mixture of revolutionary enthusiasm and intellectual curiosity.

That evening, as the Moreaus returned to their workshop, their hearts were heavy with pride and an unspoken anxiety. The streets of Paris, now quiet, seemed to whisper of changes yet to come, of ticking clocks and the ticking time bomb of revolutionary scrutiny that might one day demand more from them than they had ever anticipated.

In his report to Robespierre, the agent concluded, "The demonstration, while impressive, has undoubtedly sown seeds of thought amongst the populace—seeds that could grow into either staunch support for our cause or dangerous dissent."

As the day faded, Robespierre lingered in his office, the trembling candlelight casting long shadows over the numerous reports on his desk. "Keep a close watch," he whispered into the stillness, "For even the slightest detail can ignite the fires of revolution."

—

On the morning of 24 Brumaire, Year II (14 November 1793), a grim fog had settled over Paris, matching the sombre mood within the halls of the Committee of Public Safety. Maximilien Robespierre convened an urgent session with his closest deputies, a palpable tension filling the air as they gathered around the cluttered oak table with reports and dispatches.

Robespierre, his face etched with the lines of relentless vigilance, spoke first. "The matter of the Moreau's clocks continues to intrigue as much as it concerns us. Their innovation, while brilliant, skirts the edge of what some might call subversion. We must discern their true intent."

Jean-Lambert Tallien, one of his deputies, interjected with a note of caution, "Citizen Robespierre, while we must safeguard the Republic from the dangers of counter-revolutionary thought, must we also guard against progress that promises to elevate our new society?"

Robespierre regarded Tallien with a piercing gaze. "Progress, Citizen Tallien, is our aim, but not at the cost of security. The Republic cannot afford the luxury of unchecked innovation that might cloak darker motives."

The debate continued, with another deputy, Bertrand Barère, adding, "Perhaps we might consider a more thorough investigation into the associations and patrons of Monsieur Moreau. If his work is as innocuous as it appears, such scrutiny should reveal nothing untoward."

Agreeing with this course of action, Robespierre, whose paranoia about counter-revolutionaries was beginning to crack his outward veneer, focused his insecurities on the Moreaus. He tasked his agents with deeper surveillance of the Moreau workshop and their clientele. "We must peel back the layers of this clockwork mystery," he declared, "and ensure that the gears of these devices grind in our favour, not against us."

Across the city, in their workshop, Pierre and Henri were oblivious to the intensifying scrutiny. They were deeply engrossed in their craft, the ticking and tocking of their clocks a symphony of industry. Today, however, their work was interrupted by an unexpected visitor, Mademoiselle Élise Girard, a patron and supporter of their endeavours.

Élise, her cheeks flushed from the brisk air, greeted them warmly. "Monsieur Moreau, Henri, your work has quite the admirers among my acquaintances. Yet, there are whispers, concerns that your creations might draw unwanted attention."

While wiping his hands on his apron, Pierre responded with a weary smile. "Mademoiselle, in these times, innovation often walks hand in hand with suspicion. We build clocks, not conspiracies."

Listening intently, Henri added, "We aim to understand time better and to synchronise the Republic with a rhythm that benefits all. Surely, such goals align with revolutionary ideals?"

Élise nodded, her eyes reflecting the flickering candlelight. "Indeed, they do. But be wary, for even the most noble intentions can be twisted by fear or malice."

As the day wore on, Robespierre's agents mingled discreetly among the populace, gathering murmurs and moods, the general sentiment towards the Moreau's clocks being one of awe and a hint of unease at their precision. One agent, disguised as a tradesman, lingered near the workshop, his ears tuned to the district's pulse.

That evening, as the streets of Paris whispered with the secrets of the day, the agent made his way back to the Committee's headquarters, his report a mixture of innocuous praise and subtle suspicion regarding the influence of Moreau's timepieces.

Upon reviewing the agent's findings, Robespierre felt a twinge of uncertainty. "Keep a watchful eye," he instructed. "If these clocks do indeed mark a turning point, let us ensure it turns in favour of the Republic."

Back at their workshop, the clockmakers discussed their next presentation at the *Académie des Sciences*, unaware of the watchful eyes that lingered just beyond their candlelit sanctuary.

"Father, are we pioneers or pawns in this new era?" Henri asked, a trace of concern threading his voice.

Pierre, placing a reassuring hand on his son's shoulder, replied, "We are craftsmen, my boy, caught in the gears of a revolution. But let us ensure our legacy is enlightenment, not suspicion."

As the night deepened, the streets of Paris settled under the watchful stars, and the Moreau's clocks ticked on, each second a steady beat in the heart of a city caught between time and tyranny.

—

On 28 Brumaire, Year II (18 November 1793), a piercing chill had settled over Paris, intensifying the underlying unease that permeated the revolutionary city. At the Committee of Public Safety headquarters, the air was thick with suspicion and cold drafts that snaked through the cracks of the ageing edifice. Maximilien Robespierre, ever vigilant, convened an impromptu meeting with his deputies, the atmosphere fraught with the gravity of their discourse.

"Today, we consider the case of Pierre Moreau and his family," Robespierre began, his voice low and measured, reflecting the tension of the dimly lit room. "Their endeavours in timekeeping, while innovative, warrant our scrutiny for the implications they hold beyond mere mechanics."

Georges Couthon, a loyal ally and a member of the Committee, responded with a nod, "Indeed, Citizen Robespierre. It is prudent to question whether their clocks serve a purpose beyond the communal. Could they, in their precision, be a symbol for counter-revolutionary coordination?"

Louis Antoine de Saint-Just, another of Robespierre's trusted deputies, interjected, his youthful face betraying a hint of impatience. "We must dissect their associations and the clientele they entertain. It is possible that under the guise of progress, they weave dissent against the Republic."

Robespierre considered these points; his fingers tented in contemplation. "Arrange discreet surveillance of their activities. Let us not precipitate action without cause, but be prepared to act decisively should the need arise."

In their humble workshop elsewhere in the city, Pierre and Henri were wholly absorbed in building a new series of decimal clocks. Spread out on their wooden workbench were the complex parts of these clocks. Interest in their work had surged after the decree of 29 Vendémiaire, Year II, and they now had several commissions to fill.

Henri, his brow furrowed in concentration, broke the silence. "Father, the precision we aim for—it's revolutionary. To redefine how people perceive and measure their lives?"

Pierre paused, looking up from his work. "It is, Henri. And in that revolution lies our peril. As we seek to mark time anew, we must be mindful of those who might interpret our ambition as subversion."

Unbeknownst to them, their discussions were being closely monitored. Jacques, a newly appointed agent of the Committee, discreetly noted every workshop visitor, compiling reports that would inevitably find their way back to Robespierre.

That evening, as Paris lay cloaked under a sad twilight, the tension in the Moreau workshop heightened with the unexpected arrival of their friend Étienne Rochefort. His entrance was swift, his expression grave. "Pierre, Henri, you must tread carefully," he warned, his voice calm. "Whispers of your work have stirred interest among patrons and those who watch from the shadows."

Henri looked towards his father, a flash of anxiety crossing his youthful features. "Are we in danger, Father? For merely advancing time?"

Pierre's response was calm and resolute. "Étienne, come in and join us for a coffee. There is nothing to fear; we have done no wrong." He gestured towards the small table by the window, inviting Étienne to sit.

As they settled with their cups, Pierre spoke with a quiet conviction that seemed to fill the room with a sense of security. "In times like these, innovation can be as threatening as a loaded musket. But we must navigate these waters with care and confidence. Our work is for the betterment of society, and we must not let fear dictate our actions."

They talked for a while longer, the atmosphere gradually easing as Pierre's strength of conviction imbued the conversation with hope and determination. When Étienne finally rose to leave, his expression was notably calmer, his earlier anxiety softened by Pierre's unwavering assurance.

Robespierre reviewed Jacques' report, which showed increasing unease at the Committee of Public Safety. "Keep a close watch on them," he instructed firmly. "We must ensure their timekeeping dedication doesn't compromise their loyalty to the Republic. Also, place an agent near Claire Fountaine; we must understand her social interactions."

As the clocks within the Moreau workshop ticked on, marking the relentless passage of revolutionary time, the winds of suspicion and fear mingled with the cold night air outside. Each tick of the clock was a reminder of the fragile balance between progress and peril, a balance that Pierre and Henri, caught in the gears of their creations, strove to maintain amidst the tumult of the Reign of Terror.

Undeterred by the tensions of the era, the Moreaus continued their ways. Claire still hosted a friendly salon in the back of the workshop once a week, where politics, philosophy, and the Enlightenment were common themes, though in no way subversive. Pierre and Henri worked diligently, filling orders for their clocks, and their dedication to their craft was unwavering.

Meanwhile, the Committee's scrutiny intensified, the line between protection and oppression blurring under the watchful eyes of the Republic's guardians. As the gears of the Moreau clocks moved in precision, so too did the machinations of Robespierre and his deputies, each moment meticulously noted, each movement carefully analysed, in the shadowed corridors of power where the future of the Moreau's clocks—and perhaps their very lives—hung precariously in balance.

—

By 4 Frimaire, Year II (24 November 1793), the chill of late autumn had deepened, casting a longer shadow over the streets of Paris. Maximilien Robespierre presided over a tense assembly in the austere chambers of the Committee of Public Safety. His deputies, a collection of the Republic's most ardent protectors, gathered around the heavy oak table that bore the weight of their collective responsibility.

"The matter at hand is delicate," Robespierre began, his voice steady yet imbued with an underlying sternness. "The Moreau father and son continue their work unabated, spreading their decimal clocks throughout Paris. We must consider the implications of this proliferation."

Georges Couthon, ever loyal, leaned forward, his wheelchair creaking slightly under the shift. "Citizen Robespierre, their intentions may not be malign, yet the symbol of their work could indeed rally those less favourable to our cause."

Saint-Just's sharp and unyielding features added, "Indeed, Georges. It is not merely their intent but the interpretation thereof that concerns us. Their clocks could become icons of dissent, whether they mean for it or not."

Robespierre nodded gravely. "Then we proceed with caution but resolve. Jacques, continue your surveillance of the Moreau workshop. Report any convergence of suspicious individuals or discussions that may suggest more than a mere fascination with horology."

Back in their workshop, nestled in the heart of a busy Parisian district, the Moreaus remained blissfully defiant of unwarranted scrutiny from the highest echelons of revolutionary power. Their workspace was cluttered with tools and clock parts, the air filled with the metallic tang of oiled gears and the soft ticking that echoed like a heartbeat through the room.

As Henri adjusted the pendulum of their newest creation, he pondered aloud, "Father, the Committee's silence on our submissions is troubling. Should we not seek their endorsement with increased determination to ease their concerns?"

Pierre, wiping his hands on a cloth, paused. "Henri, to press them might invite deeper suspicion. We walk a razor's edge—our work revolutionary in both spirit and function, yet potentially seen as a threat."

The door to their workshop suddenly swung open, causing both Moreaus to startle. Étienne, their long-time friend and occasional collaborator, stepped inside briskly, his eyes darting nervously.

"Étienne, what brings you here in such haste?" Pierre inquired, noting his friend's agitation.

Étienne closed the door behind him, lowering his voice. "I've just left a meeting with a few like-minded colleagues here in Marais. There's talk, Pierre, that your clocks are being watched not for their ingenuity but for the threat they might pose."

Henri frowned, "A threat? Our clocks only seek better to align the Republic's time with its principles."

"Ah," Étienne sighed, "but therein lies the rub. Your alignment may not be the alignment envisioned by those in power. Be wary, both of you. Caution is your best ally now."

After Étienne's departure, the workshop felt suddenly more confining, the ticking of the clocks now a stark reminder of the passing time that might also be counting down to a confrontation they were ill-prepared to face.

Meanwhile, at the Committee, Jacques delivered his latest observations. "The Moreaus attract many visitors, Citizen Robespierre. Not all are clients—some are known critics of our methods."

Robespierre received the news with a nod, his expression unreadable. "We shall keep a close eye on this. Let us not act rashly but be prepared to intervene should their influence stray from the path of revolutionary virtue."

As the day faded into evening, the streets of Paris grew colder, and the lights in the Moreau workshop burned late into the night. Each stroke of the hammer, each turn of the gear, though meant to mark time, now seemed to Pierre and Henri to be marking their fates, entwined inexorably with the ticking of their revolutionary clocks.

Within the walls of his austere office, Robespierre penned a note for his next day's agenda. The Moreaus and their clocks that ticked with a rhythm that could either harmonise with or disrupt the Republic's heartbeat would be discussed again. For in the heart of the revolution, nothing that influenced the measure of time could be left unchecked, lest it measure their downfall.

—

The cold dawn of 5 Frimaire, Year II (25 November 1793) saw the streets of Paris veiled in a dense fog, mirroring the growing opacity of political alliances and enmities. The Committee of Public Safety, now a fortress of revolutionary zeal under the steely command of Maximilien Robespierre, was a hive of activity as deputies gathered to deliberate on the threats looming over the Republic.

In the chill of the committee room, Robespierre addressed his most trusted deputies, his voice cutting through the murk of uncertainty. "The Republic teeters on the brink of greatness and destruction. We must shepherd it with a firm hand," he declared, his eyes scanning the documents across the table.

Saint-Just unfolded a sheet of paper and handed it over. "Pierre Moreau and his son Henri have been advancing the concept of decimal time through their clocks. While this aligns with revolutionary ideals, the undercurrents of their gatherings suggest a possible misuse of their influence. They discuss more than mere mechanics."

Robespierre pondered this, stroking his chin thoughtfully. "Time is a weapon as much as it is a measure. We must ensure it serves the Republic, not the ambitions of concealed royalists or counter-revolutionaries."

Elsewhere, in the shadowed confines of their workshop, Pierre and Henri were fully aware of the growing scrutiny from the corridors of power. As mere clockmakers and artisans, they knew they had but one task: to continue their work. The clang of metal and the soft ticking of gears filled the air as they laboured on their newest creation, a clock designed to symbolise unity and progress.

Ever the idealist, Henri remarked, "This clock will be our testament, Father. A beacon of the new era, measuring out hope and reason."

Pierre, however, tempered by experience, maintained a cautious outlook. "Hope, yes, but also a reminder, Henri. Every creation of ours must be beyond reproach, lest it be seen as a challenge to those who wield real power."

Their conversation halted abruptly with the entry of a mutual friend, Marc Chevalier, a fellow artisan bearing news from the streets. "Pierre, Henri, you must proceed with caution," he cautioned, his breath misting in the chilly air of the workshop. "Your discussions at the café last night did not go unnoticed. There are eyes and ears everywhere."

In his typical manner, Pierre invited Marc to sit, offering him a warm drink. "Marc, we cannot control the paranoia around us; we can only control our actions. There is nothing subversive about what we are doing. Our work and discussions are rooted in our craft and the betterment of society. We have nothing to hide."

Back at the Committee of Public Safety, Robespierre continued discussing with another deputy, Bertrand Barère, known for his eloquent oratory. "Barère, what have you read about this situation with the Moreaus? Could their work truly pose a risk?"

Barère, ever measured in his response, suggested, "While their intentions may be pure, Citizen Robespierre, the perception of their work could indeed stir unrest. If the populace sees their clocks as symbols of a new order, it might incite actions we cannot control."

Robespierre nodded slowly, a plan forming in his mind. "Then we shall keep them under surveillance. Let us not act hastily but prepare to intervene should their influence extend beyond the acceptable boundaries of innovation."

As night descended on Paris, the Moreau workshop glowed faintly, a beacon of industry and invention. Inside, Pierre and Henri were engrossed in their work, oblivious to the encroaching shadow of surveillance. Outside, the city murmured secrets into the cold air, secrets that held the power to change destinies and the passage of time itself.

In the quiet of his study, Robespierre penned instructions for his spies, his words meticulous and cold. "Observe and report back. Let us not be the architects of our demise by ignoring the gears of change, whether they turn in our favour or against us."

—

The brisk morning of 10 Nivôse, Year II (30 December 1793) brought a biting cold that seemed to seep into the very bones of Paris. At the headquarters of the Committee of Public Safety, the air was charged not only with the chill of winter but also with the paranoia of revolutionary zeal and suspicion that had come to characterise the reign of Robespierre.

Inside the austere meeting room, the warmth provided by the hearth did little to thaw the frosty atmosphere as Maximilien Robespierre convened with his deputies. The subject at hand was the continued surveillance of certain citizens whose innovations, though outwardly benign, might mask deeper subversions.

"Surveillance must be intensified," Robespierre declared, his gaze piercing each of his deputies. "The Republic is beset by enemies both within and without. We cannot afford to overlook anyone, not even a clockmaker."

One of his deputies, Georges Couthon, known for his loyalty and severity, responded with equal gravity, "Citizen Robespierre, the Moreau father and son, have garnered attention not just for their craftsmanship but for the gatherings they host. Discussions meant to focus on timekeeping increasingly verge on the philosophical implications of our new order."

Robespierre's eyes narrowed thoughtfully. "Philosophy breeds ideas, and ideas breed action. We must ensure these actions align with the ideals of the Republic. Arrange for another report on these gatherings. We must understand the full scope of their discourse."

Meanwhile, in their workshop across the city, the clockmakers remained engrossed in their world of gears and springs. Each tick of their revolutionary clocks was being matched by the silent tally of suspicions accumulating in their dossier.

With a filer in hand, Henri paused in his work, sensing his father's distraction. "Father, you seem distant today. Are the gears of our clocks not aligning?"

Pierre sighed, setting aside his tools. "It is not the gears, Henri. I fear our very pursuit may not align with the current sentiments of our leaders."

The conversation was abruptly halted by a soft knock at the door—a rarity, given the usual bustle of their trade. Pierre cautiously approached, peering through the peephole before unlocking the door to reveal Étienne Rochefort, his features drawn with concern.

"Good day, Pierre, Henri. I bring news," Étienne began, stepping inside and lowering his voice. "There's talk at the market, whispers that the Committee is increasing its watch over those who frequent your shop. Your discussions have not gone unnoticed."

Henri's expression hardened, his youthful optimism clashing with the burgeoning reality of their situation. "Our discussions? We speak of time, of science—not of politics."

"That may be," Étienne replied, "but even time is political in these times. You discuss the reordering of society through the reordering of time. To the Committee, that could seem as radical as any political manifesto."

Pierre, ever composed, responded calmly, "We are aware of the scrutiny, Étienne. We are artisans committed to our craft. Our clockmaking poses no threat to the Republic. We seek only to bring order and precision to our citizens' lives. If that is seen as provocative, then it is a misunderstanding we are prepared to face."

Robespierre and his deputies continued their deliberations at the Committee of Public Safety. Couthon brought forward a dossier outlining the Moreaus' recent activities and associations.

Robespierre reviewed the dossier intently. "We must proceed with caution," he pondered aloud. "Taking direct action against them could provoke public sympathy. After all, they are just clockmakers, and the son is still young—a detail that the public will surely not overlook."

"But influential clockmakers, Citizen Robespierre," interjected another deputy, Antoine Saint-Just. "Their influence on the concept of time resonates with the populace, intertwining with the fabric of our Republic. We cannot dismiss the power of such symbolism."

The meeting concluded with a decision to keep a closer watch on the Moreaus, documenting their interactions and the nature of their discourses without immediate confrontation. As the deputies dispersed, the weight of governance and the paranoia that came with it hung heavily in the air, starkly contrasting the ostensibly simple life of clockmaking.

In the quiet of their workshop, as Pierre and Henri resumed their work, the room filled once more with the familiar ticking of clocks. Each sound was a reminder of the passage of time and, now, a reminder of the scrutiny they were under—a scrutiny that measured not just the hours but the pulse of their loyalty to the new order of the French Republic.

—

On 14 Nivôse, Year II (3 January 1794), winter's icy grip clung tightly to Paris, its chill penetrating the thick walls of the Committee of Public Safety's chambers. Inside, Maximilien Robespierre convened an urgent meeting with his most trusted deputies, his eyes reflecting the relentless drive that defined his leadership.

"Citizens, the fabric of our Republic is under threat not merely from external foes but from within," Robespierre began, his voice resonant in the cold, stark room. "Ideas, as much as armies, possess the power to overthrow regimes. We must guard against innovative minds that cloak their treacheries in the guise of progress."

Antoine Saint-Just, a fervent advocate of Robespierre's strict policies, leaned in, his gaze intense. "The Moreaus' clocks are a prime example. Their conversations border on philosophical subversion. His wife, Claire Fontaine, associates with the wives of several other potential subversives. We need to determine our next steps."

Saint-Just continued, his voice laced with suspicion. "Claire's weekly salons in the back of the workshop have not gone unnoticed. While they claim to discuss literature, philosophy, and enlightenment, there is a growing concern that these gatherings serve as a cover for more insidious discourse. The intellectuals and artists who frequent these meetings are known for their critical views. It is possible that under the guise of cultural enrichment, they are fostering dissent against the Republic."

Robespierre, his face a mask of contemplation, nodded slowly. "We cannot ignore the potential threat posed by these salons. Claire Fontaine's influence extends beyond mere social gatherings. Her connections and the ideas exchanged within those walls could be breeding grounds for counter-revolutionary sentiments. We must approach this delicately, yet decisively, ensuring we uncover the true nature of their intentions without inciting unnecessary panic."

Saint-Just's expression hardened further. "The Moreaus' clockmaking is not just a craft; it symbolises the reordering of time and, by extension, the reordering of society. If their work and Claire's gatherings continue unchecked, they could inspire others to challenge our authority. We need to infiltrate these meetings, gather evidence, and, if necessary, take action to dismantle this network before it gains momentum."

Louis Antoine de Saint-Just's tone underscored the severity of their situation, prompting Georges Couthon to interject, "Indeed, the clocks themselves symbolise a new order, but the minds behind them concern me more. Pierre Moreau's influence grows; his son Henri's enthusiasm for their work does not go unnoticed among the young intellectuals."

Robespierre nodded, his hand resting on a pile of surveillance reports. "It is not the clocks but the conversations around them that we must monitor. Have our agents confirmed any direct subversion in these gatherings?"

Saint-Just responded with a mix of caution and resolve in his voice. "No direct subversion, but the subtext of their rhetoric could inspire dissent. They speak of equality through time, of reshaping society's structure through the division of hours and minutes."

The discussion shifted towards implementing a more strategic surveillance operation. "We will not arrest them yet," Robespierre decided, his strategy clear. "That would martyr them. Instead, let us weave a web around their activities so tight that they cannot reveal their true intentions to us."

Meanwhile, fully aware of the potential persecution, Pierre and Henri continued their work, placing their ultimate faith in justice as upstanding citizens. The steady ticking of their clocks provided a constant backdrop to their conversations. On this particularly chilly afternoon, Henri voiced his worries while piecing together a clock mechanism.

"Father, do you feel the walls closing in? Our talks of time and its implications… could they be misconstrued?" Henri's question hung heavy in the air, mixing with the metallic scent of machinery.

Pierre paused his tools momentarily still. "Every word we speak, every concept we explore, carries weight. We tread a fine line, Henri. But fear not; our purpose is just. We advance timekeeping, not treason."

At their residence, Étienne arrived urgently, cutting through the evening's calm. "Pierre, Henri, I've overheard talk at the markets. The Committee grows suspicious of your meetings. They're planning more stringent observations."

The news was a stark reminder of the danger lurking beneath their intellectual pursuits. Pierre responded with measured calm, "Thank you, Étienne. We must be more careful. Perhaps it is time to restrict our discussions to time alone."

As the sun set on 14 Nivôse, Year II, casting long shadows over the snowy streets of Paris, the Moreaus adjusted their clocks for the evening, each tick marking not just the passage of time but the pulse of an era fraught with tension and suspicion.

In the shadows of their workshop, as they prepared to close for the night, Henri's resolve hardened. "Let them watch," he whispered to his father. "Our clocks will continue to tick, and truth, like time, will not be silenced."

—

On 17 Nivôse, Year II (6 January 1794), the icy cobblestones of Paris reflected the deep coldness that had gripped its citizens' spirits. In the solemn chambers of the Committee of Public Safety, Maximilien Robespierre convened a crucial meeting with his deputies, their pressing task casting a grave silhouette in the flickering candlelight.

"We stand at a precipice," Robespierre declared, his voice cutting through the murmurs of his colleagues. "The Republic is besieged by enemies visible and hidden within the machinations of progress. Our vigilance must be absolute."

Bertrand Barère, a key ally and skilled orator, leaned in his expression grave. "Citizen Robespierre, the surveillance reports on the Moreau workshop suggest nothing but a passionate dedication to the ideals of our new time measurement. Yet, this dedication could mask deeper dissent. How shall we proceed?"

Robespierre's gaze was steely as he responded, "Continue our observations, but hold back on direct action. We must not make martyrs of mere clockmakers unless their guilt is irrefutable. The Republic requires not just justice, but prudence."

Meanwhile, the clockmakers continued their work with a quiet intensity. Their workshop, filled with the steady ticking of clocks, had become a sanctuary of gears and springs—a stark contrast to the suspicion brewing outside its doors.

Henri, his fingers stained with oil, spoke to his father with a tinge of defiance. "If our clocks symbolise the march of progress, why should we fear? Our work aligns with the Republic's principles."

Placing a gear within the belly of a grand clock, Pierre replied thoughtfully, "True, Henri, but remember, even the most rational minds can falter under the shadow of fear. Our clocks measure more than time; they challenge the very perception of it."

As the day waned, a hurried knock echoed through the workshop. It was Étienne, his breath clouding in the winter air as he entered. "Pierre, Henri, the committee grows impatient. Their eyes linger longer upon your endeavours. Caution is now your best ally."

Pierre, sensing the rising tension, stepped forward with a calm demeanour. "Étienne, we appreciate your concern. But remember, we are artisans, not counter-revolutionaries. Our work is transparent and aims to improve society. We must not let fear dictate our actions."

The warning struck a chord, and that evening, as they covered the clocks and doused the lanterns, the weight of their situation settled heavily upon them. Henri's resolve was evident as he spoke, "Father, perhaps it is time we considered the implications of our visibility. Might we be safer in the shadows?"

Pierre, locking the door behind them, pondered this as they walked through the quiet streets. "Perhaps, Henri, but to retreat completely would mean abandoning our principles. Instead, Let us tread carefully, fully aware of the eyes upon us, yet steadfast in our commitment to our craft and integrity."

Back in the shadowed corridors of power, Robespierre met with Saint-Just, his trusted confidant. "Keep a close watch, but act only if their actions prove a definitive threat. The Republic cannot afford missteps in these precarious times."

As 17 Nivôse, Year II (6 January 1794) drew close, the cold seeped through the walls of homes and hearts alike. Paris slept under a blanket of frost while its guardians, cloaked in the righteousness of their cause, prepared for whatever the new dawn might bring.

Chapter Seven

As dawn broke on 18 Nivôse, Year II (7 January 1794), a frost-laden mist enveloped the streets of Paris, creeping along the cobbled stones like a silent spectre. Within the confines of their modest workshop, nestled in a narrow alley of the Marais district, Pierre Moreau and his son Henri were already at their benches, the rhythmic tapping of their tools a comforting melody against the backdrop of a city on edge.

Henri paused, a delicate gear held between his fingers, as he sensed his father's gaze heavy upon him. With lines of worry etched deeply into his face, Pierre glanced at the window where the first light of morning cast long shadows across the cold floor.

"The eyes of the Committee grow ever more intrusive," Pierre murmured, his voice barely above a whisper as if afraid the walls themselves might listen. "Robespierre's decrees have sown seeds of paranoia that now bloom unchecked throughout Paris."

Henri nodded, placing the gear down gently. "I feel the weight of their gaze, father. Each tick of our clocks marks not just the passage of time but the tightening noose of suspicion."

Outside, the faint murmur of the city awakening, the distant calls of the vendors setting up their market stalls, the clatter of hooves on stone, and the ever-present whispers of a populace shadowed by fear.

In these early hours, the Committee's informers were most active, blending into the dawn's dim light as they marked the doors of those who whispered too freely of liberty.

The workshop, filled with the evidence of the Moreaus' trade in timekeeping and mechanics, was a testament to the Enlightenment's push against the boundaries of science and art. Clocks in various stages of assembly lined the walls, their pendulums still awaiting the master's hand to set them in motion. Yet, these creations, once symbols of progress, now stood as potential evidence of subversion in the eyes of the state, each tick potentially counting down to their undoing.

As Henri turned back to his workbench, a soft knock echoed through the room, causing both men to stiffen. The sound was light, almost hesitant, but in the charged air of revolutionary Paris, even such a gentle tap carried the weight of dread.

Pierre motioned for his son to stay quiet as he moved towards the door, his steps measured, his hand steady as he reached for the handle. Pulling open the door revealed Étienne Rochefort, his face pale under the brim of his hat, eyes darting nervously.

"They are rounding up those they deem 'enemies of progress'," Étienne said, stepping inside calmly but urgently. "The Committee for Public Safety has listed Pierre. Names of those who work too closely with the gears and springs of change. Your name, my name—we are on those lists."

Henri's grip tightened on his tools; the metal was cold and unyielding beneath his touch. "What are we to do, Étienne? We cannot simply stop our work, our inquiries into the nature of things."

Pierre, ever the peacemaker and thinker, spoke with calm conviction. "Étienne, Henri, we must approach this with logic and clarity. Our work does not oppose the Republic; it exemplifies the essence of revolution—progress, knowledge, and enlightenment. We must articulate this clearly and convincingly."

Étienne nodded, pulling from his coat a small stack of papers—pamphlets that argued for the role of science and innovation as pillars of the new France. "Then let us arm ourselves with the mightiest weapons we possess: our words, our convictions. Let us sway the hearts and minds of the people and the Committee."

Pierre's steady voice continued to instil a sense of calm. "We must prepare our case carefully, demonstrating how our innovations align with the Republic's ideals. We will show that our intentions are pure, and our work is not a threat but a boon to society."

Together, in the quiet rebellion of their intellect and passion, the three men plotted the survival of their crafts and the defence of their very lives against the creeping shadow of tyranny that threatened to engulf them all.

—

On the morning of 19 Nivôse, Year II (8 January 1794), the air in Paris was thick with frost and fear, a combination that settled over the city like a suffocating blanket. Pierre Moreau peered out from behind the faded curtains of his workshop, his eyes scanning the lonely streets as Henri arranged the tools on their workbench, each movement deliberate, echoing the tension that filled the room.

Pierre was acutely aware of the need to take steps to ensure their security, as well as the security of those with whom they interacted. Despite this, he maintained an air of calm while he attempted to apply logic to the scenario.

The previous day's warnings from Étienne had not been taken lightly. Pierre knew that their circle of trust must tighten even further to avoid the fate that had befallen so many of their peers—imprisonment or worse. Each visitor to their shop, each transaction, could no longer be about commerce; it was now about survival.

"Father, should we not cease our meetings with the others?" Henri's voice broke the silence, his tone laced with concern as he set down a gear wheel, the metal cold and unyielding under his touch.

Pierre shook his head, his gaze still fixed on the street. "To retreat completely is to admit defeat, Henri. We must be cautious, but we must also continue our work. It's not just our livelihood but our mission. We advance timekeeping and science but cannot allow fear to halt progress."

As they spoke, the distant sound of boots on cobblestones grew louder, rhythmic and foreboding. Seeing a detachment of soldiers marching in formation down their street made Henri tense. Their blue coats and Tricolour cockades, which once symbolised liberty, now heralded a reign of surveillance and control.

"They increase their patrols," Pierre murmured, drawing the curtains closed with a careful motion. Turning to his son, he added, "We must be more discreet in our comings and goings. Use the back streets; vary your routine."

Their conversation was abruptly interrupted by a sharp rap at the door—a coded knock they had agreed upon with their closest associates. Pierre cautiously opened it to reveal Étienne, his face drawn, eyes darting anxiously.

"They've arrested the Jouberts this morning," Étienne announced in a hushed tone as he stepped inside, shaking off the cold. "The

Committee accuses them of hoarding and counter-revolutionary activities. Their workshop was searched, everything seized."

Henri felt a chill that had little to do with the winter air. "The Jouberts? But their loyalty to the Republic…"

"Loyalty matters little if you are perceived as a threat," Étienne cut in, his voice low. "Or if someone decides to settle an old score under the guise of patriotism. We must protect ourselves, prepare for the worst."

The trio gathered around the old oak table that had served more discussions of revolutionary science than meals in recent times. Maps were unrolled, lists of safe contacts reviewed, and escape routes meticulously planned and revised.

"Our next meeting cannot be here," Pierre decided, finger tracing a route on the map leading out of Paris. "We'll meet at the old mill outside the city. Fewer eyes and ears there."

Henri nodded, absorbing every word. The workshop that had been his world was shrinking into a cage. "And the new chronometer prototype? If they find it…"

"We'll move it tonight," Pierre resolved. "Étienne, can you arrange for your cousin's cart? We must transport it discreetly."

As they set their plans, each was acutely aware of the risks they faced. The walls of their world seemed to close in, tightened by the invisible grip of Robespierre's Committee for Public Safety. Yet, within this constriction, their resolve hardened, not just to survive but to ensure the survival of their ideals.

Étienne left as quietly as he had arrived, blending back into the shadowed streets of a city that no longer felt like home. Pierre and Henri returned to their work, their hands mechanically resuming their tasks while their minds raced with strategies for evasion.

The clocks ticked on, indifferent to the turmoil of their creators, marking the relentless passage of time towards an uncertain future.

—

On 20 Nivôse, Year II (9 January 1794), a suffocating silence enveloped the streets of Paris, starkly contrasting the usual vibrant chatter that characterised the city's daily life. Within the confines of the Moreau residence, the air was thick with apprehension. Claire Fontaine crept about the kitchen, preparing a modest breakfast, her movements methodical. Though she had ceased hosting her weekly salons due to increased scrutiny, Claire remained an emotional rock, keeping her worry hidden from Henri while providing the calm guidance he needed.

Having barely slept, Henri joined his mother at the small wooden table, his eyes weary and his thoughts troubled. "Mother, the streets are too quiet today," he murmured, glancing out the window with a frown. "It's as though the city itself is holding its breath."

Claire nodded, her hands steady as she poured tea. "It feels like the calm before the storm, Henri. We must remain vigilant."

At that moment, a quiet but urgent knock sounded at the door. Henri quickly stood, his chair scraping against the cold tile floor. He moved to the door cautiously and opened it to reveal their neighbour, Madame Durand, her shawl pulled tightly around her against the chill.

"Madame Durand, what brings you here at this hour?" Henri asked his voice a blend of concern and surprise.

The older woman stepped inside, her eyes darting nervously. "Henri, Claire," she began, her voice quivering, "you must be careful. The gendarmes have been asking about Pierre. They were at the market this morning, questioning the vendors and the shoppers. They're looking for something or someone."

Claire's face remained composed as she clasped her hands tightly. "Thank you for letting us know, Marguerite. We will be vigilant."

As Madame Durand left, Claire turned to Henri, her expression severe but calm. "We must warn your father. He was going to the market this morning for supplies."

Henri nodded, his jaw set with determination. "I'll go, Mother. It's safer if I do. Father must be warned, and we must ensure he doesn't fall into a trap."

Grabbing his coat, Henri hurried out into the chilled air, the streets eerily deserted as he made his way towards the market. Each step felt heavier than the last, his mind racing with potential dangers. Upon arriving, he spotted his father near a stall, examining some tools. Henri quickly approached, eyes scanning the surroundings for any sign of soldiers or spies.

"Father," Henri said, gripping his father's arm, "the gendarmes are asking about you. It would help if you were careful. Madame Durand saw them at the market this morning."

Pierre Moreau looked at his son, his expression of resolve mixed with a hint of fear. "Thank you, Henri. We must be cautious but not cower. We will continue our work, but we will also prepare. It's clear they are stepping up their efforts."

Together, they quickly purchased what was necessary and left the market, their pace brisk and conversation hushed. As they walked home, Pierre spoke of plans for increased security and perhaps even preparing a haven should they need to escape in haste.

"We may need to find a more secluded place for our meetings and work," Pierre suggested, his mind working through logistics and possibilities. "Somewhere out of sight, where we can continue without interference."

Henri nodded, his family's situation heavy on his shoulders. "I'll start making arrangements, Father. We'll be ready."

As they neared home, the quiet of the streets seemed even more oppressive, a stark reminder of the tense atmosphere that had taken hold of Paris. Inside, they found Claire waiting anxiously, relief flooding her features as she saw them return safely.

Together, the Moreau family prepared for the storm they knew was coming, their unity a beacon of hope amid the growing shadows of suspicion and fear enveloping their world.

—

The dim light of early morning filtered through the workshop's dusty windows as the clockmakers continued their work amidst an oppressive silence that had settled over Paris. The ordinarily rhythmic clinking of their tools now echoed ominously in the enclosed space, each sound a stark reminder of the scrutiny they were under.

With a furrowed brow, Pierre paused and glanced towards the window, his eyes tracing the movement of a shadow that flitted across the street. "They're watching us more closely than ever," he whispered to Henri, who nodded grimly, tightening his grip on the wrench.

"Father, we must be cautious with every word and gesture," Henri replied, keeping his voice low. "The walls have ears; the smallest slip could bring them to our door."

The conversation was interrupted by a sudden knock, causing both men to startle. Pierre gestured for silence, his eyes communicating a warning as he moved cautiously towards the door. Peering through the peephole, he saw a familiar face — Marcel, one of their trusted associates, his face etched with urgency.

Pierre quickly ushered him into the workshop by opening the door just enough to allow Marcel inside. Marcel glanced around nervously before speaking. "I've come with news," he said breathlessly. "The Committee is increasing their raids. They're rounding up anyone suspected of counter-revolutionary activities. Your names have been mentioned, Pierre. They're coming closer to linking you to the dissidents."

The news sent a chill through Pierre. He had long feared this day would come, and now the threat loomed more significant than ever. "Thank you, Marcel. We must think of a plan to protect ourselves and our families."

Turning to Henri, Pierre's expression hardened with resolve. "We need to secure all our documents and correspondence, including any diagrams or materials that could be misconstrued as subversive. Everything must be hidden or destroyed."

Henri nodded, understanding the gravity of the situation. "I'll start moving the sensitive materials to our secondary location tonight. The hidden cellar beneath the mill should be secure."

Claire entered the workshop as they spoke, her face pale with worry. "I heard the news from the market," she said, trembling. "The gendarmes are arresting people at random. Our friends, our neighbours… no one is safe."

Pierre took her hand, offering a squeeze of reassurance. "We will get through this, Claire. We are cautious, and we are prepared."

The rest of the day, they passed in a blur of activity. Henri and Pierre worked to conceal their most sensitive projects, transferring diagrams and prototype parts to hidden compartments and off-site locations. Marcel helped where possible, and his knowledge of the city's back alleys proved invaluable.

As night fell, the tension in the air grew thicker. Pierre watched from the window as patrols increased on the streets. Turning back to his family, he spoke with a quiet intensity. "Tonight, we stay vigilant. Henri, once it's dark enough, you move what's left to the cellar. Marcel, can you ensure the route is clear?"

Marcel nodded. "I'll scout ahead. No one will see Henri if I can help it."

After gathering a small bag of necessities, Claire added, "I'll prepare a quick meal. We'll need our strength." Her hands were steady, and her resolve was a testament to the strength that had carried her family thus far.

The Moreau family and Marcel ate in subdued silence, their ears tuned to any sound out of the ordinary. Each creak and whisper of wind seemed to carry the possibility of danger.

As they cleared the table, Henri prepared to depart with crucial materials. He clasped his father's hand, the unspoken fear evident in their tight grip. "I'll be back before dawn," he promised, a determined glint in his eye.

Pierre nodded pride and fear mingling in his chest. "Be safe, my son."

With one last look at his family, Henri slipped out into the night, the shadows swallowing his figure as he made his way towards the uncertain safety of the hidden cellar. The fate of the Moreau family hung precariously in the balance, their every action a calculated step in their bid for survival amid the Reign of Terror's suffocating grip.

—

As dawn broke on the 22nd of Nivôse, Year II (11 January 1794), a tense atmosphere pervaded the streets of Paris. Within the humble confines of the Moreau family workshop, Pierre and Henri reviewed every detail of their inventions, ensuring nothing could be construed as provocative. The news of increased detentions was a grim reminder of the precarious thread by which their fates dangled.

Henri glanced over at his father with a furrowed brow. "We need to ensure every document is accounted for. The slightest oversight could be disastrous," he said, his voice heavy with concern.

Pierre nodded, his eyes scanning the stacks of diagrams and notes. "Indeed, my son. Let's categorise everything that could be misunderstood or seen as incriminating. It needs to be moved to the hidden cellar by nightfall."

As they worked, the door creaked slightly, and Claire entered, her face drawn and pale. "The neighbours were whispering about the patrols last night," she whispered, her eyes darting nervously. "Two more families were taken. No reason given, no return. Henri, please reconsider your plan to stay."

Henri met his mother's gaze, his resolve hardening. "I must stay, Mother. Leaving now would only draw more suspicion to us. We have to stand together and face whatever comes."

The conversation was abruptly cut short by the sudden arrival of their old friend and loyal customer, Monsieur Lefèvre. His unexpected presence brought a brief moment of normalcy to the charged atmosphere. "Pierre, Henri, I've come for the usual adjustments to my equipment. But more importantly, how are you holding up?" he asked, lowering his voice as he glanced around the cluttered workshop.

"We manage, as always, Monsieur Lefèvre," Pierre responded with a forced smile, leading their guest to the back where the less sensitive work was displayed. "Let's discuss your needs."

As Henri and Claire continued to sort through the paperwork, their discussion was intermittently punctuated by the low murmur of voices from the back of the workshop. Henri paused, his attention caught by a particular set of designs. "These are too risky to keep. If they were to be found…" His voice trailed off as he considered the implications.

"Then we must destroy them," Claire said decisively, her hands trembling slightly as she took the documents from Henri. "Better ashes than chains."

The day wore on, and the shadows grew longer, casting a gloom over the room as the sun dipped below the horizon. The air grew colder, mirroring the chill that had settled in their hearts. After Monsieur Lefèvre left, reassured yet unaware of the full gravity of the situation, the family gathered once more.

"We've done all we can for today," Pierre announced. "Let's prepare for the evening. Henri, you and I will move the critical items to a safe location tonight. Claire, please make sure everything else appears normal here."

As night fell over the city, Henri and Pierre, shrouded in darkness, moved the final batch of sensitive materials to an old mill on the outskirts of Paris. This long-abandoned mill acted as their clandestine storage, concealed from watchful eyes. They travelled separately to avoid detection by the Revolutionary Guards' patrols.

Each movement was calculated, and each step was measured to avoid detection. The silence of the night was a stark contrast to the turmoil that churned within them. Every snapped twig or rustle of leaves sent a jolt of fear through their spines.

Henri took the lead, and Pierre followed shortly after. They completed their task and headed home through the enveloping darkness, the burden of their deeds weighing heavily upon them. The city, once a beacon of innovation and progress, now seemed to constrict around them like a tightening noose.

At home, Claire remained resolute by the window, keeping a constant vigil. As she saw Henri and Pierre emerge separately from the shadows, a brief surge of relief swept through her, but it quickly passed.

The circle was tightening, and dawn was nearing, heralding the arrival of uncertainties. As they settled in for the night, the persistent ticking of the clocks transcended its usual role, marking not just the passage of time but a countdown to an undetermined fate. Their determination to safeguard their legacy and each other stood firm as the sole certainty in a world upended.

—

As the city of Paris slept on the night of 22 Nivôse, Year II (11 January 1794), the streets and buildings transitioned into shadowy silhouettes against the darkened sky. Having left the hidden cache where he and Henri safeguarded their most sensitive documents, Pierre Moreau felt the weight of each step towards his home. The documents, a mixture of correspondences with foreign intellectuals and philosophical treatises, were damning in the wrong hands. Their last hope was that these critical papers remained undiscovered, as discovery would surely seal their fate under the current regime's scrutiny.

Pierre's route took him through narrower, less frequented alleys, a path he had memorised to avoid the prying eyes of the Committee's spies. However, tonight, the air was thick with an ominous chill beyond the winter's cold—a sensation that tugged at the edges of his nerves, alerting him to danger. His heart pounded with dread and resolve; he was no stranger to this dance of shadows and whispers, yet tonight, it bore a heavier, more sinister tone.

Unbeknownst to Pierre, a pair of eyes watched from the darkness. The Guard, informed by an anonymous tip-off, had been tracking his movements with predatory precision. As Pierre turned into a particularly secluded lane, the shuffling of feet echoed off the cobblestones behind him. Before he could react, a cold hand clamped over his shoulder, spinning him around to face the dim light of a lantern held by a stern-faced soldier.

"Monsieur Moreau, you are required to accompany us," the soldier announced, his voice devoid of emotion yet carrying an undercurrent of grim satisfaction. The lantern's flickering light revealed two more figures flanking him, their expressions obscured by the shadows but their intentions clear.

Pierre, though startled, maintained his composure. "On what grounds am I being detained?" he demanded, his voice steady but his mind racing with a million scenarios.

"The Committee for Public Safety requires your presence for questioning regarding activities counter to the principles of our Republic," the soldier replied mechanically. "Resistance will only complicate your situation."

Pierre, a pacifist and artisan influenced by Enlightenment ideals, knew better than to resist the towering guards before him. Aware that any attempt to fight back would be futile and likely disastrous, he slowly nodded, concealing his rising panic beneath a façade of resignation. "Very well, lead the way," he said, his mind quickly considering how he might warn Henri and Claire.

Pierre's thoughts raced as the guards led him through the winding streets toward their headquarters. Each step away from freedom deepened his uncertainty, strengthening his resolve to protect his family. He knew he had to think and devise a plan, even under these dire circumstances. However, espionage and deception were not skills Pierre had mastered, so compliance became his only option, driven by fear for the safety of his wife and son.

Meanwhile, Henri grew increasingly uneasy as the time for his father's return had long passed. Deciding to follow his father's usual route, he shared his plans with Claire and stepped out into the cold night. Looking at Henri, Claire saw not the man he had become but still the boy she wished to protect. With a hesitant nod, she agreed to his decision.

The streets carried the whispers of revolution—echoes of fear, betrayal, and courage. As Henri moved stealthily, blending into the shadows, he overheard snippets of a conversation among three men speaking in subdued tones. Although hard to discern, he caught phrases like "The Clockmaker" and "Three Guardsmen." These fragments led him to a chilling conclusion. His heart sank as he realised his father had been captured, the pieces of the puzzle falling into place with a dread that tightened his chest.

Back in their home, Claire waited, each tick of the clock a sharp reminder of the danger they faced. When Henri's hurried footsteps finally echoed through the hall, her heart leapt, only to sink again at the sight of his grave expression.

"They've taken him," Henri said, his voice tinged with anger and fear. Claire steadied herself against the mantle, her mind whirling as she processed the shock and prepared to shift from fear to action. Sensing Henri's anger, she struggled to control her emotions. Her most immediate concern was that Henri might act rashly, and she knew she needed to be his anchor, the calm presence to steady him.

"We must remain calm," Claire said, her voice unwavering. "We cannot afford to act impulsively. We need a plan, and we need to stay united."

Henri nodded, the tension in his shoulders easing slightly at his mother's calm resolve. "What should we do, Mother?"

"We will gather what remains of our sensitive documents and ensure they are well hidden," Claire replied. "And we will seek help from our trusted friends. We must be strategic and cautious."

As they settled in for the night, the persistent ticking of the clocks transcended its usual role, marking not just the passage of time but a countdown to an undetermined fate. Their determination to safeguard their legacy and each other stood firm as the sole certainty in a world upended.

The morning of 23 Nivôse, Year II (12 January 1794), she enveloped the city of Paris in an eerie silence that hung heavily in the streets like a dense fog. Inside the Moreau household, the tension could be cut with a knife as Claire moved around the dimly lit kitchen, her movements mechanical and her thoughts distant. The usual bustling sounds of the neighbourhood were conspicuously absent, replaced by the haunting quiet of a city bracing for more of the Committee's unpredictable actions.

Claire gazed through the frost-covered window, watching as the weak sunlight struggled to break through the grey Parisian winter clouds. She hoped for a miracle—that Pierre would appear and this nightmare would be undone. Time seemed to stretch endlessly, each second echoing the last. Turning away from the window, she saw Henri hunched over the table, intently scouring a list of names of those detained or questioned.

"Claire's voice was a whisper, barely audible above the faint ticking of the wall clock. "Henri," she said, "you should eat something. You've barely touched your food." Though Claire hadn't eaten anything, her concern lay elsewhere; as a mother, her priority was Henri's well-being.

Henri looked up, his eyes bloodshot and weary. "I can't, Mother. Not while Father and the others…" His voice trailed off as his gaze returned to the papers scattered before him.

The silence was abruptly broken by a soft knock at the door, causing both Henri and Claire to startle. With a caution born of recent experiences, Henri moved slowly towards the door, his hand on the handle feeling cold and heavy. Peering through the peephole, he saw Monsieur Dubois, their neighbour, his eyes wide with fear and urgency.

Opening the door just enough to speak, Henri greeted him with a nod. "Monsieur Dubois, what brings you here at this hour?"

"Dubois glanced nervously over his shoulder before speaking. "Henri," he said in a low voice, "I am sorry about Pierre. He truly embodies the Enlightenment and has become a symbol of the revolution. It would help if you were careful. There are whispers that the Committee is planning to target anyone who has shown even the slightest dissent. They're no longer focusing only on the obvious suspects."

Dubois handed Henri a small, folded piece of paper before quickly departing. Henri unfolded it carefully, his fingers trembling slightly as he read the hastily scribbled message warning him of a possible raid scheduled for the next day. The reality that his family could be next sent a shiver down his spine.

Henri returned to the kitchen and shared the news with Claire, who responded with a resigned nod. "We must prepare," she said firmly. "Gather anything that could incriminate us or our friends. We need to hide or destroy it before they have a chance to discover anything."

Claire and Henri spent the day in a flurry of activity, meticulously sifting through every document, letter, and scrap of paper that could link them to revolutionary ideals now seen as damning. Henri focused on preserving his father's legacy, safeguarding the innovative diagrams and notes that might be misinterpreted as subversive. Only now did he fully grasp the extent of Pierre's documentation—every correspondence and idea was recorded in detail. Despite their recent efforts to conceal these items, documents still cluttered the space.

Once innocuous notes are barely worth a second glance, these papers now took on a menacing significance in Henri's eyes. To those determined to find fault, each page could be twisted into evidence of subversion, casting a shadow over everything Pierre had worked for.

As the sun set, casting long shadows across the room, Claire and Henri packed the last of the papers into a false bottom in an old chest. They stood back, looking at the seemingly innocuous piece of furniture that now showed their precarious existence.

That night, the Moreau household was cloaked in a vigil of silence, the kind that preludes a storm. Henri watched by the window, eyes scanning the shadowy street for any sign of approaching danger. Claire tried to rest, but sleep eluded her, the weight of impending doom pressing down like a physical force.

In the stillness of that foreboding night, the silent hours ticked by, each drawing closer to the dawn of an uncertain day. The Moreaus, bound by blood and crisis, faced the unknown with stoic resolve, ready to protect each other at all costs. The city's silence was a grim reminder of the isolation they now felt, enveloped by literal and metaphorical darkness, as they awaited the first light of day that might bring with it the full fury of the revolution's shadow.

—

As morning broke, adrenaline surged through Claire and Henri, sustaining them through their exhaustion. The day passed in a tense silence, each moment tinged with the expectation of an ominous knock at the door. By the evening of 24 Nivôse, Year II (13 January 1794), a heavy silence enveloped their home. Henri paced the length of the living room, casting anxious glances toward the window with every sound. The fear that had been simmering throughout the day reached a boiling point, with the dread of the soldiers' arrival looming over the household like a dark cloud.

Claire sat by the hearth; her knitting needles idle in her lap, the yarn tangled and forgotten. Her mind was occupied with thoughts of Pierre, wondering if there was any way to shield her family from the storm they knew was coming. Every minute that ticked by deepened the dread that gripped her heart.

Suddenly, the quiet of the evening was shattered by a firm knock at the door. The sound echoed ominously through the house, causing Henri and Claire to freeze. Henri's hand reached instinctively for a hidden dagger under his shirt as he moved towards the door, his mother's whispered caution trailing behind him.

"Be careful, Henri," Claire said, her voice a strained whisper.

Henri nodded, pressing his eye to the peephole. Outside stood several soldiers, their red caps barely visible in the dim light of dusk. Steeling himself, he opened the door just enough to speak; his body tensed for any sign of aggression.

"Bonsoir," the lead soldier said, his tone authoritative. "We are here by the orders of the Committee of Public Safety. Are you Henri Moreau?"

"Yes, I am," Henri replied, his voice steady despite the adrenaline coursing through his veins. "How can I assist you?"

The soldier's eyes narrowed slightly. "We need to speak with both you and Madame Moreau. It is about the security of the Republic."

Without waiting for an invitation, the soldiers stepped forward, pushing past Henri into the foyer. Claire rose to her feet, her expression one of resigned determination. She had prepared for this moment, though no amount of preparation could truly ready one's heart for the cold march of soldiers' boots in one's home.

"Madame Moreau, we must ask you to come with us," another soldier stated, his hand resting on the hilt of his sword.

"And my son?" Claire's voice was firm, demanding an answer.

"He stays," the soldier replied curtly. "For now."

Henri's mind raced as he watched the soldiers escort his mother towards the door. His initial impulse was to fight and protect her, but he knew any resistance would only end in bloodshed. Claire's reassuring glance back at him quelled his rising panic. She was composed, her demeanour calm and unyielding even in captivity.

As the door closed behind them, leaving Henri alone in the echoing silence of the now-empty house, the weight of his solitude pressed down on him. The night had fallen completely, and with it, the last rays of hope seemed to dim. Henri moved to the window, watching as the soldiers led his mother away into the night, her figure a small, resilient shadow against the torch-lit darkness.

The house felt cavernous and eerie, filled with the ghosts of whispered conversations and laughter now stifled by the harsh reality of their situation. Henri knew the coming days would test him in ways he had never imagined. As he turned away from the window, his resolve hardened. He would do whatever it took to save his parents and clear their name, no matter the cost.

The night air was cold as it seeped through the cracks of the old wooden house, carrying the sounds of a changing city, its precious revolution now a mask for fear and suspicion. Henri sat at his father's desk, pulling out a hidden drawer to reveal the papers and plans he knew could save them or condemn them further. His fingers brushed over the documents, the ink barely dry, the words a testament to his family's legacy and their undying commitment to a cause that threatened to destroy them.

—

The morning of 25 Nivôse, Year II (14 January 1794), they dawned bleak and unforgiving. Pierre Moreau and his wife Claire Fountaine confronted the grim reality of their predicament, each confined to separate cells within the cold, stone walls of La Force prison—one of Paris's most notorious prisons during the Reign of Terror. The harsh conditions of their imprisonment mirrored the severe measures the revolutionary government employed against those it deemed enemies.

Claire sat on a thin straw mattress, the bleakness of her surroundings underscoring the drastic turn their lives had taken. The damp air seeped into her bones while the distant sounds of other prisoners' despair echoed hauntingly through the corridors. Despite the fear gnawing at her, Claire's thoughts remained with her family, especially Henri, who was alone, facing the turmoil outside. Her worry that he might act impulsively weighed heavily on her mind.

Meanwhile, Pierre paced back and forth in his cell, his mind racing with thoughts of escape and rescue. The reality of their circumstances was harsh, yet his resolve hardened. "I must find a way to protect Claire and Henri," he murmured, his responsibility bearing on him. Every echoing step in his cell reminded him of the time slipping away.

At home, Henri faced his struggles. Word of his parents' imprisonment had quickly spread, causing friends and allies to distance themselves, wary of the Committee's extensive reach. While Henri understood their fear, he couldn't shake the feeling of abandonment in his time of need. Nevertheless, this did not shake his determination; it steeled his resolve to fight even harder for his parents' freedom. His guiding thought was the memory of his mother's calm composure during her arrest. He knew that if he acted rashly, she might never forgive herself.

As the day progressed, Henri scoured the city for anyone who would openly oppose the Committee. His journey led him to the dimly lit back rooms of taverns and the shadowed alleyways where whispers of resistance flickered like the fragile flames of candles. Here, Henri met with disillusioned revolutionaries and desperate citizens, each conversation a delicate dance of trust and danger.

In the depths of La Force, Pierre and Claire's thoughts often met in silent solidarity, each drawing strength from their shared resolve. Claire, ever the nurturer, worried incessantly about the toll this ordeal would take on Henri. She whispered into the darkness, "Stay strong, my son. We will be together soon." Her voice, though soft, was tinged with a mother's unwavering love and conviction.

The conditions in the jail were harsh, and the jailers indifferent or cruel, yet the spirit of the Moreau family remained unbroken. Using his charm and wit, Pierre began to weave a network within the prison walls, gathering snippets of information and planting seeds of doubt among the guards about the legitimacy of the charges against him.

As night fell over Paris, the chill within the cells grew colder. Claire wrapped her shawl tighter around her shoulders, her thoughts drifting to the past, to days filled with laughter and love, a stark contrast to the shadowed present. Meanwhile, Pierre lay awake, staring at the stone ceiling, plotting, planning, and always thinking ahead.

Outside, the streets of Paris simmered with unrest. Moving through the city under the cover of darkness, Henri met with a secretive group committed to justice, or at least opposed to the current reign of terror. They spoke in hushed tones, their plans ambitious and dangerous. Henri knew the risks but saw no other path forward. He was ready to gamble everything to save his parents.

In the quiet solitude of his cell, Pierre finally drifted into a restless sleep, dreaming of reunions and revolts. At the same time, Claire clutched a small locket, a remnant of better days, her silent prayer for protection echoing off the walls. Both knew the dawn might bring judgment, but they also knew their son was fighting for them.

—

As the dawn of 27 Nivôse, Year II (16 January 1794) broke over Paris, the city awoke to another frigid morning; its streets were blanketed in a thin layer of frost. Henri Moreau faced the day with a heavy heart, his thoughts consumed by the plight of his parents, Pierre and Claire, now locked away in the harsh confines of adjacent cells.

Henri had spent a restless night pacing his family's apartment, formulating plans and considering every conceivable avenue to aid his parents. His resolve was firm, but the paths to success were uncertain. The weight of his family's legacy bore down upon him, a lineage now tainted by accusations and imprisonment.

La Force prison, a stark edifice of despair, was notorious for its harsh conditions and the brutal treatment of its inmates. Pierre and Claire were subjected to the same cold indifference that all prisoners faced. Their cells were small, damp, and poorly lit, the iron bars cold to the touch, a constant reminder of their grim reality.

Pierre attempted to maintain a semblance of dignity and strength in his cell. He spent his days pacing back and forth, rehearsing arguments and speeches in his mind, clinging to the hope of a public trial where he could speak the truth. Despite the bleakness of his situation, his spirit remained unbroken, fuelled by the thought of seeing his family reunited.

Claire, on the other hand, found solace in quieter reflection. She whispered prayers and composed letters she knew she could never send, each word a testament to her enduring love and hope for her family. Her resilience was a quiet force, her faith unspoken but evident in her jaw set and the resolve in her eyes.

Outside the prison, Henri's efforts to gather support intensified. The young Moreau met clandestinely with old family friends, former political allies, and even sympathetic strangers, each meeting held in whispered tones in the shadowed corners of dimly lit cafes or secluded back alleys. The risks were immense, but Henri's determination drove him forward. He knew that public sentiment could sway the scales of justice, but it was an inconsistent and dangerous ally.

One such ally was an old friend of Pierre, a former deputy of the Assembly who had managed to avoid the purges. This friend, Monsieur Lefèvre, had connections that could prove invaluable. Hesitant at first, moved by Henri's impassioned pleas, Lefèvre agreed to help, suggesting they seek the assistance of a well-known lawyer who was discreetly opposed to the extremities of the current regime.

Henri and Lefèvre dedicated countless hours to planning, acutely aware that time was of the essence. They needed to move quickly to mount a robust defence. The task was daunting and complex, yet Henri's resolve remained unshaken. Despite the overwhelming odds, the thought of his parents facing their grim fate alone was intolerable. His impulses to act rashly were continually tempered by the memory of one of the last things his mother said during her arrest: "Be careful, Henri." It lacked the enthusiasm of his father's speeches to the assembly or the crowds at Place Royale. Still, its simplicity and starkness carried a profound meaning that steadied him.

Back in the prison, as the day waned, Pierre and Claire shared a silent moment of connection across the cold expanse separating their cells. In that brief exchange of glances, filled with love and mutual reassurance, they drew strength from each other, their bond unbroken by iron bars.

As night descended upon Paris, enveloping the city in darkness, the Moreau family, each in their way, prepared for the challenges of the coming days. They understood the stakes were high, and the morrow could bring changes, for better or worse. In the silent watches of the night, Henri continued his work by candlelight, the flickering flame a beacon of hope in the encroaching darkness, his spirit bolstered by the thought of justice and the dream of freedom for his beloved parents.

In the darkest hours, the Moreau family stood resilient, a testament to the enduring power of love and the unyielding desire for justice. The dawn would soon arrive, bringing new challenges and opportunities to fight for what was right in the shadow of the guillotine's blade and the watchful eyes of a revolution that consumed its own.

—

The sombre grey skies of 28 Nivôse, Year II (17 January 1794) mirrored the mood that had settled over Paris, a city now deep in the grip of Terror and suspicion. For Henri Moreau, the day marked another gruelling attempt to navigate the turbulent waters of political alliances and potential betrayals, his every move shadowed by the unseen but ever-present eyes of the Committee of Public Safety.

In the dim light of early morning, Henri left the confines of his modest home, his breath visible in the icy air, his steps determined yet cautious. The streets, usually alive with the sounds of market traders and citizens, felt subdued, as if the city was holding its breath in anticipation of the tempest brewing. Henri's destination was a secluded meeting place, an old bookshop owned by a sympathiser, Monsieur Dubois, whose once-thriving business had become a covert hub for those who dared to question the Committee's relentless purges.

Dubois' bookstore, a labyrinth of narrow aisles and towering shelves, was a sanctuary for forbidden ideas and banned literature. The scent of aged paper and leather-bound volumes filled the air, a comforting contrast to the cold, harsh reality outside. Dust motes danced in the slivers of morning light that pierced the grimy windows, adding a touch of ethereal beauty to the otherwise shadowy interior. The walls were lined with books on philosophy, science, and revolutionary thought, their spines worn and titles faded from years of eager handling by seekers of knowledge and truth.

Inside the cramped, book-lined space, Henri met with a small group of loyalists, each connected by their shared desire to see justice served, not by the guillotine's blade but through the fairness of the trial. Among them was Madeline Giroux, a sharp-minded journalist whose anonymous pamphlets criticising the revolution's excesses had made her a target. Her dark, piercing eyes and sharp features reflected her relentless pursuit of truth. She had agreed to help Henri craft a narrative that could sway public opinion in favour of his parents, Pierre and Claire.

With her raven-black hair pulled back in a tight bun, Madeline was a formidable presence in the dimly lit room. Her voice, though low, carried a steely determination that matched the fire in her eyes. She wore a simple, practical dress suitable for blending into the background while navigating the dangerous streets of Paris. Her tattered notebook was filled with notes, observations, and drafts of her biting critiques against the government, each word a potential death sentence if discovered.

As they conferred, their voices low, Henri laid out the pieces of his plan. "We must shift the narrative," he insisted, his hands animated as he spoke. "The people of Paris must see my parents as victims of circumstance, not enemies of the state."

Madeline nodded in agreement, her pen hovering over a tattered notebook. "The story needs to resonate with everyday people, Henri. We must highlight your father's dedication to low-income people and his advocacy for reform. He was a true product of the Enlightenment—his only 'crime' was trying to rationalise time. He had no subversive affiliations. His motivation was always the pursuit of wisdom."

Their strategy was to disseminate the articles through covert channels, relying on the underground network of dissidents that Madeline had cultivated. Each article would subtly undermine the credibility of the charges against the Moreaus, painting them as pawns in a giant political game played by those hungry for power at the Committee.

Dubois, a man of quiet strength with a greying beard and kind, knowing eyes, added, "We can distribute these articles discreetly through my network. The people trust me, and they will listen." He had an air of wisdom about him, his demeanour calm and steady despite the chaos outside. With its dim lighting and musty smell of old paper, his shop seemed to envelop them in a protective embrace, offering a sanctuary from the oppressive atmosphere outside.

Henri's meeting was interrupted by the sudden arrival of a trusted ally, Jean-Luc, a former soldier turned resistance fighter. Jean-Luc brought with him dire news—the authorities had intercepted one of the pamphlets before it could be distributed. The window for action was closing rapidly as Robespierre's agents tightened their grip on the city.

With his rugged, battle-scarred face and intense blue eyes, Jean-Luc starkly contrasted the scholarly atmosphere of the bookstore. His presence brought a sense of urgency and reality to their discussions. "We must act now, Henri," he urged, his expression grave. "Time is a luxury we no longer possess."

As storm clouds loomed overhead, foretelling a literal and metaphorical deluge, Henri faced the gathering storm with a blend of dread and resolve. With few options remaining and the fate of his parents hanging in the balance, he decided to take a drastic step. On the eve of their trial, he organised a public demonstration at the Place de la Révolution—a bold, last-ditch effort to sway public opinion and save his parents from the guillotine's blade. Despite Claire's words of caution, "Be careful, Henri," resonating in his mind, his determination to act overshadowed his fears. This was a fight for his family and a stand against what he saw as a gross miscarriage of justice.

That evening, as Henri readied himself, he pondered the path that had brought him here—the critical choices, the fragile alliances, and the considerable risks. The atmosphere was tense; Paris seemed like a grand chessboard, with his family's destiny in balance. As the first snowflakes fell, silently blanketing the cobblestones in a serene white, Henri braced himself for the upheaval. Despite the weight in his heart, his spirit remained unbroken. He was ready to confront the storm, to fight tooth and nail for the lives of his beloved parents under the dark, brooding skies of a city deeply divided.

The demonstration took place at the historic Place de la Révolution, a site laden with the echoes of past upheavals. Standing at the spot where many had faced the blade, Henri's voice rang out, cutting through the chilly air and the colder spirits of the gathered Parisians. He spoke of justice, enlightenment, and the true meaning of revolution—a return to reason, not a descent into blind retribution. However, as his words floated over the crowd, it became painfully clear that appeals to logic or compassion did not sway the public's mood. The fear of being seen to oppose the Committee's will, coupled with a general weariness of political strife, rendered his pleas for understanding and mercy ineffectual. The faces in the crowd were primarily impassive, their expressions hardened by years of upheaval.

Desperation tinged Henri's final words as the demonstration concluded with little to no apparent impact. The citizens dispersed, leaving Henri in the rapidly deepening snow, feeling more isolated than ever. The failure of the demonstration was a harsh blow, not just to his hopes but to his belief in the power of collective action. As he trudged home through the snow-blanketed streets of the Place de la Révolution, the reality of his situation settled in. His attempt to draw public support had fallen on deaf ears, and now he faced the grim prospect of confronting the trial without the backing of a swayed public opinion. His parents' fate seemed increasingly sealed, dictated not by justice but by a regime's desire for control and retribution.

—

As the grim dawn of 29 Nivôse, Year II (18 January 1794) broke over Paris, the city was calm and softened by a fresh layer of snow from the day before, mirroring the icy despair settling in Henri Moreau's heart. With his parents' trial looming and the city under the tight surveillance of the Committee, Henri's options were rapidly diminishing.

In the dim light of his attic room, Henri poured over the documents and notes he had gathered, each piece a fragment of the puzzle he hoped would clear his parents' names. Around him, the papers whispered of desperation: testimonials from those who had witnessed his father's charitable acts, character statements from neighbours, and legal precedents that might offer a loophole in the charges against them.

While sifting through his father's papers in the study, Henri's attention was suddenly drawn to a hidden stack of letters tucked away in a desk drawer. He hadn't noticed them before, perhaps overlooked in the flurry of previous searches.

As he carefully read the correspondence, Henri's heart raced with hope and dread. Among the letters, he discovered a particularly damning one from a known radical, suggesting a meeting with his father—a meeting that the prosecution had cited as evidence of Pierre Moreau's involvement in a subversive plot. This letter had been critical evidence, casting a dark shadow over his father's reputation.

However, Henri's hands trembled as he found another letter, previously unnoticed and still sealed. Upon opening it, he realised it contained crucial information—the meeting had been cancelled. This new evidence could undermine the prosecution's claims and prove his father's innocence. Filled with relief and urgency, Henri prepared to present this newfound evidence at the trial, hoping it would sway the outcome in his father's favour.

Armed with this new evidence, Henri knew he had to act swiftly. He arranged a meeting with an influential, albeit risky, contact within the judiciary—Judge Armand, known for his secret disapproval of the Committee's extreme methods. Under the guise of night, they met in the shadowed recesses of a quiet tavern, away from prying eyes.

Judge Armand, a man with a stern visage and a reputation for integrity, exuded a quiet confidence that belied the dangerous tightrope he walked. His tall, imposing figure cast a long shadow in the dimly lit room, his well-groomed hair streaked with grey, and his sharp eyes reflecting a lifetime of navigating the treacherous waters of revolutionary politics. Armand's presence was commanding, yet there was a palpable tension about him, a constant awareness of the retribution that could fall upon him should his disapproval of the Committee become known.

"Judge Armand," Henri began, his voice low and urgent, "these letters prove my father's innocence. The meeting they claim he attended never occurred. This is the proof we need to challenge the prosecution's narrative."

Armand studied the documents intently, his stern features deepening into a thoughtful frown. The lines on his face spoke of countless sleepless nights and the burden of decisions that had far-reaching consequences. After a long moment, he nodded slowly. "This could sway the tribunal, but it's risky. The Committee does not take kindly to being challenged. Are you prepared for the consequences?"

"I am," Henri affirmed, his resolve steeling. "It's a risk we must take for justice's sake."

Armand's expression softened slightly, a hint of respect flickering in his eyes. "Very well. I will bring this evidence forward at the trial, but know this—once we start down this path, there is no turning back. We must be prepared for whatever may come."

As they parted, the task's weight hung heavily in the air. Armand walked away with the documents, his back straight, projecting an aura of steadfast determination. Yet, Henri could see the subtle tension in his movements, the cautious glances he cast around the tavern. The judge was a man of honour and bravery, but even he could not escape the ever-present fear of retribution that came with opposing the Committee.

Henri watched him go, the flickering lantern light casting long shadows on the tavern walls. The impending danger loomed large, but so too did a glimmer of hope. Armand's involvement meant there was a chance, however slim, to save his parents from the guillotine's blade. As Henri stepped out into the cold night, his breath visible in the air, he steeled himself for the battles yet to come, each step bringing him closer to the uncertain dawn.

—

Meanwhile, in their adjacent, dimly lit cells, Pierre Moreau and his wife Claire Fountaine struggled against the cold, their spirits lifted by their enduring love and loyalty. La Force was a place of despair, its thick stone walls suffocatingly close and the air damp and smelly. The meagre light seeped through the small, barred windows, barely illuminating the squalor. Rats scurried along the floor, and the constant water drip echoed in the silence, a cruel reminder of their dire circumstances.

Pierre and Claire's cells were barely large enough to stand in, with straw-covered floors that did little to keep the chill at bay. Their bodies ached from the complex, uneven surfaces they were forced to sleep on, and the thin, ragged blankets offered scant protection against the biting cold. Despite the physical hardships, the emotional strain weighed most heavily on them.

Despite the grimness of their situation, the knowledge that Henri was out there fighting for their freedom offered a glimmer of hope amid the overwhelming darkness. They whispered reassurances through the walls, drawing strength from their unbreakable bond even in the bleakest moments. "We will endure this, Claire," Pierre would murmur, pressing his lips to the cold stone that separated them. "For Henri's sake, we must hold on."

The day before the trial, Henri visited his parents. The sight of them in their cells was a heart-wrenching ordeal. Pierre's once-strong frame had withered under the strain, his eyes hollow but still burning with determination. Claire, always the beacon of their family, seemed frailer, her face drawn but her spirit unbroken. Her hands trembled slightly as she reached through the bars to touch Henri's face. Her fingers were cold, but her touch was warm with love.

Henri conveyed the news of the evidence and Judge Armand's support, trying to infuse hope into their dire situation. Their reunion was bittersweet, marked by tears and tender embraces. "We are so proud of you, my son," Claire whispered, her voice cracking with emotion. "No matter what happens tomorrow, know you have done everything possible."

Pierre added, his voice rough with pride and sorrow, "You have given us strength, Henri. Whatever comes, we face it with you."

As Henri left the prison, the city around him felt oppressive, the cobbled streets echoing with the ghosts of revolution. The weight of the impending trial bore down on him, each step feeling heavier as he walked away from the cold, forbidding walls of La Force. The stage was set for a dramatic confrontation in the courtroom, where the fate of the Moreau family would be decided under the watchful eyes of a nation torn by upheaval and fear.

The echoes of justice were faint but persistent, and as the sun set on Paris, the fires of resolve burned brightly in Henri's chest, ready for the day of reckoning that awaited. Shrouded in twilight, the city seemed to hold its breath, mirroring the anticipation and dread that filled Henri's heart.

As he wrote and practised his speeches, every memory of his father returned to him: his speeches at the Assembly and the Contention, in Place Royale and the streets of Paris. All these memories drove him on. Henri imagined what his father would say in his situation as he wrote and rewrote passages, trying to capture Pierre's eloquence and conviction.

Approaching the eve of what would be the most critical day in the lives of the Moreau family, the streets of Paris lay blanketed in a deep, oppressive silence, mirroring the heavy heart of Henri Moreau as he paced the length of his dimly lit room. Outside, the soft murmur of a cold wind whispered through the barren branches of winter trees, a sad prelude to the dawn of judgment.

Henri had spent the last hours before midnight pouring over every document, every piece of evidence he had gathered, his eyes burning with the tireless determination to save his parents. The weight of his family's legacy pressed upon him with a palpable force, the clock ticking in the corner a constant reminder of the fleeting time.

As the clock chimed, Henri's thoughts were abruptly interrupted by a cautious knock at his door. He opened it to find Madeleine, a loyal friend and the daughter of a fellow artisan. Her face, usually so composed, was etched with concern.

"Henri," she said, her voice barely above a whisper, "there's news you need to hear." She stepped inside, closing the door softly behind her. She held a small, crumpled piece of paper in her hands, which she passed to Henri with a solemn nod.

It was a message from one of Henri's contacts within the revolutionary tribunal, warning him of a last-minute change in the panel of judges for the trial. This shift was not in their favour; the new judge was notorious for his harsh sentences and unwavering support for the Committee of Public Safety.

"The trial… it's going to be a farce, Henri," Madeleine's words cut through the thick air with sharp clarity. "They're stacking the tribunal against you."

Henri clenched the paper in his hand, his resolve hardening. "Then we must be prepared to fight even harder," he responded, his voice steady despite the turmoil. He knew the road ahead was perilous, but he was not ready to give up when his parents' lives were at stake.

The subsequent hours were a whirlwind of activity. Henri busied himself formulating a strategy, contacting anyone who might be moved by justice or compassion. He wrote speeches and crafted statements driven by desperation and hope.

As dawn broke over the city, painting the sky with streaks of grey and pale blue, Henri stood by his window, looking out over the rooftops of Paris. The city he loved was caught in the throes of revolution, where justice was as elusive as the morning mist.

In a quiet, solemn moment, Henri allowed himself to think of his parents—Pierre and Claire, separated and alone in their cells, yet undoubtedly strong in their dignity and love for their family. Henri drew strength from their resilience, from the love that had been the cornerstone of his upbringing.

Meanwhile, in their adjacent, dimly lit cells, Pierre Moreau and Claire Fountaine struggled against the cold, their spirits lifted by their enduring love and loyalty. La Force prison was a place of despair, its thick stone walls suffocatingly close and damp and smelly air. The meagre light seeped through the small, barred windows, barely illuminating the squalor. Rats scurried along the floor, and the constant water drip echoed in the silence, a cruel reminder of their dire circumstances.

Pierre and Claire's cells were barely large enough to stand in, with straw-covered floors that did little to keep the chill at bay. Their bodies ached from the complex, uneven surfaces they were forced to sleep on, and the thin, ragged blankets offered scant protection against the biting cold. Despite the physical hardships, the emotional strain weighed most heavily on them.

The day before the trial, Henri visited his parents. The sight of them in their cells was a heart-wrenching ordeal. Pierre's once-strong frame had withered under the strain, his eyes hollow but still burning with determination. Claire, always the beacon of their family, seemed frailer, her face drawn but her spirit unbroken. Her hands trembled slightly as she reached through the bars to touch Henri's face. Her fingers were cold, but her touch was warm with love.

Henri conveyed the news of the evidence and Judge Armand's support, trying to infuse hope into their dire situation. Their reunion was bittersweet, marked by tears and tender embraces. "We are so proud of you, my son," Claire whispered, her voice cracking with emotion. "No matter what happens tomorrow, know you have done everything possible."

Pierre added, his voice rough with pride and sorrow, "You have given us strength, Henri. Whatever comes, we face it with you."

The streets began to stir as the city awoke, the sounds of distant carts and early risers muffled by the thick walls of Henri's room. He turned from the window, his gaze falling on the stack of papers on his desk, each page a testament to the fight he was about to undertake.

"Today, I fight not just for my parents but for truth," Henri murmured to himself, his voice a mix of resolve and fatigue. He donned his coat, the fabric heavy on his shoulders, and tucked the papers under his arm. Giving one last look around the room, he stepped out into the cold morning, the door closing with a soft click behind him.

The streets awaited him, the tribunal awaited him, and history awaited him. Today, Henri Moreau would challenge the might of the Committee, armed with nothing but his wits and the righteousness of his cause. In the heart of revolutionary Paris, the pendulum was ready to swing once again under the watchful eyes of Robespierre and his deputies.

—

As the first light of dawn crept over the horizon, casting long shadows across the frosted cobblestones of Paris, the day of the tribunal had arrived. 1 Pluviôse, Year II (20 January 1794) would be a day etched in the annals of the Moreau family's history. Pierre and Claire, having spent the night in separate, chilling confines, were roused by the clanking keys of the gaolers. Today, they would face the revolutionary tribunal, as formidable and unforgiving as the winter itself.

The journey to the tribunal was solemn. The streets, usually teeming with the relentless flow of the city's populace, were hauntingly quiet, reflecting the day's solemnity. Wrapped in threadbare cloaks, Pierre and Claire were escorted under heavy guard through the winding alleys, their breaths visible in the cold air, each exhale marking the fleeting moments.

Having been up all night, Henri had gathered at a small café across from the courthouse with a few staunch allies. They huddled around a worn wooden table, maps and papers strewn about, finalising every possible argument to sway the judges. Despite the preparation, the heavy pit in Henri's stomach grew as the time drew near. His parents' legacy, their very lives, hung precariously in the balance.

Inside the courtroom, the atmosphere was thick with anticipation and dread. The wooden pews were filled with spectators, some out of morbid curiosity, others out of genuine concern for the revolutionary justice being meted out. At the front, the judges sat elevated above the rest, their expressions grim and unyielding. The head judge, known for his stringent adherence to Robespierre's doctrines, surveyed the room with sharp, discerning eyes.

A hush fell over the crowd as Pierre and Claire were brought in. Hand in hand, they walked to the stand, their stance defiant yet dignified. Henri, catching a glimpse of his parents, felt a surge of resolve. He whispered to Madeleine, "No matter what happens, we fight until the end."

The trial began with the prosecutor presenting the charges: conspiracy against the state, collusion with foreign powers, and inciting dissent against the Committee of Public Safety. The evidence presented was largely circumstantial, consisting of out-of-context excerpts and testimonies from witnesses under duress. Additionally, unfounded accusations were made against Claire, alleging that her social interactions with the wives of other men targeted by the Committee amounted to subversive activities.

The prosecutor, a man with a stern countenance and a voice that echoed with authority, laid out the allegations systematically yet impassioned. He painted a picture of Pierre and Claire Moreau as dangerous elements within the society, cloaking their treacherous activities under the guise of innocent gatherings and intellectual pursuits. "These salons," he declared, "were not merely social interactions. They were breeding grounds for dissent orchestrated by Madame Claire Moreau. The fact that no concrete evidence was found only proves the cunning nature of these conspirators. They knew how to cover their tracks."

When it was time for the defence to present their case, Henri rose. His voice, clear and resonant, echoed throughout the courtroom, capturing the attention of all present. He argued vigorously against the flimsiness of the evidence provided by the prosecution, emphasising not just the absence of concrete proof but also highlighting his parents' steadfast dedication to the revolutionary principles of liberty, equality, and fraternity.

"Ladies and gentlemen of the tribunal," Henri began, his tone steady and vibrant, "my parents stand accused of heinous crimes based on conjecture and innuendo. The prosecution's case is built on a foundation of sand, with no solid evidence to support these grave charges. My mother's salons were places of intellectual and cultural exchange, where the ideas of the Enlightenment flourished, not plots of subversion."

Henri shared vivid examples of how his parents had consistently supported their neighbours, engaged in charitable activities, and devoted themselves wholeheartedly to the welfare of their community. He recounted stories of Pierre's tireless work as a clockmaker, often repairing clocks for the less fortunate without charge, and Claire's efforts to provide food and comfort to those in need, especially during the harsh winters.

"Pierre Moreau," Henri continued, "has always been a man of integrity and principle. His passion for rationalising time was not a provocative act but an endeavour to bring order and precision to our society. And Claire Moreau, my mother, has been a beacon of compassion and generosity. Her gatherings were nothing more than a celebration of knowledge and friendship, a far cry from the sinister activities the prosecution would have you believe."

Henri's eloquence reminded him of the many impassioned speeches his father, Pierre, had delivered over the years. Pierre had once used his rhetorical skills to advocate for rationalising time. Still, Henri was now using his learned oratory prowess in a far more critical fight—defending his parents' right to live. This was no longer about academic debates or community meetings; it was a desperate battle to sway public opinion and save his family from the fatal consequences of a politically motivated trial.

The crowd listened, rapt, as Henri painted a picture of Pierre and Claire not as conspirators but as pillars of the community wrongly accused in these tumultuous times. Their allies distributed copies of signed petitions vouching for the Moreaus' character among the spectators, swaying public opinion in real time. Each testimony and signature was a lifeline, a tangible sign of support that echoed through the courtroom.

Henri concluded his defence with a powerful plea. "We must not let fear and paranoia dictate our actions. My parents are not enemies of the state; they are devoted citizens who have dedicated their lives to the betterment of our society. To condemn them based on such flimsy evidence would be a grave injustice, a betrayal of the very principles our revolution stands for."

As Henri sat down, the murmurs in the courtroom grew louder. The prosecution's case seemed less confident, their arguments fraying under the weight of Henri's passionate defence. The tribunal's decision hung in the balance, the fate of the Moreau family poised on the edge of a knife.

—

As the morning sun illuminated the stained glass of the courthouse, the head judge announced a recess for deliberation. The tension was palpable as Henri joined his parents, squeezing their hands in silent solidarity. After what seemed an eternity, the judges returned, but rather than deliver the verdict, the head judge declared that the tribunal would adjourn and reconvene the following day to read the verdict. The room, filled with anxious anticipation, fell silent as everyone awaited the decision to determine the fate of Pierre Moreau and his wife, Claire Fountaine.

Outside, the streets of Paris lay quiet, the city seemingly holding its breath for the outcome that would send ripples through the foundations of revolutionary society. Inside, Henri stood with his parents, bracing themselves to face whatever decision would come. Their fate, deeply entwined with the revolutionary ideals they had once so fervently supported, hung in the balance.

That night, Henri experienced a restless anxiety, the weight of the impending verdict tormenting him. Tossing and turning, he found no comfort in sleep, his mind replaying the day's events and speculating about the possibilities of the next morning. Each scenario was more foreboding than the last, leaving him to await the dawn with a sense of dread.

CHAPTER EIGHT

On the morning of 2 Pluviôse, Year II (21 January 1794), a solemn silence filled the courtroom as the final gavel resonated through the air with grave finality. The tribunal, symbolic of the Revolution's merciless justice system, delivered its irreversible verdict on Pierre Moreau and his wife, Claire Fountaine. Once respected citizens, they were now condemned as enemies of the state, sentenced to meet their fate at the sharp edge of the guillotine. The head judge, his voice devoid of empathy, declared in a firm tone, "By the laws of the Republic and by the power vested in this tribunal, Pierre Moreau and Claire Fountaine are to be executed in six days. There will be no appeal." This pronouncement left no room for hope or reprieve, sealing their fate with chilling efficiency.

The head judge, a gaunt figure with cold, steely eyes, delivered the verdict with finality that struck like a tonne of bricks. The words seemed to hang in the air, suffocating any remaining hope. The courtroom, filled with the echoes of past trials, now reverberated with the damning decree. The judge's flat and unwavering voice held no hint of mercy or doubt. It was as if he were reading from a script, each word a nail in the coffin of the Moreaus' future.

Standing amidst the shadowed onlookers, Henri Moreau felt his heart pound with a mix of dread and disbelief. The air was thick with despair, the grim reality of his parents' impending execution hanging heavily in the room. As the crowd began to disperse, their murmurings of sympathy and subdued whispers barely registered with Henri. His thoughts were fixed solely on the ticking clock leading up to his parents' execution, each second echoing louder in his mind.

Henri watched as his parents were led away, their steps measured and their dignity intact despite the chains that bound them. Claire, always composed, gave him a final look of unwavering love, her eyes communicating what words could not. Pierre, his face lined with exhaustion but still holding a spark of defiance, nodded once at his son, a silent gesture of strength and solidarity. The sight of them being taken away, mere shadows against the oppressive stone walls, was almost too much to bear.

Feeling desperate to act, Henri pushed his way through the crowd and stepped out into Paris's cold, indifferent streets. The city, usually bustling with life, now felt like a ghost town, each corner shadowed by the spectre of fear. Henri knew he could not afford to give in to despair. He needed allies, influential voices that could sway the Committee of Public Safety's powers and perhaps even reach Robespierre's ear.

His first stop was the home of Monsieur Fournier, an old associate of his father and a minor official within the revolutionary government. If anyone could intervene, it would be him. Henri's steps quickened as he navigated the narrow, cobbled streets, rehearsing his plea with every stride.

Upon arriving, he was hastily ushered into Fournier's modest study. The room was cramped, with books and papers about busier, more hopeful times. Fournier, looking older and wearier than Henri remembered, greeted him with a strained smile.

"Henri, this is a dark hour indeed," Fournier began, his voice heavy with unspoken understanding. "But you must know that challenging this verdict is akin to signing one's death warrant. The tribunal does not err in its judgements—or rather, it does not admit to errors."

"But there must be something we can do," Henri implored, his voice cracking with urgency. "Surely, someone of your standing—"

"Henri," Fournier interrupted a note of finality in his tone. "Robespierre's decree is absolute. The Committee would not dare oppose him, and neither can I. I am truly sorry."

The dismissal was polite but firm. Henri left Fournier's house with a cold dread settling in his chest. Realising that his father's old allies were either too afraid or powerless to act was a bitter pill. His isolation grew heavier as he made his way to another potential ally. With each refusal, each well-meaning but fearful rejection, the walls of Henri's hope crumbled a little more.

Continuing his efforts, Henri next visited Madame Beaumont, a former colleague of his mother and known sympathiser of the revolutionary cause. The Beaumont residence in a quieter part of Paris offered a stark contrast to the bustling city centre. Henri arrived with hope and trepidation, hoping that Madame Beaumont's respect for his mother might influence her decision to help.

Upon his arrival, Henri was greeted with a warm yet cautious welcome. Madame Beaumont led him to her sitting room, where the remnants of revolutionary fervour adorned the walls—portraits of prominent revolutionaries and faded Tricolour ribbons. She listened intently as Henri outlined the circumstances of his parents' arrest and the subsequent trial, his voice laden with desperation.

"Madame Beaumont, you knew my mother, her integrity, and her passion for justice," Henri pleaded. "Isn't anything that can be done to sway the Committee, to delay the execution?"

Madame Beaumont sighed, a gesture of empathy tinged with resignation. "Henri, my dear boy, your mother was indeed a woman of great principle, and I hold her in the highest regard. However, challenging Robespierre or the Committee's decisions in these times could prove disastrous. I fear my standing isn't what it used to be, and the risk of retaliation is too great. I am sorry, but my hands are tied."

Disheartened yet determined, Henri left Madame Beaumont's home as the evening shadows grew longer. His journey through the city felt increasingly sombre as each attempt failed. The cold reality that his efforts to find support through legitimate means proved futile became ever more apparent.

As Henri walked the cobbled streets towards his lodgings, his mind raced with alternatives. Each conversation with his father's former allies revealed a web of fear and compliance that Robespierre had intricately woven through Parisian society. The once fiery spirit of the Revolution seemed smothered by an oppressive air of surveillance and suspicion.

As the night deepened, Henri's resolve hardened. He understood the monumental risks involved in continuing his quest, yet the thought of doing nothing was excessive. He knew the odds were stacked heavily against him, but the memory of his parents' strength and dignity spurred him on. Henri was not ready to give up the fight; the stakes were too high, and the cost of failure was too great. He would exhaust every possible avenue, no matter how slim the chance, to save his parents from their unjust fate.

—

Henri's efforts went well into the evening, driven by desperation and a dwindling sense of hope. His next stop was the residence of Monsieur Lefèvre, an influential former colleague of his father. Henri was received in a lavish study, the walls lined with books that spoke of a time when reason and debate held sway over the guillotine's swift justice. Lefèvre, with his grey hair and solemn eyes, listened intently to Henri's pleas, his face a mask of sympathetic helplessness.

"Henri, my boy," Lefèvre began, his voice low and grave, "I understand your pain, but you must realise the power Robespierre wields over us all. The fear he instils is too great, and his orders are as binding as the laws of nature. I dare not oppose him, for my family's and my own."

Henri's heart sank. "Monsieur Lefèvre, you knew my father. He stood by you during the darkest days of the revolution. Can you abandon him now? My mother, Claire—she looked up to you. Please, there must be something, anything you can do."

Lefèvre's eyes softened, but he shook his head. "To challenge Robespierre is to commit suicide. His reach is long, and his vengeance is swift. I am truly sorry, Henri, but I cannot help you."

Frustration tightened around Henri like a vice as he left Lefèvre's opulent home. The shadows of the evening seemed to mock his plight, deepening as his options dwindled. He hurried to another potential ally, a former judge known for his once fiery rhetoric against tyranny, but the response was the same: a blend of pity and fear but no promise of action.

The biting air seemed to seep into Henri's bones as he moved from door to door, each knock a pulse of fading hope, each rejection a nail in the coffin of his parent's fate. The city around him felt alien, a labyrinth of cold stones and colder hearts, each turn reminding him of the revolution's cruel betrayals.

It was late in the evening when Henri reached the home of Madame Renault, a friend of his mother's and a widow whose husband had fallen victim to similar political machinations. Madame Renault's quarters, usually a place of warmth and lively discussion, now felt like a sanctuary on the edge of despair.

"Henri, to stand against Robespierre is to stand against the revolution itself," Madame Renault said as they sat in her dimly lit drawing room, the fire crackling a mournful accompaniment to their conversation. "I grieve with you; truly, I do. But to speak out is to invite the guillotine to my door. I cannot help you, not against him."

Henri's voice broke as he pleaded, "Madame Renault, please. My parents are good people. They don't deserve this. There must be a way. Can't you see? We can't let fear dictate our actions."

Madame Renault shook her head, tears welling in her eyes. "I wish I could, Henri. But Robespierre's grip is too tight. He watches everything and knows everything. Any move against him would be signing my death warrant. I'm so sorry."

Henri's desperation grew with each refusal, twisting into a sharp, hard knot of resolve. The Paris he had loved, the city of light and enlightenment, now seemed a dark maze of fear and submission. The revolutionary ideals of liberty and justice once filled the streets with fraternity songs now rang hollow in the face of blind obedience to tyranny.

As Henri walked back through the sleeping streets, the weight of his isolation pressed down upon him. The echoes of the day's failures whispered cruel truths: he was alone, his parents were condemned, and their fate was sealed not by justice but by the whim of a tyrant. The city around him, wrapped in the darkness of a winter night, was as silent as the grave that awaited his father and mother.

Henri's mind whirled with dark thoughts as he crossed the Pont Neuf, the Seine below as black as the thoughts he now harboured. If the law would not protect his parents, if the so-called champions of the people crouched in the shadows of power, perhaps it was time for the shadows to fight back. The thought of taking justice into his own hands, once unthinkable, now flickered in his mind like a candle in the wind—dangerous, yet undeniably alluring.

The rebukes he received that night planted a deep-seated hatred for Robespierre in Henri's heart. In Henri's eyes, the man who had been a symbol of revolutionary purity was now a despotic tyrant, an enemy of everything the revolution had promised. The sense of betrayal was complete, and it festered in his soul like a wound that would never heal.

As the clock tower chimed midnight, signalling the close of a day overshadowed by the crushing verdict against his parents and his unsuccessful attempts to garner support, Henri's determination intensified. Tomorrow, he resolved that he would take a different approach. If the light of reason could not save Pierre Moreau and his wife, Claire Fountaine, perhaps he would find salvation in the shadows.

—

As 3 Pluviôse, Year II (22 January 1794) dawned, the morning sun barely penetrated the heavy winter clouds over Paris, mirroring the sombre mood that had enveloped Henri since the previous day's devastating verdict. The cold seemed to seep into his bones as he walked through the deserted streets, each step an effort in the face of overwhelming despair.

Henri's night, he had been restless, haunted by images of his parents behind bars and the relentless ticking of the clock counting down to their execution. The echo of the judge's gavel continued to resound in his ears, a grim punctuation to the nightmare that had become his reality.

Determined to exhaust every possible avenue, Henri arranged a meeting with an influential journalist known for his fierce critiques of the government. If public opinion could be swayed, it might pressure the authorities to reconsider. The journalist, Monsieur Girard, had once been a vocal advocate for justice and the rights of the accused. However, Henri soon discovered that the fear of Robespierre's retribution had dampened many spirits.

Monsieur Girard's office was cluttered with papers and books, the air thick with the smell of ink and tobacco. The man who greeted Henri was a shadow of the fiery editor he once admired. His eyes, once sharp and challenging, now flickered with caution.

"Henri, I grasp the reason behind your visit," Girard said softly and hesitantly. "However, you must realise that the circumstances are different now. To oppose Robespierre's rulings... it's much like walking into the lion's den."

Henri's fists clenched at his sides, his frustration boiling over. "So we are to do nothing?" he challenged, his voice rising. "We are to let innocent people be slaughtered because we fear for ourselves?"

Girard sighed, passing a weary hand over his face. "It is not just about fear for oneself, Henri. It's about survival. I have a family, employees... if I speak out, I endanger myself and all of them."

The desperation in Henri's plea was palpable as he leaned forward, his hands spread on the cluttered desk. "My parents are going to die, Monsieur. In days. Does their blood not weigh on your conscience?"

The journalist met Henri's gaze, a flash of the old fire returning momentarily. "It does, and heavily so. But the power to change this does not rest with me. Robespierre has made sure of that. The Tribunal is his tool, and we, my young friend, are merely subjects under his rule."

Leaving Girard's office, Henri felt the last vestiges of hope beginning to wane. The reality was stark and brutal: the machinery of the revolution had become an instrument of tyranny, and their fears shackled those who might have the power to intervene.

As he walked back through the streets, the murmurs of the city seemed to mock him. The whispers of the market sellers and the clatter of carriages all seemed oblivious to the tragedy unfolding in the city's heart. Henri's mind raced as he considered his next steps. If the pen and voice of reason would not suffice, what was left but to appeal to darker forces?

The thought was chilling, yet it clung to him with the tenacity of a shadow. Henri knew that turning to such measures could lead him down a path without return. Yet, the image of his father, proud and unyielding even in the face of death, urged him on. If the light of justice would not illuminate their path, perhaps the cloak of night would offer its form of redress.

By the time Henri returned to his modest lodgings, the day had aged, and the shadows had grown long. In the privacy of his room, he penned a list of names and contacts on the fringes of the revolution —those disillusioned, angry, and bold enough to consider what polite society would not. He would walk a line from which there could be no turning back tomorrow.

—

Before the first light of dawn had broken over Paris on 4 Pluviôse, Year II (23 January 1794), Henri Moreau found himself wandering the dimly lit streets that led to the small, inconspicuous café where he was to meet Étienne Rochefort. The chill of the morning seeped through his cloak, a piercing reminder of the bleak thoughts that plagued his mind. As he walked, his steps were hurried, driven by a desperate need for counsel and, perhaps, a way to alter the grim fate awaiting his parents.

The café, a usual haunt for artists and thinkers who still dared to discuss philosophy and politics despite the ever-watchful eyes of the Republic, was nearly empty. A lone candle flickered at a table in the corner, casting long shadows that danced across the walls. Étienne was already there, his face shadowed and thoughtful, a steaming cup of coffee in hand.

Henri approached, wearing his hat in greeting, his face etched with the strains of the last few days. "Thank you for coming, Étienne," he started, his voice low, almost lost amidst the soft murmurings of the few early risers scattered around the room.

Étienne nodded, gesturing to the chair opposite him. "I came as soon as I received your message," he replied, his usually composed features now marked by concern. "What is it, Henri? You sounded most urgent."

Taking his seat, Henri leaned forward, his eyes scanning the room before speaking. "It's my parents," he confessed, the weight of his words laden with emotion. "I... I am considering all possibilities, Étienne. I cannot just watch them be taken from me."

Étienne's expression shifted from concern to alarm. "What are you saying, Henri? What possibilities?"

Henri's hands trembled slightly as he reached for his cup of coffee. "I've been thinking about taking action against those responsible. Against Robespierre himself." The words, once spoken, seemed to hang heavily between them, fraught with danger and the weight of their implication.

For a moment, Étienne was silent, his eyes fixed intently on Henri. Then, carefully, he set his cup down. "You must think this through, Henri. To strike against Robespierre is not just dangerous—it is almost certainly a death sentence. And what would it achieve? Would your parents want this for you?"

Henri's gaze faltered, dropping to his hands wrapped around the warm cup. "I don't know," he admitted, his voice a whisper. "But what am I to do, Étienne? Accept their deaths as just another casualty of the Republic's paranoia?"

Étienne leaned in, his voice insistent yet gentle. "You must find another way, Henri. Your anger, while justified, could lead you down a path of no return. And I fear it would not save your parents but only add to the toll of this madness."

The conversation drifted then to the nation's state, to the fear that gripped Paris where friends turned on one another at the whisper of disloyalty, where justice was not impartial but blindingly partisan. As they talked, the café began to fill, and the noise of the arriving patrons was a curtain of sound that shielded their conversation from prying ears.

As dawn broke outside, bathing the room in a grey, sober light, Henri felt the weight of Étienne's words. He was torn between the desire for vengeance and the principles his father had instilled in him. The meeting did not give him the answers he hoped for, but it anchored him enough to reconsider the drastic measures his tortured mind had contemplated.

Finally, as they rose to leave, Étienne placed a firm, reassuring gesture on Henri's shoulder. "Think about what we discussed, Henri. Remember who you are and the legacy your parents would wish for you."

With a heavy heart, Henri stepped back into the cold morning, the early light filtering through the narrow streets, casting long shadows that seemed to echo his sad thoughts. The decision lay before him, fraught with peril and shadowed by grief.

Leaving the dimly lit café with the echoes of Étienne's caution still reverberating in his mind, Henri walked through the awakening streets of Paris, the city's daily tumult slowly coming to life as vendors opened their stalls and the early workers made their weary way. His mind churned with a turmoil that mirrored the overcast skies above—dark and brooding. Henri pondered the implications of his contemplated path, the potential for violence that could lead not just to his demise but potentially harm those he sought to protect.

As he wandered, Henri's feet led him to one of the less frequented parts of the city, where the grim shadows seemed a refuge for those with heavier hearts and darker intentions. Here, Henri knew, he could find the more radical elements of society, those disenchanted souls who whispered of revolution within the Revolution, of turning the tide against the tyrants who had hijacked their ideals.

In a secluded tavern behind a row of dilapidated buildings, Henri met with a man known only as Anouk, an agitator whose hunger for change was matched only by his disdain for Robespierre and his ilk.

The tavern was dim and smelled of stale ale and older secrets, a fitting backdrop for the clandestine nature of their meeting.

"Étienne tells me I should seek justice, not revenge," Henri confessed as he sat across from Anouk, the wooden table between them sticky with the residue of spilt drinks.

Anouk snorted derisively, his eyes sharp as flint. "And what justice would that be, Henri? The justice that condemns your parents without a fair trial? The justice that sees enemies in every shadow?" He leaned forward, his voice dropping to a conspiratorial whisper. "No, my friend, the justice Étienne speaks of is a phantom, a spectre waved by those too afraid to grasp the nettle."

Henri listened, his heart heavy, the weight of Anouk's words sinking like stones in his soul. He knew Anouk spoke some truth—the justice that had once been the bedrock of their Revolution had been perverted. Yet, the idea of taking a life, of stepping into the murky waters of assassination, was a line Henri had never envisioned crossing.

"Think of it, Henri," Anouk pressed on, sensing his hesitation. "You have the means to reach where others cannot. A single moment of courage could shift the balance, could stop the guillotine's blade before it claims those you love."

The words tempted Henri with their poisonous promise, a siren call to his darkest desires. He imagined a Paris free from the tyranny of Robespierre, where his parents could walk free and where the ideals of liberty, equality, and fraternity were not stained with the blood of the innocent.

But then he remembered his father's eyes, the depth of conviction in Pierre's final words to him during their last visit. His father had spoken of hope, of enduring beyond the cruelty of their times. "Do not let our end be the end of who you are, my son," Pierre had said, his voice steady despite the shadows that clung to his fate.

Torn between the enthusiasm of Anouk's arguments and the foundational morals his parents had instilled in him, Henri felt as if he stood at a precipice, the winds of fate howling around him, threatening to unmoor his soul.

As the meeting concluded, Henri left the tavern with a heavy heart, the cobblestone streets slick with a dusting of snow. He walked back towards the city's heart, the weight of his impending decision bearing upon him like the grey skies above.

The clash between the revolutionary zeal stoked by Anouk and the moral wisdom imparted by Étienne painted Henri's thoughts in stark, conflicting hues. Ahead lay a path forked and shrouded in mist, each turn fraught with peril and profound consequence.

—

The late evening found Henri, approaching eighteen, hardened by the ebb and flow of the Revolution at the doorstep of Étienne, his heart pounding and his mind awhirl with dark thoughts. Étienne's home, a modest two-storey building nestled among similar structures in a quieter district of Paris, was where Henri had always found solace. But tonight, it was a battleground of ideals.

Étienne opened the door, his expression turning from surprise to concern as he saw Henri's state. "Henri, what brings you here at this hour?" he asked, stepping aside to let him in.

Inside, the warmth of the fire did little to thaw the chill that had settled in Henri's bones. He paced before the hearth, hands clasped behind his back, words tumbling out as he spoke of his meeting with the radicals, of plans whispered in shadowed corners, of vengeance against Robespierre.

Étienne listened, his brow furrowed, before finally raising his hand to stop Henri. "You must think carefully about what you're suggesting," Étienne implored, his voice steady yet tinged with urgency. "Assassination? Henri, this is not the way. You are letting grief and anger cloud your judgment."

Henri stopped pacing, turning to face his friend. "What other choice do I have, Étienne? They will kill my parents! Should I stand by and watch?"

Étienne sighed, crossing the room to place a hand on Henri's shoulder. "I understand your pain, but consider what your father would want. Would Pierre advocate for murder, or would he want you to uphold the principles he taught you? To seek justice, not revenge?"

The mention of his father's ideals struck a chord in Henri, causing hesitation. His father's voice echoed in his mind, words of justice and integrity that had shaped his childhood. Henri slumped into a chair, burying his face in his hands.

Étienne sat beside him, his voice softer. "There are other ways to fight this, Henri. Ways that do not lead down a path of no return. Remember who you are and who your parents raised you to be."

The room was silent save for the crackling of the fire. Henri felt torn, the pull of vengeance battling with the values he had always held dear. After a long pause, he lifted his head, meeting Étienne's earnest gaze.

"Then what do I do, Étienne? How do I fight this tyranny without becoming a tyrant myself?"

Étienne nodded, understanding the depth of Henri's turmoil. "We gather support, not for an assassination, but for change. We expose the injustices and rally the people who are just as disillusioned with Robespierre as we are. We fight with words and ideas, Henri, not with bloodshed."

Henri considered Étienne's words, the tempest of his emotions gradually subsiding into a determined resolve. It would not be easy to relinquish the burning desire for immediate retribution. Still, Étienne's counsel offered a different kind of courage—a courage to confront tyranny with the truth rather than violence.

"Will you help me?" Henri asked a new clarity in his voice.

Étienne smiled, relief evident in his eyes. "Of course, my friend. We will do this the right way, together."

That night, as Henri left Étienne's home, the weight on his chest felt lighter, not from resolving his predicament but from the knowledge that he was choosing a path that honoured his parents' legacy. He knew the road ahead would be fraught with challenges, but for the first time since the verdict, he felt a flicker of hope—hope that through unity and perseverance, change was possible.

---

5 Pluviôse, Year II (24 January 1794) saw Henri standing outside the dreary walls of the prison, his heart heavy as he waited to be admitted. Inside, the damp corridors echoed with the clinks of chains and the shuffles of the condemned. He was led to a small, stark room where Pierre and Claire awaited him, their faces marked by the harsh reality of their fate yet holding a serenity that Henri found both comforting and heart-wrenching.

As Henri entered, Claire's eyes lit up with sadness and relief. Pierre, ever the stoic, managed a weak smile. "Henri," Pierre began, his voice firm despite his pale appearance, "tell us, what news do you bring?"

Henri hesitated, the truth burning on his tongue. He had contemplated darker paths, and now, confronted with his parents' expectant gazes, the weight of his thoughts grew unbearable. "I've… I've been speaking with some people. People who think like me, who want to fight back," he confessed, watching their reactions closely.

Claire's expression shifted to one of concern. "Fight back? Henri, what exactly are you planning?"

"There are those who believe we could change everything—if we took more… drastic measures against Robespierre," Henri admitted, his voice faltering as he saw the alarm in his mother's eyes.

Pierre reached across the small table, placing his worn hand over Henri's. "Son, remember who you are. This path you speak of leads only to more sorrow. Do not let your anger cloud your judgment. We wouldn't want our legacy to be one of vengeance."

Henri felt a surge of emotion. "I know, Father, I am no longer—"

"Henri," Claire interjected softly, her voice steady despite the shimmer of tears in her eyes. "We raised you to stand for what's right, uphold the values of justice and mercy, and not succumb to hatred. This man, Robespierre, has spread enough darkness. Don't let it consume you, too."

The clarity in Claire's words pierced the fog of Henri's rage. The thought of further staining his hands with the very violence that condemned his parents was jarring. He looked into his father's eyes, finding the resolve and integrity that had defined Pierre Moreau all his life.

"You must promise us, Henri," Pierre continued, his tone imbued with a quiet urgency. "Promise us that whatever you do, you'll act in a way that you can live with, in a way that would make us proud."

Henri nodded, the fight draining from him. He whispered, "I promise."

The guards signalled that time was up. Henri stood, his eyes lingering on his parents. He memorised every detail—the lines of worry on his mother's face and his father's steadfast calm. As he turned to leave, Claire called out, "We love you, Henri. Never forget that."

Outside, the cold air felt sharper as it filled Henri's lungs. The promise he made echoed in his mind, a solemn vow to seek a path that honoured not just his parents' wishes but their very essence. As he walked away from the prison, the weight of his responsibility settled upon him, not just to avenge but to advocate, not to destroy, but to rebuild.

Henri knew the road ahead would be fraught with challenges, perhaps even more daunting than confrontation. Yet, as he walked through the quiet streets of Paris, a plan began to form, requiring all the courage, intelligence, and compassion he could muster. It was a path that would not lead to the guillotine's shadow but towards the light of change, driven by the legacies of Pierre Moreau and his wife, Claire Fountaine.

—

Two days passed, and the atmosphere in the sombre, grey corridors of the prison was thick with despair. Henri shuffled through the halls, the clanking of the guard's keys echoing off the stone walls, each sound a stark reminder of the reality his family faced. Today's visit, however, held a sliver of unexpected hope amid the pervasive gloom.

As Henri entered the visiting area, he was greeted by the sight of his parents, Pierre and Claire, waiting behind the barred partition. Claire's eyes lit up with a complex mixture of relief and sorrow at the sight of her son. "Henri," she began, her voice barely above a whisper, "they've commuted my sentence to thirty days of imprisonment."

Unbeknownst to many, Claire's commutation was not a mere act of mercy by the judiciary but the result of a concerted effort by the women in her social circle. These women, who had long admired Claire for her integrity and benevolence, had worked quietly yet persistently behind the scenes. They leveraged their social gatherings as a platform to discuss Claire's situation, eventually pressuring their husbands to use their influence. These men, connected in various professional and political capacities, began to exert subtle pressure on their contacts within the government, advocating for Claire's cause.

The group was realistic about their limitations; they knew changing Robespierre's mind about Pierre was unlikely given his deep-seated animosity. However, they believed that Claire was essentially an innocent, caught up in the political crossfire aimed at her husband. Their strategy hinged on this perception, hoping to appeal to any remnants of leniency in the hearts of those close to Robespierre. They argued that while Pierre might be seen as a threat, Claire was merely collateral damage, undeserving of such a harsh fate. Their persistent efforts, a blend of social manoeuvring and subtle political pressure, eventually led to the commutation of Claire's sentence, reflecting a partial yet poignant victory for their quiet campaign.

Henri's heart, heavy with the dread of their impending fates, felt a momentary lift. The decision was a rare mercy in these ruthless times, yet the unchanged fate of his father overshadowed the joy. "That's some relief, at least," Henri replied, managing a strained smile. He grasped his mother's hands through the bars, their touch a bittersweet comfort.

Looking older than his years, Pierre wore a sombre expression that deeply contrasted with the slight relief that had momentarily brightened Claire's features. "It's a small mercy in these harsh times," he said, his voice steady but low. "But we must discuss what comes next, Henri."

The three of them huddled close, speaking in hushed tones. Henri relayed his failed attempts to sway any influential allies, each effort thwarted by the pervasive fear of Robespierre's wrath. Pierre listened intently, his face etched with resignation. "It's as I feared," Pierre sighed. "Robespierre's grip is too strong. Our friends are too frightened to act."

Claire squeezed Henri's hand, her resolve clear. "Then we must face what comes with dignity, my son. Do not let our fate darken your heart or your future," she urged her voice firm despite the tremble that hinted at her underlying fear.

Henri nodded, the resolve from his mother's words bolstering him slightly. "I will try, Mother. For both of you, I will try not to let hate consume me."

The conversation shifted to memories, to better days before the revolution had turned friend against friend, neighbour against neighbour. They reminisced about Henri's childhood, about the lessons of justice and integrity that Pierre had always emphasised. These memories, precious and painful, were their rebellion against the despair of their situation.

Leaving the cold confines of the prison, Henri felt the weight of his solitude more acutely than ever. The brief joy from his mother's commuted sentence did little to ease the dread of his father's unchanged destiny. The walk back home was long and contemplative, Henri's mind a whirl of fear, sadness, and a flickering hope that somehow, through his actions, he could honour the principles his parents had taught him, even in the face of their looming absence.

—

As the night of 7 Pluviôse, Year II (26 January 1794) enveloped the city of Paris, a chilling silence settled over the streets, contrasting starkly with the tumult within Henri's heart. He sat alone in his small, dimly lit room, the flickering candle casting long shadows that seemed to dance with his mounting anxieties. With his father's execution merely hours away, Henri's thoughts churned with despair and helplessness, each moment passing with the heavy tick of the old clock on the mantelpiece.

Compelled by a restless urge to preserve his thoughts and emotions, Henri pulled out his journal—a worn leather-bound book that had seen the best and worst of his days. He dipped his quill in ink and began to write, his handwriting shaky as he tried to capture the essence of his torment.

"7 Pluviôse, Year II, the eve of what may be the harrowing day of my life," Henri scribbled, pausing as he sought the words that might express his sorrow. "Tonight, I am haunted not by the spectres of the revolution but by the impending loss of my father, Pierre Moreau, whose dignity and resolve in the face of unjust condemnation have only deepened my respect and love for him."

Henri wrote of his recent visits to the prison and how his mother, Claire, had shown a resilience that belied her delicate appearance. "Mother though spared the guillotine's blade, remains shackled by grief and dread for father's fate. Their last moments together, bound by the inevitability of separation, were marked by a poignant blend of tenderness and despair."

His pen moved fervently as he recounted the conversations with his father—each word Pierre had uttered about life, legacy, and the importance of standing by one's principles, even in the face of death. Henri's father had implored him to live a life of purpose, to ensure that his passing would not extinguish the ideals they cherished.

"Father spoke of the revolution, not with the bitterness of a man wronged, but with the perspective of a philosopher who sees beyond the immediate tumult to the broader arcs of justice and reform. He urged me to fight, not with weapons wrought from anger, but with the tools of dialogue and democracy."

As he wrote, Henri's thoughts turned to the dark conversations he had entertained with radicals, driven by a lust for retribution against Robespierre and his tyrannical reign. He remembered Étienne's words of caution, the heated debates over the soul of the revolution, and the thin line between justice and vengeance.

Henri detailed these internal conflicts, pouring his doubts and fears onto the pages. Writing provided a temporary respite, a way to organise the chaos of his mind. Yet, no amount of ink could fully encapsulate the dread of the looming dawn nor the profound sense of duty instilled by his father's final teachings.

The hours he waned as Henri continued to write, each paragraph a step through his past, each sentence a bridge to the uncertain future. When the candle burned low, casting the room into semi-darkness, Henri finally set his pen down. He leaned back in his chair, eyes closed, his father's words echoing through the silence, mingling with the soft, persistent sounds of the Parisian night.

Tomorrow would bring with it the harsh light of reality, the execution of a beloved father, and the irrevocable alteration of his path. But tonight, in the solitude of his room, surrounded by the written reflections of a son's love and a patriot's resolve, Henri found a fragile peace, clinging to the hope that his father's legacy would guide him through whatever lay ahead.

With dawn mere hours away, Henri finally succumbed to a fitful sleep, his journal lying on the desk, a testament to a son's vow to honour his father's life and sacrifices through his own deeds.

—

He had arrived in a sombre mood on the fateful day of 8 Pluviôse, Year II (27 January 1794). Before the first light touched the streets of Paris, Henri was awake. His sleep had been fitful, a restless dance of shadowy dreams and haunting memories. With the gravity of the day weighing on his shoulders, he dressed quietly in the dark, his movements automatic, driven by a dreadful sense of duty.

The streets were eerily quiet as he approached the Place de la Révolution. The dawn was grey, the clouds hanging low as if to mourn the day's grim purpose. Henri's steps echoed on the cobblestones, each footfall a sharp reminder of what lay ahead. He pulled his coat tighter around him against the biting January chill, his breath visible in the air, mingling with the faint mist that rose from the Seine.

As Henri walked, his mind replayed the events that had led to this moment. The trial, the verdict, his desperate attempts to alter the course of what now seemed inevitable. He thought of his last visit to the prison, the way his father had looked at him with both love and resignation, the strength he had tried to impart with his final words. Henri clung to those words now, a lifeline in the tumult of his emotions.

The square was slowly coming to life as the city awoke to another day of spectacle. Henri felt disgusted as he noticed vendors setting up their stalls and selling trinkets and refreshments to the gathering crowd. It was a macabre festival atmosphere that had become all too common in these times of revolution.

The scaffold was set against a backdrop of stark grey buildings, the morning fog still clinging to the edges of the rooftops. Henri moved through the crowd, his presence almost ghost-like, unnoticed by those who had come to watch the day's grim spectacle. His eyes were fixed on the platform where his father, Pierre Moreau, would soon make his final stand.

As the appointed hour approached, the square began to fill, the noise level rising as people jostled for a better view. The hum of conversation, the clatter of wooden clogs on cobblestones, and the distant sound of a dog barking all seemed surreal to Henri. His heart felt heavy, each beat a painful reminder of what was to come.

Pierre was led to the scaffold, his hands bound yet his posture defiantly erect. Amid the grim circumstances, a profound dignity enveloped him—a quality Henri had always admired, now even more evident as Pierre confronted his imminent demise. The crowd fell into a deep hush as he ascended the steps, his calm demeanour sharply contrasting with the cruel purpose of the guillotine awaiting him.

Ironically, the guillotine was a product of the Enlightenment—the intellectual movement that advocated for reason and human rights. Introduced as a humane execution, it was meant to be quick and equal, devoid of the barbarity of previous methods. Yet, in this dark moment, it stood as a grim icon of the Reign of Terror, employed to suppress the ideals it was meant to uphold. This stark irony was palpable among the onlookers and deeply felt by Henri as he witnessed his father approach a fate marked by philosophical contradiction.

Henri positioned himself to maintain eye contact with his father. Their gazes locked, transmitting a silent exchange laden with love, regret, and profound sadness. Pierre's nod, barely noticeable, conveyed a message of strength and the importance of clinging to the values he had instilled in his son.

Given a chance to address the crowd, Pierre's voice sounded clear and resonant. "Citizens," he declared, "I stand before you not as a criminal but as a man unjustly accused. I bear no ill will towards those who have decreed my fate. Instead, I urge you all to seek truth and justice within your hearts and remember that the values of our great revolution are betrayed, not served, by violence and oppression."

The crowd remained silent, deeply moved by Pierre's words. Even the executioner appeared affected, hesitating momentarily, seemingly struck by the condemned man's dignity and courage.

Finally, Pierre turned to face the blade. He knelt, placing his neck on the block with a composed finality. The executioner positioned himself, and the crowd held its breath. Henri felt that time had slowed, each second stretching into an eternity. He wanted to close his eyes, to shut out the horror of what was about to happen, but he forced himself to watch, to bear witness to his father's courage.

The blade descended with a swift, cruel precision. A collective gasp rose from the crowd as it thudded into the wooden base. Henri felt a visceral pain as if the blade had sliced through his flesh. Tears streamed down his face, but he stood resolute, his gaze never leaving the place where his father had just given his life.

As the executioner held up Pierre's head to show the crowd, a few cries of "Justice served!" were drowned out by a wave of murmurs and uneasy shifts. The spectacle was over, and the crowd began to disperse, many faces etched with conflict and confusion.

Henri remained frozen, his body numb. The space around him felt empty, the departing crowd a blur of colours and movements that made no sense. Slowly, he turned away from the scaffold, each step heavy with grief and exhaustion.

He walked home alone, the streets of Paris echoing with the hollow sounds of a city that moved on too quickly from its daily dramas. Inside him, a storm of emotions raged—grief, anger, helplessness. But beneath it all lay a flicker of something else, a determination forged in the fires of this profound loss. Henri knew that his path forward would not be defined by vengeance, but by a pursuit of the justice and truth, his father had died defending.

Upon reaching his home, the emptiness of the house enveloped him. Every corner remembered conversations, laughter, his father's wise words, and his mother's gentle admonishments. Now, only silence greeted him, a silence so profound it seemed to suffocate. Henri wandered through the rooms aimlessly, touching objects his father had once held, half-expecting to turn a corner and find Pierre there, reading a book or scribbling notes.

He ended up in his father's study, the room left untouched since Pierre had been arrested. The air was stale but still carried the faint scent of his father's pipe tobacco. Henri sat at the desk, laying his head down amongst the scattered papers and books, each a fragment of Pierre's interrupted life.

Here, surrounded by the remnants of his father's existence, Henri allowed himself to break down completely. The sobs that wracked his body were loud in the quiet, each one a release of the pent-up emotions he'd held at bay. Grief, anger, helplessness, and an aching sense of injustice flowed through him, leaving him drained and hollow.

As he cried, Henri felt as if he were shedding part of himself, the naïve belief that justice and righteousness always prevailed. In its place, a hardened resolve began to form, a resolve to ensure his father's beliefs and dreams did not die with him on that scaffold. Henri did not yet know how to achieve this, but the path forward would be one that honoured Pierre Moreau's memory, not with revenge, but with a commitment to the ideals he had died for.

The solitude was overwhelming, and Henri sank into his father's chair, the leather worn and comforting. The quiet was oppressive and suffocating, yet there was also a strange form of companionship—as if in the absence of sound, he could almost hear his father's voice, imparting the wisdom and strength he so desperately needed to continue.

Henri's thoughts drifted to the lessons his father had taught him, the discussions of justice, liberty, and the commoner's plight that had animated many of their evenings together. Pierre Moreau had been a man of principles, often at odds with the revolutionary government's methods, advocating for a revolution that upheld the true ideals of freedom and equality rather than descending into terror and revenge.

The loss felt monumental, not just a personal loss for Henri but for the cause his father had believed in. How could he move forward, Henri wondered, in a world that seemed so irrevocably altered? How could he continue to fight for the ideals that had led to his father's death?

But as the night deepened and the silence stretched, Henri began to feel a burgeoning sense of resolve. His father's life could not be in vain; his ideals and visions for a fairer society needed a voice now more than ever. Henri knew he could not let grief paralyse him—not what his father would have wanted, nor what the nation needed.

Resolute, Henri stood up, a plan slowly forming in his mind. He would speak out, not just to honour his father's memory but to rekindle the true spirit of the Revolution, one that championed justice without succumbing to tyranny. It would not be easy, and the path would undoubtedly be fraught with danger and opposition, but Henri felt a renewed sense of purpose, a drive to act that his father's teachings had instilled in him.

As dawn broke, casting a pale light through the windows, Henri prepared for the days ahead, fortified by the love and lessons of his father, ready to face a new day with courage and a clear vision for the future.

—

The sad shadows of the evening of 9 Pluviôse, Year II (28 January 1794) drew longer across the modest confines of Henri's home, mirroring the palpable grief that seemed to permeate every corner of the room. The day had been spent in silent reflection, and Henri was physically and mentally exhausted. He had tried to formulate a plan for the days ahead but had ultimately succumbed to a few hours of desperately needed sleep. Now, with his father's execution still vivid in his mind, Henri was left alone in the enveloping silence, the stark absence of family voices rendering the space unnervingly hollow. The house's stillness was oppressive, starkly contrasting the chaotic rush of emotions that surged within him.

Sitting in the dim light of the candle that flickered on the mantelpiece, Henri contemplated the profound loss that had befallen him. The house once filled with his family's lively discussions and warm laughter, now echoed with the quiet hum of solitude. It was in these quiet moments that the reality of his father's absence became most acute, the silence a harsh reminder of the void Pierre's death had left behind.

As the night deepened, Henri's thoughts wandered through the tumultuous events of the past days. The rapid descent from hope to despair, from action to helplessness, seemed almost surreal. The grief was not just for his father's death but for the death of the ideals that Pierre had so fervently believed in—ideals that now seemed as distant and fragile as the flickering candlelight that barely illuminated the room.

The solitude forced Henri to confront the depths of his sorrow and the immense burden of his newfound responsibilities. As the son of a man who had stood firm in his convictions, even in the face of death, Henri felt overwhelming pressure to live up to Pierre's legacy. The expectation to continue his father's fight for justice and equality weighed heavily on his shoulders, a daunting task amidst the prevailing atmosphere of fear and repression.

Compounding his sorrow was the helplessness he felt about his mother's plight. Claire's imprisonment, though temporarily stayed by a commutation to a mere thirty days, was a constant source of worry. Henri longed to provide her comfort yet knew that the brief visits to the prison were but a paltry solace in the face of their shared grief.

As the hours passed, Henri's solitude was intermittently pierced by memories of his father. Each recollection was a double-edged sword, bringing comfort and a renewed sense of loss. Pierre's principles, his unwavering commitment to his ideals, and his profound love for his family—these memories steeled Henri's resolve but also deepened the ache in his heart.

Henri moved to his father's desk, seeking some respite from his thoughts. The papers and books, so often the tools of Pierre's intellectual pursuits, now served as a tangible connection to the man who had been his father, mentor, and guide. Henri picked up a book on the principles of democracy—a volume Pierre had often quoted—and leafed through it, each page a testament to his father's vision for a fairer, more equitable society.

The night slowly gave way to the grey light of dawn, and with it came a sad acceptance of the tasks ahead. Henri knew that the path forward would require mourning his father and embodying the principles Pierre had died for. It was a monumental task, but as the first light crept through the curtains, Henri felt a quiet resolve solidify within him.

He would continue his father's legacy, not through vengeance as he had once contemplated, but by advocating for justice and reform. The road ahead would undoubtedly be fraught with challenges, but Henri was determined to forge a path honouring his father's memory and the ideals he had fought for. In this quiet dawn, amidst the sorrow and solitude, Henri Moreau found the strength to face the future, his spirit kindling a flame of hope and determination in the cold morning air.

—

In the muted light of the early afternoon, 12 Pluviôse, Year II (31 January 1794), Henri navigated the sombre corridors of the prison where his mother, Claire, was being held. Each step echoed with a cold, hollow sound that seemed to underscore the gravity of his family's ordeal. As he approached the designated visiting area, the weight of recent days appeared to press more heavily upon him, the lingering grief for his father blending with the anxiety of seeing his mother in such circumstances.

Upon entering the visiting room, Henri found Claire sitting behind a simple wooden table, her posture composed but her eyes revealing a deep, unspoken sorrow. The stark setting only heightened the poignancy of their reunion. The harsh realities of imprisonment now marked Claire's usually impeccable appearance. Her once vibrant auburn hair, now streaked with grey, was loosely tied back, and her face bore the signs of fatigue, with dark circles under her eyes and lines etched by worry and sleepless nights.

Despite her dishevelled state, Claire's inherent dignity remained intact. She wore a plain, worn dress that contrasted sharply with the elegance she once effortlessly exuded. Yet, even in this austere environment, her presence was commanding. Though shadowed by recent hardships, her eyes still held the steely resolve that had carried her through so many trials.

Their greeting was a poignant mix of relief and pain—relief at being reunited, even under such harrowing conditions, and pain from the emotional wounds that were far from healed.

"Mother," Henri began, his voice barely above a whisper as he sat opposite her. "How are you holding up?"

Claire managed a weary smile, reaching out to clasp his hands across the table. "I am managing, Henri. It's not easy, but knowing you are safe gives me strength," she replied, her voice steady but tinged with sadness.

The conversation that followed was a delicate dance around the more painful subjects. They spoke of daily trivialities at first, but it wasn't long before the discussion turned to Pierre. Henri watched as his mother's face lit up with pride and melancholy as she recounted anecdotes of their earlier years together, her words painting a picture of a man deeply committed to his ideals and family.

"Henri," Claire said, her tone shifting to solemnity, "your father was a man of great principle. He believed in justice, in fairness, and though his life was cut tragically short, his beliefs do not have to die with him."

Henri nodded, feeling the familiar stirrings of resolve within him. "I know, Mother. I also want to continue his work and advocate for the changes he deeply believes in. I want to ensure his sacrifices were not in vain."

Claire squeezed his hands tighter, her eyes glistening with unshed tears. "That's all I could ever ask for," she replied. "But remember, Henri, do it with the same compassion your father had. He fought for what was right, but never with hate in his heart."

Their conversation gradually deepened, exploring Henri's paths to effect change. Claire's insights were invaluable, grounded in her experiences and intimate knowledge of Pierre's ideals and strategies. She urged Henri to think critically about whom he trusted, to build alliances wisely, and to always keep the greater good at the forefront of his actions.

Henri felt a renewed sense of purpose as the visiting hour drew close. The comfort he found in his mother's words and presence fortified him against the uncertainty of the days ahead. They parted with a promise to keep the lines of communication open, no matter what.

Stepping out of the prison into the chilly air of late January, Henri felt the burden of his grief lighten slightly, replaced by a burgeoning sense of duty. The conversations with his mother had not only provided solace but had also rekindled a fire within him. He was ready to step into the role that fate had thrust upon him, to honour his parents by championing the cause of justice and reform.

Chapter Nine

The bitter cold of 13 Pluviôse, Year II (1 February 1794) seemed to pierce straight to the bone, but it was the chill of grief that gripped Henri Moreau more tightly as he pushed open the door to his late father's workshop, *Moreau Horlogerie*. The familiar creak of the hinges sounded almost like a mournful sigh, echoing Henri's sombre mood. The tools and half-finished projects lay exactly as Pierre had left them, each piece a stark reminder of the future they had planned together, now irrevocably altered by the blade of the guillotine.

As Henri's fingers brushed against the cold metal of a clockwork mechanism, he felt a visceral reaction coursing through him. Once a place of warmth and innovation, the workshop now felt like a mausoleum of unfulfilled dreams. Yet amidst the shadows of loss, a fierce determination kindled within him. Henri knew that his father's ideals and hopes for a just society were worth fighting for, even if that meant standing against the terror Robespierre's regime had unleashed.

After all, Henri was Pierre Moreau's son, and lineage dictated that he, too, was always thinking and planning. The familiar sights and smells of the workshop reignited a spark within him. Here, surrounded by the remnants of his father's life's work, Henri found a renewed sense of purpose. He realised that the fight for justice, not vengeance, was the path he must tread.

Resolutely, Henri cleared a space on the cluttered workbench, setting aside his sorrow to focus on the task. The revolution had consumed many, but he vowed not to let it devour the principles his father had died defending. He began to pen a list of names—close family friends, former allies of his father, anyone who might still harbour a desire for a genuine republic free from the tyranny of the Committee of Public Safety.

With each name, Henri felt a connection to his father, as if each act of defiance against the regime brought him closer to Pierre's spirit. He envisioned a network of like-minded individuals, a silent resistance formed in the shadows of oppression. The workshop would become their meeting place, a haven for plotting a course towards a more just government.

As the last light of day faded, casting long shadows across the dusty floor, Henri lit a small oil lamp. Its flicker was a beacon of hope against the encroaching darkness. He knew the path ahead would be dangerous—Robespierre's spies were everywhere, and the guillotine was ever hungry. But as Henri sat alone in the dim light, surrounded by his father's trade tools, he felt a resolve harden within him.

This workshop, a place of creation and life, would not turn into a tomb of despair. Instead, it would be the birthplace of a new revolution, one that sought to reclaim the ideals that had sparked the people's uprising in the first place. Henri Moreau, bolstered by the memory of his father's unwavering courage, was ready to fight for a future where liberty, equality, and fraternity were more than just empty promises.

With a final glance around the workshop, Henri blew out the lamp and stepped into the cold night air. The streets of Paris shrouded in darkness, seemed to hold their breath, waiting for the winds of change that Henri and his allies would soon bring. The silent tide was rising, and with it, the hopes of all who dared to dream of a better tomorrow.

—

The day before 16 Pluviôse, Year II (4 February 1794), Pierre had been entirely engrossed in his work on decimal time when news of the decree abolishing slavery reached him. For a moment, he sat stunned, taken aback by the sudden announcement. Under normal circumstances, such a monumental event would have sparked vigorous discussions for days. However, in the relentless pace of the current reality, it was but a fleeting moment of reflection for him.

On 17 Pluviôse, Year II (5 February 1794), Henri Moreau convened the first of many clandestine meetings in a dimly lit corner of his father's workshop. A hush fell over the room as the door shut softly behind the last of the attendees. These individuals had known and respected Pierre Moreau—family friends and former political associates who shared a simmering discontent with the ruthless trajectory of the Revolution under Robespierre.

Henri looked around the circle of familiar faces, feeling comfort and immense responsibility. "Thank you for coming," he began, his voice low to avoid carrying beyond the thick stone walls. "I know each of you understands the risks involved in merely being here tonight. But I know you shared my father's vision for a Republic built on justice and reason, not terror and suspicion."

The room filled with nods of agreement. Henri's gaze met that of Monsieur Lefort, a seasoned journalist whose pen had grown increasingly silent in the face of the Committee's censorship. Lefort was a tall man with a thin frame and perpetually furrowed brows. His eyes, sharp and intelligent, still held a spark of defiance, a testament to his once-vocal opposition to tyranny.

"We are at a crossroads," Henri continued, "where silence becomes complicity. My father's death must not be in vain. It should catalyse us to restore the ideals the Revolution initially stood for."

Monsieur Lefort's words lingered in the dim light of the workshop, his voice a reminder of the days when Pierre Moreau's visions first inspired hope for a rational republic. "Henri, your father was a visionary; his dreams must not die with him. It's time to act, but we must strategise carefully."

Henri, absorbing the gravity of the moment, nodded in agreement. "Exactly, Monsieur Lefort. We begin by rallying a network of like-minded individuals. We need support not only from Paris but across France. We must reach out to other groups who share our vision and feel the strain of the Committee's grip."

The conversation transitioned into a broader discussion. Madame Durand, a former salon hostess known for intellectual gatherings, proposed a solution. "Let us use my salons as a cover. Though they are watched, they remain places where free thought can masquerade as casual conversation. We can spread our message under the guise of academic debate."

Henri and the others gathered around the old oak table that had seen countless plans and projects unfold. "Your salons would provide the perfect façade, Madame Durand. Meanwhile, we must establish a secure method of communication that evades the Committee's surveillance."

Gaston, a young engineer with a knack for mechanics, chimed in with practical enthusiasm. "I've been working on a cypher disguised within ordinary objects—perhaps books or clocks—that only we can decode. It would allow us to send messages without arousing suspicion."

The group, invigorated by the plan, began to map out the details. They discussed potential codes, the logistics of message transmission, and the strategic placement of their communication nodes. Each member took on a role that leveraged their unique skills, from Madame Durand's social influence to Gaston's inventive prowess.

As the meeting drew close, Henri felt a renewed sense of purpose. They were not just resisting an oppressive regime; they were laying the groundwork for a new phase of the revolution, one that would honour his father's legacy and reshape the future of France.

The conspirators left the workshop under the cover of night, their spirits buoyed by the plans they had set in motion. Henri stayed behind, gazing at the clock his father had nearly completed. It was no longer just a timepiece but a symbol of their resistance—a beacon of hope in a time of darkness.

Henri Moreau stood in his father's workshop on 1 Ventôse, Year II (19 February 1794), the air thick with the anticipation of change. Dust particles danced in the slivers of light that penetrated the tiny, grimy windows, each beam spotlighting the clutter of mechanical parts and tools that had once been the lifeblood of his father's craft. Today, however, the space was being transformed for a different purpose, far more aligned with whispered revolution than with the ticking of clocks.

As Henri swept the wooden floor, his mind raced with preparations for the covert gathering planned for the evening. Claire's release from prison was only a day away, and the workshop needed to be ready to serve as a family reunion spot and a nexus for their growing network of dissenters. The workbenches were pushed to the walls, creating a makeshift meeting area, while a heavy curtain was draped over the main window to obstruct prying eyes.

Henri's meticulous attention to detail was interrupted by a soft knock at the back door—a prearranged signal among the members of what had informally become known as "Anonyme." He opened it to find Monsieur Bellamy, a trusted ally and a former legal scholar whose expertise would be invaluable in navigating the complexities of their covert operations.

"Good to see you, Henri," Bellamy said, stepping inside and brushing off the cold. "I've brought some additional papers that might help us better understand the legal boundaries we're flirting with. We need to be sharp, cautious."

"Thank you, Monsieur Bellamy," Henri replied, accepting the stack of documents. "Tonight's meeting must set the foundation for how we operate—carefully, smartly, without attracting the Committee's attention."

They reviewed the workshop layout, discussing potential escape routes and contingency plans. Henri had installed a false back in one of the larger cabinets, a hidden space where sensitive documents or, in the worst case, a person could be concealed if the authorities ever raided the place.

The final touches were implemented as the afternoon waned into the evening. Candles were set up to provide adequate, yet subdued, lighting. Chairs borrowed from various acquaintances were arranged semi-circular, fostering collaboration and openness. Henri also laid out several copies of a brief manifesto he had drafted, inspired by his father's writings on liberty and justice, which he hoped would unify and encourage their group.

The workshop, once a place of punctual rhythms and precise mechanics, had transformed into a hub of revolutionary thought and planning. Henri felt a surge of nervous energy as he anticipated the challenges they would face and the potential to ignite meaningful change.

As dusk settled over Paris, the first of the attendees began to arrive, cloaked not only against the winter chill but against the watchful eyes of the regime. Each member of Anonyme was greeted at the door by Henri, who felt a mix of pride and apprehension with each handshake and nod of solidarity.

The group assembled that night was diverse—a mix of former military officers disillusioned by the government's promises of glory, intellectuals starved of free expression and ordinary citizens whose lives had been upended by constant surveillance and fear. Each person there shared a common desire: to see the tyranny of Robespierre replaced with a governance that genuinely reflected the revolutionary ideals of 1789.

With the workshop doors bolted and the windows secured, Henri stood before the gathered group, his heart heavy with the gravity of their task but buoyed by the collective spirit of resistance in the room. "Friends," he began, his voice firm despite the underlying tremor of emotion, "tonight, we stand together not just as rebels against a regime that has betrayed its people but as bearers of hope for a Republic that answers to justice and reason rather than fear and oppression."

The meeting that unfolded was charged with cautious optimism. Strategies were debated, roles were assigned, and the groundwork was laid for a campaign of subtle subversion aimed at undermining the pillars of Robespierre's power without sparking an overt rebellion that could lead to unnecessary bloodshed.

As the clock in the corner quietly marked the passing hours, Henri felt a stronger connection to his father than ever. The workshop—where Pierre Moreau had once carefully repaired the intricate cogs and wheels of Parisian timepieces—was now the setting for his son to work on something far more complex and delicate: the mechanisms of revolution.

When the last of the attendees had left, and Henri was alone in the quiet aftermath, he allowed himself a moment of reflection. The path they had chosen was fraught with peril, but for the first time since his father's execution, Henri felt a flicker of hope—a sense that, together, they might steer the course of history back towards the light of the ideals that had sparked the Revolution in the first place.

—

On 2 Ventôse, Year II (20 February 1794), the day Claire Fontaine was released from prison and returned to the quiet sanctuary of her home, the atmosphere was imbued with a bittersweet mixture of reunion and resolve. The house, marked by the absence of Pierre's presence, felt empty and comforting as Claire stepped through the door, her eyes scanning the familiar surroundings that spoke of a cherished and irrevocably changed life.

Henri, who had been preparing for this moment, greeted his mother with a warm, enveloping embrace. The relief of having her home was palpable, but so too was the undercurrent of urgency that had taken root in the days of her absence. After allowing a few moments for quiet reacquaintance, they sat down in the dimly lit living room, where the flicker of a single candle cast shadows that danced across the walls, mirroring the flickering uncertainties of their shared future.

"Mother," Henri began, his voice a careful blend of warmth and seriousness, "I've begun to lay the foundations for a resistance. It's what Father would have wanted—not just to grieve, but to act."

Claire, her expression composed yet tinged with sadness, nodded slowly. "I sensed as much in your letters," she replied, gently touching Henri's. "Tell me everything, Henri. What plans are in motion?"

Henri detailed the gatherings that had begun in the workshop and the covert meetings with those disillusioned by Robespierre's tyrannical grip. He spoke of the coded communications, the whispers of dissent slowly knitting together a network of allies. Each word was weighed with the gravity of their endeavour; each pause filled with the heavy breath of potential consequences.

"As it stands, we're growing cautiously but steadily. Our aim isn't just to rally voices but to inspire a movement grounded in the ideals Father fought for—justice, reason, liberty," Henri explained, his eyes reflecting both the fire of determination and the shadow of risk.

Claire listened intently, her mind processing their path's dangers and necessity. "We must tread carefully, Henri," she cautioned, her experience and maternal instinct framing her every word. "Robespierre's spies are as pervasive as the fear they wield. We'll need to spread our message without drawing the eye of the Committee of Public Safety."

Together, they strategised into the late hours of the evening, Claire bringing her insights into play—her networks from the salon days, her understanding of the political undercurrents, and her subtle insight in navigating the treacherous waters of revolutionary politics. They discussed ways to extend their influence, using the subtlety of art, literature, and salon gatherings as veils for their revolutionary discourse.

The plan was to weave their resistance so tightly into the fabric of everyday life that it would be invisible until it was undeniable. "We'll need to communicate our vision in a manner that resonates widely, stirring the hearts of those who've grown weary of the bloodshed and tyranny," Claire suggested, her mind already crafting the framework of their message.

As the candle burned lower, casting the room into deeper shadows, Henri and Claire discussed the need to maintain appearances. Claire decided to seek work with Madame Durand, who was re-establishing her salons—a hub for Paris's intellectual elite. Together, they planned to use these gatherings as a façade, creating a seemingly innocent environment while subtly coordinating efforts to fuel the discourse of dissent.

The night grew deep, and the discussions detailed, with Henri outlining the next steps for expanding their covert operations. Plans for distributing pamphlets, encoded with criticisms of Robespierre's policies, were set into motion. These writings would question the legitimacy of the oppressive measures suffocating Paris, sowing seeds of doubt and defiance under the guise of philosophical debate.

By the time they retired for the night, the paths before them were lined with a clear direction and myriad cautions. Claire's return had brought a renewed sense of hope and familial comfort and fortified the resolve needed to challenge the despotic rule that had cost them so dearly.

As Henri extinguished the candle, the room's darkness seemed to echo the uncertainty of their endeavour. Yet, within that uncertainty, there lay a steely thread of determination woven by Pierre Moreau's legacy and his family's unbreakable will. They would continue their quiet rebellion tomorrow, armed with the power of whispered words and the strength of shared convictions.

—

On 6 Ventôse, Year II (24 February 1794), as the Parisian winter clung with a lingering chill, Henri Moreau, his mother Claire, set about crafting a web of secrecy to shield their burgeoning resistance. In the dimly lit confines of Henri's workshop, which had become the nucleus of their operations, the pair devised a system of coded communications to connect their discreet network of collaborators.

The morning had been spent perfecting a series of ciphered messages, a method Henri had adapted from old diplomatic codes once discussed by his father. These messages were designed to be innocuous to any unintended observer, yet they carried the weight of revolutionary intent to those who knew how to decipher them.

"Each message will be a drop of water in a silent tide," Henri remarked as he demonstrated the coding technique to a small group of trusted associates gathered around the sturdy oak table that served as their makeshift command centre. These individuals, a mix of old friends of Pierre and new allies drawn by Henri's fervent yet reasoned approach to change, listened intently. The air was thick with the musty scent of old wood and iron, and the walls were lined with the tools of Henri's trade, which now served a dual purpose.

Claire oversaw the proceedings with a measured eye as they practised encoding and decoding the messages. During her years hosting salons, she honed her ability to read people, a now invaluable skill. "We must be careful to keep our circle tight but informed. Trust is our currency, and it is as precious as it is fragile," she advised her voice a soft yet firm reminder of the stakes at play.

Later that afternoon, after their allies had left, Claire and Henri refined their communication network. They established a series of drop points around Paris for message exchange—a discreet nod to the spy tactics of old, repurposed for their cause. These points were common enough to avoid suspicion but known only to their inner circle. A loose brick in a nondescript alley, a hollowed-out book in a public library, and a false bottom in a market stall—each was a link in their chain of silent rebellion.

As dusk fell and the city's noises dimmed to whispers, Henri and Claire sat together, mapping out the routes for their message couriers. They used a faded map of Paris, its edges frayed but the streets still clear. Pins and threads marked their nodes and lines of communication, a visual testament to their careful planning.

"Our words must move like shadows through the city, unseen but present, stirring the thoughts of those who feel as we do," Henri mused, his finger tracing a route from the Latin Quarter to Montmartre.

Claire nodded, her mind racing with contingencies. "We'll rotate the couriers weekly. No pattern should emerge that might draw the eye of the Committee's spies."

The discussion moved to the content of their messages. Each pamphlet and coded letter would carry critiques of Robespierre's policies, questioning his reign's moral and political legitimacy. They planned to cloak their criticisms in philosophical queries and historical analogies, making them thought-provoking rather than overtly seditious.

"It's not just about dissent, Henri," Claire emphasised, her eyes reflecting the flicker of the candle between them. "It's about awakening a dialogue, about making people reflect on what the Revolution promised and what it has, unfortunately, become."

Henri absorbed his mother's words, his respect for her understanding deepening. "We'll be the spark, Mother. But it will be the people's will that fans the flame."

The night deepened as they continued their work, the candle burning low, casting long shadows across the paper-strewn table. The coded messages they created were more than mere words; they were vessels of hope and change instruments set to sail on the undercurrents of a city teetering on the edge of further upheaval.

By the time they retired for the night, their network of silent whispers was set in motion—a testament to their resolve and a challenge to the oppressive atmosphere that had gripped Paris. In the quiet solitude of the workshop, as Henri extinguished the last candle, the shadows seemed less menacing, as if the very darkness was with them, cloaking their cause in secrecy and promise.

—

By 14 Ventôse, Year II (4 March 1794), Henri Moreau had steadily expanded his covert operations, capitalising on the growing disillusionment among Paris's intellectuals and political figures. The icy grip of winter had begun to loosen over the city, but the chill in the political atmosphere only intensified as the Reign of Terror continued its ruthless course.

In a dimly lit back room of a quiet café near the University of Paris, a gathering of minds, weary of Maximilien Robespierre's draconian measures, convened. Henri had chosen the location for its discretion and its clientele; the café was a known haunt for thinkers and scholars who, under the veil of academic pursuit, discussed matters of state with a critical eye.

As the men settled around a scarred wooden table, their faces etched with the fatigue of living under constant suspicion, Henri patiently presented his case. "The Republic has strayed far from its ideals," he began, his voice barely above a whisper yet carrying a sharp intensity. "Robespierre's vision of virtue and terror has become a tool for personal vendettas and mass paranoia. It's time we reclaimed the principles for which we first fought."

Among the attendees was Professor Émile Renard, a respected historian whose lectures on the Republic's ideals had been subtly critical of the current regime. His keen mind and influence over young intellectuals made him a valuable ally. "You speak truly, Henri," he responded, his eyes glinting with a mix of fear and resolve. "Many of us have watched with growing dismay as the Committee of Public Safety's grip tightens. But what, precisely, do you propose?"

Henri leaned forward, his hands clasped tightly in front of him. "We must forge a network of like-minded individuals, a coalition rooted in the original spirit of the Revolution. Not to overthrow the Republic but to steer it back to its rightful course. We will begin by spreading information, encouraging critical thought, challenging the propaganda that fuels Robespierre's power."

The plan was met with nods of cautious approval. The intellectuals understood the power of ideas; many had seen their students spirited away for mere whispers of dissent. Henri's proposal to circulate pamphlets, essays, and articles that questioned the government's policies without overt sedition was a strategy they could endorse.

Dr. Lucien Favre, a former member of the Legislative Assembly and now a law professor, raised a practical concern. "The risk is substantial. If we were caught, it wouldn't just be a matter of imprisonment. The guillotine has been the answer to far less than what we're contemplating."

Henri acknowledged the risk with a grim nod. "We will operate in the shadows. Meetings such as this will be rare and untraceable. Our communications will be coded, and our writings will be anonymous. We must be the ghost in the system, unseen yet pervasive."

The group agreed to begin their campaign quietly. Professor Renard offered to draft the first series of essays, using historical parallels to highlight the dangers of autocratic rule subtly. Dr. Favre would use his contacts to distribute these writings among legal circles and beyond.

As the meeting drew to a close, Henri felt a surge of both anticipation and anxiety. Their path was fraught with danger, but the alternative—a silent acquiescence to tyranny—was unthinkable. They parted with the understanding that each step forward would be taken with the utmost care, their conspiracy shielded by the anonymity of Paris's shadowy corners.

Walking back through the cobblestone streets, Henri's mind raced with the possibilities and perils ahead. Now set in motion, the network would grow to challenge the oppressive regime, each member a critical part of a more significant movement towards justice. In the quiet of the night, as the city of Paris lay blanketed under a pall of fear and suspicion, the seeds of a quiet revolution were sown, watered by the whispers of those who dared to dream of change.

Henri's plans for resistance were meticulously detailed. They would begin by disseminating pamphlets and essays that subtly questioned the legitimacy of Robespierre's policies. These writings would be carefully crafted to avoid confrontation, instead employing philosophical debate and historical examples to encourage critical thought among the populace. Henri planned to use clandestine presses and discreet couriers to circulate these materials, ensuring they reached influential circles without drawing undue attention.

To bolster their network, Henri and his allies would cultivate relationships with disaffected members of the National Convention and the Jacobin Club, seeking to sow seeds of doubt and discontent within the very heart of the government. They aimed to create a ripple effect, where whispered conversations and private doubts would slowly erode the monolithic support for Robespierre's rule.

Henri also recognised the power of the arts in shaping public opinion. With her extensive connections from her salon days, Claire would play a pivotal role in this aspect of their plan. They would support playwrights, poets, and artists who could embed subtle critiques of the regime within their works, reaching a broader audience through culture and entertainment. Salon gatherings would be revived under the guise of literary and philosophical discussion, providing a cover for their revolutionary discourse.

Furthermore, Henri intended to leverage his background in mechanics and engineering. He would develop hidden compartments and coded mechanisms to safeguard their communications and documents, ensuring that even if one cell were compromised, the network as a whole would remain intact.

Each step of their plan was designed with the utmost caution. The use of coded language and encrypted messages would be standard practice. Meetings would be infrequent and held in ever-changing locations to avoid detection. The goal was to create a decentralised network that could operate autonomously, reducing the risk of total collapse if any one part was exposed.

As Henri and Claire refined their strategy, they knew the difficult road ahead. Yet, in the face of tyranny, their resolve was unyielding. They would fight not with swords or guns but with ideas, words, and the indomitable spirit of those who believed in a future where liberty, equality, and fraternity were more than just hollow slogans.

With each passing day, their quiet rebellion gained momentum, a growing force of intellect and courage poised to reclaim the Revolution's ideals. And so, beneath the surface of a city gripped by fear, a new hope began to flicker, fuelled by the determination of those who dared to resist.

—

On the 18th of Ventôse, Year II (8 March 1794), Henri Moreau found himself in the cluttered, shadow-filled basement of his father's old workshop. This place had seen the birth of many a mechanical marvel and was now the cradle of a nascent revolution. The air was thick with the scent of oil and metal, but the discussions this evening were fueled by a different kind of urgency.

Gathered around an old oak table, under the dim light of flickering candles, were members of the newly dubbed group "Anonyme." The name was a nod to their need for anonymity, a crucial veil against the prying eyes of Robespierre's increasingly paranoid regime. Henri surveyed the room, taking in the determined faces of his compatriots —men and women drawn from various walks of life, each united by a shared disdain for their beloved Republic's despotic trajectory.

"As we expand our efforts, coordination and discretion must be our watchwords," Henri began, his voice unwavering yet subdued enough to blend with the murmur of the stone walls. "Our aim is not merely to criticise, but to enlighten—to remind our fellow citizens of the ideals that sparked our revolution in the first place."

Henri had delivered a similar speech several times before. Since it was impossible for all members of Anonyme to meet simultaneously, he and Claire had crafted a strategy to segment the group into smaller cells. This structure was designed to enhance the safety and effectiveness of their operations, ensuring each cell could operate independently yet remain interconnected, thus safeguarding the entire group.

A map of Paris lay sprawled across the table, marked with various symbols that indicated safe houses, meeting spots, and routes for message delivery. Henri pointed to several locations marked discreetly with red dots. "These are where our pamphlets will be distributed next week. Each point has been chosen for its high foot traffic yet low surveillance. We must spread our words without drawing the eyes of the Committee of Public Safety."

Marianne Dubois, a former bookseller whose establishment had been shuttered by the authorities for harbouring 'subversive literature,' was tasked with overseeing the distribution. "I've secured several reliable couriers, all skilled in avoiding detection. They understand the risks and the importance of what we're doing," she confirmed, her voice a blend of nervousness and excitement.

Henri then turned to Lucas Girard, a young but brilliant strategist who had once served as a junior aide in the military. "Lucas, how goes the recruitment within the army ranks?"

Lucas shifted uncomfortably, the weight of his task evident in his furrowed brow. "Progress is slow but promising. Discontent is rife, especially among the lower ranks. Many are disillusioned with Robespierre's purges. They fear for their families and their comrades. We're tapping into that fear, turning it into a call to action. But we must be cautious—trust is scarce, and betrayal is often a matter of survival."

The group nodded in understanding. Trust was a luxury few could afford in these treacherous times. Henri appreciated the gravity of Lucas's work; the military could be a powerful ally or a devastating foe.

The meeting continued with discussions on security measures, contingency plans, and the circulation of their latest series of essays, which subtly denounced the excesses of the current regime. Ever the pragmatist Claire Fontaine emphasised the need for a contingency plan. "If one of us is arrested, the rest must remain protected. Let's agree now—no written records of our members, no direct references in our communications. We must think like ghosts, seen in effect but never grasped."

As the candles burned lower, casting long shadows across the earnest faces of the assembled group, Henri felt a surge of pride and trepidation. They were few, under threat, but their resolve was firm. The spirit of liberty that had ignited the Revolution was not yet extinguished; it lived on in the hearts and actions of those gathered here.

The meeting disbanded with a collective sense of cautious optimism. Each member slipped away into the night, their movements as silent as the pact forged in the flickering shadows. Henri lingered a moment longer, his gaze fixed on the map—a web of hope and defiance spread across the city he loved. The road ahead was fraught with danger, but the cause was just. In the silent communion of those shared moments, Anonyme was no longer just a group of rebels but a beacon of the silent tide rising against tyranny.

—

By the 26th of Ventôse, Year II (16 March 1794), Claire Fontaine had discreetly helped transform Madame Durand's salon into a nucleus of dissent against Robespierre's oppressive regime. This once-bustling centre of Parisian intellectual and cultural life, now masked as innocent social gatherings, served a more clandestine purpose under Madame Durand's direction, with Claire playing a pivotal role in its operations.

With a natural grace that belied the intensity of her mission, Claire began to use her weekly tea parties as venues for quiet subversion. Each event, while outwardly a simple congregation of the city's literati and minor nobility, was carefully designed to sow the seeds of resistance among those disillusioned with the current state of the Republic.

This particular afternoon, the drawing room was abuzz with the soft clinks of china and the murmur of cultured voices. The attendees, a mixture of old friends and new acquaintances, were carefully chosen by Claire for their potential sympathy for the cause or their influence within their respective circles.

As she moved through the room, her demeanour was calm and her conversation light, but her eyes were sharp, gauging the subtle reactions of her guests to the carefully phrased critiques that floated through the air. She played a dangerous game, but the stakes could not be higher.

"Indeed, it is said that the very essence of our Republic is the will of the people," Claire remarked to a group gathered around a set of settees. "Yet, how often are those voices truly heard amidst the clamour of the Committee's decrees?" Her tone was thoughtful, inviting contemplation rather than confrontation.

Across the room, a small cluster of guests debated the latest policies enacted under Robespierre's rule. Their discontent was palpable, though spoken in hushed tones. Joining them, Claire listened intently, offering nods and smiles, encouraging further confidence.

"Marcel, you have always been a keen observer of political tides," Claire said to a well-respected journalist among the group. "What is your take on the recent arrests? It seems anyone might be next." Her question, innocent on the surface, was a deliberate probe for loyalty and perspective.

Marcel, a sharp-eyed man with a reputation for intelligent commentary, lowered his voice. "Claire, it is as if suspicion alone has become grounds for accusation. The air in Paris is thick with fear and chokes the truth before it can be spoken."

As the afternoon waned, Claire knew she had gathered valuable insights and, perhaps, more critically, identified those who might soon be ready to support their cause openly. The importance of discretion, however, could not be overstressed. Each new ally was a potential risk but also a beacon of hope.

After the guests had departed, Claire and Henri convened in the study, a room filled with the lingering scent of her husband's pipe tobacco—a reminder of Pierre's absence and the reason for their struggle.

"Henri, the salons are proving more fruitful than I dared hope," Claire began her voice a mixture of excitement and caution. "There are many who share our dissatisfaction with Robespierre's methods. But we must be selective in whom we trust."

Henri, who had been busy organising the distribution of their latest pamphlets, looked up from his papers, his expression serious. "Mother, your ability to read the room is unmatched. If you believe they are ready, we will bring them closer to the heart of our planning. But we must ensure their absolute commitment—half-hearted allies could doom us all."

Claire nodded in agreement, her mind already calculating the next steps. "I will arrange a few private meetings with the most promising. In smaller, more intimate settings, we can perhaps reveal more of our intentions."

As night fell over Paris, the Moreaus were a study in quiet determination. Once a beacon of intellectual and social exchange, their home had morphed into the command centre of their resistance efforts. Each whispered conversation, each shared glance between mother and son, fortified their resolve.

The revolution within the Revolution was gaining momentum, propelled by the silent undercurrents swirling through Claire's drawing room. In the heart of a city gripped by tumult and terror, a new hope was kindling, fragile yet fierce in its quiet intensity.

—

On the 5th of Germinal, Year II (25 March 1794), Henri Moreau and his mother Claire took decisive steps to broaden their influence. They were now focused on constructing a distribution network for their subversive pamphlets—a task that required cunning and immense caution.

The pamphlets, carefully worded to question the legitimacy of Robespierre's policies, were designed not to incite immediate rebellion but to provoke thought and doubt among the populace. Henri had spent countless nights drafting and redrafting these documents, ensuring each line could withstand scrutiny yet leave a lasting impact on the reader.

The morning was brisk as Henri and Claire sat in the dim light of dawn, discussing the logistics of their operation. "We need a system that allows these pamphlets to reach as many sympathetic hands as possible without leading the authorities back to us," Henri explained, spreading a map of Paris on the kitchen table.

Claire, ever the strategist, pointed to several key locations on the map. "We should start with the northern districts. The mood there is ripe for our words. My contact at the market can get us in touch with the cart drivers—they're always moving around the city and hear everything."

Henri nodded in agreement, marking the locations with a pencil. "We'll need to create secure and constantly changing drop-off points. Maybe the back rooms of friendly taverns or bookshops?" he suggested, his mind working through the possibilities.

"Exactly," Claire replied, her eyes alight with the strategic challenge. "And we should use coded messages to inform our distributors of the pickup points. Something innocuous that won't draw attention if intercepted."

The rest of the day was spent in preparation. Henri contacted trusted allies who could act as distributors, each chosen for their loyalty and ability to remain unnoticed by the authorities. They were given instructions on collecting and distributing the pamphlets discreetly, with strict warnings about the consequences of carelessness.

By evening, the first batch of pamphlets was ready. They were simple sheets of paper, but each bore a message potent enough to stir the thoughts of those disillusioned with the current state of the Republic. Henri watched as the first of their quiet missives left the safety of the workshop, tucked away in the false bottom of a market cart.

As night fell over Paris, Henri and Claire sat back in the workshop, the air thick with the scent of ink and paper. "Do you think it will make a difference?" Henri asked, a trace of doubt creeping into his voice.

Claire reached over to squeeze his hand reassuringly. "Every revolution starts with a single act of defiance, however small," she said. "We are planting seeds, Henri. And seeds, given time, will break through even the hardest soil."

The operation grew over the following weeks, becoming more refined with each batch of pamphlets. Drop-off points were rotated regularly, coded messages were changed frequently, and their network of distributors slowly expanded.

Feedback from the streets began to trickle in. The pamphlets were sparking discussions, some heated, some reflective, but all pointing to growing unrest with how Robespierre handled the reins of power. People began to whisper, question, and doubt in tavern backrooms and quiet corners of public squares.

Henri felt a cautious surge of hope. Each whispered conversation, each nod of agreement that their pamphlets received, confirmed that the tides of opinion were slowly turning. In the cover of darkness, with quiet words and the rustle of paper, a revolution within the Revolution was taking shape, guided by the silent determination of Henri Moreau and his mother, Claire.

This quiet network, born of a son's grief and a mother's resolve, was now a whisper of revolution, echoing through the streets of Paris, waiting for the moment to raise its voice against tyranny.

On the 15th of Germinal, Year II (4 April 1794), the clandestine network Henri Moreau and his mother Claire had painstakingly built came under a sudden and alarming threat. A close encounter with the Committee of Public Safety almost compromised their entire operation, forcing them to reassess and fortify their security measures.

The day had begun uneventfully as Henri made his way through the narrow alleys of Paris to deliver a new batch of coded messages to one of their trusted couriers. However, the air was tense, charged with the whispers of spies and informers who lurked in every shadow, eager to report any hint of dissent to the authorities.

As Henri approached the rendezvous point, a nondescript tavern in the heart of the Marais district, he noticed a group of Committee agents interrogating a local shopkeeper. His heart raced; the Revolutionary Guards were not known for their subtlety or discretion, and their presence in the area could spell disaster.

Henri ducked into a nearby alley, his mind racing with contingency plans. He watched from a distance, his hand clenched around the small package of messages hidden inside his coat. The interrogation intensified, and Henri knew he had to make a quick decision.

With no clear path to the tavern without risking detection, Henri decided to abort the mission. He took a circuitous route back to his workshop, constantly looking over his shoulder for any sign of pursuit. The streets felt like a maze designed to trap the unwary revolutionary.

Once back in the safety of his father's workshop, Henri and Claire convened an emergency meeting with their closest advisors. The brush with the Committee agents was a stark reminder of the dangers they faced. "We've been too careless," Henri admitted, his voice heavy with frustration. "It's time we tightened security around all our operations."

The group agreed on a series of measures to enhance their operational security. First, they decided to implement a vetting process for all new members. The network had increased, and while this had many advantages, it also increased the risk of infiltration by spies.

"We need to know exactly who is in our ranks," Claire stated firmly. "Trust must be earned, not freely given in these dangerous times."

They also agreed to increase the use of coded language and cyphers in their communications. A new codebook was to be created, with copies given only to the most trusted members of the network. Each message would now be encoded twice, ensuring that the true meaning would remain protected even if one layer was deciphered.

Moreover, Henri introduced a system of dead drops for message exchanges. No longer would couriers meet directly; instead, they would leave messages in pre-arranged hidden locations, which the recipient would retrieve later. This method would reduce the chances of members being caught in the act of exchanging sensitive information.

The day's events had shaken the group, but they emerged from the meeting with a renewed sense of purpose and caution. The threat of discovery was confirmed and ever-present, but they were not deterred. Instead, they were more determined than ever to continue their work, armed now with stricter protocols and an unyielding commitment to their cause.

As night fell over Paris, Henri sat alone in the dim light of his workshop, pondering the road ahead. The stakes were incredibly high, and the margin for error was shrinking. Yet, the resolve in his heart was firm. Inspired by his father's courage and guided by his mother's wisdom, Henri was ready to navigate the dangerous waters of revolutionary politics.

With each cautious step forward, the silent tide of their resistance grew more muscular, flowing steadily towards the day it would crash against the shores of tyranny, ready to reclaim the promise of the Revolution for the people of France.

—

By the 25th of Germinal, Year II (14 April 1794), the clandestine group known as "Anonyme" had seen its numbers swell with fresh, albeit cautiously vetted, supporters. Among them were several key military personnel, discontented with the chaotic leadership of Robespierre and his increasingly paranoid regime. These new additions brought their dissatisfaction and a wealth of strategic military experience and connections invaluable to Henri and Claire's burgeoning resistance movement.

The day was brisk, with a lingering chill hinting at winter's reluctant departure. Acutely aware of the growing surveillance and suspicion that pervaded Paris, Henri chose a secluded spot for this pivotal gathering—a derelict barn on the outskirts of the city, known only to a trusted few. The location was far from the prying eyes of the city's Revolutionary Guards, providing a temporary haven for the kind of discussions that could mean the difference between liberty and the guillotine.

As the sun began its descent, casting long shadows over the cobblestone paths leading to their meeting place, Henri reviewed the list of attendees. Each had been thoroughly scrutinised, and their allegiances were confirmed by multiple trusted sources within "Anonyme." Despite these precautions, the weight of command was palpable on his shoulders, each decision carrying potential ramifications far beyond the immediate circle of revolutionaries.

The meeting commenced with the usual precautions: lookouts were posted discreetly at vantage points, and the newest members were reminded of the secrecy upon which their lives depended. Henri opened the session with a sad nod to their shared purpose, his voice steady but low.

"Tonight, we stand together not just as dissenters but as architects of a fairer future," Henri began, his gaze sweeping over the faces illuminated by the flickering light of lanterns. "Our ranks have grown, strengthened by those with much to lose should we fail. It is with great care that we welcome our new allies from the military. Their expertise will be crucial as we move forward."

One of the military officers, a seasoned captain with a network of loyalists disillusioned by the rampant corruption and terror of Robespierre's rule, stepped forward. His uniform was worn, but his posture remained rigid, the discipline of years ingrained in his every move.

"Thank you, Henri. We are here not just as soldiers but as citizens who seek to reclaim the Revolution's initial promise," the captain stated, his voice resonant in the quiet of the barn. "Our knowledge of military strategy and internal troop movements can help us predict and counter the actions of the government forces should it come to that."

The discussion that followed was intense and detailed. Maps were rolled out across a rough-hewn wooden table with markers representing critical locations in Paris. Routes for safe passage, potential safe houses, and contingency plans for emergency communication were meticulously plotted.

Claire, ever the strategist, proposed creating a mobile communication system using trusted couriers who could move quickly and unnoticed between groups. "We must be able to adapt our plans at a moment's notice," she advised, her clear eyes scanning the map. "Flexibility and swift communication will be our greatest allies."

As the meeting drew close, Henri felt a surge of cautious optimism. The web of allies they had woven was diverse and motivated, each member linked by a common desire for change. Yet, the stakes were immeasurably high, and their path was fraught with peril.

The group disbanded under the cover of darkness, each member slipping away into the night, their movements as silent as the hope that drove them. Henri lingered momentarily, looking out over the empty barn that had witnessed the birth of a new phase in their resistance.

As he returned to the city, the lingering clouds obscured the stars overhead, a reminder of the uncertainty ahead. Yet the darkness could not wholly diminish the resolve that burned in Henri's chest— a resolve forged in the crucible of loss and tempered by the collective will of those who dared to dream of a different France.

—

On the 6th of Floréal, Year II (25 April 1794), the sprawling outskirts of Paris, with their rambling fields and secluded coppices, became the backdrop for a clandestine rendezvous that could very well change the course of the revolution. Under the cloak of dusk, Henri met with the leaders of a like-minded resistance group that had long operated in the shadows of the city's outer limits.

This group, known amongst its members as the "Liberté Collective," had gained a reputation for their daring and successful disruptions of governmental operations, making them invaluable allies. The rendezvous point was an abandoned farmhouse hidden from any main roads. Its worn appearance was a perfect cover for the evening's subversive activities.

As Henri approached the agreed location, the last remnants of sunlight slipped below the horizon, casting elongated shadows across the gravel path. His heart thudded with anticipation and wariness—forming alliances was a necessary risk, but a risk nonetheless.

Inside the farmhouse, the air was thick with the musty smell of disuse. Old farming tools hung from the walls, and dust motes danced in the beams of light that the lanterns threw across the darkened room. The leaders of the Liberté Collective—a robust woman named Marianne and a tall, wiry man known only as Jacques—stood to greet Henri as he entered.

"Monsieur Moreau, your reputation precedes you," Marianne said, extending a firm hand. Her voice carried the rasp of someone who had spent many nights whispering plots and plans.

"Likewise, Mademoiselle Marianne," Henri responded, matching her firm grip. "I've heard much of your group's exploits. Our aims align; it is time we coordinate our efforts more closely."

Jacques, who had been observing silently, nodded in agreement. "The more united we stand, the stronger we strike," he remarked sagely, moving to unroll a large map of Paris on a rickety table.

The trio bent over the map, their heads close together as they discussed potential strategies. Henri outlined the growing network of Anonyme, emphasising their infiltration into various levels of society and the military. Marianne and Jacques brought insights into logistical support, detailing safe routes for transporting messages and contraband.

"Our main objective," Henri emphasised, "is to disrupt the government's communication lines. We've identified a vulnerability in their courier system that we can exploit. Intercepting their messages could give us the advantage we need."

Marianne's eyes gleamed with a strategic fire. "An excellent plan. My group can help facilitate this. We have contacts within the postal service—disillusioned souls who despise the tyranny as much as we do."

Jacques chimed in, his tone cautious but optimistic. "We need to ensure our actions remain untraceable. The Committee of Public Safety is growing more suspicious by the day."

The meeting stretched into the early hours, with discussions diving into the minutiae of every plan and contingency. Codes and signals were agreed upon, and a communication network between Anonyme and the Liberté Collective was firmly established. Henri felt a surge of hope—this alliance might tip the scales in their favour.

As they wrapped up their strategies, Marianne touched Henri's shoulder. "Your father would be proud, Monsieur Moreau. You honour his memory with your courage."

Henri nodded, feeling the weight of her words. "Thank you, Marianne. It is for all our fathers, families, and future."

Leaving the farmhouse, Henri looked up at the stars, their light faint but persistent against the dark sky. The night felt less oppressive, the shadows less menacing. With the Liberté Collective by their side, Anonyme was more muscular, their resolve firmer. As he made his way back to Paris, the quiet of the night was a cloak around him, shielding his movements just as his newfound allies would shield their shared cause. The path ahead was fraught with danger, but now, it was a path they would walk together.

—

On the 17th of Floréal, Year II (6 May 1794), as the unrest in Paris intensified, Henri and Claire faced the necessity of evolving their tactics. The increasing scrutiny from government officials meant they could no longer afford the risk of predictable patterns. Like many others, this night found them navigating the labyrinthine back alleys of Paris under the guise of darkness, their movements shrouded in secrecy.

The city, a tapestry of shadows and whispers, felt silently tense. Feeling the weight of each step, Henri led the way to a nondescript building on the eastern fringes of the Marais district. The location was one of many they would use, a dilapidated bookshop whose owner, a staunch supporter of their cause, had offered his back room as a meeting space.

As they entered through the rear, the faint, musty smell of old books and the soft rustle of pages acted as a backdrop to their hushed conference. Tonight's gathering was small and deliberate in its selection. Alongside Henri and Claire, only three others were present: a former military officer, a young intellectual, and a seasoned messenger, all bound by a common resolve to see the downfall of tyranny.

With a map spread across a worn wooden table, Henri outlined their immediate concerns. "The patrols have been doubled. We've seen more informants lurking around our usual spots. It's no longer safe to stick to one place for too long," he explained, his finger tracing the routes they frequently used.

The former officer, a man named Léon, with a scar tracing down his forehead, nodded in agreement. "We must become like phantoms—

seen, felt, but never caught. It's about adapting to the enemy's tactics, anticipating their moves."

The intellectual, a sharp-featured woman named Élise, said, "We should consider using the catacombs on occasion. Few dare to venture there, and it could serve as a safe passage if we find ourselves cornered."

As the voice of measured strategy, Claire added, "We must also diversify our communication methods. The coded messages have served us well, but we should develop alternatives—perhaps visual signals or even coded knocks for close-range communication."

The discussion turned to the pressing issue of maintaining their network's morale. Henri could see the strain of constant vigilance wearing on his allies' faces, mirrored in his fatigue. "We cannot let fear dictate our actions," he said firmly. "We've all lost much—friends, family, a semblance of peace. But we stand together in this. Let's ensure everyone in our network feels that strength."

The young messenger, whose agility and keen sense of direction had saved many of their messages from interception, suggested more regular updates to keep the group informed. "Knowledge is as much a weapon as any sword. It will bolster their resolve if everyone understands the stakes and the plan."

As the meeting drew close, Henri felt a renewed sense of purpose pulsing through the dimly lit room. They had plans to refine, new routes to map out, and many logistical challenges to overcome. Yet, the unity and determination in each hushed voice provided a stark contrast to the uncertainty lurking outside the bookshop's walls.

Claire lingered for a moment as the others prepared to leave. "You're leading well, Henri," she whispered, her hand resting briefly on his arm. "Your father would have been proud."

With a nod of gratitude, Henri watched as his mother blended back into the room's shadows, readying herself to leave by another exit. As they dispersed into the night's embrace, the echo of their quiet resolve filled the empty spaces, a silent tide rising against the storm of oppression that raged above.

—

It was the 29th of Floréal, Year II (18 May 1794), a day marked by a breakthrough that Henri and his network, Anonyme, had silently prayed for. Gathered in a dimly lit cellar beneath an old print shop, Henri, Claire, and their closest confidants convened to discuss a significant opportunity that had presented itself—an exposed flaw within the government's communication infrastructure.

"The lines that carry dispatches between the Committee of Public Safety and its outposts are not as secure as they believe," Henri began, his voice a low murmur as he unrolled a map across the table. The map was dotted with various locations, marked and connected with lines that traced the government's communication routes. "Here and here," he pointed, "the couriers are fewer, and their paths cross less patrolled areas. It's a vulnerability we cannot ignore."

Léon, the former military officer, leaned over the map, studying Henri's highlighted points. "If we can intercept their messages, we could gather intelligence and sow discord. Misinformation could lead them to misallocate resources or distrust their own channels."

Élise, instrumental in devising their coded language, added, "We could draft false orders, perhaps even halt some of their operations temporarily. It would give us and the people a much-needed respite from their constant pressure."

The room buzzed with cautious enthusiasm as the potential of this new strategy unfurled. However, ever the voice of prudence, Claire interjected, "We must proceed with utmost caution. The moment they detect any tampering, they'll tighten security even further. We'll likely only get one chance at this."

Henri nodded in agreement. "Exactly why our first move must be a calculated one. We'll need volunteers to track the couriers' routes for the next few days. We must know their schedules down to the minute before we act."

A plan began to take shape. Two of their most reliable messengers were tasked with shadowing the government couriers from a safe distance, noting their timings and any potential gaps in their routines. Meanwhile, Henri and another small team would prepare the false messages they intended to inject into the government's stream.

As the meeting drew to a close, the group felt a mix of excitement and trepidation. This was their chance to tip the scales, even slightly, in their favour. "Remember," Henri said as they prepared to leave, "absolute discretion. If you suspect you've been seen, abandon the task. We cannot afford to be exposed."

The following days were tense. Henri found himself grappling with the weight of their undertaking. The success of their plan could encourage their efforts and possibly attract more to their cause. Failure, however, wasn't something he allowed himself to dwell on, though it lurked in the back of his mind, an unspoken shadow among their whispered strategies.

In the secrecy of the early hours, before the first light of dawn had begun to touch the sky, Henri and Claire would meet, reviewing reports brought back by their scouts and adjusting their plans accordingly. Though fraught with the anxiety of their high stakes, these moments also brought them closer. They were comrades in arms, bonded by blood and conviction.

When the assigned day arrived to execute their plan, the air was thick with nervous energy. Henri reviewed every detail and every contingency plan with his team. They were ready, as ready as they could ever be. As they dispersed to their respective posts, Henri felt a resolve settle over him, solidifying his determination to see this through, for his father, for their future.

That night, under the cloak of darkness, Anonyme would make their move, attempting to weave their threads into the tapestry of revolution that enveloped Paris. Whether it would hold or unravel would depend on the events of the next few hours, hidden beneath the city's restless heart.

—

On the 12th of Messidor, Year II (30 June 1794), Henri Moreau found himself narrowly escaping the clutches of the Revolutionary Guards during what should have been a routine procurement of printing supplies. The encounter had been too close for comfort, a stark reminder of the dangerous game he and his fellow conspirators were playing against the oppressive regime of Robespierre.

Earlier that day, Henri had ventured into a less familiar part of Paris to collect ink and paper—a mundane task that had suddenly turned perilous. As he navigated the narrow, bustling streets, he noticed a pair of guards scrutinising passersby more closely than usual. The tension in the air was palpable, and Henri's instincts screamed for caution. He quickened his pace, clutching the nondescript parcel tightly under his arm.

Just as he rounded a corner, one of the guards called out, demanding he halt and present his identification. Henri's heart pounded in his chest as he contemplated his limited options. A confrontation would be foolhardy, yet compliance might lead to a search of his parcel and discovery of the materials intended for anti-government pamphlets.

In a split second, Henri made his decision. Feigning a stumble, he dropped the parcel, and as the guards approached, he seized the moment of distraction to dash into a narrow alley. His knowledge of the city's labyrinthine backstreets, honed through countless secretive meetings and late-night escapades, now proved invaluable.

Darting through shadowed passageways and over fences, Henri's breath tore at his throat, each gasp sharp in the cool air. Behind him, the shouts of the guards grew fainter as he distanced himself from danger. Finally, after what felt like an eternity, he slipped into the cellar of a sympathetic tavern owned by a discreet supporter of Anonyme.

The incident weighed heavily on Henri in the safety of his own workshop. The encounter was a stark reminder of the increased surveillance and paranoia that permeated Paris. It was clear that their operations needed to be even more cautious. That evening, Henri convened an emergency meeting with the core members of Anonyme.

Claire, who had heard of her son's narrow escape, greeted him with a tight embrace before turning to the assembled group. "This close call shows that we must halt all physical gatherings for now," she declared, her voice firm despite the worry that earlier clouded her features. "We will move to coded correspondence only. We cannot afford another risk like today."

Henri nodded in agreement, his recent fright still chilling his spine. "We'll need to improve our security protocols," he added, addressing the group. "Each of you will receive a new cypher by the end of the week. Memorise it, then destroy the document. Do not write it down or speak of it outside these walls."

The meeting unfolded with a heightened sense of urgency. Plans were rapidly adjusted, with new measures to safeguard the members and their families. Feeling the weight of responsibility, Henri emphasised the importance of discretion and vigilance.

"We are in the heart of a storm," he said, his gaze meeting each of theirs. "But we must remain steadfast. Our cause demands courage, and our safety demands cunning."

As the group dispersed, each member left with a renewed commitment to their cause and a greater awareness of the risks involved. The revolution they were fostering was not just against the tyranny of a despot but also against the apathy of despair. Henri spent the remainder of the night reviewing their network's communication strategies, determined to ensure that their silent tide of resistance could continue to rise, undetected and unstoppable.

—

The 7th of Thermidor, Year II (25 July 1794) dawned with a sense of heavy expectancy hanging in the air as the streets of Paris whispered with the winds of change. Henri Moreau and the clandestine group he had forged in the shadows now stood on the precipice of a pivotal moment that could alter the course of the Revolution and their lives.

Throughout the past months, Henri and his mother, Claire, had meticulously orchestrated the growth of their underground network, "Anonyme," to challenge the despotic rule of Robespierre. Their careful planning and discreet manoeuvring had culminated on this day when murmurs of discontent within the government suggested that Robespierre's power might finally be waning.

In the dim light of dawn, Henri reviewed the final preparations. His small workshop, once a place of simple craft, had transformed into the nerve centre of their resistance movement. Maps of Paris, marked with strategic locations, lay spread across a table, and next to them, a stack of hastily written notes detailed last-minute communications from their allies.

Claire, ever the vigilant co-conspirator, adjusted the distribution of leaflets that critiqued Robespierre's regime without inciting direct rebellion. These were to be scattered in public squares and slipped into newspapers and pamphlets across the city. "Remember," she told the young runners, their eyes wide with a mix of fear and determination, "discretion is your shield. Move quickly and blend in."

As the clock ticked closer to midday, Henri met with his closest advisers in a back room, their faces etched with the strain of impending action. They discussed the signals from various factions within the city—signs that today, the government's grip might finally loosen enough for a significant push against the tyranny that had suffocated Paris.

"The air is ripe with revolution, once again," Henri mused aloud, his voice a low murmur. "But this time, we must steer it towards true liberty, not replace one tyrant with another."

The group nodded, understanding the weight of their task. They were not merely to act as catalysts for change but as architects of a more just system. Henri's thoughts briefly wandered to his father, Pierre, whose ideals had sown the seeds for this day. "We do this in his memory," he whispered to himself, "and for the future of our republic."

Chapter Ten

On 8 Thermidor, Year II (26 July 1794), the atmosphere in Paris was thick with tension and anticipation. The sweltering heat of summer seemed to magnify the sense of unease that permeated the streets as the citizens whispered of Maximilien Robespierre's scheduled address to the National Convention. It was a city balanced on the knife-edge of hope and fear, where the ordinary sounds of day-to-day life were overlaid with the murmurs of discontent and the rustle of secretive movements.

In the heart of this bustling metropolis, Henri Moreau, a young clockmaker by trade but a revolutionary at heart, navigated the cobbled streets with a purposeful stride. His mother, Claire, accompanied him, her presence a calming influence in the swirling chaos surrounding them. They were crucial figures in Anonyme, a clandestine group committed to dismantling Robespierre's authoritarian regime.

The day had begun early for them, in the dim light of dawn, as they meticulously prepared bundles of leaflets in the back room of their workshop. Each pamphlet was a carefully crafted piece of rebellion designed to stir the hearts and minds of those who felt crushed under the weight of the ongoing terror.

"Mother, do you think the people will heed our call today?" Henri asked, his voice low as he bundled another stack of the crisp papers. His hands were stained with ink, a testament to their morning's labour.

Claire looked up from her work, her eyes meeting his with an intensity that spoke of her unwavering commitment to their cause. "They must, Henri. The city is a tinderbox waiting for a spark. We must provide it," she replied, her voice steady despite the uncertainty ahead.

As they stepped out into the morning light, their first destination was the bustling market in the Place des Vosges. Even at this early hour, the area thrummed with activity. Vendors hawked their wares loudly, trying to drown out the undercurrent of anxious conversations that flowed around them like a hidden stream.

Henri and Claire moved discreetly through the crowd, slipping leaflets into the hands of sympathetic shopkeepers and leaving stacks tucked away in nooks where they knew they would be found by those hungry for change. Each exchange was brief, and the understanding was immediate and unspoken. Their message was clear: "Stand with us at the turning of the tide."

As they walked, the murmur of the city seemed to grow, fueled by the leaflets they had distributed. Whispers followed in their wake, a growing wave of discontent that threatened to break at any moment.

The Rue Saint-Antoine was busier, the crowd thicker. Henri's keen eyes scanned the faces they passed—faces marked by hardship and the shadow of fear that Robespierre's rule had cast over the city. Here, he felt the pulse of Paris most acutely, beating a rhythm of suppressed rage and desperate hope.

"Will they listen, Mother?" Henri asked again, handing a leaflet to a young woman who clutched it like a lifeline. The question was more to himself than to Claire, reflecting the doubt that gnawed at him despite their preparations.

"They will," Claire affirmed, her voice a soft but fierce whisper. "They must. We have laid the groundwork, Henri. Now, we must trust in the people."

Their morning's work took them across the city, from the Marais to the Latin Quarter, each step, each leaflet, another seed of revolution sown on fertile ground. By midday, the energy of the city had shifted palpably. The whispers had grown into conversations, conversations into heated discussions that spilt out from the cafes and taverns onto the streets.

As they made their way towards the Palais Royal, the epicentre of political discourse, Henri felt a stirring of hope. The Paris he knew, the Paris of artisans and workers, mothers and fathers, young and old, seemed to awaken from the enforced slumber of fear.

The stage was set, the players in motion, and as Henri and Claire blended into the crowd gathering to hear Robespierre speak, they knew today would be pivotal. Today, Paris would either rise in defiance or sink deeper into despair. But whatever the outcome, they had ignited the flame. Now, it was up to the people to fan it into a fire that would cleanse or consume.

—

As the 8th of Thermidor, Year II (26 July 1794) unfolded, the palpable tension that permeated the National Convention only intensified. The hall, a grand chamber within the Tuileries Palace, was awash with a sea of deputies, their faces etched with concern and suspicion. The room buzzed with whispered strategies and wary glances as everyone awaited Robespierre's much-anticipated address. Among the spectators in the crowded public gallery stood Henri and his mother, Claire. They blended seamlessly with the rest, their expressions masked with the same cautious anticipation that filled the air.

Keenly observant, Henri noted the shifting dynamics within the hall as crucial figures of the Convention exchanged covert nods and silent messages. The political theatre was not lost on him; it was a dance of power and fear, each player acutely aware of the stakes.

"Citizens," Robespierre began, his voice resonating through the hall, commanding immediate silence. His presence was imposing, his gaze sweeping the assembly with an unsettling mix of paranoia and authority. "The Republic is at peril from within. Conspiracies weave their threads through the very fabric of our society, sown by the enemies of freedom."

As Robespierre's speech unfolded, Henri felt Claire's subtle grip on his arm tightens. Her concern was evident; the speech was more than just rhetoric—it was a veiled warning, perhaps even a prelude to another purge. Robespierre's words, draped in patriotism, spoke of unseen enemies and the need for vigilance and sacrifice. The underlying message was clear: trust was a commodity as scarce as peace.

"We cannot falter in our vigilance," Robespierre continued, his tone escalating fervently. "The Revolution must defend itself against all who would see it undone, even if they hide within our ranks."

Henri exchanged a look with Claire. They both understood the gravity of the moment; Robespierre was stoking the fires of fear, possibly to justify his next wave of terror. The assembly responded with genuine applause and murmured dissent—a discordant symphony mirrored the Republic's fractured state.

As the applause slowly faded into a buzz of whispers and unsettled murmurs, Henri leaned towards his mother, his voice low and urgent. "Robespierre's response is excessive; the public won't tolerate another wave of purges. It's time for Anonyme to act."

Claire nodded, her eyes scanning the room for allies and potential threats. "Watch the ones who are too enthusiastic in their applause. They're either true believers or the most dangerous kind of opportunists."

The speech ended with Robespierre's call for unity and strength, but the words felt more like shackles than a rallying cry. As the assembly dispersed, the atmosphere was charged with a volatile blend of fear and defiance.

Henri and Claire lingered in the gallery, observing the departing deputies. Their plan needed adjustment in light of Robespierre's ominous address. They needed to balance caution and action, aware that any misstep could lead to disaster.

"The whispers we've sown will soon bear fruit," Claire said quietly as they exited the hall. "Let's make sure we're ready when they do."

The streets of Paris, under the midday sun, seemed to pulse with the unrest stirred within the Convention's walls. Henri and Claire made their way through the crowds of people, each step taking them deeper into the heart of a city on the brink of another upheaval.

Their next task was straightforward: rally their network, strengthen their resolve, and prepare for the night ahead. The leaflets they had distributed earlier were already igniting discussions and debates in cafes and street corners across Paris. The seeds of dissent germinated, fed by the growing discontent with Robespierre's reign.

As they walked, the echoes of Robespierre's speech lingered in their minds, a reminder of the delicate line they walked. Henri felt the weight of their cause pressing down on him, a burden he bore with a resolve forged in the fires of past struggles.

Tonight, they would meet with the core of Anonyme to plan, strategise, and kindle the flames of revolution. The city that had once risen to overthrow a king was now poised to reclaim its freedom from a tyrant who had once been its champion. The irony was not lost on Henri; it was a stark reminder that the fight for liberty was never truly over, merely passed like a torch from one generation to the next.

—

The clock struck late into the evening of 8 Thermidor, Year II (26 July 1794), as Henri and Claire navigated through the dimly lit streets of Paris, their shadows merging with the darkness that enveloped the city. The tension from the day's events at the National Convention lingered in the air, thick as the fog that rolled off the Seine. The whispered words of Maximilien Robespierre had set the wheels of fear and suspicion in motion, but for Henri and Claire, these hours were for preparation, not paranoia.

They reached their safe house, an unassuming building tucked away in a less frequented part of Marais. The wooden door creaked softly as they entered, the sound starkly contrasting the quiet determination that filled the room. Inside, the dim glow of candles cast long shadows on the walls, illuminating the faces of the few trusted members of Anonyme who had already gathered.

Henri addressed the room, his voice low but persistent. "Tonight, we mobilise our efforts. Robespierre's speech today has only confirmed what we feared—he's preparing to strike out against us, to silence any dissent. We must act swiftly to spread our message further."

Claire unfolded a map across the wooden table, her fingers tracing the routes their couriers would take. "We've prepared a new batch of leaflets—more provocative, designed to awaken those still swayed by Robespierre's rhetoric. These must be distributed before dawn."

The room buzzed with a quiet intensity as plans were drawn. Every member knew their part; the stakes of their clandestine efforts mirrored in the grim set of their jaws. Henri and Claire, with practised precision, delegated tasks, pairing couriers with routes that exploited their knowledge of Paris's labyrinthine alleys.

As the group dispersed, Henri pulled aside a young man named Luc, whose agility and stealth had proven invaluable in past missions. "Luc, take the northern district. It's heavily patrolled, but your familiarity with it is unmatched. Be cautious—the night is friend and foe alike."

Luc nodded the weight of his assignment clear on his young face. "I won't fail you," he said, determination lining his voice, the maps etched in his mind providing a silent guide through the city's heart.

Meanwhile, Claire prepared small packages of leaflets, her hands steady despite the fatigue that edged her movements. Each packet was a potential spark for the fire they hoped to ignite—a fire that would cleanse Paris of the tyranny that threatened to choke its soul.

Henri watched his mother, pride and worry mingling in his chest. "Be careful, Mother," he said softly, his voice barely a whisper over the rustle of paper.

Claire looked up, a smile touching her lips despite the gravity of their situation. "We are beyond the reach of careful, my son. Now, we must be bold."

They worked through the night, the candlelight flickering as if in rhythm with their racing hearts. Outside, the streets of Paris lay quiet, the oppressive silence a stark canvas awaiting the dawn's chaos.

As the first light of morning tinged the horizon with grey, Henri and Claire stepped out into the cool air, their cloaks pulled tight against the chill. The city that awaited them was a different Paris than the one they had left the night before—one teetering on the edge of revolution, its fate intertwined with the success of their night's endeavours.

As the first light of morning painted the streets of Paris, Henri and Claire merged into the awakening city, their actions deliberate and discreet. They circulated among the burgeoning crowd, subtly distributing leaflets. Each piece bore excerpts from Robespierre's speeches, ingeniously repurposed to illuminate his tyranny and rally the citizens to their cause. The leaflets found their way under café tables, slipped inside newspapers, and left on benches—silent heralds of the brewing storm, urging the populace to see the urgency of ending his reign.

By the time the sun fully rose, casting a golden glow over the city's rooftops, Henri and Claire's part was done. They retreated to the shadows again, their hearts heavy with hope and fear. The revolution they sought was no longer a distant dream but a palpable reality, its success hinging on the hearts and minds of a city that had endured too much.

As they vanished into the maze of streets, the leaflets they left behind fluttered like the wings of doves, each one a bearer of the dawn's new light, a call to arms for those who yearned to breathe free. The day of reckoning was upon them, and Paris, once the stage of kings, would now decide the fate of its tyrant.

—

As dawn cast its first grey light over Paris on 9 Thermidor, Year II (27 July 1794), Henri Moreau was already standing by the window of his small room in their current safe house. The risk of returning home had become too great after the events they had set in motion. He watched the city awaken; the streets below were quiet, but this silence was deceptive—it was the calm before the storm that Henri knew was inevitable.

Claire was in the kitchen, the clink of porcelain and the smell of brewing coffee filling the small flat with mundane sounds and smells that belied the tension between them. Today would be decisive, and both mother and son were acutely aware of the dangers they would face.

Henri turned as Claire entered the room with a steaming cup. Her eyes, usually so calm and commanding, flickered with the same nervous energy that Henri felt pulsing in his veins. She handed him the coffee, her hand brushing his briefly—a touch that spoke of comfort and warning.

"Today, we'll see the fruits of our labour," she said, her voice steady but her face pale in the early morning light. "The leaflets have been spread, and the whispers of dissent are growing louder. We must be prepared to guide when the people are ready to act."

Henri nodded, sipping the coffee, its bitterness a sharp reminder of the task ahead. "The streets will be dangerous," he replied, setting the cup down and meeting his mother's gaze. "Robespierre's supporters are not just the zealots at the Convention. They're in every district, every quarter. We'll need to be cautious."

Claire moved to the window, her eyes scanning the horizon. "Our allies are in place across the city. From the Faubourg Saint-Antoine to the Palais-Royal, every word we've sown will start to take root. We must ensure that it leads not to blind chaos but to a revolution that will rebuild, not just destroy."

As they prepared to leave, Henri checked his pistol, a necessary precaution he wished he didn't have to consider. Claire watched him, her expression hardening. "Remember, we are not just fighting for freedom from Robespierre's tyranny. We are fighting for a new France. Every action we take today must reflect that."

They left their flat as the city began to stir, joining the flow of citizens heading towards the heart of Paris. The tension in the air was palpable, a mix of fear and anticipation that charged the atmosphere like electricity before a storm.

Their first stop was a small printing shop in an alley off Rue Montorgueil, where they met with several members of Anonyme. The shop was cramped and dim, the air thick with the smell of ink and paper. The owner, a stout man named Georges, greeted them with a nod, his face grim.

"We've printed another thousand leaflets," he informed them, gesturing to the stacks of paper that lined the walls. "They're ready to be distributed."

Henri helped load several bundles into a cart waiting outside. The streets were filling up now, the crowd's murmur a constant backdrop as the city woke to another day of unrest.

As they dispersed to their various tasks, Henri felt the weight of his responsibility settles on his shoulders. Today, his actions could change the course of his city and country. He wasn't just a clockmaker anymore; he was a revolutionary, fighting not just against a tyrant but for an ideal.

Throughout the morning, Henri and Claire moved through the city, from the bustling markets of Les Halles to the quieter, more residential streets of the Marais, each step taking them further into the heart of the unfolding revolution. The seeds of discontent they had sown everywhere were sprouting, visible in the discussions at cafés and the furtive exchanges between citizens.

As the clock struck midday, the tension in the crowd had built to an almost palpable intensity. Henri was at the centre of a restless crowd near the Hôtel de Ville, surrounded by a chorus of passionate voices filled with anger and hope. Seizing the moment, he stepped up onto a nearby cart, drawing all eyes to him. His decision to enter the spotlight was fraught with risk, fully aware of the dire consequences should their movement falter.

"Citizens of Paris!" Henri called out, his voice carrying over the crowd. "Today, we stand at the brink of a new dawn! Today, we can cast off the chains of fear and oppression! Join us, and let us reclaim our city, our liberty!"

The response was immediate and electrifying. Shouts of agreement rose from the crowd, a solidarity wave sweeping through the streets. Henri stepped down from the cart, his heart pounding with adrenaline and hope. Beside him, Claire smiled, her eyes shining with tears and pride.

Together, they moved through the crowd, their spirits buoyed by the knowledge that they were no longer alone in their fight. Paris was rising, and they were at the heart of its awakening.

—

As 9 Thermidor progressed, the atmosphere in Paris had grown tumultuous as the sun climbed higher in the sky. The streets hummed with anticipation and dread, resonating with the enthusiasm of revolutionaries and the anxious whispers of the wary. Henri Moreau and his mother, Claire, now found themselves in the city's pulsing heart, outside the stoic façade of the National Convention.

Henri, cloaked in the nondescript garb of the common Parisian but with eyes that burned with revolutionary zeal, wove through the growing crowd. Beside him, Claire's composed demeanour belied the torrent of strategies and contingencies swirling in her mind. Each step they took was calculated to stir the crowd further towards action.

Within the crowd, dissent had turned into loud conversations about change and justice. Henri and Claire stopped near a large gathering where a street orator passionately voiced grievances against Robespierre's reign of terror. Henri listened intently, gauging the mood, and then stepped forward, ready to escalate the spirit of rebellion into outright defiance.

"Citizens!" Henri's voice cut through the murmur like a blade, drawing eyes towards him. "How long shall we live under the shadow of a tyrant? Robespierre claims to protect the revolution, but who shall protect us from him?"

Murmurs of agreement bubbled up from the crowd, and Claire watched with a sharp eye as the faces around them flickered with the fire of rebellion. She nudged Henri, nodding subtly towards a group of agitated young men who looked ready to take up the cause.

As the day progressed, the weariness from continuous vigilance under the Reign of Terror evaporated, replaced by the energising spirit of a renewed revolutionary zeal. Standing elevated on a makeshift platform, Henri's voice carried across the square, "We are told to guard against enemies of the state, but he has turned the Republic into his dominion. We must rise, not just to safeguard our lives, but for the very essence of France!" His words resonated deeply, sparking an immediate response. The crowd's reaction was spirited and enthusiastic, their collective energy now a formidable force ready to confront the structures of tyranny.

Claire and a select group of trusted Anonyme members fanned out through the crowd, each step and whisper part of a carefully orchestrated plan they had anticipated for days. Their words, seeded with the ideals of liberty and justice, were sparks setting aflame the dry tinder of the populace's deep-seated rage against Robespierre's despotic rule. Each phrase was a calculated thrust, pushing the gathered Parisians towards the brink of action—a deliberate crescendo to ignite the moment of revolt.

As the crowd's anger peaked, the doors of the National Convention burst open. A group of deputies faces drawn and anxious, stepped out onto the steps, their appearance in stark contrast to the seething mass before them. One of them, a man known for eloquence, raised his hands, calling for silence.

"People of Paris!" he shouted, trying to be heard over the din. "We hear your cries; we know your sufferings! The Convention is not blind to the injustices that plague our Republic!"

His words, meant to soothe, only stoked the fires higher. Henri used the moment to solidify the crowd's resolve. "They hear us, yes, but will they act? Or will they placate us with promises as they have done before?"

As the shouts began to crescendo, the square filled with a tumultuous blend of voices. Some were spontaneous outbursts from the gathered public, fueled by the charged atmosphere and shared rhetoric. Others, meticulously planned, came from the members of Anonyme, strategically positioned throughout the crowd to stir the unrest further.

"No more promises!" a woman near the front shouted, her voice clear and robust across the crowd, capturing the collective sentiment of frustration and desire for change.

Echoing her, another voice rose, "No more tyranny!" This call resonated deeply, voiced by another member of Anonyme, weaving through the crowd's rising tide of discontent.

Henri and Claire exchanged a glance, a silent communication between them that now was the critical moment. Henri clambered atop a nearby cart, his figure now raised above the crowd, visible to all.

"This day," Henri proclaimed, his gaze sweeping over the crowd, "will be remembered as the day we reclaimed our revolution! Follow us, not to destruction, but to build a new foundation for France—one of true liberty and justice!"

The response was overwhelming. The crowd surged forward, a massive force converging on the doors of the National Convention. Inside, the deputies scrambled, their earlier composure shattered by the undeniable power of the people united.

As the first stone was thrown, shattering the calm with the sound of breaking glass, Henri jumped down from the cart, Claire at his side. Together, they led the charge, not just in physical space but as symbols of a people's revolution reborn in the fire of righteous indignation. Their voices merged with the cries around them, a chorus of defiance and hope that would echo through the history of France.

—

As the day progressed into the late hours of 9 Thermidor, Year II (27 July 1794), the energy of Paris remained unyielding. The sun began to set, casting long shadows over the cobblestoned streets, but the passion that had seized the city showed no sign of waning. Henri Moreau and his mother Claire, the silent architects of this burgeoning revolution, found themselves at the heart of a movement swiftly gaining momentum.

The streets near the National Convention were packed, a sea of bodies moving as one organism, chanting and calling for justice. With his mother Claire at his side, Henri moved through the crowd, their purpose clear. Each interaction, every shouted slogan, was a carefully placed thread in the fabric of their plan.

With her keen strategist's mind, Claire directed their followers with a series of subtle signals. Her experience navigating the treacherous waters of political intrigue allowed her to anticipate the responses of the Convention's guards. She knew that the real battle was not just against the stone walls of government buildings but against the complacency and fear that had held the city in its grip.

As they approached a makeshift barricade, Henri climbed atop, his figure illuminated by the flickering light of torches. He looked out over the crowd, his heart swelling with pride and gravity.

Throughout the crowd, members of Anonyme had carefully prepared for this pivotal moment, strategically positioning themselves to turn the attention of the assembled Parisians towards Henri as he climbed onto a makeshift platform. Their coordinated effort was crucial, directing the energy of the gathering towards a singular focal point, transforming Henri into a symbol of the collective desire for freedom from oppression.

"Friends, patriots!" Henri's voice rang out, clear and compelling against murmurs and restless movements. "This night is ours to challenge tyranny and affirm our commitment to liberty, equality, and fraternity. We do not seek vengeance but the restoration of a Republic that serves all its people!"

His words, amplified by the strategic placement and subtle cues from Anonyme members, resonated through the crowd, turning individual frustrations and isolated dissent into a unified call for change. The atmosphere, electric with the potential for pivotal change, was charged with a renewed sense of purpose and possibility.

The response was electric. Cheers erupted, and the air was thick with renewed determination. The crowd, encouraged by Henri's words, pressed forward, their chants becoming a mighty chorus that resonated through the evening air.

Meanwhile, Claire manoeuvred through the crowd, her eyes sharp for any sign of retaliation from the Convention's guards. She approached a group of young men eagerly discussing their plan's next phase.

"Keep your focus," Claire advised them, her voice firm yet inspiring. "Remember, we win not when we overpower our enemies, but when we convince them and the onlookers of the justice of our cause."

Her words were calming, and the men nodded, visibly organising themselves with more discipline.

As the crowd's murmurs turned into a resonant thrum, Henri, standing defiantly atop an improvised platform, took in the sea of faces before him. It was a moment charged with the potential of what could be—a pivotal night under the stars of Paris, where hope could be rekindled or extinguished.

"Tonight," Henri began, his voice carrying across the gathered masses, "we stand on the precipice of change. We gather not for battle but for enlightenment, not to spill blood but to reclaim the heart of our Republic. Our movement is born from the will of the people, tempered by the lessons of the past. It is a delicate balance we strike this evening."

He paused, letting the weight of his words sink in, then continued with a clarity that cut through the chilly night air. "We seek to awaken the spirit of liberty, equality, and fraternity—that which the Revolution promised but has been denied by those seeking to suppress it. Let us move forward with a measured and mindful resolve, ensuring that our actions tonight reflect our desires for freedom and our commitment to peace."

The crowd, stirred by Henri's oratory, buzzed with renewed energy. Here was a leader who spoke not just of change but of cautious revolution, a man who understood the razor's edge upon which they all now stood.

Back at the barricades, the atmosphere was charged with a heady mix of fear and exhilaration. The crowd watched anxiously as a line of guards appeared at the entrance of the Convention. The stand-off that ensued was tense, with both sides uncertain of the other's intentions.

It was Henri who broke the stalemate. Stepping forward into the open space between the crowds and the guards, he raised his hands, a universal gesture of peace.

"We come not for blood but for justice!" Henri called out, his voice steady and commanding. "We stand for all who have suffered under oppression!"

One of the guards, a young man with a face too weary for his years, locked eyes with Henri. After a moment that stretched out like a tightrope, the guard slowly lowered his weapon, his actions rippling through his comrades.

The crowd erupted in a mixture of relief and jubilation. Cheers and applause filled the air, drowning out the clatter of weapons being set aside. Henri turned to the crowd, his face reflecting both the weight of the moment and the hope it represented.

As the impromptu celebration grew, Claire stayed vigilant, her eyes scanning the surroundings for any sign of backlash. But as the night wore on, it became clear that the tide had turned. The people of Paris had spoken, not just with their voices but with their presence and resolve.

Henri and Claire, standing amidst the crowd of their fellow citizens, knew that the events of this day would echo through history. They had ignited a spark that could potentially reshape the nation—not by violence but by the shared desire of a people for a fair and accessible society. The revolution had been reborn, not in the shadow of the guillotine, but in the light of the ideals it had initially been promised.

—

As dawn approached on 10 Thermidor, Year II (28 July 1794), the streets of Paris, previously alive with the powderkeg of a city on the cusp of change, now lay in a suspenseful calm. The previous day's events had set a fire in the hearts of its citizens, a fire that the morning light could not dispel. After a night of little rest, Henri Moreau and his mother Claire stood before the imposing structure of the Hôtel de Ville. In this stronghold, Robespierre and his remaining loyalists had barricaded themselves.

The building stood defiant against the pale sky, its aged stones whispering histories of Paris that had seen many such dawns. The air was crisp, charged with the electric buzz of anticipation. Today would be pivotal, Henri knew. Today, the revolution could teeter on the edge of victory or spiral back into chaos.

Claire, her face showing the strain of relentless nights yet, with a resolve that seemed to strengthen with each challenge, addressed the small group of Anonyme members and guardsmen who had rallied to their cause. They gathered in the shadow of the old city hall, united by the people's will to support them.

"We strike at first light," she instructed her voice a soft yet penetrating whisper that carried more authority than any shout. "Robespierre's forces are dwindling, cornered but dangerous. Remember, we aim to capture, not to kill. We end this with honour."

Standing beside her, Henri surveyed their group's faces, each set with determination. These were not soldiers by training but citizens by choice, each drawn into the vortex of revolution by the gravity of their convictions. Henri felt a kinship with these men and women, a bond forged in the furnace of shared ideals.

As the first rays of sunlight touched the tips of Parisian rooftops, casting long shadows down the narrow streets, Henri led a contingent towards the main entrance of the Hôtel de Ville. Their approach was silent, a ghostly procession amidst the morning fog, their movements calculated and precise.

The door loomed at the front of the building, unyielding and foreboding. Henri paused, his hand on the cold metal, feeling the weight of history push back against him. With a nod from Claire, he went forward, the door giving way with a groan that seemed to echo through the ages.

The interior of the Hôtel de Ville was a labyrinth of corridors and staircases, each turn and shadow potentially hiding an enemy. Henri and his group moved cautiously, their footsteps a soft patter against the stone floors. With another team, Claire took a side entrance, her strategy to surround and squeeze the loyalists gently but firmly.

The building was eerily silent; the only sounds were the distant shouts from outside and the occasional scuffle as they encountered small pockets of resistance. These were quickly and quietly subdued, the loyalists too surprised and outnumbered to mount any adequate defence.

Henri's heart raced as they ascended towards the upper floors. Each step took them closer to their quarry, to the man who had once been their leader, now their foe. The air grew heavier, the musty smell of old paper and forgotten promises filling their lungs.

Finally, they arrived at the main chamber. The door was slightly open, casting light into the dimly lit hallway. Henri paused to listen to the desperate, heated arguments coming from inside. Taking a deep breath, he pushed the door open and stepped into the room, projecting an assertive calm. Flanking him were two guardsmen who had joined their cause, their presence a silent testament to the moment's seriousness.

The chamber was a vivid tableau of chaos. Maps and papers were strewn across every surface, creating a disordered landscape. As they entered, a handful of men turned, their faces etched with surprise and fear. In the centre stood Robespierre, embodying the image of a man confronted by his inescapable fate. His face bore a gruesome wound

—a botched suicide attempt from the previous night had left his jaw injured. In his expression, there was the unmistakable mark of defeat.

"You are surrounded," Henri announced, his voice steady. "Lay down your arms. There's no need for further bloodshed."

Robespierre's eyes met Henri's, and for a moment, there was a flicker of something like recognition, a shared memory of a revolution that had once promised so much.

Grimacing with pain, Robespierre, his jaw visibly disfigured, struggled to utter, "Henri Moreau," before managing to add, "So it ends with you."

"It ends with justice," Henri replied. "Not vengeance. Surrender, and you will be treated with the honour due to any citizen of France."

The room fell silent, the tension a tangible shroud. Slowly, achingly, Robespierre nodded, his shoulders slumping as he released his last weapon. A small pistol clattered to the floor, its sound a knell of finality.

As Henri's team secured the room, Claire entered, her presence reassuring. Together, they watched as the sun fully rose over Paris, its light not just a herald of a new day but a beacon for a new era.

The arrest of Robespierre was a culmination of months of mounting discontent and political manoeuvring. His address on the 8th of Thermidor had backfired spectacularly. Instead of rallying support, it had alienated many of his former allies. By speaking generally about the threats to the Republic, Robespierre failed to name specific enemies, casting a shadow of suspicion over the entire Convention.

This vagueness created a sense of imminent danger among the deputies; many feared they might be next on the list of traitors.

Figures such as Tallien, Billaud-Varenne, and Collot d'Herbois seized the moment to galvanise their efforts against him. The following day, Robespierre and his closest supporters found himself arrested. His speech had inadvertently united his enemies and sparked the events that would lead to his execution and the end of the Reign of Terror.

Henri and Claire had worked tirelessly with their resistance group, Anonyme, to bring about this moment. Their clandestine meetings with Convention and National Guard members had forged a fragile yet necessary alliance. They understood that only a coordinated effort could successfully challenge Robespierre's grip on power. The address of the 8th of Thermidor was a catalyst. It turned apprehensive whispers into decisive actions, uniting disparate factions in a common cause against tyranny.

Henri and Claire's collaboration with the guards and Convention members was instrumental. They planned meticulously, using their network to gather intelligence and orchestrate the arrest. Their strategy was to strike at the heart of Robespierre's stronghold, the Hôtel de Ville, ensuring a swift and decisive blow. This coordination was crucial in overcoming the loyalists' resistance and minimising casualties.

For Henri and Claire, the address was a stark reminder of the unpredictable nature of revolutionary politics. It underscored the need for vigilance and adaptability, traits crucial in the turbulent days ahead. As the sun set on Paris, the Moreaus prepared for the next chapter in their struggle, knowing that the fall of one tyrant did not guarantee the rise of a just and lasting peace.

—

The morning of 10 Thermidor, Year II (28 July 1794), unfolded with a palpable sense of finality over Paris. The shadows that had clung to the streets during the night's turmoil began to dissipate, chased away by the bold strokes of the rising sun. Within the walls of the Hôtel de Ville, the aftermath of the siege left a heavy silence—a silence that spoke louder than the clamours of conflict that had filled the air mere hours before.

In the quiet of the conquered hall, Henri Moreau watched as Robespierre, now a shadow of the formidable figure he once was, was led away by a group of Anonyme members. The revolutionary leader's steps were unsteady, and his figure diminished due to physical injury and the immense weight of his fall from power. Henri's gaze lingered on the man who had once inspired such chaos and fear across France. Now, Robespierre looked merely human, his ideals undone by his extremism.

Claire Fontaine stood beside her son, her presence a steady force amid so much uncertainty. She observed the proceedings with a critical eye, aware of the significance of their actions not only for their immediate future but for the historical record.

"This is a pivotal moment, Henri," Claire murmured, her voice barely rising above a whisper. "How we handle the aftermath will shape the Republic's path forward."

Henri nodded, his thoughts aligning with his mother's. "We must ensure that justice, not vengeance, guides us. Robespierre's trial must be fair, a testament to the principles we fought for."

Outside, the city was stirring, the populace awakening to the news that the tide of the Revolution had turned once more. Word of Robespierre's capture and the success of Anonyme spread rapidly, a current of relief mingling with the undercurrents of ongoing fear and suspicion.

As they exited the Hôtel de Ville, Henri and Claire were met with the sight of Parisians gathering in the streets, their faces marked by joy and exhaustion. The air was filled with a cacophony of voices—cries of triumph, impromptu discussions about the future, and the persistent hum of a city too long accustomed to turmoil.

Henri felt a pull in his chest as he and Claire entered the crowd. Every shout, every cheer for Anonyme, underscored the weight of responsibility now resting on their shoulders. They were no longer mere insurgents fighting a tyrant; they were leaders in a city desperate for direction and healing.

In a quiet square, away from the crowd, Claire stopped to address a small gathering of citizens who recognised her from Anonyme's spread leaflets.

"Fellow Parisians," she began, her voice firm, carrying through the morning air, "today marks a new dawn for our Republic. But let it be a dawn of peace, of justice. We must not replace one tyranny with another."

Her words seemed to resonate, calming some of the rawer emotions in the crowd. People nodded, their expressions thoughtful, as they digested the weight of her message.

Henri took up the thread of his mother's discourse, his youthful energy tempered by the gravity of his experiences. "We stand at a crossroads," he declared. "Let us choose the path of liberty and law. Let our Revolution finally honour its promise to all citizens, not just those with power."

Their speeches, impromptu yet impassioned, served as a salve to the wounds of a battered city. As they spoke, the crowd grew, drawn by their words and the promise of stability they represented.

After addressing the gathering, Henri and Claire continued their walk through the streets of Paris, taking them past landmarks that bore the scars of the Revolution's darker days. They passed walls still plastered with faded posters proclaiming liberty, equality, and fraternity—ideals tested in the fires of conflict and chaos.

The morning wore on, and as they walked, they discussed their next moves—forming a provisional government, organising fair trials for Robespierre and his associates, and restoring public trust.

"We have a long road ahead, Henri," Claire said, her gaze taking in the sweep of the city around them. "But today, we begin to mend what was broken."

"Yes," Henri agreed, a persistent note in his voice. "Today, we build anew."

Their discussion, muted amid the broader chaos, was a subtle yet powerful signal of change—a reflection of a nation desperately clawing out of the shadows of the Reign of Terror. Paris thrummed with the pulse of a revolution reborn, centred around Henri and Claire Moreau. As they stood ready to steer their people towards a future grounded in the freedoms they had championed, their voices merged with the collective cry for justice and reform. Now, as the fate of Robespierre hung in the balance, dictated by the will of the populace, Anonyme's influence was one voice in the complex chorus of a country scarred yet spirited, hopeful yet cautious.

—

By midday on 10 Thermidor, Year II (28 July 1794), as Robespierre and his closest allies, including Saint-Just and Couthon, were led to the Place de la Révolution, the overwhelming surge of public sentiment was beyond what Henri, Claire, and the members of Anonyme could moderate. They had advocated for fair trials, but the collective trauma and fury unleashed by the Reign of Terror spurred the crowd to demand swift, visceral justice. The site, once a hub of vibrant discourse and trade, had transformed into a stark symbol of political retribution, its air now heavy with the sad anticipation of executions.

Amid the gathering, Henri Moreau and Claire observed not just the imminent executions but the broader public reaction, a complex tapestry of relief, vindication, and foreboding. Despite their emotional push for systemic change, the sight of Robespierre, diminished and bandaged from a botched suicide attempt, did not satisfy them. Instead, it underscored the grim realities of revolutionary zeal turning cannibalistic.

Claire, consistently the more stoic, felt the moment's gravity, recognising its historical weight but also the fragile hope of a new beginning it represented. She knew well the deep-seated roots of tyranny that wouldn't be easily eradicated with the fall of a few leaders.

Henri, his instincts honed from years of navigating revolutionary politics, whispered to Claire amidst the tumult, "Mother, will this truly mend our Republic?"

Claire's response was tinged with wisdom and caution, "It marks an end to overt terror, Henri, but it's merely the start of another chapter of rebuilding and healing. True change requires more than removing tyrants—a steadfast commitment to the principles of liberty and justice."

As the guillotine's blade fell, sealing the fate of Robespierre and his deputies, the crowd's reaction—a cacophony of cheers and gasps—reflected not just the release of pent-up emotions but also the anxious uncertainty about what lay ahead.

Henri and Claire did not join the cheers. They watched solemnly as Robespierre's life ended, the finality of the moment marking the undeniable conclusion of his reign of terror. Henri felt relief and a profound, unsettling question about the future. Having dedicated so much of his life to this moment, he pondered his role in the new world they had fought to achieve.

As the crowd began to disperse, shifting from collective catharsis to individual reflection, people left the square in small, thoughtful groups, discussing the implications of what had occurred and what it meant for their future.

Claire gently touched Henri's arm, signalling it was time to leave. They walked away from the square, their steps slow, each lost in their thoughts.

The streets of Paris, though quieter now, still resonated with the energy of change. Henri and Claire passed walls where the morning's leaflets fluttered in the breeze, silent witnesses to the enduring power of words and will.

As they walked, they discussed what came next—for themselves and France. "We need to ensure the Republic doesn't falter into chaos," Henri mused, his voice low.

Claire nodded, her thoughts echoing his. "We'll need to be vigilant, Henri. We cut down a tyrant today, but tomorrow, we must cultivate liberty."

Their conversation was a steady stream of strategy and philosophy as they debated ideas for safeguarding the fragile democracy they hoped to build, aware that the real work was beginning.

When they returned to their quarters, the sun was lower in the sky, casting long shadows on the cobbled streets that had witnessed so much history. Inside, they sat down to draft plans, reach out to their contacts, and prepare for the coming days.

Outside, Paris continued to buzz with the news of Robespierre's execution. But inside the small, modest room where Henri and Claire planned their next moves, the focus was firmly on the future—a future they hoped would be defined not by the shadow of the guillotine but by the light of liberty they had fought so hard to secure.

As the days of Thermidor unfolded, the atmosphere in Paris shifted palpably. From the 11th to the 22nd of Thermidor, Year II (29 July - 10 August 1794), the city seemed to be holding its breath, waiting for what the new dawn would bring. The fall of Robespierre had left a vacuum that was filled with both uncertainty and opportunity. In this transformative period, Henri Moreau and Claire found themselves reconsidering the role of Anonyme in this new era.

In the subdued light of their workshop, which had long served as the nerve centre for their secretive operations, Henri and Claire were deep in discussion. Maps and papers were strewn across the table, but these were no longer extended plans for covert actions; they were civic engagement and reform proposals.

"Mother, we've spent so long in the shadows; it feels almost alien to step into the light," Henri remarked, his fingers tracing the lines of a draft for a new civic education programme. "But it's necessary. The people must be informed and involved to ensure the Republic thrives."

Claire looked up from a list of potential candidates for a proposed advisory council. "Indeed, Henri. The real revolution begins now—not with weapons, but with words and wills united for the common good. We must be educators and facilitators, helping to guide our fellow citizens towards a more participatory form of government."

Their conversation was interrupted by a knock at the door. Marianne entered her presence, constantly reminded of the youthful energy that had fuelled their movement. She brought with her the pulse of the city—the concerns, the hopes, and the rumbling undercurrents of a populace eager to shape their future.

"Henri, Claire, there's a gathering at the Place de la République," Marianne reported. "People are confused, some are afraid. They're looking for direction, assurance that the terror is over and that what comes next will be better."

Claire exchanged a glance with Henri, a silent agreement passing between them. "Thank you, Marianne. We'll go. They must see us not as orchestrators from the shadows but as fellow citizens committed to the Republic."

Dressing in plain attire, Henri and Claire set out for the square, blending into the crowd. Voices raised in debate filled the air, a vibrant tapestry of ideas and emotions. As they moved through the crowd, listening and occasionally speaking, Henri felt a profound connection to these people, his people, in a way he had never felt while hidden behind the mask of Anonyme.

One particularly heated debate caught his attention. A small group was arguing about the role of the government in regulating trade. Seeing an opportunity, Henri stepped into the circle.

"Consider this," Henri began, drawing on his own experiences of cause and effect as a clockmaker. "If the government imposes too many restrictions, it stifles innovation and growth. Yet, without any oversight, the market can become a place of exploitation rather than competition."

The crowd listened, intrigued by his practical perspective. Henri continued, weaving in principles of fairness and equity, his words bridging the gap between idealism and practicality.

As the debate wound, Henri and Claire continued to mingle, answering questions, offering reassurances, and, most importantly, listening. They stayed until the square began to empty, the setting sun casting long shadows over the cobblestones.

Walking back through the quiet streets, Claire spoke thoughtfully. "Today was important, Henri. We helped to calm fears and spark hope. But there's so much more to do."

Henri nodded his thoughts on the road ahead. "I know. But today, he reminded me that we're not alone in this. The city, the people—they're ready to be part of something greater. We need to keep the dialogue open, keep the momentum going."

Back at their workshop, as they stored away their papers and plans, the mood was contemplative but hopeful. They were no longer just survivors of a dark time; they were shapers of a brighter future. As each day passed, Henri Moreau and his mother, Claire, continued to stand with their city, guiding, supporting, and participating in the grand experiment of democracy just beginning to unfold in the heart of Paris.

—

In the days following Robespierre's fall, Paris seemed to awaken as if from a long slumber. As the French Republican Calendar ticked from 10 Thermidor, Year II (28 July 1794) onwards, Henri Moreau and his mother Claire navigated a landscape brimming with hope yet tinged with uncertainty. Streets once shadowed by fear of spies and the swift justice of the guillotine now buzzed with lively discussions and debates about the future.

One late afternoon, with the sun casting golden hues across the rooftops, Henri and Claire strolled through the bustling Place de la Révolution. This square, previously silenced under Robespierre's regime, was now vibrant with the spirit of debate, reflecting the newfound freedom of speech. As they walked, Henri absorbed the myriad ideas and concerns voiced by his fellow Parisians, deeply engrossed in thought until a familiar voice interrupted him.

"Moreau, what will Anonyme do now? With Robespierre gone, what's left for your shadowy brigade?" It was Lucien, a former member of the Commune and a regular in political debates.

Henri responded with a slight smile, "Anonyme was never just about a single man or tyrant, Lucien. Our fight is for justice, a Republic that embodies the ideals of liberty, equality, and fraternity. Our work continues." Claire, joining in, added, "The fall of a tyrant doesn't spell the end of tyranny. We must remain vigilant to ensure that what replaces Robespierre is not simply another form of oppression."

Their dialogue quickly drew a small crowd, eager to hear from those who had played a role in the recent upheaval. Henri spoke passionately about the need for ongoing public vigilance and active governmental participation.

"We must all be guardians of our liberty," Henri declared, his voice unmistakable. "Every citizen has a role in shaping our country's future. We must educate, engage, and, most importantly, empower the commoner to have a voice in government."

Nods and murmurs of agreement rippled through the crowd as the discussion shifted to practical steps. Suggestions for local councils to enhance civic duty education and the establishment of a free press were all eagerly debated.

Claire watched her son with pride and concern as the conversation wound down. She knew the road ahead would be fraught with challenges, but she also believed in Henri's ability to help steer their city into this new era. As they walked home in the fading light, she spoke softly, "Henri, remember that power can corrupt as subtly as it can overtly. We must focus not only on changing structures but also on nurturing integrity and humility."

Henri nodded, acknowledging the depth of her words, "I understand, Mother. We will set examples, not just make promises. Anonyme will evolve, from the shadows into the light, to guide, not govern."

At *Moreau Horlogerie*, which doubled as a workshop and Anonyme's headquarters, Henri and Claire sat down to draft a manifesto. This document was designed to outline their vision for a transparent, just, and inclusive government and was intended to spark discussions and encourage active participation across all sectors of society.

That night, as Henri penned the final words of the manifesto, he felt a profound sense of responsibility wash over him. He recognised that the real work was beginning—the revolution they had fought was about more than just overthrowing a tyrant; it was about redefining the nation's soul.

As he sealed the manifesto, ready for distribution the following day, he gazed at the flickering city lights. Paris stood on the brink of something monumental. Henri Moreau, once a humble clockmaker turned revolutionary, now saw his role as not just a liberator but as a builder—a creator of both timepieces and futures, with each tick marking a step towards a new dawn.

—

In the tranquil days that followed the tumult of Thermidor, Paris seemed to be reborn. The city, stretching from the 11th to the 22nd of Thermidor, Year II (29 July - 10 August 1794), vibrated with a cautious optimism. The oppressive air that had once choked its streets had lifted, and in its place was a burgeoning sense of hope and renewal.

Henri Moreau and his mother Claire found themselves at the centre of this transformation, not as the shadowy figures of Anonyme but as public advocates for a reformed Republic. Each morning, as the city awoke to the possibilities of a new era, they walked through the bustling streets, engaging with citizens, discussing plans for civic improvement, and participating in assemblies where the future of France was vigorously debated.

One late afternoon, Henri stood at the edge of the Seine, watching the sunlight dance on the water, reflecting the city's newfound lightness. Claire joined him, her presence comforting in the whirlwind of change.

"Henri, do you feel it?" Claire asked, her voice tinged with a mixture of hope and solemnity. "The shift in the air, the way people speak, their eyes brighter, free from the shadow of the guillotine."

Henri nodded, his gaze lingering on a group of children playing nearby, their laughter a clear sign of the city's slow healing. "I do, Mother. It's like we've stepped out of a long night into dawn. But with Robespierre gone, the real challenge begins. How do we ensure that what follows is not just a different shade of tyranny?"

Claire looked thoughtful, her eyes scanning the horizon. "We lead by example, Henri. We stay involved; we keep the conversations going. We help frame the laws that will govern us all, ensuring they're built on the principles of liberty, equality, and fraternity we fought so hard for."

Their conversation was interrupted by the arrival of Marianne, who approached with a brisk step and an earnest expression. "Henri, Claire, there's a gathering at the town hall tonight. They're discussing forming a new legislative body and asking representatives from all districts to join. They want you there to share your insights."

"Thank you, Marianne," Claire responded, a spark of determination lighting her eyes. "We'll be there. It's exactly what we need to be involved in to shape this new Republic."

That evening, under the vaulted ceilings of the town hall, Henri and Claire joined a diverse group of citizens, each passionate about the role they would play in framing the new government. The hall buzzed with spirited debate and the rustling of papers as proposals were examined and re-examined.

When it was his turn to speak, Henri stood, his voice clear and steady. "We stand at a crossroads," he began, the room falling silent. "Down one path lies the return to old ways, to power concentrated in the hands of the few. Down the other lies a path we've yet to tread — one of true democratic governance, where every citizen's voice has weight."

The assembly listened intently as Henri articulated his vision for a balanced government, one that learned from the past's mistakes. His words resonated with their idealism and grounded understanding of the practical steps needed to achieve such ideals.

As the meeting drew close, Henri and Claire felt renewed purpose. They walked home under the starlit sky, the streets of Paris quieter now, and Thermidor's tumultuous events slowly receded into memory.

"Mother, whatever comes next, I believe we're ready for it," Henri said with a quiet conviction.

Claire smiled, squeezing his hand. "Yes, we are, Henri. Together with the people of Paris, we'll build something lasting. This is just the beginning."

And so, as the French Republican Calendar turned and the streets of Paris whispered of change, Henri Moreau, his mother Claire, continued their walk, not just as survivors of a dark chapter in history but as architects of a brighter, more hopeful future. In the whispers of Anonyme that had once fuelled a revolution, there was now a promise — a commitment to nurture the fragile roots of liberty and guard vigilantly against the rise of new tyrants. The task was daunting, but the journey was beginning for Henri and Claire.

Chapter Eleven

On 10 Thermidor, Year II (28 July 1794), the atmosphere in Paris was thick with a mix of relief, anxiety, and the lingering scent of revolution. The Place de la Révolution, where the guillotine had claimed the lives of Robespierre and his closest allies just hours before, was now slowly emptying. The citizens, who had come to witness the end of the tyrant's reign, were dispersing into the city's labyrinthine streets, each step heavy with the weight of a new era.

Henri Moreau and his mother, Claire, walked side by side through the narrow alleys, their faces reflecting the complex emotions of the day. The sun had set, leaving the city bathed in the soft glow of twilight. The crowd's murmur faded into a distant hum as they passed by shuttered shops and dimly lit windows.

"Today was a turning point, Mother," Henri said quietly, breaking the silence. His voice was filled with a mix of exhaustion and determination. "But I can't shake the feeling that this is just the beginning of another struggle."

Claire nodded, her gaze fixed ahead. "It is, Henri. The execution of Robespierre has closed one chapter, but it has opened another. We must be vigilant and guide the people through this transition. The fear that has gripped Paris won't vanish overnight."

The streets were alive with whispers and hurried footsteps. Groups of citizens huddled together, hushedly discussing the day's events. The tension that permeated the city during Robespierre's reign was still palpable, but there was also a sense of cautious optimism.

As they walked, they passed a group of children playing in the shadow of a grand building. Their laughter starkly contrasted the sombre mood that had dominated Paris for so long. Henri paused for a moment, watching them with a faint smile.

"It's strange, seeing them so carefree after everything that's happened," he mused. "It's a reminder of what we're fighting for—their future."

Claire placed a hand on his shoulder, her touch comforting and grounding. "Yes, Henri. And it's up to us to ensure their future is one of liberty and justice, not fear and oppression."

The familiar sight of *Moreau Horlogerie* came into view, its sign barely visible in the dim light. The workshop had been their refuge and the heart of Anonyme's operations. As they approached, the wooden door creaked open, and they were greeted by Marianne, her face a mixture of relief and concern.

"Henri, Claire, thank goodness you're back safe," Marianne said, her voice trembling slightly. "The city is on edge. People are hopeful, but there's fear of what comes next."

"We know, Marianne," Claire replied, her voice steady. "Today was a significant victory, but we have much work to do to ensure that the Republic doesn't fall back into chaos."

Henri and Claire stepped inside, the familiar scent of wood and metal mingling with the faint aroma of ink from their recent pamphleteering. The workshop was dimly lit, casting long shadows on the walls lined with clocks and revolutionary paraphernalia.

Henri sank into a chair, his body finally succumbing to the day's fatigue. "Marianne, can you fetch us some water?" he asked. "We need to regroup and plan our next steps."

Marianne nodded and disappeared into the back room. Henri leaned back, closing his eyes for a moment. The image of Robespierre's final moments played in his mind, a stark reminder of the fragility of power and the cost of tyranny.

Claire sat across from him, her expression contemplative. "Henri, we must be careful. The people look to us for guidance but are also desperate. Desperation can lead to rash decisions."

Henri opened his eyes, meeting his mother's gaze. "I know, Mother. We need to focus on rebuilding trust and ensuring justice is served. The Republic must be more than just a change in leadership; it must be a change in how we govern and care for our citizens."

Marianne returned with a pitcher of water and two cups. She poured them silently, her hands shaking slightly. Henri took a cup and sipped the cool water, feeling it revive his spirits.

"We'll start by reaching out to our allies in the Convention," he said, setting the cup down. "We need to ensure that the trials for Robespierre's supporters are fair and just. We can't afford to let the Revolution descend into another cycle of vengeance."

Claire nodded, her resolve firm. "Agreed. We must also work on educating the public and helping them understand their rights and responsibilities in this new Republic. Only through informed and active participation can we hope to build a lasting democracy."

As the night deepened, the sounds of the city quieted, leaving only the occasional distant shout or the soft rustle of leaves in the breeze. Henri and Claire continued to plan, their words weaving a vision of a future where liberty, equality, and fraternity were not just ideals but lived realities.

In the quiet of the workshop, amid the ticking of clocks and the whispered hopes of a reborn Paris, they prepared for the challenges ahead. The fall of Robespierre was only the beginning. Now, it was up to them to fulfil the Revolution's promise of a just and fair society.

—

On 12 Thermidor, Year II (30 July 1794), the sun rose over Paris, still grappling with the aftermath of Robespierre's execution. The air was cool, yet the tension remained thick like a storm waiting to break. As the city slowly awakened, its streets began to hum with the nervous energy of a populace caught between relief and uncertainty.

Henri Moreau and Claire had spent the previous days in relentless activity, coordinating with allies and ensuring the transition from Robespierre's authoritarian rule did not descend into chaos. Their tireless efforts had begun to show results, but much work remained.

At *Moreau Horlogerie*, their workshop and the nerve centre of Anonyme were bustling with activity. Resistance members moved with purpose, their tasks clear and their resolve unwavering. Henri stood by a large table strewn with maps and papers, his eyes scanning a list of names.

"Henri, we've received word from the Marais district," a young woman named Colette said as she approached, her voice steady but her eyes betraying her anxiety. "The citizens are organising a public meeting. They want to discuss the future of the Republic and how to prevent another reign of terror."

Henri nodded, his mind already racing with possibilities. "That's good news, Colette. We need the people to be involved, to feel they have a voice in shaping the future. Have we sent someone to address their concerns?"

Colette shook her head. "Not yet. I thought you or Claire might want to go. Your presence would mean a lot to them."

Henri glanced at Claire, who was deep in conversation with Marianne about the logistics of distributing pamphlets. Sensing his gaze, Claire looked up and gave him a slight nod.

"I'll go," Henri decided. "Mother, you stay here and continue coordinating our efforts. We need to ensure our messages reach every corner of Paris."

Claire's eyes softened with a mixture of pride and concern. "Be careful, Henri. The city is still volatile, and emotions are running high. Make sure you emphasise unity and justice."

Henri grabbed his coat and a bundle of leaflets, tucking them under his arm. "I will, Mother. We can't let this moment slip through our fingers. The people need to know they have the power to shape their destiny."

As Henri entered the street, the morning light cast long shadows across the cobblestones. The city was already alive with movement, and he could hear snippets of conversations as he walked. The citizens of Paris, long accustomed to the fear and suspicion of Robespierre's reign, now spoke with hope and caution.

Reaching the Marais district, Henri found the public square filled with people. Makeshift banners calling for liberty and justice hung from the surrounding buildings, and a palpable energy thrummed through the crowd. Henri made his way to the front, where a group of citizens had gathered around a makeshift podium.

An older man, his face lined with years of hardship, was addressing the crowd. "We have seen the fall of a tyrant, but we must ensure that no new one rises in his place. The power to shape our future lies with us, the people. We must demand transparency and fairness from our leaders."

Henri stepped forward, catching the man's eye. The speaker paused, recognising Henri, and stepped aside to allow him to address the crowd. Henri took a deep breath, feeling the weight of the moment.

"Citizens of Paris," he began, his voice carrying over the crowd's murmurs, "We stand at the dawn of a new era. The fall of Robespierre is not the end but the beginning of our true revolution. We can build a Republic founded on liberty, equality, and fraternity."

The crowd quieted, their attention focused on Henri's words. He continued, his voice growing stronger with each sentence. "But we must remain vigilant. We must ensure that our leaders are held accountable and that power is not concentrated in the hands of a few but shared among all citizens. This is our chance to create a government representing the people's will."

A young woman in the crowd raised her hand, her voice trembling with emotion. "How can we trust that this new government won't become as corrupt as the last? How do we ensure our voices are heard?"

Henri met her gaze, his expression earnest. "We start by participating, staying informed, and holding our leaders accountable. We must create local councils and assemblies where citizens can voice their concerns and contribute to decision-making. We must build a system that encourages transparency and rewards integrity."

The crowd murmured in agreement, their expressions reflecting a mix of hope and determination. Henri could feel the tide turning; the people's collective will was beginning to merge into a force for positive change.

As the meeting continued, Henri listened to the concerns and ideas of the citizens. He took notes, promising to bring their suggestions back to the Convention and ensure their voices were heard. The discussions were spirited, and the air was filled with a sense of possibility rather than fear for the first time in a long while.

When Henri returned to the workshop, the sun was high in the sky, casting a warm glow over the city. He felt a renewed sense of purpose, knowing that the people of Paris were ready to take an active role in shaping their future.

Claire looked up as he entered, her eyes filled with anticipation. "How did it go?"

Henri smiled, his exhaustion momentarily forgotten. "It went well. The people are ready, Mother. They want to be involved and take ownership of their republic. We have a lot of work ahead, but I believe we can do this. Together."

Claire nodded, her expression resolute. "Then let's get to work. The future of the Republic depends on it."

In the heart of Paris, amid the echoes of revolution and the promise of renewal, Henri and Claire prepared to lead their fellow citizens towards a brighter, more just future. The challenges were immense, but their resolve was unbreakable, their vision clear. The true revolution had just begun.

—

On 18 Thermidor, Year II (5 August 1794), the oppressive summer heat clung to Paris, the city bustling with the restless energy of change. The streets were filled with citizens, their conversations brimming with cautious optimism and spirited debates about the Republic's future. The execution of Robespierre had left a power vacuum, and the people were eager to see how it would be filled.

Henri Moreau and Claire went to the National Convention, the centre of political activity, where crucial decisions about the Republic's future were debated. Its imposing facade reflected the weighty discussions as they approached the grand building.

"Stay close, Henri," Claire advised, her eyes scanning the crowd. "The atmosphere is still volatile. We must ensure our presence is felt but not provoke unnecessary attention."

Henri nodded, his mind already focused on the task ahead. The air was thick with tension inside the Convention, and heated debates echoed through the halls. Deputies clustered in groups, their faces marked with concern and determination.

Henri and Claire entered the main chamber, taking their seats among the other deputies. The room was a hive of activity, with voices rising and falling as arguments and counterarguments were exchanged.

"Order! Order!" The presiding officer's voice cut through the din, calling the assembly to attention. "Today, we must discuss the formation of a new government. The people of France demand stability and justice. We cannot afford to fail them."

Henri rose from his seat, his gaze sweeping over the assembly. "Citizens of the Convention," he began, his voice steady. "We have overthrown a tyrant, but our work is far from over. We must establish a government that embodies the ideals of our revolution—liberty, equality, and fraternity."

A murmur of agreement rippled through the chamber, but voices of dissent quickly drowned it out. A deputy from the far side of the room stood up, his face flushed with anger.

"Moreau, your words are noble, but how do we ensure this new government won't fall into the same traps as the last? How do we prevent another Reign of Terror?"

Henri met his gaze, his expression resolute. "We start by decentralising power. We must create a system where local councils and assemblies have a voice in governance. Transparency and accountability must be our guiding principles."

Claire leaned forward, her voice clear and firm. "We also need to establish checks and balances within our government. No single individual or group should hold absolute power. We need a constitution that guarantees the rights of all citizens and ensures that power is distributed fairly."

The room fell silent as the deputies considered their words. The presiding officer nodded, his expression thoughtful. "These are important points. We must learn from our past mistakes and build a system that protects our Republic from corruption and tyranny."

Henri continued, his voice growing more passionate. "We must also focus on education and civic engagement. The people of France need to understand their rights and responsibilities. An informed and active citizenry is our best defence against tyranny."

A deputy from the front row, a middle-aged woman with a determined expression, stood up. "I agree with Moreau. We must empower our citizens and ensure they have a stake in our Republic. But we also need to address the immediate needs of our people—food, security, and justice."

Henri nodded, acknowledging her point. "You're right. We need to address the basic needs of our citizens while building a strong and fair government. This is not an easy task, but it is necessary to honour the sacrifices made for our revolution."

The presiding officer raised his hand, calling for a vote. "Let us put these proposals to a vote. Those who favour creating a decentralised government with checks and balances focused on education and civic engagement, raise your hands."

Hands shot up across the room, a clear majority in favour. The presiding officer smiled a rare moment of unity in a divided chamber. "The motion passes. We will begin drafting the necessary documents and forming committees to implement these changes."

As the assembly began to disperse, Henri and Claire exchanged a look of determination. They knew the road ahead would be challenging, but this was a crucial step towards building their envisioned Republic.

The sun began to set outside the Convention, casting a warm glow over the city. Henri and Claire returned to their workshop, their hearts buoyed by the day's progress.

"Today was a good day, Henri," Claire said, her voice filled with relief and resolve. "But we must remain vigilant. There are still many challenges ahead."

Henri nodded, his eyes reflecting the same determination. "I know, Mother. But for the first time in a long while, I feel hopeful. We're building something real, something lasting."

As they walked through the bustling streets of Paris, they could see the flickering lights of hope and determination in the eyes of their fellow citizens. The revolution was far from over, but the foundations of a new Republic were being laid. Henri and Claire were ready to face whatever challenges lay ahead, guided by the ideals they held dear and the unwavering spirit of the people of Paris.

—

On 26 Thermidor, Year II (13 August 1794), the air in Paris was thick with the scents of summer—baking bread, fresh produce from market stalls, and the faint, lingering odour of gunpowder. The city was alive with anticipation as the first steps toward restructuring the government were being implemented. The National Convention had voted in favour of the reforms proposed by Henri Moreau and his allies, and now the implementation work began in earnest.

Henri and Claire sat at a table in their workshop, which had become a de facto headquarters for Anonyme and a centre of revolutionary planning. Papers were strewn across the table, maps and documents detailing the new administrative divisions and the establishment of local councils. The atmosphere was one of intense focus and determination.

"Henri, have you finished drafting the guidelines for the local councils?" Claire asked, her eyes scanning a document in front of her.

"Yes, Mother," Henri replied, handing her a neatly written paper. "We've outlined the responsibilities and the processes for electing representatives. We want to ensure that every citizen has a voice."

Claire read through the document, nodding in approval. "This is good. We need to emphasise transparency and accountability. These councils must serve the people, not their interests."

As they worked, a knock sounded at the door. Marianne entered her expression a mix of excitement and urgency. "Henri, Claire, there's a delegation from the Marais district here to see you. They've heard about our proposals and want to discuss how they can implement them locally."

Henri stood, smoothing his coat. "Excellent. This is exactly the kind of engagement we need. Show them in, Marianne."

A group of four men and two women entered, their faces lined with determination and the weariness of recent struggles. They introduced themselves and took seats around the table, the atmosphere buzzing with the energy of potential change.

"Citizens of the Marais, welcome," Henri began, his tone warm and inviting. "We're eager to hear your thoughts and answer any questions you have about the new local councils."

One of the men, a burly blacksmith named Jacques, spoke first. "We've read your proposals and believe they're a step in the right direction. But how do we ensure the new councils don't fall into the same traps as the old regime?"

Claire leaned forward, her gaze steady. "It's crucial that we start with transparency. Meetings must be open to the public, and records must be accessible. We must also rotate leadership to prevent the consolidation of power."

A young woman named Elodie, her hair tied back in a practical bun, added, "And what about the immediate needs of our people? Food shortages and security—are urgent issues. How do we address them while building this new system?"

Henri nodded, understanding their concerns. "You're right, Elodie. We can't ignore the immediate needs. That's why we're also creating committees within the councils to address issues like food distribution and public safety. These committees will have the resources and authority to act swiftly."

The discussion flowed naturally, with ideas exchanged and plans refined. The delegation from the Marais brought valuable insights, highlighting the practical challenges of implementing theoretical reforms. Henri and Claire took notes, and their respect for these community leaders was evident in their attentive listening.

As the meeting progressed, a sense of camaraderie developed. These were not just theoretical debates but practical solutions crafted by people who understood the stakes. By the time the delegation left, there was a palpable sense of progress.

After the visitors departed, Henri and Claire returned to their work, their spirits lifted by the productive meeting. The sun was setting, casting a warm glow through the windows, and the streets outside hummed with the life of a city in transition.

"Today was promising, Henri," Claire said, her voice filled with a rare optimism. "We're seeing the first steps of real change. The people are engaged and ready to build something better."

Henri smiled, feeling a renewed sense of purpose. "Yes, Mother. It's a long road ahead, but we're on the right path. We're not just tearing down the old structures; we're building something new that truly serves the people."

As the evening shadows lengthened, they continued their work; each page they wrote and each plan they made was a testament to their commitment to the revolution's ideals. The future of the Republic was being forged in these moments, one conversation, one document at a time.

—

On 10 Fructidor, Year II (27 August 1794), the air in Paris was filled with the warmth of late summer, the sun casting long shadows over the cobblestones as citizens went about their day. The National Convention was abuzz with activity, as today was the day they would debate and vote on the new reforms that Henri Moreau and his colleagues proposed.

Henri and Claire arrived early, their presence now familiar and respected within the halls of the Convention. The grand chamber was filled with deputies, their expressions ranging from hopeful to wary. Henri could feel the weight of the moment pressing down on him, the knowledge that today's decisions could shape the future of the Republic.

As they took their seats, Henri glanced around the room, noting the critical figures in attendance. Tallien, who had been instrumental in the fall of Robespierre, stood in animated conversation with Billaud-Varenne and Collot d'Herbois. The air was thick with anticipation and the scent of ink and parchment.

The session began with a call to order, the President of the Convention banging his gavel to silence the murmurs. "Citizens of the Convention, today we address the proposals for reforming our government. As you know, these reforms have been crafted to ensure a fair and just Republic, free from the tyranny that has plagued us."

Henri stood when it was his turn to speak, his heart pounding in his chest. He had prepared meticulously, but addressing such an august body was daunting. He took a deep breath and began.

"Honored deputies, we stand at a critical juncture. The fall of Robespierre was not the end of our revolution but the beginning of its true purpose. We must now build a government that reflects the ideals of liberty, equality, and fraternity we have fought so hard to achieve."

He outlined the key points of the reforms: the establishment of local councils, the rotation of leadership, transparency in governance, and the creation of committees to address immediate needs like food distribution and public safety. As he spoke, he could see the reactions of the deputies—some nodding in agreement, others frowning in scepticism.

When he finished, there was a moment of silence before the room erupted into debate. Deputies rose to speak, their voices clashing in a cacophony of passion and reason. Henri returned to his seat beside Claire, his hands trembling slightly.

"Henri, you spoke well," Claire whispered, her hand resting reassuringly on his arm. "Now, we must listen and respond thoughtfully. This is the crucible in which our ideas will be tested."

The debate raged for hours. Some deputies raised concerns about the feasibility of the reforms, arguing that they were too radical and could destabilise the fragile peace. Others supported the changes, seeing them as necessary steps to prevent the rise of another tyrant.

Tallien stood to speak, his voice carrying the weight of experience and authority. "Citizens, we have seen the dangers of unchecked power. These reforms are not without risk, but they are essential. We must be vigilant, but we must also be bold. The Republic demands it."

As the day wore on, the tension in the room grew palpable. The final vote approached, and Henri felt a knot of anxiety tighten in his stomach. He knew this was a pivotal moment—not just for the Convention, but for the future of France.

When the President called for the vote, the deputies cast their ballots, the atmosphere thick with anticipation. Henri and Claire exchanged a tense glance, both holding their breath.

The results were announced, and a wave of relief and joy washed over Henri. A significant majority had approved the reforms. The room erupted in applause, and Henri felt tears of joy and exhaustion prick at his eyes.

Claire embraced him, her voice filled with pride. "We did it, Henri. We've taken the first step toward a new Republic."

Henri nodded, feeling the weight of the moment settle on his shoulders. "This is just the beginning, Mother. We must ensure these reforms are implemented and that the people see the benefits."

As they left the Convention, the sun setting over Paris, Henri felt a renewed sense of purpose. The road ahead would be long and challenging, but he felt a glimmer of hope for the first time in months. The Republic was theirs to build, and he was ready to dedicate his life to making it a reality.

—

On 1 Vendémiaire, Year III (22 September 1794), Paris was bathed in early autumn's soft, golden light. Once gripped by fear and uncertainty, the city hummed with cautious optimism. Establishing the Directory was a pivotal moment, marking the end of the Thermidorian Reaction and the beginning of a new chapter for the French Republic.

Henri Moreau stood on the steps of the National Convention, looking out over the Place de la Révolution. The air was crisp, and the leaves on the trees had begun to turn, their colours a vivid reminder of the changing seasons. Beside him, Claire Fountaine observed the bustling square, her gaze steady and reflective.

"Do you think we can sustain this momentum?" Henri asked, his voice filled with a mixture of hope and apprehension.

Claire turned to him, her expression thoughtful. "We have laid a strong foundation, Henri. But sustaining it will require vigilance and dedication. The people are counting on us to lead with integrity."

As they descended the steps, they were greeted by a group of citizens who had gathered to witness the historic day. Among them was Marianne, her eyes shining with pride and determination.

"Henri, Claire, the people are ready to support the new government," Marianne said, her voice filled with conviction. "We've seen what happens when power is abused. We must ensure the Directory remains true to the principles of the Revolution."

Henri nodded, feeling the weight of responsibility settle on his shoulders. "We will, Marianne. This is a collective effort; we must all play our part."

They walked together towards the centre of the square, where a stage had been erected for the day's ceremonies. The flags of the Republic fluttered in the breeze, their colours vibrant against the clear blue sky. The atmosphere was charged with a sense of renewal, the air filled with lively conversation and the rustle of documents.

The crowd quieted as the ceremony began. Tallien, now one of the leading figures of the Directory, stepped forward to address the assembly. His voice was strong and resolute, carrying the hopes and dreams of a nation weary from years of turmoil.

"Citizens of France, today we embark on a new journey. The Directory is not merely a government; it is a promise to uphold the values of liberty, equality, and fraternity. We have learned from past mistakes, and we are committed to building a future where every citizen can thrive."

As Tallien spoke, Henri felt a surge of pride and determination. He glanced at Claire, who gave him a reassuring nod. They had come so far that it was time to turn their vision into reality.

After the speeches, the crowd dispersed, their faces reflecting hope and cautious optimism. Henri and Claire remained in the square, soaking in the atmosphere of a city on the brink of transformation.

"Mother, we have much work ahead of us," Henri said, his voice filled with resolve.

Claire smiled, her eyes twinkling with pride. "Indeed we do, Henri. But we are not alone. The people are with us, and together, we will build a Republic that embodies the Revolution's spirit."

As they walked through the streets of Paris, the city seemed to come alive with the promise of a new beginning. Shops were bustling with activity, children played in the parks, and conversations were exciting and exciting.

Henri and Claire went to *Moreau Horlogerie*, their beloved workshop and the heart of Anonyme's operations. Inside, the familiar scent of wood and oil greeted them, a comforting reminder of their journey.

Henri looked around the workshop, his heart swelling with gratitude. "This place has been our sanctuary, command centre, and home. It's where we planned, dreamed, and fought for a better future."

Claire touched his shoulder, her touch filled with warmth and reassurance. "And it will continue to be our base as we move forward. We've accomplished so much, but there's still much to do."

As the sun set over Paris, casting long shadows on the cobblestone streets, Henri and Claire sat down to plan their next steps. The challenges ahead were daunting, but they were ready to face them with courage and conviction.

Together, they would work to ensure that the Directory lived up to its promise, that the Republic remained true to its ideals, and that the sacrifices of the Revolution were not in vain. As the first stars appeared in the night sky, they knew that their journey was far from over—but they felt a glimmer of hope for the first time in a long while.

The new dawn had arrived, and with it, the promise of a brighter future for France.

Milton Keynes UK
Ingram Content Group UK Ltd.
UKHW050019010724
444882UK00014B/650